PRAISE FOR
THE COUNTRY GIRL'S GUIDE TO HEXES AND HAINTS

"Some people call Oklahoma God's country, but in Mer Whinery's fiction, the land is given over to much darker forces. Whinery's prose is lean, lyrical, and visual: it puts you right in the front row of the Red Hand Theater for the creepiest midnight show you'll ever see." —Matthew M. Bartlett, author of *Gateways to Abomination* and *Where Night Cowers*

"Only nihilists and necrophiliacs will tell you romance is dead. A story, a nightmare, a laxative. *The Country Girl's Guide* succeeds on every level. Buy the book. Wear a diaper." —Jared Collins, lead singer for Mississippi Bones

"Reading Mer is like sitting on the porch with a good country neighbor for a cup of hot cider on a cool autumn day, but as dusk draws close and you've warmed your bones he begins to share the things he's seen and they're not all pleasant. Sometimes they're downright scary.

The Country Girl's Guide starts up quick and doesn't let up for one minute. A thoroughly fun read perfect for the witching season." —A.P. Sessler, author of *This Body of Death* and *Dr. Sand's Maritime Museum of Nautical Oddities*

"Grindhouse literature has a champion in Mer Whinery. *The Country Girl's Guide to Hexes and Haints* is a horror novel in the best tradition of the southern, blood-soaked Gothic." —Jonathan Raab, author of *The Haunting of Camp Winter Falcon* and *The Crypt of Blood: A Halloween TV Special*

MER WHINERY

THE
COUNTRY GIRL'S
GUIDE TO
HEXES
AND
HAINTS

JOURNALSTONE
YOUR LINK TO ARTIST TALENT

ISBN: 978-1-68510-021-6 (sc)
ISBN: 978-1-68510-022-3 (ebook)
Library of Congress Control Number: 2022931591

First printing edition: December 9, 2022
Printed by JournalStone Publishing in the United States of America.
Cover Design: Don Noble
Edited by Sean Leonard
Proofreading and Cover/Interior Layout: Scarlett R. Algee

JournalStone Publishing
3205 Sassafras Trail
Carbondale, Illinois 62901

JournalStone books may be ordered through booksellers or by contacting:
JournalStone | www.journalstone.com

A BRIEF WORD REGARDING A VERY BAD PLACE

You just never can tell, can you?

People live in the same town their whole lives and they think they know everything about it based solely upon the influence of familiarity. Particularly those who were born in the spot they live in, and their parents before them, and the brood before those people, bloodlines and friendships stretching across decades and divisions. Yet this familiarity breeds a kind of lazy blindness in some folks. They no longer notice things they should be writing down and quit listening to stories they should be worrying over. Bad things are easy to bury when nobody wants to remember them. Especially a really bad thing.

Originally known as Black Knot Camp, formally christened a township in 1866, Black Knot was a lot bigger than it appeared, sprawling across a vaster expanse of territory than advertised. The name had existed before the arrival of the pale interlopers, and had been originally built as a settlement for Confederate guerilla fighters hiding from the corpse-end of a Yankee noose. According to local fable, the Camp had been named in honor of a Choctaw medicine man of the same name, although nobody could find any mention of this alleged wizard via any reputable resource. Whether he had existed or not was hotly debated among what few Choctaw elders remained, and as these individuals slowly departed this world for the hereafter it began to be taken as gospel the man in question had never been real to begin with. Small towns are like that. Their people don't care much about chronicling their exploits on paper. Legend and lore are whispered from mouth to ear and then back through the mouth again, making dishonesties seem like viable truths and truths downplayed to fairy dust.

However, after a few decades the name had realized it wasn't going anywhere and decided to stick around, and nobody had felt the need to stir up unnecessary dust by complaining about it. It was as good a name as any and had a pleasant ring to it. Black Knot and all the land surrounding it was a right pretty lap of country, built smack up against the banks of the mighty Hootchyfalala River, which itself forked all the way up to Canada one way and down to the Texas Gulf the other. Most folks who came to visit were there for the seclusion of the forest enclosing the town, which were remarkably thick and imposing, and shenanigans often involving bass boats and guns on Bride's Lament Lake. Lots of prize catfish had been pulled from those muddy, turbulent waters and even a cottonmouth (dead) stretching out a full twenty-one feet from the tip of the nose to the point of the tail. It seemed as if every other house possessed a barbecue grill on the back porch, and to every schoolyard a battered basketball goal had been assigned. People would talk to one another at the laundromat, and boys actually had to *call* girls on the phone if they wanted to get to know them better. Men went hunting together come late autumn, and women gathering together for the purpose of weaving a county fair quilt cobbled together from deathbed sheets was a long-revered endeavor. Kids counted down the days to Vacation Bible School every summer, and the grown-ups indulged in their weekend ritual of sipping beers and two-stepping at the local Dew Drop Inn.

Yet nobody, not one soul, would ever discuss the strange noises often heard in that aforementioned forest, commonly attributed to the rare wolf or an occasional brown bear. Those glowing green lights hovering over the entrance of the long-collapsed RJ McAlester Mine # 9, locally referred to as Bloody Ben's Pit, always dismissed as the refraction of truck headlights from the nearby interstate reflecting off the stony face of Crooked Ethel's Bluff. That spectral hotrod roaring along the verified deadly twists and hollows of Reaper's Curve were just kids boosting a souped-up stock car. Strange midnight concerts emanating from a secret room deep within Lavera Lodge #2 were dismissed as a trick of the wind. The number of infants interred in the Old Fulci Burying Ground was staggering, and even the most well-read educators in town could discern neither the origin nor the meaning of the arcane symbol inscribed on the steps of Black Knot High.

No ma'am. You didn't speak of such things.

But there were other people, usually the extra colorful sort you'd find bellied up to a bar someplace with a row of empty bottles lined up before them, who might tell you a different tale about Black Knot. Tales about those same things nobody else wanted to talk about. Things that might make someone think twice about settling down there.

You might want to pay attention to those folks.

He was dressed strangely for someone chowing here, especially at this hour. Ordinarily, the tables and booths were haunted by burly good old boys in worsted denim with bristly beards and stained ballcaps, reeking of the unending highway and all of the distinctive odors customary to such a freewheeling livelihood. Men who looked like they carried a large caliber weapon hidden upon their person and had no reservations about busting it out to discourage any monkeyshines. A guy like this, though, you didn't even *see* a person even remotely like him around these parts. Dressed in a spotless white leisure suit, the lapels rimed in silver glitter and immaculately pressed, the young man looked more disposed to a wild night in some big city disco than gobbling down lukewarm waffles, day-old coffee, and bacon tough enough to use for a razor strap. He kept his head down, his long brown hair dipping into a pool of melted butter on the plate, chewing and swallowing loudly. Eating like someone who had not had a decent meal for days. Like a beast, devouring the meat and bones of its kill.

Kept close to his side was an old burlap bag. The bag looked as if it had been dragged through a lot of places and held a lot of different things.

The waitress couldn't quite place the smell coming off of the man. It was a disagreeable combination of unwashed, sweaty maleness and some kind of disinfectant. An acrid, almost medicinal stink. Probably didn't help he gave her the willies to begin with, although he had done absolutely nothing to inspire such revulsion. Indeed, he had been respectful to a fault, money being no issue, and was now on his third plate of waffles. He'd been here for well over an hour, throwing a look out the window every so often as if waiting for somebody to walk past and into the diner to join him in his booth. Pausing between bites, he'd glance at his watch, his hair a dark curtain obscuring his face. He didn't so much as even acknowledge the unkind comments from the truckers in the booth behind him regarding his possible homosexual inclinations.

The man kept his head down, fork busy back and forth from plate to mouth, like a machine.

Two hours passed.

Five full plates of waffles and bacon to go with it. A whole pot of coffee.

The waitress was confident the tip left behind would be worth it.

Just before sunrise a trio of unique individuals walked through the sliding glass door separating the diner from the rest of the truck stop. All of them were dressed similarly to the man seated at the table glutting himself on waffles and bacon. Three-piece suits, loud and flashy. Two of them, judging by their bulkier physiques, were most definitely men. However, one of them was considerably smaller than the others. Perhaps a woman, or just a very delicately proportioned male. It was impossible to tell due to the masks covering their faces. The masks of animals. Had anyone ventured forth for a closer looky-loo, they would have been horrified to learn these ornaments were not just masks, but the soggy and still bloody faces of beasts slaughtered for their skins and stretched across their faces.

Three little pigs, their crumpled snouts slick with gore and mud.

The well-dressed and foul-smelling man polished off the last of his coffee and rose to his feet, wiping his mouth across the back of his sleeve. From the bag beside him he withdrew his own mask, the scarred visage of a timber wolf, and slipped it over his head with a nauseating wet *squelch*. Calmly unbuttoning his suit, he withdrew a large handgun, stretched his arm out and clicked the hammer back.

"Nobody knows when they are going to die. That's the beauty of it all." The Wolf-Man spoke, his voice tinged faintly with a slow, syrupy Southern accent. The kind of man folks liked to listen to. A radio voice, perhaps a former preacher. "The wonderful, delightful, penetrating surprise. It's like Christmas and your birthday all rolled into one. And just so this doesn't hurt so bad, understand your blood, your dead meat, will serve a greater purpose. A purpose undreamed of."

The three little pigs now unbuttoned their coats, removing their own weapons. The smaller one withdrew a sawed-off shotgun and racked it.

The waitress wasn't so concerned about her tip anymore.

It all took less than a minute.

Before he left, the Wolf made use of the telephone in the kitchen. He took his time dialing the number. The person at the other end of the line was sympathetic to his cause and was dispatching people to perform the necessary cleanup. There would be paperwork to attend to and things done to make sure this stayed quiet. It would be quite involved. The Wolf had no use for such things and didn't care. It was not in his job description. He was merely the ferryman. That was *his* job. As he made his calls the three pigs perused the small gift shop. Most of it was useless, quaint junk. One pig took a trucker's cap bearing the logo for "Orville's 24-Hour Septic Repair," while another claimed a Route 66 snow globe. Pig number three snagged a pouch of chewing tobacco from behind the counter, saving it for later. The pig had always wanted to try it and had never had the chance. It had seen people on television do it, and it looked interesting to them.

The Wolf, his correspondences completed, gathered the swine around him.

The four killers walked away from Dot's Chow and Plow, ambling along as if they had all the time in the world. Inside the corpses of two adults and one child lay lifeless and mutilated behind the counter, in the kitchen and on the floor. Three for the way in. A handful of bones and a death song.

The Wolf walked in front of his three little pigs, as always. He cut a look back at the diner and nodded his head grimly. This was not a pleasant ritual, but necessary. The blood spilled inside the diner was the key, the very forging of it. You got to have a key when there is a door.

He then focused his eyes northward, beyond the treetops and hills and hollers, in the direction of Black Knot.

By foot, it was a seven-hour walk.

The pig promised to share his tobacco.

In Black Knot the Door in the Floor awaited.

Behind that door, the Seamstress slept. She dreamed.

The four of them, rapt with the tainted spirit, filled with Her Dark Breath, fell to their knees in dreadful worship.

THE
COUNTRY GIRL'S
GUIDE TO
HEXES
AND
HAINTS

ONE

Dad was dead, and there was no coming back from that. Hayder would never see him again until he was also dead himself. There was that consolation, unnerving as it was, he supposed. He had been told this over and over and over. At the funeral, at school, from every single neighbor who had stopped by to drop off a casserole or a pot pie or some kind of simple to heat up dessert thing. The same speech on repeat, each one cut and pasted from the same book.

He's with Jesus now.

He's with Brandy now.

The Lord's Plan is unknowable.

Be comforted in knowing he is finally at peace.

Hayder looked at the house and groaned inwardly. It was even more of a winner than Mom had let on, and a few notches below a "quaint fixer-upper," as the real estate guy had called it. It was big enough for sure, at three stories and thirteen rooms far too much house for just for the two of them. It was just a little over a hundred years old and looked every single season of it in its peeling cold blue paint, gently sagging roof, and chipped sandstone columns. It did have a really cool porch, the boy had to admit. One of those really gnarly numbers that started at the front, curved around to one side, and finished up in the back. Even had a porch swing in the front, albeit one that looked incapable of bearing the weight of a housecat, much less a human being. That could be replaced easy enough. Mom was the handiest person he knew, which was the point of buying the quaint fixer-upper in the first place.

In reality it wasn't nearly that awful. Mostly, the house just looked kind of sad, and he was feeling more than a little sorry for himself right now.

Hayder Hennessey had been used to living in a big old refurbished Civil War-era house back home in Dallas. An inheritance from his dad's side of the tree. Eight bedrooms and a game room with his very own *Gobbler* arcade machine, a pool table, and his own phone line. This was a huge step down, but he agreed with his mom it had been the right thing for the two of them. That big old house had become a cursed thing. The swimming pool where his little sister Brandy had drowned and the basement where Dad had hung himself would never let it feel like home again. Their roots had rotted, and the tree of them had withered up and collapsed upon itself. A new beginning was necessary for both their sanity and survival.

"Whatcha thinking, my dude?" Mom draped her arm across his slight shoulders. Her smell of pine soap and autumn things filled her son's head and eased his nerves. She wasn't eating enough. He could tell just from the way that one arm felt against him. A little bit more fragile than before. Her long red hair had a few faint blossoms of gray which, just a month before, hadn't been there.

"I'm thinking we got our work cut out for us." Hayder shook his head, frogging her arm. "Does it even have running water? Will we need oil lamps to read by?"

"Smart guy." Mom ruffled Hayder's hair. "I checked out the place, remember? That weekend I had you stay at Uncle Shawn's. Everything that's wrong with this house is, for the most part, cosmetic. The roof near the front of the house does have some beams that need replacing, and new shingles. I already have a quote on some aluminum siding, and amazingly there were no termites to tend with."

The boy shrugged. "You say so, lady. Squint a little harder. Think I see a nibble here and there."

"I do. Best of all, it's about a five-minute drive to the new shop. A dang sight better than the commute I had back in Texas, and it's just a couple more minutes from the shop to *your* job." Mom ruffled his hair fondly.

Hayder side-eyed her. "Jeeze, I'm only twelve. Do I really need a job?"

"Nah, not really. Dad's life insurance will take care of us for a very long time. But I do think it would be good for you, Hayder, to learn the value of a buck. Earning it will make you appreciate a lot more than just being given. Being twelve is a silly excuse."

"I was just kidding anyway. I'm kinda looking forward to it, actually." The boy dug into the front pocket of his jeans and brushed his thumb against the tie-dyed fur of his lucky rabbit's foot, something he did when he felt a little extra unsure about things. "What kind name is The Red Hand for a movie theater, anyway? Sounds a little bit fishy."

Mom laughed. "It's been here forever. It was old and creepy back when *I* was a kid, so I can imagine it hasn't changed a lot. You like spooky stuff. Should be right up your alley."

"Hey, *you* like the scary stuff, lady. Not me."

"Please. I know better." Mom rolled her eyes and rubbed her forehead with the back of her hand. "Trust me, though, you'll love it spooky or not. The concession stand is definitely the coolest job in the theater. You control the snacks, so you'll get to see all kinds of people come in and out too. Lots of…ladies."

Hayder didn't respond. A few seconds later came the expected nudge from his mom's elbow into his ribs. He didn't have to look at her to know she had shot him that weird wink, which always followed the elbowing and only occurred when the subject of females came up.

His skin was tight as a fresh snakeskin and flooded with an embarrassment of heat.

"I know." He nodded.

Mom began walking and gestured for him to follow. "Best part is the backyard. Trust me, you see this, and you'll be sold."

Hayder ambled along behind his mom as she guided him along the side of the house and into what she had referred to the backyard. It was a lot more than that. What lay before them was a massive sprawl of seemingly endless pasture, a lake of trembling golden grass dotted here and there with several tall mounds of earth swelling up a good five feet each. In the distance, almost out of eyeshot, a thick wall of trees imposed, forming a natural barrier and encircling the house on all sides like a great hand.

"Yeah, it's real pretty, but gonna be a monster to mow."

"Not if we get someone to come out and brush hog it first. I can spring for a riding mower for the stuff closer to the house, and I'll help you with it. Don't worry, your mean old momma won't do that to you." Mom walked out a few yards and knelt on the grass, digging her fingers into the dirt. "We can put in a fence here so we can have a dog. Sound good?"

"I'd rather get a cat, to be honest. Less work." Hayder jerked his chin back at the pasture. "What are those mounds? Indian graves? *Please* tell me those aren't Indian graves and you didn't just move us into *Poltergeist*."

Mom chuckled. "No, this place wasn't built on an Indian burial ground, although this is southeastern Oklahoma, and all of this was tribal land at one time. Those mounds right there are probably old mines."

Hayder shuddered. "Ok, that really doesn't make me feel any better. What if one of them gets an itch to collapse and the ground opens up and swallows up the house? And us."

"Jeeze, stop *worrying*! Both the real estate guy and the surveyor assured me they were perfectly safe. Used to have silver in them, but they've been sealed up good and tight since the thirties. They had to. Now, there's an older and bigger mine couple of miles up the road which had to be sealed up because it did collapse and killed a bunch of miners. Like almost a hundred years ago. Government put a halt on all the mining in this area." Mona Hennessey walked back over to her son and put her hands on his shoulders, tapping her forehead against the top of the child's head. "Buddy, *please* stop looking for reasons to hate it here. It will work against us and we got enough rocks to climb as it is."

Hayder was silent for several seconds. "Sorry, momma. I just miss home. My friends. Dad. Brandy."

"I get it, son. I miss them too. It was just getting too hard to stay in that house. In that city, even. Everyone always talking about your dad and sissy. It never ended. As if I need to be constantly reminded they are gone." Hayder could hear the lump in his mother's throat and felt one begin to swell in his own. He hated to cry and began thinking of other things to keep himself steady. "Besides, this was my home once. Home is good when you're sad."

"It was your home for a year, mom."

"Yeah, but it was an *amazing* year. One of the best years of my life." His mother released him and stared out into the pasture, fixated, as if gazing into an unknowable beyond. Hayder nodded but didn't comment further. The lump in his throat was still having a hard time finding someplace else to go.

With that Mom left Hayder to his thoughts and headed into the house, the porch creaking beneath her boots. Overhead a groggy belch of thunder trembled the world, tiny drops of cold rain starting to fall in response. The boy stood alone on the back porch, watching the October clouds split open wider to offer forth their waterworks. Hayder Hennessey suddenly felt very old for his twelve years. He told himself over and over, almost scolding, he was going to make this work. He *had* to make this work for the both of them. Their saneness depended on it.

He knew it was wrong, but it was hard not to hate Dad for what he had done. Then, back to hating himself for hanging on to that hate.

"I hope you're happy, daddy, wherever you are. Say hi to baby sister for me."

Out in the shadowed woods beyond the pasture, from the depths of the thick forest and hollows, the cry of an unknown creature squalled out. Was it a bird? Maybe a beast? Hayder couldn't place it. Whatever it was, it was hurting. Wounded. Something had hurt it and left to die where it lay. The summits of the ancient sycamores and oak trembled with the passage of something unseen but not unfelt. A coil of nameless horror rippled through the boy's bones, crawling beneath his flesh and tangling itself around his guts. He found himself rooted to the spot, his sneakers feeling like someone had poured cold concrete into them.

Was Dad trying to answer? Brandy?

Then, arriving on the heels of the awful wailing from the woods, a smell. Something beyond unusual and nasty to the nose. The boy had never smelled anything like it, but somehow could separate parts of the stench, isolate certain characteristics, and mold them into a vivid mental picture. The odor reminded him of the nursing home his Nana Josie had died in last winter. Old people pee and poop and dirty old skin mixed with Lysol. Beneath it all a strange…*rawness*. Like what he imagined an open wound, like a gunshot hole or a knife slash, to smell like. Something perfumed with violence, with an aftertaste of every bad thing you could worry about happening to you.

That smell was worse than the cry from the woods and the mute terror it carried with it.

Then, almost as fast as it had arrived, the sensation of dread departed, followed by the withdrawal of the odor as well. The boughs of the disturbed tree grew still and calm. Everything was as it should have been. Normal. His feet could move again, taking the memory of the experience with it, making the boy wonder if it had ever happened at all.

Hayder strolled along the side of the house to head back to the truck for his bike. Just a couple of hundred feet from their property was their sole neighbor, a ramshackle shell of a dwelling that a casual passerby would mistake for abandoned, were it not for the old pickup up on blocks out front and the girl standing outside.

From where he stood she looked to be about his age. Her long black hair was stuck to her shoulders and face from the rain, and she was only wearing flannel pajama pants and a red t-shirt. In one hand she toted a kerosene lantern, and she was so pale she almost seemed to glow in the creeping twilight. She didn't see him, however, but appeared to be focused on something in the distance. Watching her made Hayder feel weird, like he was peeking in on something private. Not wanting to be noticed but not quite ready to stop watching the girl, he knelt behind a mulberry bush and dug himself out an observation point in the mess of branches. The girl had moved now, tiptoeing toward the road outside of her house, brandishing her lantern out before her as if it were a holy symbol to ward off something unnatural. Hayder squinted to see if he could make out what she was looking at, but saw nothing but an empty country road and a dilapidated old farmhouse across the way.

He couldn't see anything, but it was obvious to him she *could*.

Seeing something she didn't want to see.

The lantern in her hand began to shake. He could actually hear the metal rattling from where he sat, spying like a thief. A scream split through the gloom, a scream from the girl, a scream which trembled the blood in Hayder Hennessey's veins. It was the scream of his mother finding Brandy's little white body floating in the swimming pool. The scream from his own throat when he had switched on the basement light and seen Daddy hanging from the rafters. The scream of a mind broken to pieces and scattered across the grave of a life lost. Disrupted blood. The girl, lantern in hand, bolted back in the direction of her dilapidated house. Whatever she was fleeing from remained behind in the coils of barbed wire, heaps of cinder blocks, and gray slats of splintered oak. He himself still saw nothing but an abandoned and unwanted place.

"Great, I live next to a crazy person. Just…my…luck." Hayder shook his head, rising from his cover. Behind him the backdoor swing open with a rusty creak, his mother emerging from within holding a flashlight.

"Welp, power's out, it looks like. Welcome to country life, city folks." Mom jerked her head over in the direction of the girl's house. "What on earth was that? Did I hear somebody scream?"

"Eh…girl next door. I think she saw a snake or a spider or something."

"Ah, a girl." The boy could feel the grin unfurling on his momma's face. "So, she about your age? Possible prospect there?"

Hayder didn't turn to answer, but kept his eyes on the girl's house. He didn't want to admit it, but he desperately wanted her to come back out and be normal. Maybe wave at him and ask if he'd like to come over and listen to music, maybe. Watch TV with her. Maybe she had an Atari they could play. Normal stuff that kids their age did. Not be some weirdo screaming at imaginary monsters on a dark and rainy autumn evening in a backwoods town a hundred million miles away from his old friends, life, and home.

"No, I don't think so." A light then came on in the girl's house, soon followed by the re-awakening of the lights in their own place. "I think there might be something wrong with her."

TWO

Cora Corbucci, age twelve, was dead.

At least that was how she felt at the precise moment that thought popped into her head. Something that had died, been left outside to rot away, and had just not bothered to crawl itself into a hole in the ground. But the autumn storm, though a mild-mannered one, made it all a bit more tolerable. Bedroom window opened just a hair, the crisp early October air whistling and seeping through the crack between the frame and the sill, rich with the odors of dug-up dirt and the melancholy damp of the rainfall, it made being confined to her sagging old bed a sight more bearable.

"One more week, sister," the child mumbled to herself. "Just seven more days and you're back in the big old bad world again." She cut her eyes to the large oval mirror next to her dresser. A light spattering of moisture from the open window had misted the lower right-hand corner of the glass. Observing her reflection, she tried to ignore her gaunt face and the smoky halos riming the undersides of her eyes. She regarded the photo of her mom and dad on her nightstand and tried to see the resemblance between herself and the woman who had toted her around in her gut for nine months. The lady in the Polaroid looked so pretty and elegant. Someone who could have been in movies or hosting the five o'clock news. Folks told her she was pretty too, but she didn't see it. What she saw staring back at her from that mussed-up reflective surface was rough, scrawny, pale as Death's Terrible Horse, with a thick headful of long snarled black hair and a traveling man's eyes set too deeply into her face.

Not to mention that eye of hers. That dang lazy left eye. Even glasses weren't helping to fix it.

Lately she found herself wondering a lot what it felt like to be dead. Was it like you just went on living like you were still here, except you didn't have any more concerns like bills and sickness and heartbreak? Were they in any pain, momma and daddy? Did they watch her from Heaven, or wherever decent folks went when their bodies gave up on them?

At least her own body hurt was gone, for the most part. She still got a twinge in her right side and in the dead center of her chest now and again. Mostly when she got up and moved around too long. But the pain had eased off enough to where she no longer needed those pain pills quite as often. She hated taking those things, and they were a risky thing to have in the house with Aunt Polly being the way she was. The doctors had told her no lifting whatsoever until she hit that next week mark. But that was easier said than done. She had a house to keep from falling down. Baba Lena was now hooked up to that oxygen tank full-time, and Aunt Polly locked in hard at the Army Ammunition plant graveyard shift. Tending to the conservation of their humble home, one of the oldest in Haggard, had fallen upon her shoulders.

Cora Corbucci was known throughout the greater Black Knot area, maybe even as far as Tulsa, as the Girl Who Survived the Massacre at Reverend Billy Tim's Feed Lot.

It was the first day of Fall Break for Mandrake Creek Middle School, so there would be no homework for Cora to catch up on. She was thankful the accident had happened at summer's end, and her being in the gifted and talented classes, her young brain like a sponge, avoiding getting left behind was not a worry for her. She almost wished for homework right now, just to have something to keep her occupied. She'd already read and re-read all her favorite books. Her boombox had been broken for months now, and Polly had long ago pawned all the albums they owned for gas, grocery, and God know what else money. The television set in the living room, planted in the same dusty corner next to the empty bookshelf for the past decade, was only capable of reaching four channels with the help of a battered set of rabbit ears. Getting a new one that worked worth a flip was out of the question. Such a thing was a luxury, and there were no frills in Baba Lena Vovk's old shotgun house.

Cora rose from the bed and wandered into the kitchen, half awake, to get a drink of water. On the way back to her room, without even thinking, she picked up the phone bolted next to the fridge and punched in Crystal's number. She let it ring a few times before she remembered everything, then quickly hung up. Her heart buzzed in her chest like a hummingbird. When the phone rang less than a minute later she reluctantly answered it, shutting her eyes and taking a deep breath. It was Mr. Compton this time. His poor wife had probably gotten her fill of these moments and had passed on this chore to the man of the house.

"Cora…honey…you doin' okay?" His voice was coarse with weariness, barely clinging to tenderness. She knew it was only a matter of time before they stopped taking her calls altogether, which was probably best for everyone. Her voice struggled to crawl out of her throat. Just a peep. A squeak. Something. She managed a weak, almost inaudible gasp. A long pause followed, so long Cora thought the line had gone dead. When Crystal's daddy spoke again, the harsh edge in his voice had smoothed out. The tenderness had found its foothold again. "It's okay, sweet pea. We want to forget too, sometimes. Now, you listen to me, girly-girl, and you best do what I tell you, 'cus I'm an old man and I know what's best. I don't want you to cry no more. Ya hear? Not one more tear. You need to get better. Get out of that bed. Get back into life. Make every hour, every *minute*, count. And if you don't mind, kiddo, please don't call over here again for a really long while."

Next, a cold plastic click, followed by the anticipated final, steady hum.

"Yes sir." The child wiped her wet eyes with the back of her palm and gently eased the receiver back onto its cradle. "A really long while. Maybe not even ever."

Cora walked back to her bedroom, slipped beneath her shelter of ragged sheets and quilts, and thought about all sorts of things for a very long while.

She had nodded off again.

The green digital read-out of the alarm clock on the nightstand glowed out the time as being a hair past five, but it felt closer to bedtime. That's the way it was when you were mending after a bad hurt, she had found. The days and shadows and hours and TV shows just sort of mashed-up together into one gray spill of blah. The brief chapters of sunlight only hastened the bleeding, and Cora, who had always loved autumn, found herself pining for the southeastern Oklahoma summertime with its seemingly eternal days and sadistic, clotted heat.

They say this sort of thing can happen to a person when they die, or even get close to dying. Something about death, it rewires their brain stuff or something. Changes them in weird ways. They start to enjoy things they used to hate, believe in things they used to think were unbelievable. Love people that they used to want to wish would drop dead.

Aunt Polly's words. She could wax quite poetic when she was of a certain mood and mind.

That was it. She'd lain in bed long enough.

Bones creaking like the gears of an old tractor, Cora swung her legs over the side of the bed and set her feet to the grimy floorboards. The cold air confined beneath the house drafted up through peeling gray wooden slats and pricked out goosebumps on her skin. She peeled off her nightgown, flung it into the corner of the room set aside for dirty clothes, and hobbled into the toilet, pretending not to notice how ripe her armpits were. The child cranked the hot water to life and eased into the shower, plopping down on her rear in the tub. Still a bit woozy, she didn't quite feel like standing right now, allowing the steaming water to wash away all remnants of the chill from her bones and soften the hurt of Mr. Crawford's final words.

"No sir. I won't call again. You'll never get to be bothered by this here gal ever again."

Visiting Crystal's grave would be the first thing she would do once she got past this last week.

First thing.

"No sir. Not ever again."

Part of her had died when the man in the wolf mask killed Crystal. Didn't Mr. and Mrs. Crawford realize that? They lost a daughter, but she had lost the only person in the world she could actually stand. The only person who had ever really listened to her.

Thunder cracked and the lights flickered, quickly followed by a sharp flash of lightning. Struggling to her feet, Cora quickly shut off the water and crawled over the side of the tub, wrapping herself in the one clean towel she could find. No sense in having God fry her in the shower.

Was a closed casket funeral, of course. Undertaker can't do much with that sort of mess but close the lid on the whole thing.

She'd overheard Aunt Polly telling Baba Lena all that in Ukrainian, the only language her granny knew. Even through the pink miasma of the pain pills, she was able to understand all of it.

Yet none of these gruesome details mattered to Cora one bit. She had been there. She had seen everything but the cops arriving to blast down the gunmen. She had *seen* Crystal Crawford die. She had seen all of them die.

The Wolf-Man in the white business suit had walked right up to her. The man had approached her calmly, as if he had all the free hours in the world to do all of his bad things, a shiny double-barreled shotgun cradled over his shoulder. His mask had been different than the other two killers'. It didn't appear to be made of rubber, but of actual beast flesh. As if a blade had been taken to a wolf, fresh and neatly slaughtered, and skinned the face tidily away from its skull. She could even smell the sour sweetness of rot the closer he got to her. He raised a thin hand encased in a red glove and made some sort of symbol in the air between them, shouldered his weapon and trained it straight on her.

That was all she remembered until she awoke in Morgana Fulci Memorial Hospital, hooked up to a half-dozen different beeping machines, tubes sticking in parts of her body she didn't think it possible to slip a tube into, both Baba Lena and Polly snoring in the plastic chairs beside her bed. She tried to say something but couldn't quite get her tongue to play nice with her brain. But she able to stir up enough life into her thumb to push the call button and get a nurse in there. Polly and Baba had been just a half-shade shy of incoherent upon her awakening, scaring the wits out of the child with their sobbing and carrying on. The nurse, a pretty redhead with the most amazing blue eyes and a serene smile, arrived and smoothed back her hair as she squirted something into one of the tubes in her arm that made every trickle-down into her body painted with grayness and calm.

Nobody explained anything to Cora until she was in a more stable condition, both in mind and body, which was a couple of weeks later. One of the police officers who had saved her came to call with a big bouquet of flowers and enough balloons to float to Kansas and back on. The girl felt sorry for the guy, having to be the bearer of such bad tidings. He was very young, a rookie, and this had been the first time he had ever even fired his gun, much less killed a person. He still seemed shook up about the whole ordeal, so much so that Cora felt compelled to take hold of his hand to offer comfort. He then proceeded to drop the bomb which she had already felt go off in her heart, that her best friend was dead, and she was lucky she wasn't in a coffin over at the Black Knot Burial Garden herself. She released his hand, thanked him for his time and tears, and then returned to her episode of *The Green Green Grass of Home* on the TV without another peep.

As for the monsters with the guns, nothing more was every said about them. They weren't here anymore, and that was good enough for her.

Everyone kept waiting for the crying to start on her end. The child welfare folks even ordered up a pretty lady in smart-looking office dress blacks to talk to her about the dry eyes. It was a genuine crisis, they seemed to think. Still didn't get things moving, and it made her feel pretty rotten that she couldn't even manage a single drop for Crystal's parents. Cora eventually got sick of trying to hash out all the whys and why-nots and just started to fake it to make everyone calm down, especially when she'd overheard talk of medications with long scary names and a possible trip to The Oaks. The Oaks was a special hospital in Coffin Mills they sent you to work on your troubles with crying, cutting your skin, and setting things on fire and whatnot. The few poor folks she'd known who had been sent there always came back home looking like they'd been escorted slowly behind a pickup by a long chain across rough back roads, patched up half-assed, then sent back into the world with a wad of drug store prescriptions in their pocket and a head full of Jesus.

People who went to The Oaks never got better, they just got distracted for a while.

After she got to thinking about it awhile, Cora came to accept maybe she'd already done her crying while she had been stuck in that place you hang around in when you're not really dead enough to die, but not alive enough to do normal living people stuff. Like eat, play video games, or cry. Once she accepted this everything seemed to smooth out. However, she kept up the crying charade just to keep the grown-ups calmed down. Didn't hurt nobody.

The evening she was discharged, mere minutes away from freedom, the sheriff himself paid her a visit. Most of Cora's encounters with Juston Matheson had been relegated to his presence on the front porch of their skeletal old house, grimly stern of countenance and banging out orders with his fist against the door, usually to come claim Aunt Polly for some trouble she'd caused or had been a party to. So even though he'd never been anything less than respectful to her, even having brought them canned food and some buck back strap when their cupboard had been extra spare, his appearance always carried with it a distinct aftertaste of panic.

Sheriff Matheson was a nice-looking guy for his age, Cora had noticed. He looked about a decade younger than he was, thirty-four, the same age as Aunt Polly. Smiling helped his face a lot, and she reckoned he didn't get to practice it all that often, considering the almost bashful way it struggled to stay put on his lips. He always smelled all manly. Some kind of musk that made her imagine hulking bearded fellows in the woods hacking down trees and stalking deer with sharp sticks. A tall man, slender around the edges with just a faint swell above the belt to indicate he liked the Sunday chicken-fried steak afternoon special at the Sizzler, he radiated a strange, almost solemn authority more akin to a man of the cloth than an officer of the law.

He'd brought her a teddy bear. A big one. One of those fluffy horrors only dying kids in Christmas movies seemed to receive. Even helped her finish packing her suitcase, making small talk about things unrelated to what had got her there in the first place. He was nice to talk to for a grown-up, and had a way of speaking that made her feel like he cared about what was being said back to him. Evidently, he and Aunt Polly had dated a few times back in the latter part of middle school, years before the Corbucci family name had taken a sharp nosedive into complete disgrace. It was weird watching Polly around him, acting all goofy, blushing and twirling a lock of her forty-times-over bleached hair around her finger. Like a kid herself. All the while Cora kept waiting for him to bring it up. That day of terror and blood. He never said a word in regard to that matter, but did give her his home number in case anything further was needed from him. This he provided for her and her alone, with whispered orders to keep the digits out of sight and earshot from her aunt. This last aside he seasoned with a sharp, knowing wink and a hand-ruffle of her hair. He then tipped his hat and was on his way, looking very much like a noble gunslinging lawman of legend as he walked away from her.

So far, she had no occasion to reach out to Juston Matheson, Sheriff of Black Knot. But she kept that phone number close at hand just the same. There'd be no need for his involvement in family matters so long as Polly kept her act together, which she had been doing for the most part for the duration of her niece's recovery. Yet she was a wild card by nature, and these moments of blessed steadiness never lasted. Eventually the drama with Cora would die down and the sick thing haunting the inside of Polly Corbucci would cry out for the trouble it thrived upon. That sad cry would turn into black deeds, and the lights would quickly grow dim upon that blessed steadiness, and Sheriff Juston Matheson would again be banging on the front door in regard to matters unrelated to an earful of numbers given to a young girl in private.

The child dried off and ran a comb through her long dark hair, still slightly damp, and dug a wrinkled t-shirt out of her chest-of-drawers. Unearthing some clean underwear and a pair of battered pajama pants, she constructed everything into something presentable and staggered into the living room. The house of Lena Vovk had stood for just a hair over a century, and the grim story of its owner's bloodline was reflected in every gloomy crook and corner of that single, commodious square chamber. The room itself was the largest in the house, boasting a ten-foot ceiling, and yet somehow still exuded suffocation, like a cardboard box set into the palm of a giant gray hand, its fingers and thumb slowly grinding inward. Almost every space not occupied by a stick of furniture was bordered and barred by heaps upon piles of things, some of it useful yet none of it valuable. Boxes of unopened jigsaw puzzles stacked with junk-fat milk crates and mangled cowboy boots belonging to men who had hit the bricks decades before, the sour sweat-stink of their feet still clinging stubbornly to the ruined leather. Scuffed and worsened tin TV trays and broken turntables held aloft tattered waist-high stacks of newspapers and magazines. In two opposite corners of the room imposed matching floor lamps, their meager dueling glares endangered by the towering pillars of refuse, casting the entire room in a perpetual dreariness.

Throughout the wreck, the damp, ruined stink of something that wasn't right within the bowels and timbers of the home. A sickness that burrowed down to the marrow.

Baba Lena was in her usual spot, settled barely more than a foot away from a prehistoric television set, entombed in the ratty hollow of her beloved garage-sale La-Z-Boy recliner. On the screen was her favorite show for as long as Cora had been alive, *Gunsmoke*, which the old woman was, true to form, snoring rowdily through. Another eruption of thunder growled overhead, the old house complaining with a cantankerous protestation of derelict boards, flickering lights and rattling glass. Baba Lena's arms flew outward as she came alive with a startled squawk, something harsh and incoherent barking from her lips which Cora was pretty sure was some sort of mother country swearword.

"It's all right, Baba. Just Jesus and the Devil closing down the bar," Cora joked, laying her hand on her granny's shoulder. She tried to ignore the brittle play of the skin and bones beneath the raggedy macramé shawl. The old woman clutched fearfully at the child's elbow with her bird-claw hands, surprisingly strong despite the frailty of their exterior. The young girl took the ancient limb in her own and gently ran her fingernails across the furrowed white flesh, whispering words of consolation. Lena calmed down after a few minutes and returned to her program without another peep, leaving her granddaughter to the primary concern of what would be for supper.

The kitchen was a pit, as expected. Greasy dishes heaped clear to the tip of the faucet and the countertops junked over with old fast food sacks, moldy pizza boxes and Dixie cups half full of mystery fluids. A thriving colony of ants marched steadily along the edge of the sink, some even having set up shop in a puddle of some sticky pink ooze on the floor. Cora opened the fridge to behold the harsh reality of leaving a sweet but crazy aunt in charge of managing the household money. Tonight's supper would be a lean one indeed, the filthy innards of the ancient icebox revealing an inventory of one plastic container of fuzzy bologna, and what appeared to be Kool-Aid in large Tupperware pitcher. The child sighed and closed the fridge door. Walking over to the cookie jar beside the hutch, she lifted the lid and dipped her hand inside, feeling around for the mad money she'd stashed there for fiascos such as this. Thirty-three bucks, mostly in ones. Enough to get some off-brand whatever to see them through another week or so. She could make it stretch. The granddaughter of Lena Vovk, although still very much a little girl in many ways, was a master of bleeding nickels dry. There would have to be a Come to Jesus moment with Aunt Polly tonight, and a trip to the Git N' Split for supplies, no matter how meager.

A massive wallop of thunder shuddered the house from the floorboards, up through the rickety windows, and spread out across the rooftop. The lights fluttered, struggled, and then gave up altogether. Matt Dillon's voice grew silent from the living room to be replaced with a chain of Ukrainian profanity. Cora slipped the cash into the pocket of her pajama pants and walked over to the sink, located the junk drawer, and found both the flashlight and a book of matches, the latter of which she slipped into the pocket to keep company with the wad of bills. Although it wasn't so late as to throw the house into full blackness, she knew Baba would start to panic if she didn't get her something to cut through the darkness. Thankfully, the flashlight worked without a hitch, but its meager output suggested a set of dying batteries. She took the device over to Lena, took the old woman's hands and curled her knobbed fingers around its handle.

"You hang on to this, Baba Lena. I'll fetch the kerosene lantern out of the shed. Just breathe nice and easy and don't get up." Cora patted her shoulder and slipped her feet into her battered sneakers. Pausing at the front door, she turned back to the old woman, who was now muttering to herself: a familiar sign she was going to get fired up and misbehave. "I mean it, Baba. Don't get up. Remember the last time you fell and what happened?" Baba's face went phantom pale, noticeable even in the eclipsed glow of the flashlight. Cora tried not to grin. All you had to do was threaten the old girl with a return trip to the emergency room and she gentled right on down.

The child opened the front door and stepped out on to the porch, pulling it closed behind her just as Polly pulled into the driveway, her prehistoric El Camino rattling like a sack of doorknobs as she came skidding to a halt just a few feet from the steps. Thunder rumbled again, the wind collecting gumption, and cold spurts of rain began slipping through the coal blushed clouds. Big cold drops threatening something prolonged and nasty. Her aunt exited the vehicle, several plastic sacks hanging from wrist to elbow crook on each arm. Cora sighed in relief and ambled off of the porch to help.

"Get your tail back in bed, lil gal! You lost your dadblamed mind?" Polly hollered over the flat roar of the wind. "Doc said you got another week before you can be up and about."

"What the man don't know ain't gonna matter, now is it? How's he gonna hear about it unless some annoying little birdie tells him?" The girl relieved a load of Git 'N Split bags from one of her aunt's arms and began heading in the direction of the shed. "Power's off inside, just so you know. Got Baba settled in her chair with a flashlight so she won't get too worked up, and I'm gonna fetch one of them kerosene lamps from out back. Best get in there, though. You know how scared she gets in the dark."

"I swear, this old barn. Even looks like it might think about raining and whole damned place gives up the juice." Her aunt struggled up the porch and set down a handful of sacks so she could crack open the front door. "And this conversation about you getting up and around ain't over, sister."

"Can't lie in that bed another second. It's just the worst!" Cora slipped off her shoes and began hopping over the chug holes scattering the driveway, relishing the feeling of being able to just *move* again. "One might argue I need to stretch myself out. Get exercise. Like, you know, a kid or something."

"Christ alive, just like your daddy. Pig-danged-headed." Polly shook her head, setting the groceries inside the door and leaning up against the archway. "Look over at me. Quit the frog-leaping around and look here. Now."

The tone in her auntie's voice put a pause in her niece's gait. Up to her ankles in mud, Cora stopped as bidden and turned to face the woman. Polly's face, its expression usually stuck in a charming halfway point between laughing and put-out, was all business. The sober woman, the grown-up of the house, was now firmly at the wheel.

"I need you. Understand me. Right now, I *need* you." Polly's eyes locked with hers. The woman popped a cigarette into the corner of her mouth, slipped a lighter from the pocket of her jeans and fired it up. "You get me?"

Cora nodded. Both of them stared at one another, hard, for a minute or a half. Another streak and rumble of lightning and thunder, the house lights responding with a flicker and feeble twinkle, only to be swallowed up by shadow again. Within, a distressed squawk from Baba Lena followed by a string of muted mumbling, then a crash. Polly smirked and flipped out her smoke into the yard, disappearing into the house.

In spite of the new weather developments, Cora took her slow, sweet time getting to the shed, muddying up her bare feet as much as she could. By the time she reached the ramshackle old lean-to, which had allegedly once been a deer skinner's shelter before the house had ever had a single board or nail put to it, she was soaked down to her bare skin. The lantern hung by a hook on the weathered pine wall, shrouded in cobwebs and leaves of countless neglectful seasons. The little girl lifted the contraption off of the hook and shook it, relieved to hear the slosh of fuel within. She sat it down on the rickety butcher's table and pried off the cap, using one hand to keep it steady as she turned the little knob on the side to coax out the flat strip of wick out. Cutting an eye back to the house, she saw the yellow orb of the flashlight going from the living room to the kitchen. Polly putting up the groceries.

"You always need me. Who's the dang kid around here? Ain't that supposed to be my job?" Cora muttered as she fished the matchbook from her pocket. Thankfully, they were still dry, eager to crack a light, and in a few seconds she had the lantern broadcasting a cheerful amber glow. As she made her way back across the yard, the rain turning extra vicious like it does right before it steps aside for its cousin hail to come knocking, she noticed something. Something in the big field across the road. The property of Gerald Jacobsen, now the sometime homestead of his son Anders since the passing of the old man two Thanksgivings ago. A sprawling pasture of dead golden grass populated by row upon row of wilted stalks of corn and, some whispered, a moonshine still very much in operation by the dreaded Fulci family buried in the dense thickets of pecan and oak in the rear of the property. The son had some kind of job that kept him on the road a lot, so the acreage had pretty much gone to pot, and he paid some of the kids in town to keep an eye on things and tend to the yard to where it didn't turn into a total jungle.

Seeing folks on the property was a rarity, but there was someone there now clear as could be. Right out in front of the cornfield standing next to the wellhouse. Cora couldn't make them out too sharp, as she'd left her glasses inside on her dresser and they were far enough away where squinting extra hard didn't cut it. A definite shape. A shape like a person.

The child began walking toward the road, down the gravel path of her driveway. She couldn't explain why she had to snatch a peek at this visitor to the Jacobsen farm, only knowing that she had to see them. She held out the lantern before her, feeling a need to have some sort of beacon or source of warding to signal her passage. As she drew closer to the edge of her driveway, her ears began to swim and fill up with noises. The muffled babble of people conversing in large groups, their words a muddle. The electronic bing-bong of machines and clanking glass plates. In her skull the floating memories of smells. Pizza...tomato sauce and frying meat. Onion and oregano and Lysol. Then a tangy and bitter taste in her mouth, overpowering all other sense of taste, a thick and hot fluid filling up her cheeks and spilling out past her lips and onto the front of her shirt.

Cora brought the lantern up close to shed the light upon her chest, which was now soaked in a shade of red so dark it shone a glossy black in the October twilight. She laid her fingertips upon the stain, quickly pulling them away to find the skin coated with the same color.

Blood?

Her blood?

She lifted her wet shirt to regard the ragged map of needlework outlining her from navel to the middle of her ribcage. Everything was still in place, nicely healing and swelling into scar tissue as predicted. Something on the inside had torn loose, maybe? Oh God, why hadn't she listened and just stayed put in that bed like she had been told? Probably a bone poking into a lung or something. Just had to get back inside, get dried off and back in bed. Maybe if she just got still things would start to mend again. She couldn't take another overnight stay in the hospital, especially not *that* hospital.

A terrible sound slit the autumn stillness. A howl. Not the cry of an animal but a man, deranged and mournful, the parodied wailing of a wolf. Shivering all over, her flesh a map of curdled bumps, Cora held the lamp back out before her and crept closer.

Across the road stood the madman from Reverend Billy Tim's Feed Lot, ghostly in his clean white preacher's suit and hellish wolfskin mask, a smoking shotgun held aloft in one hand and the convulsing, headless body of Crystal Crawford, dangling like a ruined puppet, from the other. The eyes hooded behind the flesh mask shimmered like silver coins laid upon the lid of a coffin, catching graveyard moonlight, and broadcasting out ancient profanity. Cora kept hollering at her feet to start going backwards, back toward the house with the lights out and the cursing old woman and a door that locked. But they wouldn't fall in line, keeping her locked to the earth as if roots had grown out of the soles of her feet and begun tangling deep into the dirt, finding other roots and chaining her in place. The Wolf-Man's head lolled back and another wail rang out, this one louder and more agonized. He hefted the ruined body of her sweet friend and began to shake it viciously. From the sky itself a deluge of cold blood began to shower down upon Cora Corbucci, soaking her into a grimy, rotten mess as she prayed for God or anything in between that might have been eavesdropping to just get her back into that house. Back into her bed.

Then, something else. A new, curious horror to complement the nightmare being fed into her eyes. It took a moment for Cora's brain to register the phenomena as a smell even as it slithered up into her nostrils and tickled the twitching ends of her nerves with recognition. One of those really rank odors that pulled half of the breath out of the lungs and made them beg and gasp for cleanliness again. What frightened the girl more than anything was she couldn't figure out what the smell was. It was like nothing she had ever sampled or imagined. But the feeling left behind in its wake was unmistakable. The scent carried the flavor of death with it. Not the kind of death shown on TV or even on the news. Perverse Death, long asleep, now waking up someplace very dark and quiet, left alone for years and years to dream and fantasize about all of the ghastly pleasures it would indulge in upon awakening.

The stench of the man in the wolf mask.

Now came *her* scream. A closed-eyed screech that sucked out every little bit of breath in her lungs, fueled by a heady cocktail of panic and courage. When the scream died down, her heart rumbling in her chest like something set to ignite and consume the world, she opened her eyes to find no wolfman howling from the front yard of Old Man Jacobsen's dead farm. No corpse of a dear friend. No scarlet terror weeping from the thinning autumn storm clouds. No stains on her shirt. Just a twelve-year-old girl and a kerosene lantern and the aftertaste of something truly unspeakable having just brushed up against her.

"It really happened. Oh Lord, all of that really did happen." She trembled, brushing the back of her hand across her eyes.

Cora raced back to the house, the lights returning to life a few seconds after she walked into the kitchen. Polly was putting up groceries in the pantry, cleaning out expired remnants and muttering to herself with her cig clinging faithfully to her bottom lip. Seeing the look on her niece's face seemed to do something to her. Call forth the grown-up thing that liked to hibernate. Somehow the woman knew what she was looking at was someone who had just gazed deep and hard into something unfathomable and left a tiny little chunk of their sanity behind.

"Cora...babydoll?" She set down the case of Coors and started forward, cautiously.

"I want one of my pills, please." The child smiled grimly, holding out her small white hand. "I want one of my pills, right now."

THREE

Juston Matheson, lawfully elected sheriff of Black Knot, sat on the hood of his patrol car, munching on his usual lunch of a bologna sandwich and pork rinds, sipping on a lukewarm can of orange pop. He was parked on the corner of Belladonna and Lavera, the sweetest vantage point on the main drag to observe the daily comings and goings of the Black Knot folks as they went about their afternoon shenanigans. It was a fine autumn afternoon, a bit on the cool and blustery side but decent enough to eat outside if you didn't mind a buttoned-up jacket and getting your hair messed up a little. Sunny but not bright enough to throw on the shades. The breeze had been significantly more hostile earlier in the day, the stoops and storefronts mounded with rust-kissed leaves blown in from other people's yards and lawns. Before the end of the day folks would be out and about raking and sweeping the sidewalks, bagging up the orphaned leaves for twilight burning.

Black Knot was a tidy place, and the people that lived there liked keeping it pretty. Matheson appreciated that in his people. That sense of civic pride you just didn't find in bigger spots like Tulsa or Oklahoma City. Sure, the Knot had its share of issues. What town didn't these days? Drugs, mostly, and even that was a phenomenon consigned primarily to the rougher country out around the lake and up in the hills around Haggard. He'd been the sheriff going on nearly ten years now, and had only worked a handful of violent crimes, only three of them being genuine murders. Even then, those specific acts had been offenses born of poisoned passions. Hair-trigger incidents devoid of sadism. Nothing springing from a source of something truly, naturally wicked.

Like what had happened at the Feed Lot. Nobody would ever forget that bloodbath.

That whole mess, now *that* was wickedness. To even reminisce for a second about the horrors he had witnessed that afternoon made Matheson's blood race through his veins, pounding upon the back door of his heart. The boiling summer heat and all the screaming and the stink of the gore so thick he could smell it clear out in the parking lot. He counted himself lucky he hadn't actually seen the bodies himself. He'd been over in Texarkana fishing when he'd received the call from Deputy Raab about the massacre at the Lot. By the time he'd arrived OSBI had already been on the scene, tended to the bagging the dead, and Barney Driscoll, the local coroner, had handed everything over to the state medical examiner, along with his statement. Raab, however, had seen it all. Matheson had never pressed him for details. The damaged, plagued look in his eyes was more than enough conversation.

The aftermath had been more than enough of a shitshow for him. It didn't help that the maniacs responsible were still loose somewhere, possibly planning God knew what. Maybe even cooking up a second act for Black Knot. That was the worst part of it for the sheriff. Knowing something like that happened in his peaceful little burg with nobody to put a face or name to. No concrete images or evidence. No clear motive or reason. Just the dim, death-tinged remembrances of one little girl. It was as if the killers, literally, had vanished into the same darkness which had brought them here. All those damned reporters weaseling around, some coming from as far away as California to pick at the scraps of a tragedy. A funeral a day for an entire week, it had marked him. It had marked the whole town.

Tearing the Feed Lot down had been a good thing. Nobody wanted that eyesore around to remind them of what had happened. Like a giant tombstone on the edge of town. Razing it down to dust and bare concrete had been good medicine for Black Knot.

Matheson pitched his trash into a bin in front of The Gates of Mordor Arcade, regarding the place with not a small dose of genuine contempt. That arcade was the bitter fruit from the first casualty in the Overhaul Downtown Black Knot Initiative, one of several ancient properties along the main drag to be singled out and mangled for a makeover. True, the old building had been barely hanging on even when it had been his momma's old grocery store. The sheriff still felt some guilt for not having tried to keep the place alive after she had passed. He wholeheartedly felt selling it off had been a smart move. He had worked enough after-school shifts at the old bag of bricks to verify he wasn't cut out for it. Just watching his momma struggle, barely bringing home enough cash to cover the cost of eggs and flour and the fat to fry it all in. But it hadn't been about that, really. Dottie's Grab and Go had *been* his momma. Even after she had died you could still smell her perfume drifting about the storeroom among the odors of good Christian woman cooking. That endless prattle of amazing nonsense which never stopped flowing from her mouth, Matheson swore up and down he could still hear from whenever he walked through the arcade from time to time. Juston didn't believe in ghosts, but if he did, he was for damned sure that old store had been haunted by the old girl.

People came up to him all the time and told him they missed the place, so it wasn't just him. So to see the place just up and gutted like that, its past rendered obsolete and repurposed in a matter of minutes, it had been tough.

The Gates of Mordor Arcade, commonly shortened by its regulars to simply The Gates, really wasn't that bad. Matheson knew they could have put something else in that spot which could have been a hundred times worse. The arcade had only been here a little over a year, and the sheriff had already seen a marked decrease in general teenage tomfoolery. Fewer thuggy brats hanging around in front of the Git N' Split or camping out in the shadows of Withered Oaks Cemetery. The couple that ran it, a brother and sister, were Laveras, an older than the hills and influential Black Knot family who were never crossed and rarely bested. They had already snatched up most of the older buildings on the strip, and Matheson figured they would have probably found a way to easily wrest it out from under him if they wanted to. Better to wash his hands of it now while they were playing nice and dropping coins from a really big piggy bank.

He had to admit theydd really turned the look of the place around quite nicely. The huge picture window in front had finally been replaced after sporting the wounds of a BB gun assault of several years prior. Nice paint job and a really nifty neon sign out front. Most impressive of all was the mural decorating the picture window. Now, that was something! That little girl, Polly Corbucci's niece who had been in that horrible business at the Feed Lot, its sole survivor in fact, had been the hand behind the brush on that. One would never believe a kid that age could be capable of something that polished or coherent. But there it was all the same. In keeping with the motif of the arcade's moniker, it was a montage of fantasy stuff. A bearded sorcerer in deep gray robes etched upon the glass of the big picture window in front, electric blue skeins of lightning rippling from his fingertips to form the logo of the store. One of those creatures which had the top bits of a man and the nether parts of a horse rearing back from a coiled sea serpent. A foreboding knight in black armor menacing a cowering damsel with golden braids and a shimmering crown. Of course, there was a dragon, an impressive serpentine horror of glittering crimson scales and drooling fangs, its mighty head reared back, jaws yawning open and brewing a belly full of flaming death to spew forth.

Good stuff there. The kid really had more than talent. She had a bona fide gift.

Matheson often wished he had had some sort of talent. Not simply a hobby, but something he was good enough at to earn his keep doing it all time. Not that it wouldn't have mattered much. His fate had been set in stone the day his daddy had gone and got himself killed. The summer when he had been forced to give up all of his daydreams to follow in the old man's path. To honor him. At least, that's what he had thought he had been doing. Now, he wasn't so sure it had really ever been his idea. So many folks at daddy's funeral telling him it was what *needed* to be done. To venerate his daddy's memory. Momma herself walking his little three-piece-suited tail right up to the edge of the coffin and informing his father's dead body that their little boy was gonna wear a badge just like his one day. A shiny silver number polished to glowing, like a holy symbol held up before something unnatural slithered up out of a grave.

And so it was said, and so it was done. He went to the academy, as fated. Acquired the badge, as fated. Elected sheriff, as fated.

Not long after the badge came Becky. No kids to speak of, thank the Lord. Not that he hadn't wanted for any. Just hadn't been in the cards for them. Good thing in retrospect, really, given the current state of affairs with his beloved bride and her half-her-age boy toy. A kid would have just complicated things, given the two of them more to tussle over. Matheson, in contrast to the often-rambunctious nature of his vocation, loathed conflict. Hell, he didn't even like to correct the kids at the drive-thru when they got his order jacked up. He didn't just choose his battles wisely, but left them to the side of the road to wonder what if, time and time again.

Matheson belched and slid back into the patrol car by way of the driver side window. It wasn't a totally comfortable squeeze, and he knew it going into the whole affair, but it made him feel like a kid again and he really didn't give a fiddlediddle-damn. Once inside he keyed the car to life and snapped on the radio. The channel was set to the local radio station, and right now the broadcast was smack in the middle of their daily *Radalicous Midday Powerplay*. Matheson hated to admit it, but he enjoyed a lot of the music he heard on the *Powerplay*. Mostly the edgier stuff like Iron Tiger and Slaymaster. Even the more lightweight tunes the kids liked to slow-skate along to at the roller rink weren't too bad. Like the one playing at the moment, "Hold On to Me". He couldn't remember who sang it, The Starlight Twins or something like that. It was all right. Something about it made him think about being young and goofy and hurting over a girl that had stopped taking his phone calls. The lonely part of being a kid.

He grinned and turned the volume up just a bit louder.

As he listened to the song, immersed in the solaces of the past, he didn't realize his hand had already crept up to his earlobe and begun tugging at it: a quirk he had fostered since childhood indulged only when he was really locked into a heavy, thoughtful disposition. But the girl had noticed it. She had seen him doing it when he'd been standing at her hospital bedside, clutching that absurd, gargantuan teddy bear. He must have really been deep down the rabbit hole, as he hadn't even heard her grind her skateboard to a halt next to the door of his patrol car. The song on the radio was one she had heard before. She liked it too. It had a nice chorus that made her want to sing it even when she didn't feel like singing anything at all. She gave him a few minutes, up until the lingering strains of the song evaporated, then merged into some screechy heavy metal number, to see if he would turn the ear loose. The fingers remained hard at it, pinching and kneading the flesh, which was already beet-red.

"You're gonna rip that little guy clean off, you keep after it like that."

Matheson startled, dialed down the volume on the radio and turned to regard the little Corbucci girl grinning at him through the car window. Last time the sheriff had seen the child had been right before she had been discharged from the hospital, still both looking and feeling quite poor. Her appearance was much improved since that afternoon, although she still wore that gloom which all folks who cheat the grave seemed to hang on to for the remainder of their living days.

The kid had the eyes of an old lady, a deep smoky brown so dark they almost melted into their pupils, widely set upon a finely boned, borderline gaunt face. The left eye was lazy to the point of distraction and more than likely officially beyond the corrective guidance of eyeglasses. She was a pretty kid, but needed some serious attention from someone who gave a damn. The raggedy off-yellow sundress she had on was obviously a hand-me-down several times over, the knees of her green leggings worn down to the bare kneecaps, and her Converse sneakers barely clinging to usefulness. Her long snarl of black hair was in desperate need of a comb, her lips dry and peeling. Grinning at him, Matheson was dismayed to see that same gloom found in her eyes mirrored in her smile as well. Poor thing, between living out there in that Haggard hellhole with her screwball Aunt Polly and what had happened to her at the Feed Lot, Cora Corbucci didn't have a lot of cards to play with.

"Whatcha doing so far from home, kiddo?" Matheson leaned out the window, grateful for a reason to keep his lunch break on the rails a bit longer. "Long way to roll on a skateboard, and I believe you're still on bedrest, if I'm not mistaken."

"I didn't come all the way here on it. Ain't got that kind of steam. Polly had to come into town to the Bargain Shed, so I just brought this contraption to tool around on. Kind of rusty, though. Almost fell about a hundred times already." The girl perched herself on the skateboard and practiced at balancing herself. "And I got the all-clear from Doc Jenkins day before yesterday. My days of confinement have ended, praise Jeebus."

"Y'all doing all right up there?" Matheson asked. The patrol car CB radio hissed at him, a series of beep issuing forth indicating a message from Deputy Raab. It could wait. Prob busted some stoners again over at the old McAlester Mine selling weed.

"Tolerable enough, I guess. Why?"

"We busted some dudes cooking out behind the old Anderson stockyards couple weeks back. Rough bunch of boys. Had to shoot one of them, and Deputy Raab had a close call with one of their fighting dogs. Almost lost a finger. Took almost ten stitches, I think, to keep it attached and working proper. Thankfully, it wasn't his gun hand. Not that he can shoot straight to start with."

"That's a good ten miles or so from our place. Almost to the Mills. Ya kill the bad guy?"

"Still close enough to make me ask if y'all are okay. And no, he's alive. We try not to kill people, even the bad ones, if we can help it."

"I appreciate that, mister Officer, sir." Cora smiled, leaning against the patrol car door. "Whew...I'm already tired. Maybe I did overdo it getting out on this thing."

"Easy to do that when you're young."

"It looks real cute, by the way."

Matheson cocked a brow. "Come again?"

"That teddy bear you got me when I was sick. It looks cute in my room. I got it propped up in a corner next to my dresser where I can look at it from my bed. Next to my big plastic jar of pennies. It's too big to fit in bed with me. Bed barely holds me."

"Glad to hear it. See, I always wanted to buy one of those big old bastards, just never had a cause to do so. Pardon my French." The CB honked again, the beeping dragging out a bit longer than earlier. It was most definitely Deputy Raab, which meant whatever he wanted was hot, at least by his standards.

"The look on your face makes me think the person on the other end of that radio has something important to tell you, so I best let you get to it. Aunt Polly is taking too long, so I'm afraid she might have got to talking the cashier's ear off." Cora retrieved the skateboard and secured it in the crook of her arm. "Later on, copper."

"Here. Wait up." Matheson dug around in the console in the middle of the front seat and located a couple of wadded-up dollar bills. "Go get yourself a pop or something over at the Git N' Split. You're looking a little yellow around the gills. Probably a little dehydrated, I wager."

"My, but ain't you a sweet talker." The child smirked, dismissing the offer with a flutter of her fingers. "No thanks. I got cash of my own."

"Nah, you go on and take mine." Matheson insisted, unfurling the dollars and smoothing them out. "If you don't my ex-wife will just end up getting her mitts on it. Rather it go toward an orange pop than her bar tab."

"Oh, she's like that, huh? I've seen her out and about. In her tight pants that show off her coochie. If it means anything to you, she ain't much to write home about. She has a really big butt, and those pants are not the right sort of thing to wear when your butt is all big like that. You could do lots better, you worked out a little. Get a haircut by someone who went to school to learn about doing things like that. Snip that beard a little here and there." Cora reached out and accepted, reluctantly, the pair of bills. "Nah. If I were you I think I'd just stay single. At your age it's probably more hassle than it's worth, all this wooing and buying ladies drinks and supper and such."

"That's the plan, little gal. A bachelor's life for me, soon as the ink's dry on the paper." Matheson chuckled. He really liked this kid, and could tell she didn't have much kindly interaction with folks outside her own house. Kind of felt bad to have to shoo her off. Another series of bleeps chirped from the radio. "It's Deputy Raab. Must be somewhat serious."

"You advise that deputy to keep an eye on that finger of his. He'll be a-needing something to pick his nose proper with. You be careful too." With that Cora Corbucci set her banged-up old skateboard to the cobblestone and rolled away in the direction of the Git N' Split. Matheson grinned as she departed. Such a cool kid. He resolved himself to check in on her later on in the week, just to see how things were going.

The sheriff of Black Knot started his patrol car and got Raab on the radio. Ever prompt, his deputy answered even as the echo of the first blast of static still drifted around in the empty air.

"All right, Raab. What're you blowing up my damn radio for? Remember what I told you about my lunch break. Break means stop. It means 'stop work until said break is done'. Same goes for you, pal. Take. A. Break."

"Boss, we got a bad deal here. A real bad deal." Something in Raab's voice was all wrong. Shaky. Not his usual stern, all-business tone. Matheson tasted the definite flavor of fear. "Need you out here at Camp Azalea, the burned-out part of it on the Bava Crag side, right now. Better get Barney. He's probably over at the gas station having his sammich."

The mention of the coroner's name sent Matheson's heart down into his gut. Last time he'd even had to interact with Barney Driscoll was when little Afton Maxwell had drowned in Lake Hootchyfalala three summers back. But something in the way Raab had used the man's name seemed to hint at something else. Something truly, impressively ominous. Then there was the matter of Camp Azalea itself. Nobody went out there on purpose, not even individuals who made their livelihood in the southeastern Oklahoma criminal underworld. Ever since the murders of those three little Girl Scouts almost a decade before, when it had been called Camp Red Hand, it had become known locally as more than just a haunted place, but a shunned one as well. Matheson did not look forward to going out there.

"I'll call him. On my way." Matheson set the CB back in its cradle and reclined his head against the head rest of his seat, his skin slicking over with cold sweat. This was not a good day for something like this to happen. The lawman eased his patrol car out on to the main drag and waited for the light to go green. While he waited, he noticed some men working on the roof of what used to be Muldrow's Drugstore, a small rock building directly across the street from The Gates. They were re-shingling the roof, a couple of them down below caulking the windows. A pretty lady with long red hair and a butt that looked great in jeans was putting the finishing touches on the painted logo of what appeared to be a new café. The woman turned to give orders to the men working on the windows and Matheson was struck by the familiarity of her profile. She was very distinctive-looking, and he swore he had seen her before, but couldn't hang a clear memory on her. Sitting cross-legged to one side of the entrance of the café was a young boy of around eleven or twelve, head down and scrawling intently on a Big Chief notepad. His rust red hair hinted at him possibly being the woman's son, or at least someone of her blood.

The light shifted from yellow to green, and Sheriff Juston Matheson swerved onto Hemlock Avenue, heading toward his duty.

When Matheson arrived at the campground, he found Deputy Raab hunkered down in a tall patch of Creeping Jenny, his hat off in the grass and face buried in his palms. The familiarity of his body language immediately set the lawman on edge. It very much mirrored his condition when Matheson had arrived at the Feed Lot, months back. The sight of him made Juston want to linger a bit longer in the squad car. He didn't feel ready to face whatever it was that had humbled his deputy straight down to his knees. Yet go to him he did. He put his arm around the young man and allowed him to cry hard into his shoulder until the fabric of the sheriff's uniform was soaked dark at the shoulder. They talked about what Raab had seen and a little about God and Jesus and why the world was such a horrible place to be in sometimes. Barney Driscoll, county coroner, pulled up not long after that, and the three of them walked into the gutted ruin of what had once been the Head Counselor's Lodge of Camp Red Hand.

The three men stood over what was left of the child's body. A little girl, maybe of around ten or eleven. Now it was impossible to tell where the living began, and death ended. Matheson had only ever seen eight corpses in his entire life. All of them, other than his daddy, were folks who had died relatively easy. Nothing like the savaged horror scattered across the scorched floor of the old lodge like a ruptured garbage bag. The girl's skin was desiccated almost to the point of mummification, and from head to toe the dead child's cold gray face was sheathed in a gauzy shroud of what appeared to be a layer of thick gray spiderwebs, her glassy eyes rimmed with horror and mouth opened so wide the lower jaw would have had to have been broken and unhinged from her skull. Matheson extended an exploratory finger and gave the webs a quick poke. Whatever this gunk was, it most definitely did not come from a spider, or at least not any creepy crawler he had ever encountered. Looping his index finger around a loose strand, he found its surface to be chilly as graveyard moss, not at all sticky and insanely tough to pull away from the corpse. Pulling back his fingers he found them to be coated in a pale, almost silvery dust. Disgusted, he wiped his hand on his pants and stood up.

"Jesus…" Matheson leaned against the archway of the fellowship hall, pushing his hat back off his brow. He wasn't sure if he was going to puke or scream or maybe pull off a little of each. The room was starting to tilt on its side and threatened to take him down with it. He closed his eyes and took several deep breaths. "Who found her?"

Raab took a hesitant step toward the body, shining his flashlight at it. "Hiker lady from the city. Not a local. One of those nuts we get every now and then out here looking for a ghost story."

"This would be the place to find them," Barney commented dryly. Even the county coroner was looking a little green around the gills. "No bugs on her. Very odd for the state of her decay."

"Where is she now? The hiker lady?" Matheson returned to the corpse and knelt beside it, removing his pocketknife from its sheath below his gun holster.

"I got her over in the squad car. She's a mess." The deputy walked across the room to where an old window had once been and peered out. Matheson followed. From the window he could see the top of the woman's head in the back seat, inclined forward with a blanket wrapped tightly around her. She had a really striking hair color. The deepest, darkest black Matheson had ever seen. Thick and luxurious. So black it burned azure in the right light. He contemplated this for a few seconds before returning to the child.

"Reckon who she is? Nobody's reported any missing kids I know of."

"Doubt it's local for that very reason you just gave. Gonna make this a bit tougher." Matheson lifted a handful of the webbing, pulled it away from the body and began sawing on it with his pocketknife.

"Might not want to mess around too much there, Chief. Got a crime scene here," the coroner advised. He had not come forward himself, but kept a good five to six feet back as he scribbled entries into the little red notebook he kept with him at all times.

"I'm good, Barn. You just keep a-scratching that pencil of yours. I want to get a closer look at her, and this stuff all over her."

The substance he was attempting to carve a path through was resilient; each tendril, upon being severed, actually appeared to be trying to mend itself. After a good ten minutes and slashing and pulling, Matheson was able to expose the lower jaw and upper chest of the dead little girl. As he pulled the webbing away a weak expulsion of dusty yellow motes drifted up from the newly exposed area, scrunching up his nose. The lawman noted the body didn't smell dead. It didn't really smell bad at all. Drawing air into his nostrils, Matheson mulled the scent around a bit, tasting it in his mind for recollections. Images popped into his brain of wet November leaves, gutted candles and the dust of long-ago places. Secret smells.

"Looks like most of her innards are scattered around her," Raab observed. He laid a battered cigarette on his bottom lip but didn't light it. "You reckon some dogs turned wild been at her? Can't image a person doing something like this. Something this nasty."

"In a place like this, where so much bad has already happened, I can't quite agree with that." Barney toed closer and knelt beside the sheriff, using the eraser end of his pencil for a pointer. "Strange, there's no wound as far as I can tell. Not even any blood on her skin. Almost like she'd been cleaned up after what was done to her. She'd be all torn up, the way everything inside of her is all over the place. Cut down the front of her dress a bit, will you, Sheriff?"

"Hey, this is a little girl, man. I don't…"

"Just do it, please." Barney leaned in closer and pulled away the last of the gunk covering her face and breast. "Humor me."

Frowning, Matheson pinched a piece of cloth from the child's dress and began to gently slice a jagged path along her breastplate. Barney unfolded the fabric to one side and investigated further, poking and prodding. A few minutes passed before he abruptly stopped, gasped, and reared back away from the corpse.

"Something is not right about this…" He whispered, wiping his hand on his slacks.

"Damn right, some crazy son of a bitch gutted her and yanked out all of her insides. That's about as not right as you can get." Raab finally lit his Newport and took a quick puff.

"What did you feel?" Matheson asked. Barney didn't answer but nodded down at the body. The lawman reached out and parted the cut in the dress and observed. In the middle of little girl's chest from just under her sternum down to her navel a thick, deep pink scar looked back at him. Upon closer inspection he observed the scar was more like a furrow, like a rut you would find in a freshly plowed field. He pressed a hesitant hand upon the furrow and noted it was as hard and smooth as polished rock. A flick of a finger upon it verified its solidity, as if her breastbone somehow extended down into her belly. Matheson stood up, speechless, and turned to regard the coroner.

"What the hell is that?"

"Your guess is about as worth as much as mine right now, boss." Barney shrugged. "I would lean toward some sort of deformity. Probably congenital."

"What's that mean?" Raab had ventured closer, lingering behind Matheson.

"Means she was born with it," Matheson answered. He wiped a thick sheen of sweat from his forehead. The old shack felt as if the temperature had risen at least ten degrees.

"Affirmative. I won't know until an autopsy has been done, which will need to be done by the State Medical Examiner. This is way out of my wheelhouse." Barney looked over at Raab. "You contact OSBI?"

"No. Was wanting you boys to have a gander first."

"I'd keep it away from the paper as long as you can. Folks here will be sitting on their porches with their shotguns, pinging every stray cat that knocks over a garbage can. People are still on edge after that nastiness at the Feed Lot. I'll see y'all over at the hospital." Barney Driscoll returned to his car, fired it up and was gone.

"Scared me to see old Barney act like that. That old boy's seen it all and then some. He was cutting up bodies up in St. Louis for years before he came here. He was at the Feed Lot too." Raab shook his head and headed back to his squad car to radio someone back at the station for an ambulance. Matheson grabbed his arm.

"Don't fool with having somebody at the office call OSBI. Better if you go on and make the call. We'll look a little less bumpkin, we do it ourselves. Call the ambulance yourself too. I'll stay with her until they get here. See if you can get anything out of that lady once you get her settled down. Get the bottle of Old Crow I got stashed in my file cabinet and help yourself, if you need to." The sheriff pulled up an old wooden stool and parked himself there, wary of the fading daylight. Raab nodded and returned to the car, his tires throwing gravel a couple of minutes later and the sound of the engine growing fainter and fainter as he drove away. Matheson hoped the ambulance wouldn't take too long. The thought of lingering in this terrible place with the child's body chilled him. He wondered if the animal responsible for this savagery and the murder of those three little girls so many years back were the same person. It was entirely possible, as that monster had never been caught. Had they returned again to take the lives of more kids?

He didn't want to admit to himself that he didn't really buy into that theory, as much as he wanted to. Something about this just felt different. A fresh horror. He wasn't too sure which option was worse.

It took a little more than an hour for the ambulance to arrive. It was a new bunch of boys Matheson had never seen before. For the past three years it had been the Charleston twins almost exclusively, and then Maud Samuels the optometrist's daughter or Blondie from the Git N' Spit when the twins were unavailable. But they were nice enough and got to it jiminy quick when he had asked for a sheet to cover the corpse with before they saw it. He didn't want anyone else witnessing this awfulness. Right now, he thought it best to keep this one closer to home. Wouldn't do for the story to get out and gossip started. They didn't question him and dutifully loaded their dead cargo into the vehicle without fanfare.

With the body gone, the sheriff felt a bit more at ease, even inclined to help himself to a brief stroll before heading out. An avid hunter, he very much enjoyed the outdoors. He headed out what remained of a side door, passing through a short breezeway, through another archway opening out onto a large concrete patio area. It was a fine autumn evening, and the patio kind of reminded him of Becky and their lake house they had shared on the banks of the Hootchyfalala. They'd hosted a lot of barbecues from the deck of that old cabin, back in the days when he'd been a regular churchgoer and still cared about having friends. Out there by himself, everything all quiet and still, he decided he liked it better like this. Being alone and not having to always *be somewhere*. That was the way it was when you were married. Folks always expected you to be somewhere. Be available for a chat or a drink or an ear to listen to their bullshit. Now he didn't have to worry about any of that. All of their friends had been through his soon to be ex-wife. All of their commitments and connections began and ended with her. He really should have been obliged to her for pulling him out of all that. Giving him a get out of jail card for being hospitable.

Now the cabin had been all but abandoned and he was living in a cramped three-room apartment over his buddy Nick's hardware store. Still better than living with that piece of work he'd once promised until death they did part.

The sheriff sighed and shook his head. The whole time he had been pinching his earlobe, and now it was sore and agitated. The little Corbucci girl was right, he was going to rip it right off the side of his face if he didn't get that little nervous habit under his thumb.

"This is a nice place to live. This doesn't happen to people who live here."

He looked down at his watch.

It was ten till five.

FOUR

Hayder spent the next couple of days helping Mom finish setting up the café, mostly running little errands like snagging a hammer from the hardware store or fetching her an iced tea from the Git N'Split. She had even asked his opinion on the layout of the dining room, as if his input actually mattered, which made him feel pretty special. He kept hoping, in secret, she would change her mind about letting him work at the café instead of the Red Hand Theater. However, she was firmly set upon hiring another kid to help her and was adamant he break out from under her watchful eye, even just a little bit, and he sort of agreed. It was a bit scary, but he didn't want to trouble her with any of that. Being away from her too long made him anxious. The therapist back home had told him this was perfectly normal after losing a parent, and double normal after the death of a sibling. He was thankful for that. Being told you were normal by someone who understood how things like that worked.

By Wednesday evening mom was as ready as she ever would be, and opening day would be Monday promptly at six in the morning. She hoped some of the old-timers, usually early risers as well, would pop in and check the place out. Hayder had to admit Mom's biscuits and gravy were the best ever, and those old dudes were always serious about the quality of their breakfast. Once you locked in a handful of regulars, in a small town like this, you stood a good chance of not only surviving, but thriving.

"Baby boy, why don't you go do something fun? I've kept you busy since we got here with the house and the café, you've barely had time to explore. I'm absolutely the worst mom ever." She pulled a chair from one the tables and sank down into it. "Go get my purse from the back and have a five, or a ten if there is one, and mosey across the street to the arcade. I've seen you eyeballing it since we opened up."

Hayder's heart immediately pulsated with fresh life. He *had* noticed the arcade, and was intrigued by the size of it. It was a remarkably large place for such a small town, and unlike the places back home, stayed open way past sunset. The boy did as bidden, returning with a single five and two ones, more than enough to kill an hour or so or maybe longer if the arcade had a couple of games he was good at. Before he left he felt that pang of guilt and asked mom if she needed him for anything else, only to be ushered wordlessly out the café door and hearing it locked behind him. Across the street The Gates of Mordor Arcade teemed with kids, flowing in and out of the open doors in a flood of laughter, howls of frustration and cussing.

Yup, just like back home.

The innards of The Gates of Mordor Arcade were just as impressive as its outside shell. Within the wood paneled chamber Hayder found a glory of bleeping and flashing amusements. Decked out in orange and black crepe, cut-out paper frights of skeletons and sheet-ghosts in reverence of Halloween, the arcade consisted of one huge open area, easily spanning an acre, with a section set aside for the more old-school diversions like pool, ping-pong and foosball directly to the left of the entrance, a shimmering fleet of pinball machines to the right. A deeper journey forward revealed a snack bar illuminated in pink neon, a six-lane bowling alley close by, and in the very back the mother lode, the area reserved for the video games. The entire room reeked of stale cigarette smoke, dried beer, grease-soaked cheeseburgers and dirty feet. It was pure heaven. Hayder made for the cashier, broke all of his bills into rolls of quarters, and made a beeline for the hallowed region in the back.

The arcade was well-stocked. Not quite the bounty of digital goodness to be found back home in Dallas, but all of the esteemed staples were present. *Blood Warriors*, *Kung Fu Psycho*, *Dungeon Dwellers*, *Gobbler* and many more. The boy wandered through the crowd, mostly kids his age, until he found himself staring at what he had hoped would be there, his favorite game, *Necromania*.

His heart sank. There was someone else playing it.

The boy looked a little closer. It was a girl.

A girl *playing* video games. Not just watching.

He'd never seen a girl play a video game before. Not even on television.

The girl turned to rub her cheek on her shoulder as if tending to an itch, revealing her profile. His heart crawled up into his throat and sucker punched his Adam's apple.

This was no ordinary girl. It was *the* girl. The crazy kid next door he had seen screaming from her front yard on his first rainy day in Black Knot. Although he had only caught a glimpse of her from his own yard, he could tell it was her. Hayder was conflicted. On the one hand, he really wanted to saunter up to the machine, slap his quarter down on the cabinet panel and claim next game. On the other, it would mean having to actually speak to this girl, a possibly insane one to boot. He wasn't sure he was up to the challenge. What if she talked back? What if she said something weird he wasn't ready for? Maybe even attacked him? People with mental problems were known to flip out and often kill people without provocation. But the siren's call of 8-bit vampire slaying and ghost banishing conquered his better judgment, and he found himself padding over one tiny step at a time until he was standing at her side.

She was really pretty, which accelerated his discomfort from zero to five hundred in a heartbeat. It was a strange and uncommon sort of pretty. Not at all like the girls back home in Texas with their designer jeans, massive pyramids of hair and a jillion layers of makeup. Everything about her, from her long black locks and clean face, radiated a casual, natural magnetism. Then she turned to him, and they locked eyes. What Hayder Hennessey saw gazing back at him sent a peculiar shudder through his body, rattling his veins and gnawing down to the bone. For all her prettiness the girl's eyes, one of which was seriously lagging behind the movement of the other, reflected a very dark, almost mournful affectation. She looked as if she hadn't had slept for days, and her gaunt white cheeks suggested a steady ritual of malnutrition. She was even dressed like a crazy person, a pale blue ballerina skirt around her scant waist, white leggings, battered red sneakers and a torn black Mercyless Destiny t-shirt.

This last article gave him special pause. Mercyless Destiny were a heavy-metal band notorious for encouraging teen suicide, devil worship and black magic. At least that's what his Sunday school teacher back in Dallas had told him.

The girl continued to stare. A minute or so passed and she allowed a curious eyebrow to travel upward.

"I...I got next," he stammered, hesitantly placing his coin on the cabinet panel right below the screen. She took a step forward. They were both exactly the same height. The girl smelled of Ivory soap and cigarette smoke and her eyes behind her thick glasses were of such a deep brown hue they looked completely black in the shadowed cast of the flickering arcade neon. She shrugged and stepped aside, yet not leaving altogether. It was obvious she was going to hang around and gawk. Hayder took her place and rolled his quarter into the slot, the game springing to life with the acceptance of his sacrifice. The creepy girl was standing so close to him the cold flesh of her elbow often brushed up against his arm. This game was going to be over very quickly if she kept that up. Every couple of seconds he would sneak a glance at her to see if she were checking him out. Her focus, however, appeared to be upon the game and his every little button push and joystick twitch.

"Don't mind me. I've had the high score on this baby for the past four months. Four months today, exactly." Her voice was surprising low and raspy for both a kid and a girl. Hayder glanced up at the leaderboard and saw the initials *CLC* with an astonishingly awesome score of almost a million points. He'd never seen a score that high on *Necromania*, not even back home in Dalla,s where he had attended actual gaming tournaments. His own personal best had been an embarrassing by comparison ninety-eight thousand and three. Her nearness made him both excited and nauseated at the same time, and he wasn't sure he liked the feeling. The boy kept peeping at her out of the corner of his eye, looking for reasons to observe her.

"That's a rad score for sure. I don't know anyone who's even got close to that. You must practice a whole lot and go through a bunch of quarters." He barely dodged a swipe from a set of pixelated talons, sweat breaking out all over his body.

"Better watch out for those gargoyles. They do more damage than the other monsters and can't be killed without rolling around a lot. That rolling around stuff, that's the key to wiping them out without getting hurt, and every roll gets you ten extra points if you avoid their attack," the girl advised, tapping the screen with her finger. "And that there score, that's just from one quarter."

"They're dang hard to avoid," Hayder agreed. He wasn't sure if he believed her about the one quarter boast, but he let it go. No sense in getting into it with a total stranger, especially a girl he suspected of being some kind of maniac. Another gargoyle plunged in for the kill, and he responded by sending his noble knight rolling from left to right over and over until he landed an attack squarely on the creature's back, vanquishing it in a cloud of flickering red mist. She had been correct; his score had increased dramatically when factoring all of the rolling in. He couldn't help but smile, and when he glanced at her again she was smiling too. The nausea began to melt away, shifting into an easy comfort.

"I think the ghosts are the worst enemy of all of them. They're totally overpowered, and it's kinda dumb you can kill them with a sword. I mean, they're see-through. A sword is not going to do anything to something you can't even touch." Pulling up a chair, she sat down and crossed her legs, kicking her foot up and down spastically. She was breathing heavy, as if standing up and talking to him had expended excessive effort.

"Well, maybe it's some kind of blessed sword," Hayder reasoned. A ghoul, its long green tongue lolling, vaulted out from behind a graveyard shack and pounced upon his knight, reducing him to a shambling skeleton in a rusted suit of plate mail armor. "They have things like that in *Warriors and Warlocks*. There is a character you can play called a crusader. They're like holy fighter-type guys who can kill demons and undead. There is a sword they can get called a Hallowed Blade which can cut through vampires, and even ghosts, like butter."

The girl furrowed her brows and seemed to contemplate this new morsel of lore. She shook her head. "Nah, I think the dudes who built the game didn't really think it through or care much. They thought the ghost looked cool and just slapped it in there."

Hayder was unsure of how to respond to that, electing instead to focus upon getting through the graveyard level, which he had never managed to conquer. Today was no exception, and within a few minutes his valiant knight, armor and all, collapsed into a pile of bones and dirt, a small tombstone sprouting up from his pitiful remains. He looked up at his final score and enjoyed a warm tingle of pride. One hundred and twenty-two thousand and nine points, a personal best. The girl giggled and applauded loudly, making every head in the arcade turn to him and embarrassing him a bit. He looked at her, suspecting some kind mockery. Instead, he found her to be genuinely pleased for him, her eyes wide and smile genuine.

"Good game. See…I told you about that rolling stuff. Keep doing that and you'll be a genuine contender for that high score. The queen can't rule forever, ya know." She stood up, wincing as if it took effort, drawing in a deep breath. "Rats. Shouldn't have done so much today. Got my insides stirred up."

Hayder desperately wanted to ask her what was hurting her so, but held his tongue. It was none of his business and she was a stranger. He pointed at her shirt. "You like Mercyless Destiny?"

Shrug. "I like anything spooky. Movies. Music. Books especially. I really like Halloween too."

"Yeah but those guys are devil worshippers!" Appalled, Hayder gestured to her shirt again. It was pretty hard to argue with him based upon the fiendish image presented on faded black cotton. A quartet of shapes in hooded black robes gathered before a flaming inverted cross, the monstrous visage of a ghoulish demon leering down at them.

"No, they don't. It's just a gimmick like all of those heavy metal guys use to sell records." The girl dismissed him with a flutter of fingers. "Trust me, I've seen the Devil. I know what he looks like."

Another potential conversational thread severed in mid-weave.

"So, what's your name? Where are you from?" She drew closer to him until they were almost nose to nose. This person really had no sense of boundaries or personal space, another clear indicator of lunacy. "I've never seen you here, and pretty much the same people haunt this dump. Black Knot is a really small place, and I would have seen you at some point. Unless you're new, then of course I wouldn't be seeing you until right now."

"Hayder Hennessey. I just moved here from Dallas with my mom." He began racking his brain for an excuse to make a hasty departure. There would be more questions after this one, each more invasive the one before it, and he wasn't in the mood to spill out his life story to this weirdo.

"*Eeek*! I'm very sorry for you, then." She seemed genuinely troubled for him.

"Why?"

"'Cus nobody moves here on purpose, and most regret it as soon as they get here." She stated this matter-of-factly, without a hint of drama "I'm Cora. Last name's not important really. How old are you?"

"Twelve. What did you mean by that?" he asked, both interested and just a pinch unnerved.

"Oh good! I'm twelve too. Thirteen in July, so remember that." She offered a small white hand for him to shake, which he did. "Mean by what?"

"About people regretting moving here. That part."

"Nice job. You were listening. Most boys have a problem with that when a girl is saying something." She reached out and patted his head. "Let's just say Black Knot is different than other places. Weird stuff just happens here. Things that can't happen in big cities."

"What kind of stuff?" Hayder began to feel a peculiar cold crawling up his spine, pulling up tiny mounds of heebie-jeebies on his skin. "How weird? What kind of weird?"

"You'll find out soon enough, you hang around for long." Cora answered nonchalantly, as if she had had this same conversation a million times before. "So, what made you move here? You moved from a fun place to Black Knot, so something had to have happened. Your mom and dad get a divorce or something? I hear that one a lot."

Hayder took a few moments to ponder his answer. Something about the girl made him *want* to tell her about Dad and Brandy. Talk about it with someone besides Mom and his doctor. But it still hurt so bad, and even thinking about it made him sick at his belly and want to cry, and he didn't want to cry in front of a girl. Crying in front of a cute girl was like death.

"We had some bad stuff happen to us, my mom and me. She's opening that café across the street. The Kiss My Grits Café."

Cora didn't press him for more information, simply nodding, for which he was grateful. "That's a really cool name for a café. She make good pancakes?"

"Hmmm?"

"Pay. Attention. Hayder." Cora sounded each word out loudly, slowly, one at a time as if speaking to a little kid being taught how to spell. "Your momma. Does she make good pancakes? That's important for a café. A well prepared, tasty breakfast."

"You bet she does. My mom can make pancakes taste the way gold shines." Hayder smiled. He had to admit he liked this girl, in spite of her borderline impoliteness and brash approach to friending someone up. It was a refreshing switch from the giggling, looks-obsessed girls he'd grown up with and been accustomed to back in Texas.

"That's a real big brag. Pancakes are nothing to joke about." Cora walked forward and retrieved her skateboard from behind the *Necromania* cabinet. "I might just have to investigate this claim myself, in person, tomorrow morning. Will you be working there?"

"She won't be for real open until Monday morning. I won't be working there, though. She got me another job." Hayder suddenly lit up with an idea, and before he could stop himself he blurted it out. "Hey, maybe *you* could work for her! If you want, that is. She told me she wanted to hire a local kid."

Cora's dark eyes lit up, her white cheeks staining pink. "Oh my gosh! That would be so bitchin'! You think she would hire me? I can do a lot! Not just clean up. I can even cook really good. Work the register. And I work *real* hard too. Oh, that would be the best…"

Hayder held up his hand for silence. Cora nodded and made a zipping gesture across her lips.

"Let me ask her. I don't see why she'd ever say no. But can I ask *you* something?" He hesitated, sucking in his breath, afraid to go any further. However, he felt it best to get it out of the way and off of his chest. "I just want to know…are you weird?"

Cora's face scrunched up, appearing to be genuinely confounded by the request. The girl seemed to be savoring the question in her mouth, mulling it over like a peach seed.

"Well, yeah. Of course I'm weird. But I can still fry bacon and tote food to someone's table. Weird folks are just fine for doing things like that, I reckon." She shrugged. Question answered.

Hayder nodded, scrounging for something clever to say. He came up lacking, ending up with a simple: "I'll talk to her tonight."

"Yay! Here, let me give you my number so you can call me. If you want." She scored a gel-pen from her backpack and took hold of his wrist. "You better write this down as soon as you get home, so you don't accidentally wash it off. I've had that happen a kajillion times! People seem to lose my number. Like, tons of people." The girl painted her digits onto boy's skin in neon purple glitter ink. Huge, impossibly to ignore numerals.

Should I tell her she lives right next door to me?

The glitter beckoned.

Nah.

Without a further peep, not even a goodbye, the girl named Cora flounced away from the boy and out the doors of Mordor. Hayder didn't care. He couldn't stop staring at his wrist. A girl had actually given him her phone number! To call her. On the phone! A girl. He wanted to both do a back flip and hurl his lunch at the same time.

Hayder played a few games of *Kung Fu Psycho* before deciding to call it a day. The girl still fresh on his mind, his belly turning delightfully as he began to ascend the steps leading out of the arcade. Looking down at the glittering numerals on his skin, he grinned.

"You'd do well to steer clear of that one, lil buddy."

The boy paused and turned to regard the voice, finding it belonging to a man who could have been anywhere from fifty to one hundred and fifty. A chubby fellow with a chaotic cloud of gray-black hair, frizzy pork chop sideburns with a battered corncob pipe dangling from the corner of his mouth. He was wearing a discolored Hawaiian shirt three sizes too small, the buttons straining against the flaccid distension of his gut, Bermuda shorts and flip-flops. Hayder could almost taste the reek of beer from where he stood, a good ten feet away from the man.

"Sorry, sir?"

"That lil gal. You would do well to not let her know your business. Nor you hers. A bad child from a bad family plagued by trouble." The man sparked the pipe with a BIC lighter and indulged in a puff. "Corbucci family is cursed. Ask anyone. Nobody here will tell you different."

Hayder was both intrigued and scared. "That stuff isn't real. Curses."

"You new to the Knot?" the man asked. Hayder nodded.

The man spent the next several minutes telling Hayder a story. A dark tale about an even darker deed. A tale of a beautiful late summer afternoon in which seven people went to enjoy a quiet Sunday lunch at a beloved local chowhouse, ending with only one person leaving that place barely alive.

That one person was Cora Corbucci, current *Necromania* champion of The Gates of Mordor Arcade and possible future employee of the Kiss My Grits Café.

"She got shot with a damn scattergun, man! Right in the chest. They didn't think she was going to make it." The old codger shook his head as if still shocked by the entire affair. "But she pulled through, and folks are saying ever since she ain't been right in the noodle. A black cloud hangs over her, and trouble follows her. She stabbed a dude in the face for just looking sideways at her. Also heard she's become a loose girl. Doing the sort of stuff with boys only married people are supposed to do."

"I don't believe that!" Hayder snapped, surprised at his reaction. Somehow, he just didn't believe that. He *wouldn't* believe that.

The man shrugged and puffed on his pipe. "Believe what you want, junior. Ask around about her. About the whole Corbucci lot. You'll get the same story, word for word, every time."

"I have to go. Have a good day, mister." Hayder lifted a hand in parting and continued up the stairs. Behind him the old fart began cackling, choking on smoke.

"You'll regret it, boy." The man wheezed. "You're going to regret ever laying eyes on that girl."

Of course, Mom had teased him about it. Even more so when she discovered it was the girl next door he was asking her to look into hiring.

He had almost decided against even mentioning Cora once he and his mother were in the truck, on the way back to the house. But he felt obligated to the girl and brought it up once they were at the supper table. Greasy fast-food burgers tonight. Mom had been worn to a frazzle.

Ultimately, she was relieved. It was one less detail to attend to. In the morning she wanted him to personally walk over to Cora's house, not call, and bring her over for breakfast. He agreed, grateful to have the matter off of his chest for the time being, and collapsed into his bed, into slumber, almost immediately.

Hayder awoke sometime a little after two in the morning. He had heard voices coming from the kitchen. One of the voices was most likely his mother, judging from the higher resonance. The other one was much deeper. Familiar somehow. Mom had company, it sounded like. But who would be paying her a visit at this time of the morning? The thought scared him a little.

Rising from his bed, the boy wandered along the dark hallway, crept down the stairs and into the kitchen.

The voice had sounded like Dad.

Mom was sitting alone at the kitchen table. Before her was a cup of tea which she stirred with her finger. She looked up at him and grinned, barely awake herself.

"Get back to bed, mister," she murmured sleepily, covering the cup with her hand. "Your 'ol Ma is having her a moment."

He nodded and walked back up the stairs.

Maybe he had dreamed the voices.

He hadn't dreamed the smell of the booze.

INTERLUDE ONE:

Excerpt from Frogman's Field Guide to the Unnatural Phenomena of Little Dixie: REEL ONE (8 MM film and audio recording estimated to have been made sometime in the mid to late 1960s. Used with permission of current owner, who wishes to remain anonymous.

*The cheap film stock is faded to a frosty yellow, pockmarked with imperfections inflicted from the decay of time. The audio, miraculously, is astonishingly clear. Before us is a man seated in a lawn chair. He is in what appears to be some sort of den or game room. There is a pool table and a large wet bar behind him. The bar is well-stocked.

The man himself is unremarkable looking. Tan, weathered, and wiry, he most likely works outdoors for his paycheck. He could be anywhere between thirty-five and seventy; his raggedy mop of greasy black hair looks to have been combed with fingers. Dressed in battered Wranglers tucked into a pair of worsened Ropers and an oversized flannel shirt, he sits holding a can of beer in one hand. In spite of his inconspicuous appearance there is something in his eyes which begs your attention. The expression in those eyes is that of a normal human being who has suddenly found themselves thrust into the realm of the uncanny, barely clinging to stability.

The gentleman speaks. The coarse caress of his voice is spiked with nicotine, a very palpable tinge of fear, and untold sleepless nights.

It's taken me almost three decades of living in this shithole to get it all figured out.

It's all in the way the town is laid out. It's not random. No sir. You gotta really look at it close.

You see, I read books nobody in this place would ever think to stick a nose in. Books I had to order through the mail. Stuff about black magic and sacred geometry and all that jazz. I learned that magic and math and architecture go hand in hand. Hell, the entire city of Washington D.C. was built this way. Assembled right up from the guts of the swamp by satanic engineers guided by demons! You can go on and say it's just a dying old man off his nut, blabbing nonsense and looking for a little attention in his waning years. But I know better. I know! Hopefully, this will make it into the hands of someone with some pull. Someone who will expose the dirty deeds and secrets of this small town for what they are: huge secrets which could possibly bring about the end of the world itself. Doomsday, USA, Baby. Doomsday USA.

I won't bore you with the history of this town. It's all typical Manifest Destiny shit. This was probably a real shithole even when the Indians were the only ones here. Before those two Dago witch families, mortal enemies even back then, sloshed across the ocean and planted their Satanic flags in the soil here almost three centuries ago.

I think the really bad started with the murders at the Red Hand Theater. Christ, the name alone is a red flag somethin' ain't right with the place.

Although folks are slow to talk about it, everyone who's lived here even for a little while has at least heard about the Little Dixie Strangler. It's one of those creepy old campfire stories kids like to spook one another with at slumber parties, its details and facts changing with every set of lips and ears the tale passes from and into. Now, most people just know the basics. The stuff the papers were allowed to talk about. From July until November of 1945, seven people were strangled to death in various parts of the Red Hand Theater. Six women and one man. All of these dead folks were outsiders to Black Knot. Complete strangers, a couple of them coming from as far away as Florida. Nobody was ever caught, or even suspected in their deaths. The lack of police attention and news coverage was minimal, the crime treated as if it had been no more critical than the Halloween toilet papering of a tree. Nobody here wanted to talk about it, so digging deeper into the matter was a waste of time. Hell, the theater itself didn't even see so much as a hiccup in its ticket sales even as they were loading corpses out the fire exit.

So, I forgot about it.

Until I got Johnny Castor a-talkin' about it. Once that old boy got to talking, turns out he had a whole lot to say. Johnny was the county coroner from 1940 until his retirement in 1960. I had gone to school with his son Melvin, Johnny's wife having passed some years before, and Melvin had got hisself killed his first tour in Korea. After Melvin's death the old dude and I had grown pretty close. Johnny was the one who told me the truth about the Little Dixie Strangler. You see, there were a few colorful details missing from what was reported by the news. Stuff that was kept from the public by persons unknown, although suspected by yours truly. I'll get to that in a bit. Turns out the Strangler was a little bit more productive than both the cops and news let on. Johnny told me this as he lay a-dyin' in the old folks' home over in Coffin Mills, ate up with cancer of the liver. Guess he wanted a clean slate for his Christian soul before death flushed him out into the afterlife.

True, six women and one man met their end at the hands of the Little Dixie Strangler. That wasn't the worst of it, though. Johnny Castor told me thirteen *children* also had the ghost choked out of them as well. Six boys to seven girls. Now, here's a really important detail to know, one omitted from every single diddlydamned police report and even the official coroner statement. All of them bodies, *every single goddamned one of them*, had their innards torn right out their bellies, slung all over the theater aisles, over the backs of the seats, and yet not one drop of blood was to be found *anywhere*. The bodies looked to have been sliced open, relieved of their insides, then closed back up with just a big old healed-over wound in their chests. An impossibly healed mutilation of the flesh. Even stranger, these bodies were covered in spiderwebs and muck. Top of the head to the tips of their toes. Johnny said it reminded him of the mummies he'd seen on *Creature Feature*. The upper brass at the Red Hand, aided by the police, kept all of this on the down low. To us, to the real world, these extra details never, ever happened.

The morning Johnny Castor went to meet his maker, he kept a-callin' for me, in a panic. I was out tilling my side pasture so didn't hear the phone ringing, so they sent some kid out to my place to fetch me. When I got to the hospital I noticed a lot of people hanging around outside Johnny's room. Some of them were strangers, but a couple of them I recognized straight off as Fulcis. Not the big cheese Fulcis like Fantasma or Infestato, but some of their goons. And man, they was a-fussin' something awful to get into that room with that old man. They was up to no good, and *that* fucking scared me. At that time, I didn't believe in witches, but I did believe in evil people, and the Fulci family, witches or not, were not something to tussle with. They don't know another ballgame except a hard one, and they play for keeps. I waited for them to clear out, which after about an hour or so of carrying on they departed.

Our last shared words weren't much in the way of coherent conversation. Johnny was so doped up by that point he could barely manage even a whisper. He gave me a small envelope containing the number of a safety deposit box at Cold County Bank down in Rust River, and a key to go with it. Told me to go to the bank, only on a Sunday, and gave me the telephone number of a good Christian woman working there who would open the bank up special for me. Then, with a relieved little grin, the old man left to join his son, my friend, in the hereafter. I think right then was when I was starting to believe in things bigger than us, than regular people. I could feel it plain as day. Got to say, I didn't much care for it. There was something dangerous about all of this, and to be honest I almost drove out to Pier 7 on the Hootchyfalala and threw the envelope, box number and key and all, right into that muddy, angry lake water. But I didn't. Whether or not that was the right decision, I can't rightly say at the moment.

That following Saturday evening I called up the young lady Johnny had told me to, and the next afternoon I was down in the vault of the Cold County Bank, the safety deposit box open and its treasures exposed to me. Everything changed for me that morning. I saw photos of them murdered kids and the nasty state of the dead growed-up people. It was true. I seen their guts and other insides draped across the theater seats and hanging from the goddamned balcony. The shiny troughs of their scars. Webs, or whatever the hell they were, plastered each and every one of them from head to toe. I really had me a good long look at that. They really did look like mummies from a scary movie. They almost didn't look like real corpses either. More like extra realistic props from a carnival spookhouse. There were other things in that safety deposit box besides pictures of dead. There was more.

Along with the folders holding the pictures there were some notes from Johnny. A couple dozen notebooks and a really nice leatherbound journal. The notebooks were mostly just a bunch of rambling scribblings with one common thread: they all entwined around matters concerning the Fulci family. You see, old Johnny Castor was already one step ahead of those garlic-eating sorcerers. He knew somehow those devils were involved in the murder of all those folks and a whole hell of a lot more. Crimes going back hundreds of years. The things Johnny wrote about in them notebooks hinted there wasn't just one Little Dixie Strangler, but a whole family of them. This explained a lot about why those Dagos were a-sniffin' and pawin' around his hospital room as he lay in there about to cash in his chips. They knew he had some serious scuttlebutt on them, and they wanted to wash his mouth out with their own nasty soap before he spilled the beans about their antics to the world at large. As powerful as the Fulcis are, embarrassing pictures can be pretty powerful in the right hands. Even old Lucifer has to answer to something at the end of his time.

Whoever might be watching this, make no mistake, the Fulcis are true servants of darkness. I don't mean the Devil either. I mean the weird shit that was around before Hell was even thought about. Before God maybe. Horrors so old no words had been created yet to give names to them. Now, thanks to Johnny Castor, I believe in those horrors and all the mess that go with them. Witchery, goblins, the restless dead and everything unnatural.

But you see, I don't think the Fulcis actually knew about Johnny's pictures; else they would never have never made it to that safety deposit box and then to my sucker ass. They for damn sure knew about it after the fact, though. A little over a week later I was looking in the Rust River Tattler auction page for a replacement blade for my tiller. It's the best local rag to find that kind of shit. I just happened to glance at the obituaries, and…I seen her.

I seen *her*. That good Christian woman who'd opened the bank for me that one Sunday. I knew soon as I seen her smiling face stuck in that little black and white rectangle it had been the Fulci fuckers who put her there. It being an obit, it didn't go into detail on just how she died. But she was young and looked real healthy to me. Word was it had been a robbery gone south. She'd been shot in the head in her living room, point blank and dead upon arrival. Place had been messed up some, maybe to make it look like a robbery. But I knew better. This was Rust River, and Rust River wasn't the kind of town where people got themselves killed in their living rooms.

This got me to thinking, did she talk to them before they put a bullet between her eyes? Tell them about Johnny's safety deposit box and my little Sunday afternoon visit to the bank? That's when I started to worry. It wouldn't be long before they found me. Before their hellhounds sniffed me out.

I'm about out of film here. I'll say a little bit more on the next reel and then hide all of this shit away for good. Been debating burning all of it, the notes and the film and everything, but I figure some good might come of Johnny Castor's research. I think he had some kind of special vision into things like this. He knew what was going on and was trying to whip up the blueprints for someone to fight back. Witches aren't invincible. Not by a longshot.

Now, you may be asking why? The deaths at The Red Hand, the pretty lady from Rust River, and Lord knows who or what else. Just killing for the sake of killing?

Nah, witches don't work that way. Killing, murder, all of these deaths were part of a sacrifice. A mass offering to whatever foul creature these wizards bow down to. That's the way their magic works, you see. You ask for something, you give something, and then you get something else in return. I don't know what it is them Fulcis want, but I got a feeling it's something real bad. Real fuckin' bad.

FIVE

A skeleton crew.

To Molly Simmons, licensed registered nurse and recently promoted night-shift manager, this meant trouble.

Perhaps she should have paid closer attention at the beginning, when the call had first come in from the medical examiner at OSBI. She hadn't recognized the voice and hadn't felt the need to question things. She had simply taken her word for it the woman on the other end of that phone line was on the up and up. For at least the past five years the contact had been Milton Ferguson. The person she had spoken with, after she had hung up the phone, Molly couldn't even recall the name. The woman's instructions had been very clear, however. Very easy to remember and follow through on. She had the kind of voice that sounded like it was used to getting what it asked for, no questions asked.

This is a case of a very sensitive nature and there is to be absolutely no publicity of any kind. Paperwork will be faxed over requiring signatures of all hospital staff present, to be signed and promptly faxed back over to OSBI HQ within the hour. The deceased in question will be left in its HRP, stored in the morgue under lockdown with the charge nurse tasked with holding the key. There are to be only two nurses on duty until eight AM, one of which must be the charge nurse, and absolutely no physicians or orderlies will be present. If the skills of a physician are necessary, please call the phone number noted at the bottom of the form and the appropriate personnel will be dispatched. A representative from the OSBI forensics team should arrive sometime between one and seven AM to retrieve the specimen. You are not to speak with the representative about the deceased, nor any other matter, for that fact.

Paramount of all, do not, for any reason, open the HRP, nor allow anyone else to open the HRP.

Not even old Barney Driscoll was to be permitted in the morgue. Strange, considering he had most likely already seen the corpse, along with Sheriff Matheson and Deputy Raab as well.

Molly had dealt with odd requests from OSBI before, but nothing of this magnitude or with such a boldly authoritative directive. She suspected the crime had involved something especially perverse. Something awful which could scar a person for the rest of their days if they knew or saw too much about it. The faxes arrived, as indicated, and were signed and faxed back as instructed by both Molly and Lorna Littledove, the nurse she had asked to remain on duty. Molly had picked Lorna because the young girl was quiet as a church mouse and not given to gossip. She would do as she was told, punch in and punch out, and keep everything on the down low.

Yes, if Molly Simmons had been paying closer attention, had chased after that little prickle of dread in her belly she had sacked away in the depths of her gut, things might have worked out differently.

Having only two nurses on staff for the night wasn't too much of a problem. Morgana Fulci Memorial Hospital wasn't exactly a bustling beehive of activity. True, the facility didn't handle folks from just Black Knot, but folks from Coffin Mills, Haggard and Rust River as well. But it was all pretty much the same backwoods clientele. Boozy bust-ups via fist or wrecked pick-up truck. Animal bites and the occasional drug overdose or farm accident. The usual bugs and seasonal sniffles. Death visited in the form of heart attacks and strokes. The inevitable consummation of old age. Normal, ordinary, common death.

The last time this level of secrecy had been levied upon the hospital and its staff had been late this past summer. The bloodbath at the old Feed Lot. It had very much been the same story, though not with the ridiculous level of security requested tonight. For the incident at the Feedlot OSBI had only wanted their own people working the case, including the nursing and support staff. This hadn't been all that unusual, really. Rural cops and health care workers, as Molly herself well knew, tended to not take things seriously enough and were bound to mess up things. There were just some things you *couldn't* mess up.

Molly and Lorna sat together at the nurses' station, drinking coffee and trying to find something fun on the radio. Molly was already glimpsing the bottom of cup number three and was struggling to suppress the urge to go for number four. Since quitting smoking a few weeks back she had really doubled up on the coffee. She'd also gained almost ten pounds in that short span, and that wasn't going to do. Not. At. All.

"How long you gonna fiddle with that thing?" Lorna set her now empty cup down on the notepad she used for a coaster. "Got a mood for something in particular?"

"Wanna find something spooky. It being almost Halloween." Molly continued to dial through the list of AM frequencies, most of them small bursts of static. "Ugh! It's all rock and roll or pop crap. What about Monster Twist? Or that haunted house song?"

Lorna's thick eyebrows crinkled. "Which one is that? Haunted House one? Lots of those."

"You know that one. From the 60s, I think. About the dude moving into a haunted house and there's like a man from outer space sitting on his stove drinking hot grease from a frying pan."

Lorna shook her head, eyes narrowed. "No'm, can't say I know that particular number. I do know that other one you mentioned."

"Monster Twist?"

"Yes'm. The same. That's a good one."

"Damn near everyone's heard that one. It's a keeper for sure." Molly felt a pause creep out in the hiss of static, toggled the dial a little, and began to receive a clear signal of something. "Got something here, I think. Yep…"

"Welcome, Guys and Ghouls, to The Midnight Opry Oldtime Horror Hour! I am your host, The Reverend Winchester B. Gross. Prepare yourselves for an hour of thrills, chills, and HORROR!"

The voice on the radio struck a bell in Molly's head. A familiarity from long ago when she was a little girl. An older man's voice, tinged with a syrupy, too-hick-to-be-real accent. The voice was bathed in a weird, hollow resonance, as if the gentleman might have been broadcasting from within the musty corridors of a sealed mausoleum. A withered pair of lungs channeling gruesome fairy tales from the great beyond via a spirit board.

"Sounds like one of them old radio shows from when my granny was little," Lorna commented thoughtfully.

"Tonight's episode is a terrifying fiction of family ties gone horribly, tragically awry. A dark fable of fatherly love, and how the bond between a man and his daughter can take an unfortunate, unholy turn into the realm of the eldritch. I call this story, the Tale of…"

Molly's hand darted out and switched off the radio. She backed away, glowering at the device as if it were a scorpion hiding beneath a recently lifted stone, angry and ready to dispense venom into a careless palm. Her heart fluttered like a hummingbird trapped in a boiling tea kettle, cool sweat breaking out in an oily sheen across her forehead.

"Oh…I remember this show. I was just a little bitty thing when this was on. My stepdaddy…" Molly's voice choked. She lifted a hand to her mouth, extended her thumb and inserted it between her slack lips. It took her only a few seconds to realize what she had just done. The thumb was hurriedly removed and concealed in a pocket of her hospital jacket. "He loved this show. He liked to listen to it with me after momma went to work. It was our show. He said that. I…I…remember that."

"Daddy Gerald paused at the door. He was wearing his bed costume and had Cindy's favorite movie watching snack, a bowl of popcorn and Milk Duds and a tall glass of punch. She had made sure she was wearing her bed costume as well, as daddy liked for them to match when they watched movies together. He came closer…"

Lorna looked up at her, puzzled at first and then a little bit anxious. The younger nurse didn't like the expression on her friend's face one bit. It was the look of someone who was really scared would make right before they threw up all over the place.

"Hey, we can find something else ya like. Or we can just talk if you want." Lorna stood up and ventured a step in Molly's direction. The charge nurse was still staring at the dead radio, her body tense and wound up, as if expecting the small rectangular contraption quiet before to suddenly liven-up and lunge for her.

"No. I don't like that show. I never liked it. Not then. Not now either." She reached behind the table the radio sat on and unplugged it. "No music. I don't have to talk about it either. Just don't turn it back on. Don't plug it back in. Just don't do that and it will all be hunky-dory morning glory."

Molly glanced over at Lorna. Her dark eyes were filled with such an overwhelming air of panic Lorna felt it bleeding into her as well. Being a simple woman who had always led an equally simple, drama-free life, this distressed her. Luckily, her friend returned to the regard the radio once again. Studying it. Leaving her out of it.

"Look, I think I'll take my lunch break now, Mol, if you don't care. Gonna run home and see if my mom is feeling any better." Lorna retrieved her shawl from the back of her chair and draped it over her shoulders. "Listen, I got a little something special stashed in the trunk under the spare tire. Something to take the edge off things. I can get it if you like. I keep it in case I have car trouble and it's cold out."

Nurse Simmons nodded, not answering, still staring at the silent radio. "Don't be gone too long, Lorna. It's a strange night, and we're a skeleton crew, remember?"

It was a little past three in the morning when Molly Simmons began to hear the funny noises.

At first, she had thought it was Lorna joking around with her. Trying to spook her. You know, in the spirit of the season and all. The younger nurse had still not returned from her lunch break, and it was well past the hour allotment set aside for the respite. Ordinarily Molly wasn't a stickler about such specifics, nor was she a clock-watching kind of boss. But when it was a crew this small, she had to tighten the knot a bit. What if there had been a wreck, a shooting or something like that? It being close to Halloween, anything was possible, if unlikely. She tried not to worry about it. Once Lorna had returned, they would have a lowkey yet official conversation concerning the matter, where Molly would be pleasant but moderately firm as well. Lorna was such a goody-two-shoes it would most definitely not be a repeat offense.

That was before the noises. If Lorna was the prankster behind that particular tomfoolery, then that lowkey yet official conversation might end up having a bit more of a bite to it.

Molly had been reading her book, a murder mystery, when she had heard the first noise. Her first impulse was to look over at the radio. But after Lorna had split, Molly had taken the damn thing and stashed it in one

THE COUNTRY GIRL'S GUIDE TO HEXES AND HAINTS

of the bottom cabinets in the break room. This was an innocuous sound. All she could affirm was that it seemed to be coming from one of the back rooms, more than likely the records archive, as it sounded very much like the dry scrape of cardboard against the granite floor. She had heard that same aggravating racket about ten million times a week when the hospital was fully staffed. Nurses, clerks, orderlies were constantly in and out, in and out. Pulling paperwork from file cabinets or moving boxes of patient documents from one end of the room to the other. Yet there was something unusual about this. There was a strange insistence to it, like whoever was rifling around in there was looking for something specific.

Could have been rats. That was another possibility, and not as far-fetched as you would think. Earlier in the summer Mike Corey, the day janitor, told her he had seen a rat's nest big enough to cradle a bowling ball out in the warehouse before. The doors to the rear shipping docks were constantly opening and closing, it would be easy for a couple of lovelorn rodents to slip in and set up housekeeping in the hospital proper. This ruckus persisted for just a few minutes before the shuffling around stopped, followed by an abrupt drift of silence Molly found more uncomfortable than the preceding commotion.

I should get up, she thought. *It's my hospital, and I am in charge of the damn place.*

Despite her internalized bravado, Molly's backside remained fused to her well-used, charge nurse's station chair. She wasn't going anywhere until Lorna got back. Tried as she might, she couldn't help but keep thinking about the radio. That voice. That spooky old show.

"That couldn't have been the same show. That was damn near twenty years ago. No…possible…way," she murmured to herself. The old panic was starting to creep back into her. Entombed feelings she'd thought successfully boxed-up, labeled and locked down.

Maybe you should plug it back in. Catch an encore performance.

She could hear the pounding of her heart in her damn throat, bulging out her eardrums.

Quiet reigned for almost a full half an hour, and now Miss Lorna Littledove was officially added to Molly's shit list, first entry of the evening. There would be an official write-up regardless of the excuse, in addition to the serious behind closed doors ass-chewing to precede the paperwork. The charge nurse rose and shoved her chair back angrily, cursing under her breath. She fumbled with the metal ring attached to her belt until she located the archive room key and made her way around the front desk, soldiering out in the hallway leading toward where she needed to go.

"The Bird Says…Tweet Tweet…Tweet Tweet…"

A yellow, quivering tremor rippled up Molly's arm and throughout the rest of her body, the key slipping from her hand and landing on the cold floor with a too-loud *clank*. Had she heard that? Had she *really* just heard that?

Daddy Gerald, looking quite handsome in his bed costume, gave Cindy the sleepy drink. It tasted just like cherry Kool Aid but there was something special in it, he said. Something that would make her start giggling until she couldn't stop. Then, she would feel like flying. He put the See 'N Say in her lap and told her by the time the little arrow got to the cow she would be in a fairyland. They would be in a fairyland, far away from earth, flying into another realm…together. No momma, no granny…. just daddy and daughter and sleep forevermore.

But no…she had turned the radio off. How was it still…

"The Cow Says…Moooooooooo…"

Daddy Gerald had been dead a long time now. Damn near twenty-five years. Momma had sold that See N' Say at one of her many summer garage sale. Molly couldn't remember exactly. One year, two years, three years…they all started to bleed together after Daddy Gerald was gone.

How did the radio know about Daddy Gerald? About the See 'N Say?

"You didn't hear that. Stop it," she growled under her breath.

But ya did. YOU stop it.

Trembling from the top of her skull to the toes of her shoes, Molly Simmons knelt down and retrieved the key and struggled to stand back up. As she rose, she heard the archive room door swing open, banging hard against the wall behind it. Footsteps, clumsy and uncertain, scurried away. A low, disturbed mumbling permeated the silence, accompanied by the jangling of keys. It was then that Molly remembered what she had forgotten to do earlier. The *only* thing out of that whole goddamned list.

She had forgotten about the set of spare keys stored in the archive.

All keys were to be in the sole possession of the charge nurse. The directive from OSBI had been quite clear about that.

Good job. First huge dose of responsibility and a big fat zero. Goose-egg. Nada.

"Shut it. I got this."

Hidden in the top drawer of the black writing desk next to the accounting cabinets. Nobody knew about those keys except for the hospital director and herself, of that Molly was reasonably certain. Unless Nurse Littledove had been snooping around, which she supposed wasn't totally out of the question. It certain wasn't in the younger nurse's nature to snoop, at least for the almost six months Molly had been acquainted with her. But then again, neither were practical jokes and ill-advised pranks in Lorna's repertoire and here they were, smack in the middle of the most unamusing prank Nurse Simmons had ever been party to.

Better go after 'em, sis. They're getting away.

"I will. Leave me be. My feet are just stuck in the mud."

Yeah, their owner is too chickenshit to go do her damn job. I get it. Nurse Littledove is gonna look just dandy wearing that pretty silver boss badge you got pinned to that wrinkled-up uniform of yours. That whole quiet little mouse act is just that. An act. She wants your job. She wants you to fail.

"You're not here. Maybe I'm just imagining this too. I won't leave the desk if I don't have to."

The shuffling began to grow more distant, the mumbling even more indistinct. The corroded creak of the west wing door shrieked through the surgical quiet, then latching closed with a tinny clink. Someone *was* here, and whoever it was going to be in deeply serious shit when they met the rightful keeper of those keys.

You should have croaked with Stepdaddy Gerald. But you couldn't even do that right. You couldn't even drink all the fruit punch. That was literally all you had to do. Your one job!

Molly shut her eyes and tried to remember the trick. The trick the family counselor had taught her to help with focus after the incident, which her mom still referred to as *the accident*, to this very day.

Picture the inside of the skull as an utterly lightless room, so black you can't imagine anything blacker, or warmer, or safer.

Darkness so deep it inhales everything around it until there is just calming nothingness.

Hold on to that image.

Slowly, carefully, begin to create a picture of a flickering candle, the flame a perfect, tapered hot yellow.

Draw in the candle close, close enough to where your eyes can lock onto a single taper of fire dancing upon the wick. Inspect every burning curve, every searing, blurred edge.

Watch the candlelight until there is nothing but the flame and you. You and the flame are the same thing. There is no you…there is no you…. there is only the flame. Only flame and its light and warmth.

Astonishingly, even after all the years of abandonment, the ritual worked like a charm. Molly could hear the radio still trying to get a word in edgewise. However, the muffled words began to flatten themselves out, the disembodied syllables blending easily into the flickering flame of the candle burning within her head, until there was nothing but blessed silence. Emboldened, one of her feet edged forward, then another. Then she found herself walking at last, full speed ahead and down the dim hallway, finding her hand upon the door to the west wing, which she then flung open and passed into the dim corridor beyond.

The passageway was empty, but Molly could sense the presence of the departed intruder as if there were a mildewed, oily scent hanging in the air. She knew where they were heading, too.

They were on their way to the morgue.

Like most hospitals the morgue was located in the basement, the portal to which lay just at the end of the hallway before her. That door would have been locked for sure, but once Molly found herself at the door she found it easy to open; whoever had passed through it earlier had not bothered to lock it behind them. Nurse Simmons paused with the door half open, hesitant to venture further into the gloomy, miserable stairwell burrowing down into the decaying old bowels of the hospital. The ghostly voice from the radio was beginning to eat through the flame, begging her attention.

Molllyyyannnnnnnaaaa…

The voice sounded as if it were being spoken by someone standing directly behind her, their chin resting upon her shoulder and hand cupped over her ear, whispering her name. Startled, the charge nurse yelped and hopped through the door and into the landing beyond, then hustling down the two flights of concrete steps and into the narrow morgue hallway.

Above, up the stairs, Nurse Simmons heard the door close, latch, then lock itself.

There were only two doors in the morgue annex, both unlabeled. One on the left and almost to the end of the hallway by the emergency exit, which led to the hospital crematorium. This door was shut tight, almost blending into the faded yellow wall which held it. The other door, just a scant eight to ten feet on the right, led to the autopsy room and the refrigerated drawers, this door was open. Widely and invitingly open, with the lights on within. Whatever trickster had staged this prank obviously had little to no concern about being apprehended, lending enhanced credibility the entire affair was simply Lorna Littledove trying to put one over on her boss. A silly Halloween lark, no less.

"You're not funny, Nurse Littledove. This area is off-limits to everyone but me tonight, and you know that. You agreed to it when you signed up for this shift." Molly called out, her voice shimmering down the empty, cold hallway in an unnerving, hollow deluge. "You're not supposed to have those keys, either. I'll own up to that one. That's my mistake. I should have had all of my eggs in a basket. I'm also gonna say you picked a really, *really* bad night to be a comedian. You know darn well how important it was we stuck to protocol tonight. We had very specific guidance from OSBI in regard to…"

From within the autopsy room something moved, interrupting her stream of thought. It was a strange, out of place sound. Autumn wind rattling through a withered legion of dried corn husks. No…someone or something running through them. Kids playing at Marco Polo or a starving barn cat hounding a terrified pasture rat through the dead, yellowed stalks. The soundtrack of hunter and hunted.

"Moll…y…"

"Ah…there you are!" Nurse Simmons exclaimed, rolling her eyes and marching toward the open door, heartened. It was Lorna for sure. She had one of those distinctive, pipsqueak baby doll voices which grated on the nerves.

The charge nurse paused at the threshold to the autopsy room. Something was off. There was an uneasy quiver in the younger nurse's voice which disturbed her. She ventured a half step further into the room, the length and breadth of her entire skin from scalp to ankle pulled into acres of pricked-up spookflesh. To her right, past the row of closets and sinks, something was going on. The earlier sound had given way to another, one she recognized without missing a beat.

Someone had opened up one of the cold lockers and was pulling out a storage rack, and she had a pretty solid guess as to which drawer was being peeked into.

She was in charge.

This could not happen. Not on her watch!

"Okay, you just stop right there, missy! That there body is for damn sure off limits! You're gonna find yourself cuffed and on the way to spend a night in a Fed jail you don't come out here to me, away from that cooler, right now!" Molly, no longer afraid of phantom radio broadcasts and odd noises which didn't belong, marched past the closets and sinks and hung a hard right into the autopsy room. Lorna Littledove stood before the open morgue drawer where the mysterious specimen had been interred, now empty with its sturdy steel door hanging from its hinges. The cot housed within the icy cubicle had been pulled out, the black body bag upon it shredded to pieces and empty. A peculiar odor lingered: a conflicting, intermingled stench of heat-stewed roadkill and freshly-cut Christmas trees. Barnyard hay gone rotten and fried pork chops. Apples and rubbing alcohol. Smells that reminded her of being a little girl living out with granny after mom went to the nut house, that hard and ugly winter after Stepdaddy Gerald killed himself.

Lorna turned to regard her superior. Her eyes stared dumbly ahead, unseeing. In one hand she held a scalpel, shining and clean. The other hand was concealed beneath the tidy folds of her nurses' skirt, moving rapidly as she pleasured herself. Appalled, Molly looked back at the HRP. It had been completely reduced to flimsy scraps of black material. Although just plastic, the charge nurse knew cutting through those things was not an easy process. It didn't really look slashed up, either. More like *blown* out. Like whatever had been putrefying within had burst out in a solitary, vigorous eruption of necromantic energy.

The younger nurse took a lumbering step toward Molly, barely keeping her footing. It was like watching a baby deer venture forth away from its mother for the first time, nervous and uncertain. A frightened whimper burbled from the corner of the woman's mouth as the hand beneath her skirt increased its tempo. The raw smell of her arousal saturated the small room, blending comfortably with the lingering odors Molly had encountered earlier. The charge nurse then came to the realization what was happening here was not normal. This was something special, something singular, something terrible.

"You're in a lot of trouble, you have to know that. Not to mention, thanks to you, I'M in a lot of trouble too. I don't know what you're on right now, and I don't know what kind of weird kink you're getting from this, but I can tell you it's not normal and you need help. I can get that for you. But you're gonna have to put that scalpel down and come with me. You're gonna hurt yourself." Nurse Simmons held out a hand and began to back away slowly. She was confident if she could just get Lorna back to the front, into the glaring gleam of those florescent lobby lights, she would have a better shot at figuring out what to do with her.

Whatever was in that bag. It all had to do with that. There was a reason for all of this red tape. The bureaucracy in overdrive. But that's none of your business, Nurse Simmons. You just keep the keys and get your worker bee back to the hive where you both belong.

Nurse Littledove advanced, the scalpel brought up even higher. Another awkward shuffle, one that almost staggered the girl. She quickly reclaimed her balance and clumsily ventured forth a couple more steps. Molly realized, her gut squirming, she was going to have to try and overpower her somehow. The legs seemed like a good option. Trip her, get her to lose her grip on the blade, and then pin her to the floor. The charge nurse was confident she could do this. There was no time to get to the narcotics cabinet for a sedative. She would have to talk to her. Calm her down.

Probably man troubles. Only a man can make a woman act like this.

Nurse Simmons studied the younger woman, sizing up her window of opportunity, when she noticed something dark beginning to trickle down both of the woman's thighs. A slow trickle, thick like syrup. Lorna ceased her self-abuse and removed her hand from under her skirt, reaching out for Molly. The entire limb was completely smeared in a dark green slime tinged with streaks of crimson, dripping slow vines of ooze from her fingertips to pool upon the floor. The fluid from between her legs began to flow with greater force, as if whatever bled and festered within her had swollen to its bursting point, beginning to seep and leak. A dreadful gurgling boiled in the younger nurse's throat, dark fluid spilling from the corners of her mouth and splashing onto the breast of her pristine white uniform. Her eyes rolled back to the whites, the spasming pale orbs shot through with a black webbing of throbbing veins and leaching blisters. A popping sound rang out, like a circus balloon being pricked with a straight pin. Between Lorna Littledove's legs a rupture of mold-green slime gushed forth, shivering flaps of ragged membrane hanging to her kneecaps, slapping against her the bare skin of her knees and coating her sensible nurse's shoes in a mound of wet, unmentionable filth.

The front of the woman's skirt twitched. Once…then once again. A third time. A presence endeavoring to manifest itself.

From beneath the border of the garment something lifted the skirt up and peered out. As thick as a big man's wrist and serpentine in movement, it was coated in mustard yellow slime and scraps of innards gnawed free from its host; it very much resembled a bad dream cousin to a tree root, gnarled and pockmarked with dozens of blistered, unblinking eyes and thorny barbs. The horror was breathing, breathing so deeply and vigorously Molly could see the entire gnarled length of it bloat with respiration, then exhale. Scant seconds later a second appendage uncoiled itself from Nurse Littledove's gangrenous womb and joined its newly awakened sibling. Both reared themselves up erect, poised like a twosome of cobras contemplating a crippled rat.

Now Molly Simmons felt compelled to scream. Her jaws unhinged, mouth wide open, the beasts saw the door presented before them and lunged, quick as an eye blinking up at the sun. The charge nurse felt them burrowing and eating their passage through her throat, tearing away at flesh and muscle to reach the center of her. Her core. She fell to her knees, her entire body a quivering mass of flayed nerve endings and ebbing life. The beasts took their time feeding, latching on and claiming her. Barely conscious, Nurse Simmons collapsed on to her back, feeling herself being slowly dragged forward, closer to the thing that had once been Lorna Littledove, one grimy and stinking inch at a time. Her head was shrouded by a muscular wetness, warm and slimy, stretching over the top of her head, slipping over her ears and her gaping mouth, then spreading over her shoulders.

I'm being swallowed…she marveled. *Swallowed right up.*

True darkness arrived. The woman could feel what was left of her begin to crack and peel away as she was absorbed into this new abomination. This beautiful, terrible, blessed abomination.

"That's all for tonight's Midnight Opry Oldtime Horror Hour. This is your ghost with the most host, the Reverend Winchester B. Gross, signing off. Pleasant…dreams….

It was the last thing Molly Simmons, charge nurse of Morgana Fulci Memorial Hospital, heard before the gun-shot crack of her shattered spine. Then there was nothing except the commandments of her new Mother and the incessant hymns of praise offered forth for her Arcane Veneration.

The contact from OSBI arrived at precisely one-minute past five in the morning. They were pleased to find the front doors locked. This meant people were doing their job, which was a very good thing. The contact, technically a man, used their own key and let themselves in. A quick spot check was performed, yielding nothing which might be deemed suspicious. All that was left was to check on the status of the specimen. Make sure all protocols had been followed. This was a delicate matter where the rules, specifically a strict adherence to them, really were important.

The specimen was no longer on the premises. This was also a very good thing.

The mess in the morgue hadn't been that bad, for which the contact was thankful. It meant a speedy cleanup and moving on to new, more significant tasks. It all only required a mop, one bucketful of water, and a little extra elbow grease.

A quick note was left at the front desk, indicating the resignation of both nurses for various reasons. Inadequate wages, shabby medical benefits and substandard working conditions. The usual mundane quibbles and qualms of the workplace that slowly nibble away at one's sanity and sense of self-worth. Luckily neither woman had any family near enough to nose around too much. And if someone did happen to get a bit too close to the heart of the matter, there were procedures firmly in place to deal with the situation.

New personnel were already on the way to relieve them.

The person who had once been Lorna Littledove plodded and lurched through the ashen pall of early morning, the sharp bite of the autumn cold unheeded upon its numb, deathless flesh. It was slow going, as it was still gorged to bursting from its ghastly supper. The meal was taking longer than usual to absorb, still twitching inside of her and refusing to die quietly. The offering had fought a lot harder after it had died than it had before the actual dying part had taken place. Odd.

Few among the living knew of the Lodge, its whereabouts, and how to pass beyond its doors once you did gain ingress. Yet the Lorna-thing remembered. It had been dreaming of this night for time immeasurable. This night and the song of the Seamstress and the forthcoming consummation.

As Lorna passed by an old farmhouse, an old man asleep within began to dream. A vision of black-winged wolves and a flame-hollowed chapel topped with an inverted cross. Out in his pasture, every single bull toppled over dead, their spoiled guts gushing from their mouth in a procession of convulsions. Come dawn the old man would be completely blind and raving. A disgruntled neighbor would be blamed for the livestock.

Lorna-thing passed by the old Black Knot Rural Water Tower #2, drained and dry for the past two decades, the dozen or so piles of hidden bones stashed within began to tremble, draw closer, and seek out comfort from one another. Their knuckles would rap uselessly against the corroded metal walls and scratch furrows into the faded yellow paint. Nobody would ever hear them. Nobody ever ventured out into this stretch of Grinning Goblin Forest. Not even hunters or moonshiners. The bones, the dead, would be awake forever, and ever, and ever.

As Lorna-thing waded through the mossy swell of Fiendly's Creek the water thickened and took on a flat, coppery stink. The clear spill clouded red. The air was redolent of slaughterhouse memories and Halloween nights turned sadistic.

Just an hour before dawn, when Lorna-thing reached the Lodge, the Wolf was waiting. He wore the skin of a beast for a mask, as decreed in the Book of the Grieving Dusk. He received her graciously, as expected, and she allowed him to guide her to the sacred room beneath the Church. They spoke for many hours about the things to come. The dreadful splendors and delicious horrors. Plans for the awakening of the Two. When the moment of consummation arrived, it was every bit as strange and terrible as both had hoped it would be. The walls and floors of the Wolf's chambers were soaked and reeking with the putrescence and drippings of their joining. Foul, unblessed frights had already begun to materialize in the fluid. Things were growing in the plagued filth of their sodomy.

With the first rays of the sun arrived the moment of sacrifice. As the Wolf and his bride held onto one another, lapping the excrement and muck from one another's bodies, Lorna-thing began to feel her appropriated flesh begin to blister, the bones beneath weakening and given to crumble. Within seconds she was nothing more than a single gray, smoking furrow of earth. The sort of earth a man would bunch up into his fist, curl into a hard clod, then cast upon the shuttered lid of a sinner's coffin.

But the things growing in the wake of their union lived on, slithering out into the world to spread the dread gospel.

At exactly seven in the morning, just as Black Knot was stirring from a restless night of slumber, directly at the intersection of Belladonna and Lavera and right outside The Gates of Mordor Arcade, the ground began to shudder. The road and sidewalk cracked, spewing up dirt and gravel and small relics belonging to the folks who had lived there before the white people.

In a blast of smoke and rancid air, a pair of gravestones broke up and out of the asphalt of the street. Each monument was tall as a grown man, their exquisite carvings ornate enough to denote whoever the dead were these had been commissioned for had come from money.

The dates were illegible, lost to antiquity and weather. Only a single name was legible on the smooth marble surface of each memorial. A name well-known to everyone in Black Knot.

Fulci.

SIX

Matheson was out on the back deck of the trailer, a blazing fire in the rock pit, sipping his freshly brewed coffee, when the phone rang. His gut tightened. A call this time of night usually meant problems. His thoughts returned to the child's bizarre corpse, and the evening's good buzz began to slowly melt away. Setting his cup down on the railing, he jogged inside and snagged the phone, preparing for whatever.

It was only Becky. What had possessed her to call him at this hour simply to tell him everything was final, Matheson couldn't rightly say. He could tell she had been drinking more than a little herself, which was an odd state for his very straight-laced, formerly loving bride. A lot of crying on her end, another anomaly. Becky was one of the most stoic people, man or woman, the lawman had ever known. For almost an hour she rambled on about random topics which seemingly had no bearing upon their current domestic state. Talked about her mom a lot. That old biddy had been accountable for a lot of their marital issues, her damaging influence upon her daughter lethally soiling her mind. Then a brief foray into the anatomy of her new relationship with her boy-toy.

It seemed things just weren't working out with him. They had nothing to talk about. The sex had already started to go downhill. Another mention of how they never had anything to talk about.

Coach Grover's kid, barely out of high school. Yeah, of course you aren't working out. You're just a curious detour to him, lady. He's college bound and destined to be chin deep in tail from day one. You'll be that "older chick" notch on his belt...

He didn't tell her any of this. Just behaved like he had during their marriage. Nodded to himself and just said "Ayup" in every response. She didn't care. Becky was one of those people who just required a disembodied ear to listen.

"Maybe we can have lunch next week. Maybe at Bandit's Roost on the lake. Remember that place?" It was obvious to him she was really drunk now. Her words were barely clinging together. "During the day, you know. So, people won't talk or get ideas..."

Matheson sighed, returning to the deck, the fire, and his amazing cup of coffee. Even cold, it still tasted like a million bucks. "Becky, I think that is an exceptionally terrible idea."

Holy shit. He'd deviated from the script.

"You know what, buddy-boy? Fuck you! Good luck finding someone who'll put up with being married to the Black Knot PD and not a real man!"

Dead dial tone.

It was a really sad sound if you thought about it.

He went back inside, hung up the phone, and returned to the comfort of his deck.

The man just kept sipping that damn coffee and stoking the flames in the pit.

He thought about it for the first time in a very long time. Maybe it had been his encounter with the Corbucci girl which had fueled the memory.

The Feed Lot Massacre.

The Feed Lot incident, as it had come to be called, never saw much air outside of the state. OSBI had seen to that. Or someone else. Matheson had always thought it odd a crime that vicious, that strange, to have been wrapped up so nice and tidy. Hell, even he hadn't been allowed at the crime scene until it had all been mopped up. There had been nary a whisper since, not even among people in town. If the Corbucci kid hadn't survived, Matheson was convinced it would have faded from the town's collective consciousness altogether like a sour aftertaste.

Country people. Country life.

Around six that morning the lawman had grown tired of coffee drinking and fire-stoking and decided to take a drive. He'd hadn't enjoyed an off-duty excursion into the hills and hollers in a good while. This was his favorite time of the day, that hour or so just before the sun came up. It always held a dreamy, almost otherworldly quality for him, especially now when he was running on around five hours of sleep out of the past twenty-four. He brewed himself some more coffee, transferred it from the pot to his Army thermos, and was cruising along the curve of Highway 270, an almost abandoned stretch of old road separating Black Knot from the towns of Coffin Mills and Haggard. He'd almost elected to dust off the old flatbed for a spin, but decided against it. The squad car was more reliable, and when seen would be a good deterrent to anyone wishing an early morning traveler any ill will. Especially when he got around Haggard. A rough bunch up that way, the lot of them.

The exit for Haggard loomed in his headlights. Without thinking he took the exit and hugged the serpentine curves, his car descending into the secret valleys and nooks signaling one's arrival in the town everyone in Black Knot referred to as "The Armpit of Southeastern Oklahoma."

The Corbucci house was dark and settled down. Polly's El Camino was parked in what was left of an old barn, now missing most of its roof. Matheson was glad to see this. There was a good chance the old girl was inside, sound asleep, and not out and about causing problems. The lawman resolved to swing by now and again over the next few weeks and check in on them. Mosey up to the door, knock, then go inside and have a look around. It wouldn't hurt, and if he got the feeling Polly was up to something, he could possibly nip it in the bud before it got too bad. She was a decent woman at heart. Matheson had known her since second grade and had watched her predicted decline into drug abuse and ritual poor decision making with a heavy heart. He owed it to the kid, at least. She was smart and resourceful and deserved a chance at knowing finer things.

More interesting to him, however, was the status of the old Marley house next door. It appeared someone was living there, amazingly, in spite of its sorrowful state. Through one of the front window screens, he could see a faint orange glow, probably a stovetop light. There were a few ladders positioned outside the front and on the eastern side of the house, with several buckets of paint and rolls of drop cloth on the porch. Obviously, whoever lived here now was in the process of sprucing up the old place. The truck parked outside looked very familiar. Matheson killed the headlights and cruised slowly past the yard, inspecting the vehicle. It was the same truck he had seen parked outside that new café in town. The one across from the arcade belonging to the redhead with the rear end that looked nice in jeans. He wondered, for just a moment, if the woman was single. Then, almost as soon as he had thought it, he remembered Becky. The stuff with Becky, all the bullshit, had all started with one harmless little blind date.

"Yeah, big guy, don't even think about it." He smirked, turning on his headlights and heading back up the road and out of Gravetender's Retreat.

Instead of driving back to his trailer, Matheson hung a detour on 270 West and veered off into town. He wanted to see if Raab was at the station. Maybe pick him up and get some breakfast at The Skillet over in Crow Hollow. The autumn sun had crested the peaks of the Kiamichi Mountains and poured out its tender amber glow over the hillsides and treetops like a spill of flaming honey. The nip of harvest permeated every breath the lawman inhaled into his lungs, a hallowed and ancient fragrance redolent of burning leaves and bottled cold, undisturbed earth with just the tiniest hint of winter's approaching cruelty. It never failed to invigorate him.

As he pulled into the town square the sheriff noted a small cluster of people loitering around outside the arcade. Quite odd for this time of day, as the arcade wouldn't be open until noon and the new café across the street wasn't open at all yet. He maneuvered the squad car into the bank parking lot, killed the engine, and got out, heading toward the assembly. As he grew closer Joan Priddy, the police dispatcher, detected him and began shuffling in his direction. Her face was cloaked in a strange mixture of fear and excitement. Others among the gathering noticed his approach and began to wave him over.

"Juston...you have to see this!" Ms. Priddy gasped, out of breath. "I don't know what you can do about it, but you have to see it!" She grabbed his hand in her own wrinkled claw and began to half drag him toward the curiosity. The closer they drew to whatever it was, Matheson began to feel it again. That same weird, creeping dread he had experienced back at Gibble Gas. He suddenly wasn't so sure he wanted to have a gander at what they were all gawking at. He knew, right then and there, it wasn't something he wanted to look it. Not something he wanted to know about. As they approached the crowd parted like a set of curtains and revealed the marvel to him, and it was a strange marvel indeed.

Before the sheriff of Black Knot, crookedly jutting out among a fresh mound of disrupted concrete and dark earth, a duo of large tombstones imposed. Matheson had never seen funerary memorials this large, old, and ornate before. Not even up at Black Bog Confederate Cemetery, which sheltered the bones of almost a hundred Rebel dead. The monuments were shaped from deep gray granite, flecked with blue-green skeins of moss and algae and each standing a good five feet tall, coming up to meet Matheson's whiskered chin. The amount of detail etched into the stone was astounding, a level of craftsmanship the lawman had no choice but to pause and admire. Each tombstone resembled a massive chess piece, the pawn specifically, and was inlaid with graven images of howling skulls, bat-winged cherubs bearing faces twisted into masks of lunacy, and arcane symbols foreign and unsettling to him. Near the base of both tombstones the inscription denoting both the birth and death dates had faded into obscurity. The first names on the dead sleeping beneath were illegible save for the first couple of letters. On the one on the left, the letters **F**, **A** and **N** could be noted. The other revealed an **I**, a **F** and an **E**. The last name, however, stuck out loud and clear, as if the ruination of nature itself could not erase the letters.

"Fulci..." Matheson contemplated, rubbing his rough chin with his knuckles. "What on earth are these doing here? Fulci family has got their own burying ground outside town. And these look older than hell."

"I was thinking that myself. What made 'em pop up outta the ground like that too? Reckon we had an earthquake or something?" Priddy wondered, linking her arm in the crook of his. She leaned in and whispered into his ear. "You need a shave, Juston. The beard makes you look old and cranky. You won't catch yourself a nice girl looking like a troll. And watch your cussing. There's a couple of folks from the Church of Christ over yonder."

"Nah. Earthquakes here happen about once in a Hunter's Moon. One strong enough to push two buried tombstones up and out of solid concrete and asphalt, we would have felt that sucker. Would have been powerful enough to wake up people for sure," he whispered back. "And the beard's temporary. I just didn't get around to shaving this morning. And you get any notions of matchmaking right out of that scheming brain of yours. The monk life for me going forward."

"Yeah...let's see how long that lasts." The old woman chuckled. "There is a good woman for every good man. It can happen. You just got to be patient and not let one bad experience ruin romance for you altogether."

"More bothered about this at the moment." Matheson disengaged himself and knelt before the stones, brushing grit and grime away from the inscriptions with his fingers in hopes of achieving greater clarity. It was no use; the smooth stone had been weathered for too long, too completely. The lawman rose and scratched his head, casting a glance over at the new café. The familiar flatbed was parked out in front and a light was on inside. Behind drawn curtains he could see shadowy shapes bustling about within. He wondered if the woman's coffee would be any good.

"Might ask Roseanna about it. She's liable to have her shop open, and if anyone can tell you something about this, it would be her," Priddy offered hopefully. She had noticed the café as well. "You met the lady who opened up the café yet?:

"I might just do that, and no, I haven't introduced myself to this said café lady. Might need to rectify that." Matheson pondered the old woman's suggestion. Roseanna Lavera was the only member of her family sociable enough with the town rabble to even approach about it. Rumored to be something of a black sheep, she owned a cute little curio shop on the southern end of town. The sheriff had gone to school with her, although she had been two grades behind him. He liked her a lot. She always had a good story to tell, and if she was a part of the Lavera family's rumored witchery she worked on the more benevolent side of the house. Right now, Matheson felt a need to find Raab. Get him involved in this and get some tape around the spectacle. Keep folks away from it. Call the gas company and make sure the lines beneath the ground hadn't been damaged.

"I best get back to the station. You let me know if you talk to Roseanna about this. Want me to call the deputy for you?" Priddy asked. "It's his day off, so he's liable to be sleeping in today."

"Nah, let me call him. I can wake him up faster with the phone, too. You just let me know if you hear anything from OSBI about that stuff from yesterday. I mean as soon as you hear something. I'll be over in a bit." Patting Ms. Priddy on the back, Matheson made a path through the thinning mob of gawkers and began walking toward the café. Sure, he could use the radio in the car to reach his deputy at home, but the sheriff had other ideas. He would go over to that café and ask to use the phone, mostly as a pretense to meet the owner. Try out that coffee while he waited for Raab.

Once at the door, he was met with good smells. Baking bread, maybe. A little hint of cinnamon. Coffee too. Glorious, dark, freshly brewed fuel.

Feeling a bit like a kid knocking on his prom date's door, he rapped his knuckles against the cold glass. From within came a muffled voice asking for the visitor to wait a minute. A little more than that went by before the door opened in a jingling of bells and hinges badly in need of an oiling. Before him was a woman who looked as good in front of him as she did from the back. She was maybe early thirties, a natural redhead judging from the matching eyebrows, her hair twisted into two messy plaits on either side of her head. Her eyes were huge pale green orbs, flavored with apprehension as she regarded the disheveled middle-aged man standing before her. Matheson now wished he had cleaned up a bit before coming to call. Put on the uniform to look a little more respectable. Too late for that now.

"Hi?" She nodded, guard still up.

Matheson ran a hand through his greasy shock of hair, wishing he'd gotten a trim last week like he had intended to. "Good morning, ma'am. Sorry to bug you, but we got a spectacle out here, as you can see. Wondering if I can use your phone to call my deputy? Maybe buy a cup of that amazing smelling coffee you got on in there."

"Wow…my first customer." The woman smiled, warmer yet still a little wary. "I guess you're with the police, then?"

"Oh yeah. Sorry. Hold up." Matheson slipped his wallet from his back pocket, flipping it open to reveal his badge. "I'm the sheriff, actually. Juston Matheson." He held out a hand, which she filled with her small, warm, smooth one. "I apologize. I don't look too officious at the moment. It's been a long couple of days."

"Really? I can't imagine much goes on here other than kids getting busted for trying to buy beer or tipping cows." The woman laughed. By the way, I'm Mona. Mona Hennessey. Come on inside and see how you rate the coffee."

Matheson walked into the café and scanned the room. He was astonished at what the woman had done with the place in such a short time. When it had been Muldrow's Drugstore it had always been a lovable but scattershot mess. An establishment, borderline dive, run by unrepentant packrats where everything you saw lying around could most likely be purchased and usually had a spicy story to go along with it. Here, order prevailed. Every chair, the dishes stacked in the cabinets, every fragment of ornamentation and a fresh coat of deep orange paint, all of it fit together perfectly. The old fireplace, clogged for decades, had been swept and cleaned up nicely and boasted a recently kindled fire, which felt like heaven after the autumn chill outside. Everything about the café radiated coziness, comfort, and sociability. And man, that coffee smelled like a little kettle-full of heaven.

"You'd be surprised what we get up to in this place. Not much interesting really happens, true, but when it does it tends to be a doozy." Mona vanished into the kitchen as the lawman took a chair next to the fire, turned it around and settled into it, backwards. A few minutes later she returned with a little China cup full of smoking coffee and a cinnamon roll the size of a Frisbee, slathered with a generous pat of butter, on an actual plate. Matheson was impressed and thankful. His primary source of sustenance, for the past few months at least, had been TV dinners, hot dogs, and junk from vending machines at the station. Home cooking felt like a bona fide luxury. "Wow, swanky. I was expecting a little Styrofoam cup. Off to a fine start, my good lady." He held the cup up in salute and ventured a sip, his palate approving of the dark and rich brew. Extra brownie points awarded.

"So, what can I do for you? This just a social call? Like, being neighborly?" Mona asked. There was an odd edge to her tone. Suddenly Matheson felt like an intruder. A pest. Like he had interrupted something and was now very much in the way. The woman stood before him near the counter, with arms folded almost defensively across her chest. The lawman took a minute to casually observe her, something he was quite adept at. Yes, definitely impatience and annoyance. Then he took a second to ponder this, realized of course he was interrupting something. Mona Hennessey had a café to open, and he *was* very much in the way. He recalled when his momma opened her store and how much work it had been. After that it was a twenty-four by seven job. It was your *life*. He ventured another sip and set the cup down. Best to do what he had come to do.

"Mostly just wanted the coffee and the phone." He walked over to the counter and laid a couple of dollar bills down. "Hey that's your first couple of bucks. You have to frame one of them now, you know. It's a ritual for all new businesses when they open. Bad luck if you don't. Even my momma had one. Had it in a nice frame and nailed up over the griddle."

The woman smiled, pulling the cash toward her and depositing both bills within the register. The joking seemed to have thawed her a little. "Your momma have a café too? Right here?"

"Naw, it was across the street where the arcade is now. Little grocery store, but she had kind of a makeshift deli in the back. Mostly chili and sandwiches and whatnot. Biscuits and gravy. A chicken fried steak on Sundays sometimes."

"What was your momma's name?" Mona leaned against the counter, elbows planted, and her face cupped in her cheeks. Interested now.

"Dorothy. Everyone called her Dottie, though. She looked more like a Dottie than a Dorothy. She was a feisty old creature. Had more than a little bit of the Devil in her, I think. The Devil's good side, that is."

"Oh, the Devil has a good side?" She cocked an eyebrow.

"Sure, he does. And a sense of humor too. Lot funnier than the Boss Upstairs. Pretty sure old Lucifer created fart jokes."

Why…oh why had he just said that?

A moment of complete silence followed.

Thaw in progress.

"Go get your cup, officer." Mona nodded in the direction of where he had been seated. "Cus I am gonna refill it. You can have another round and then make your calls. You left your roll back there too. Better get that. Letting a home-baked cinnamon roll go cold is sacrilegious where I come from."

An hour later Matheson had gone through two more cups of coffee, savaged into the cinnamon roll like a junkyard dog let loose in a rendering plant, and learned a good deal more about his town's newest citizen. Mona had come from Dallas with her son Hayder, indicating she had lived in the Knot almost two decades ago, if only for a little over a year, with an aunt, after her own parents had passed on. Her husband had died earlier in the year and had left her some money, which she had sunk into both the old house in Haggard and the café. He suspected she came from money to begin with. She just had that air about her. Refinement or something.

"So why come back to Black Knot?" He was genuinely interested. "We don't get a lot of folks who choose to move here, since it's so far from Tulsa and Oklahoma City. Not a lot to do here unless you like high-school football and hunting. Pretty low-key bunch, to be honest."

"I would beg to differ, officer. You got something exciting going on outside. Doesn't look too low-key to me."

Unable to return with an acceptably witty retort, Matheson grinned sheepishly and sipped down the last of his coffee. She was more on the money than she knew. Nothing about the last couple of days had been anything remotely low-key. He felt the need to change the subject.

"So, where's your kiddo?"

Mona wandered over to the refrigerator and took a can of beer from it. Cracking it open, she leaned back against the counter and took a long, impressive pull. Matheson had to refrain from cheering and doing a slow clap for her. He hadn't tagged her as a day drinker, but he was not the sort to criticize. "I left him at home to finish up some painting for me in the kitchen. About noon I'll head home and bring him up here for a bit. Walk him over to his new job."

The sheriff thought about telling her it wasn't a good idea to leave a kid by themselves in Haggard, even in the daytime, but then thought better of it. Not his business and he couldn't come up with a subtle enough way in which to deliver the said advice. Better to leave it alone for now, and Matheson made a brain note to personally patrol the area, a bit of extra vigilance for the next few months.

"A job already! The poor kid. Just got here and already got mom cracking the whip." Matheson laughed, relieved to find Mona returning the mirth with equal enthusiasm. "Where's the new job?"

"Over at the Red Hand. Mostly weekend afternoon and evenings." Mona dug her purse out from under the counter, rooting around until a pack of Texas Ghost cigarettes was in her hand. She offered one to Matheson, who accepted the offering with an appreciative nod. He couldn't pass up one of those expensive hand-rolled smokes. So much for quitting after the one last night. "Concession stand too. I suspect management opportunities will be soon to follow." She slipped a matchbook out of the breast pocket of her flannel shirt, sparking it and her cigarette to life and then holding it out to him. Matheson leaned in and lit the end of his own stick with the smoldering end of hers. That first lungful of the superb Indian tobacco soaked into him like a blessing.

"Ah, nice! How'd you finagle that? You know Vera or something?"

"Not sure I know a Vera. Mr. Crowley is the one I've been dealing with."

The sheriff paused, a curl of smoke creeping up from his mouth and up into his nostrils. "Mr. Crowley, you say?"

Mona took a long drag on her smoke. Nodded.

"Ramsey Crowley?" he asked again.

Smoke curled from the corners of her mouth. "The same. Why? You sound strange when you said his name. Something wrong with him? He was perfectly lovely on the phone."

"Nothing of the kind. At least, I guess not. It's just that Vera Lawson is the one at the Red Hand who deals with the public. I know Crowley as just the owner. I personally have never met the gentleman. Hell, I don't think he lives here."

"Oh, he's there. He's always been there."

Something in the way that sounded coming out of her mouth made Matheson feel like dropping the subject for reasons he couldn't quite figure out. That little secret sense inherent to all of those folks out there who were born to enforce the law of the land twitched a little, like he *shouldn't* let it drop. But good manners and a lack of familiarity with his partner in the conversation won out. It was at this point the lawman figured he had lollygagged long enough, and rose to make his call. Mona receded into the shadows of the storage pantry to straighten up, leaving her customer to his own devices. It had been a strange experience, chatting with Mona Hennessey. He wasn't certain how, even now, it had gone. It almost felt as if the whole thing had never really happened.

"You need some sleep yourself, man," he muttered into the receiver as the dial tone echoed into his head through the earpiece of the phone. Raab still wasn't answering. Matheson gave it about five minutes, finished up the last of his coffee, and tried a second time. Then a third. Raab actually sleeping in on his day off would have been an anomaly. The younger man was a legendary early riser, both an avid jogger and hunter. Bow season had just started a few weeks ago, so perhaps that was what he was out doing. Trying to score a buck on his day off. Matheson didn't blame him. It was a fine day for it.

The sheriff called out to Mona, indicating he was leaving, thanking her for the coffee and sweet. From the confines of the pantry, she returned with a curt, professional acknowledgement of his gratitude.

Yeah, this looks to be about as far as this is gonna get right here, he thought. *Better off that way, more than likely. Shit's complicated enough right now.*

With that Matheson departed the café and headed toward his squad car to try Raab on the radio. The earlier crowd had already thinned down to just one: Madge Wolf, Black Knot's oldest living person not locked up at the Piney Bluff Rest Home. Slumped down in her wheelchair, she was gawking at the monoliths, transfixed. Mouth hanging slack with a little ooze of drool dangling from her bottom lip. Kept tilting her head left to right like she was trying to find locate any possible alternate angles in which to view the wonder. Her intensity gave Matheson pause.

"Y'all right there, Mabe?" he asked, stooping a little so he could be eye level with the old girl. "About to get something to tape the scene down with, so check it out all up close and personal while you can."

"Dis shouldn't be hair." The woman scrunched up her face like she'd taken a swig of spoiled milk. A long, knobbed finger stabbed at the Fulci tombstones. "Early yet. Somebody done something to stir the bones. Fulci devils!"

The sheriff followed her finger. In the golden wash of autumn sunlight, he could see every little blue vein squirming and pulsing beneath the paper-weak flesh of Madge's hand. She was shaking, and it wasn't just your standard-issue old-person quivering. This was the shiver of someone with a genuine scare put into them. The woman looked up and locked eyes, each as wide as a teacup, with his. He could hear her dentures rattling in her mouth.

"What you on about, pretty lady? Who's the somebody you're talking about here?" He drew closer. The woman's old breath was sour with morning coffee and cigarette smoke.

"Dem damn witches. Someone's stirred the pot and it's all bad now. Door in the Floor been rapped on and it's about to open right on up." She covered her eyes with her palms, shaking her head defiantly. "Pray. That's what I got to do. Y'all can go eat shit." With that she set her hands to the wheels of her chair, spun herself around and began rolling away in the direction of the Freewill Church of the Living Water. They had a nice senior citizens center there that served a free breakfast about this time. Old people never missed a free meal if they could help it.

Matheson knew this was about more than free grub.

Madge, even when she had been much younger, was regarded as something of the town character, so all of this witch talk really didn't ring an alarm in the lawman's head. Her past shenanigans made it hard to take a lot of what she rambled on about without a large, bowling ball-sized grain of salt. As for the witch nonsense, the allegations of black magic and country sorcery had dogged Black Knot's founding family since the very beginning. What had truly bothered Matheson was the clarity with which Madge had delivered the nonsense. Normally the old woman rambled incoherently, rarely capable of stringing together more than a couple of lucid thoughts and translating them into words that worked reasonably. She had looked at those two graves sticking out of the ground and had known *damn well* what she was looking at. Getting her to elaborate, however, would be next to impossible.

The sheriff realized, at that moment, he had witnessed something special. Something he would file away for now.

The Fulci tombstones loomed before him like a set of biblical tablets.

Yeah, might give old Roseanna Lavera a ring. Stop in for a game of checkers or something like that.

Halfway between the squad car and the arcade, Joan Priddy pulled up in her little Volkswagen Beetle and parked behind him. When she got out of the car she didn't bother to kill the engine or even shut the door. She was running toward him as fast as she could, stumbling over her Sunday heels, her mascara smeared across her brows. He jogged over to her and accepted her into his arms as she wept pitifully. Matheson felt his coffee and cinnamon roll roil in his gut, trying to slither passage up into his throat. But he held firm as he held her.

She told him what had happened. Afterwards he held her a little longer, more out of shock than any need to provide comfort. He sent Priddy home for the rest of the day and called up Gordon Jefferson, his reserve deputy, and asked him to man the station until he could get there. Gordon was an affable guy and agreed without hesitation.

Sheriff Matheson entered the squad car, keyed it to life, and began driving in the direction of further, assured dreadfulness.

OSBI was on the scene already, which was both a first and a shock. Strange, because the desk clerk at the motel was adamant the only phone call he had made was to the Black Knot Police Station, the only person he had spoken to was Ms. Priddy, which was confirmed by the old girl herself. Per the chain of command, it would have been the duty of a legal representative of the Sheriff's Office to then notify the Feds after they had secured the scene, not a private citizen. Matheson believed the clerk. Nate Longcrier was still on the better half of two years' probation for selling weed, had spent some quality time over at Stringbean Minimum Security Penitentiary, and in his time there had decided he had zero interest in visiting such an establishment ever again. In short, old Nate was watching his step very closely these days. Keeping his nose clean. A man with any sense, in his situation, wouldn't lie to someone, most of all an officer of the law, about anything.

Yet here they were, crawling over the crime scene like dutiful ants in bargain-basement matching double-breasted suits, dispatched for supplies for their hungry queen. They had pulled up in five identical black Jeeps just as Nate had hung up with Ms. Priddy. He had been provided with all of the thought-numbing legal puke and had asked no questions. These folks had badges, they didn't bother to hide their peacemakers, and every single one of them had a job to do. You didn't get in the way of that job.

Again, Nate was on probation.

Not so different from the business over at the Feed Lot. Matheson pondered. *OSBI was on the scene before anyone from town. I never even got to see the bodies. Why didn't it bother me then like it does right now?*

The Tarantula Arms was one of Black Knot's more…*permissive* motels. Even its location, nestled in an ancient valley of cedars and maples just northwest of Black Knot Lake, sort of advertised it being the kind of place appealing to people not necessarily wanting to spend the whole night there. Folding cash only, and you didn't have to sign the register unless you just felt a burning need to do so. Some folks are just like that, it would seem.

Scotty Raab was not one of those people. The kid only went three places: work, church and then back home. He would never have been caught dead in a dump like this under any circumstances other than those of a law enforcement capacity. Matheson wondered how seeing his young deputy, still not so many years away from being a child himself, in such a state would affect him. No matter how hard he tried, he just couldn't envision the scenario. It was if Raab were a character to be read about in an old country legend, easily returned to the land of the living by simply flipping a few pages back in the storybook. Even when Matheson was there, in the motel room, gazing upon the savaged bodies of both Raab and a stranger, a woman, it still wouldn't fully register.

It took some serious backward reflecting for Matheson to locate the memory he needed. It only took a few seconds to recognize the woman from the previous day. The witness from the campground who had discovered the perverted corpse of the child. Matheson recognized her by her hair. That deep dark ink spill, thick as shipyard rope and hanging down the back of the office chair, now soaked damp with clotted blood and dead muck.

Then he *saw* Raab. *Saw* the woman.

Next thing he knew, he was sitting on a leather couch in the front desk office of the Tarantula Arms. He had a glass of ice water in one hand and his sense of hearing completely turned off. He took a drink. As the cold went down his throat the sound began to worm its way back in, slowly. Creeping. He shook his head violently a few times, which seemed to improve his clarity of thought. Nate was kneeling beside him, smiling pleasantly but with an obvious glint of dread. To the desk clerk's right was one of them. One of the suits, standing. This particular guy had a much nicer suit than the others. For some reason this concerned Matheson.

It had been the most horrible thing he had ever seen.

Both of them had been naked, the woman sitting up on the bed, propped up on pillows, and Raab planted in a rickety chair next to the window with the air conditioner blasting, transforming the room into a crude morgue. Between the chill both outside and in the room it was cold enough for Matheson to see his breath cloud out before him in wispy white billows.

You better forget about it, constable. It will go badly for you...

Both corpses had been slit from gizzard to gullet, neat and meticulous, the skin of their abdomens pulled apart like the rind of some ghastly fruit, their laid-bare innards a hideous display. The guts had been ripped from their abdominal hollows and dumped upon their laps in glossy mounds of shredded white tissue and slimy purple membrane. From Raab's lap a single, sodden tendril of intestine stretched out and terminated in the woman's mouth, her cheeks stuffed to overflowing with the dead man's meat. Likewise, Raab's cheeks were swollen with his companion's tattered viscera as well, both of them connected to one another in a grisly ceremony of consumption. The woman's eyes were closed as if she had drifted to sleep in mid-chew, but Raab's eyes were wide, bulging, gazing into the void. To Matheson that was worse than anything. That horrified, suspended gape into whatever hell had claimed his deputy, his friend.

He had seen, but had been unable to remember, the strange symbols inscribed on their foreheads, written in the empowered ink of their own blood. He might have cried a little too. Maybe. If he had he couldn't remember it.

Matheson asked the agent in the nice suit how they had gotten there so fast. Who had called them?

Whatever answer he received did not fully register. The brain and flesh it commanded would not adhere. His mind simply accepted what it was told and tried to move on. But something within the lawman held fast to the reality of the predicament. In vain he kept asking questions with his mouth. Those questions, when answered by the agent in the nice suit, seemed legitimate. Reasonable, even. However, for the life of him he couldn't remember any of them. He just knew he needed to get away, get back on the road and back down into town with Ms. Priddy and Madge Wolf and the pretty café lady. This was none of his damn business.

"But I am the law here."

You're confused. You're confused and need to rest. Go back home and have a few beers.

"I don't need to rest."

But you do. You've seen some terrible, wondrous things today. Things you're not meant to see. You need to forget. You must forget. You need to let authorized personnel deal with this.

"You're not OSBI."

Yes we are.

"You're not."

"We are."

Matheson snapped to. He looked over at where Nate had been standing behind the cash register and found only dead space. The agent in the nice suit stood in the doorway, blocking the way out. Why did he now feel an overwhelming urge to run?

"Where's Nate?" he asked out loud.

Nate quit.

"Just now?" Matheson chuckled. Yeah, he'd probably quit right now too if he'd been in Nate's shoes.

These questions are getting old, constable.

"You're gonna tell me what's going on here. You're gonna talk about those tombstones in town. You're gonna tell me about the dead kid at Camp Azalea. You're gonna tell me about the Feed Lot. All of it, you're gonna tell me."

You know more than enough, man. Far, far too much.

There was a sharp, swift prick of pain in his neck and instantly every thought bouncing around in his skull went ash gray. Reduced to an empty vessel waiting to be filled. Something like sleep arrived. But this was a sleep Matheson couldn't fight off. It was an insistent, grim drowsiness. He gave over to it. He had no choice.

Be still. This is for your own good.

When Matheson returned to his senses he was sitting in his squad car, parked in the driveway of his trailer. He felt hung over and spent. The lawman looked around the interior of the vehicle, although what he was looking for he was not quite sure. Something to validate what had just happened. Or what he thought had happened.

What *had* happened?

Maybe something. Maybe nothing.

A spot on his neck ached. The sheriff pulled the rearview mirror down and felt around the spot with his finger. A tiny scab scratched against his nail, and a telltale red spot showed back at him from the reflective surface.

It hadn't been his imagination. He needed to get that train of thought derailed.

"That wasn't OSBI. Or if it was, it was a part of it all I found out about by accident." He pondered. Probably better to keep quiet, even in the car, just in case they, whoever they were, had bugged the vehicle. "No, it was something else. Something someone like me wasn't supposed to know about. Now that I've seen it, I can't unsee or un-remember it."

Matheson knew this was bad. That he had seen all of that and could remember it. At least most of it. Knowledge that could get him hurt.

He knew if he returned to the Tarantula Arms he would find a spotless scene. No crime. No evidence of any shenanigans. There would be a new desk clerk. New custodial staff. That was how these people worked. They had elevated distraction, gaslighting, and misdirection to an art form.

"Just me now, I guess. I told them in the beginning it wasn't going to work with just two guys. Even in a town this small. Not much happens here. But when it does, it's too much for just two men."

Raab had been a good man. Young and sincere. It wasn't right to lose someone like him.

The saddest thing of all, the lawman couldn't notify anyone regarding Raab's death. The deputy's parents were long dead, and he had been an only child. No aunts and uncles that he knew about. He also knew if he went looking any deeper in this mess the OSBI brass, or whoever these goons were, would have already taken care of it. The sad and horrible truth of it was Raab would be forgotten, and if someone ever got an urge to go and look for him they would have a sorry time awaiting them. Digging too deep for answers would just be a down payment on a future coffin.

Same for the woman in the motel room with him.

What had she to do with any of this?

He thought on this for a bit.

"She found the body," Matheson realized. His heart pounded in his chest like an angry fist against a door. "Got to go find that body. That dead kid has something to do with it. I knew when I saw all that bullshit it was something not normal. I *knew* it."

The sheriff of Black Knot went inside his home to retrieve his service revolver from the coat closet. Once back in the car he peeled out in his driveway, swerving back on the highway. He kept the gun in the passenger seat behind him, just in case. As he drove toward town he began to formulate a plan. Get to the hospital first and, if possible, have a looky-loo at that corpse. Then search for Barney and try and get him on his side before he turned up in a motel, mutilated and dishonored like Raab. His own possible fate, if he dawdled too long. Above all, try and keep it on the down low. Stop asking questions. Keep things neat.

You can always just leave all of this behind, Juston. Anytime you want. This town. These people. It's been holding you back a long time. Too long. Go on. Go back home and get in that truck of yours and just start driving. Maybe out west. Lots more to do out there. You can blend in easier. Start something new. Forget what you think you might have seen.

Matheson had had this conversation with himself too many times to remember. Before all of this he might have actually taken the advice. But now things had changed. The entire world felt different, electric. For the first time in years the sheriff felt alive, energized. Like his life suddenly had purpose and could affect change for the better.

"Shut it. I got this," he griped, this time out loud. "If someone is listening to me right now, you better know, I got this. This is my town. My people."

The lawman took the back way into town, skirting Coffin Mills and roaring through the dusty back roads and secret ways known only to a select few. When he reached the Knot, it was from the eastern edge of town where few people actually lived. This would give him access to the hospital from the shipping entrance, from which he could get into the hospital without a key. But he would need Barney to get to the corpse. True, if he just bulldozed in and demanded the head nurse walk him into the morgue, he would have me little or no resistance. Yet he felt in his gut, if possible, any and all hospital staff were to be avoided.

Matheson drove down Yellow Oak Avenue, quickly making a hard a right on Repentance toward the hospital's shipping entrance. He slammed on the brakes, his heart sinking. Not only was Barney's old Pinto not in its usual reserved parking space, but every available spot around it was occupied by a shiny black Jeep. Just like the ones he had seen earlier at the motel. The shipping entrance was secured by a team of men and women, probably fifteen to twenty strong, all of them in those matching dark suits. The lawman knew they would be armed to the teeth and wouldn't give a rat shit if he was law enforcement. His badge, overnight, had been rendered ineffectual.

"Damn. This must be big. Like, an insane level of big." Matheson laid his head against the steering wheel, took a deep breath and closed his eyes. He allowed himself to linger for a couple of minutes before returning to the back roads and driving in the direction of Crow Hollow, a small trucker town about 15 miles north. Once there he parked at a small grocery store he knew to have a payphone out in front. He dropped a coin into the slot and dialed Barney Driscoll's number.

Disconnected.

Matheson cursed, slammed his finger down on the receiver, held it in place, and retrieved his coin. Down it rattled again. He dialed each number slowly, carefully.

Disconnected.

No longer in service.

The sheriff let the phone slip from his hand, dangling from its long metal cable.

Matheson knew if he were to drive past the coroner's house, he would not like what he saw. He knew the house and driveway would be empty. Barney and his grandson would both be gone, and there would be an explanation in place as to their hasty departure. Nobody would question it. When people wore suits like that and drove around in black cars, it tended make people mind their own beeswax about things.

The lawman knew they were going to come for him next. In spite of his discretion, Juston didn't doubt for a second he was being watched. These people could spy on a man from places, distances, which would surprise you. They had told him to forget, had even *helped* him try and forget, and had seemed to believe he would play ball. Why else would they had let him live back at the motel? They could have put a bullet in his brain and dumped his body in a hog pen and nobody would have been the wiser.

But they hadn't.

Maybe they wanted him. A trusted figure in the community to reassure a suspicious community everything was perfectly fine. Nothing to see here. Keep moving. It made sense.

What did they want? Whoever they were.

He decided a visit to Roseanna Lavera was in order. Matheson was disturbed to admit it, but guidance from someone well-versed in this sort of thing was necessary. Things not of this earth. Hopefully, nobody had got to her already, providing she wasn't already a partner in their lunacy.

But first, another trek out to the remnants of Camp Azalea. The lawman knew the OSBI, or whatever they really were, had probably run a fine-toothed comb over the place. The chance of finding anything of use, of value, would be slim. But he had to try, for the sake of Black Knot and the people he had sworn to protect and the law he was bound to uphold. But he was scared. Scared almost to death.

SEVEN

Cora had noticed the pickup yesterday evening. She'd recognized it as the same one she had noticed yesterday parked outside of the new café across from the arcade. The boy, Hayder, had gotten into the truck with a pretty redheaded woman, whom Cora assumed was his momma. The girl had been spying on him, hidden from sight behind one of the gargoyle statues in front of the library, waiting until he had left The Gates. When she and Aunt Polly had come home from town, she had seen the same truck parked in the weed-choked driveway of the old Marley place. It was a very old model of truck. The chance of another truck like it around these parts was slim. Also, a very odd house to live in, that drafty old barn. It was the sort of place poor people with nowhere else to go would squat in. A lost cause house. Hayder and his mom definitely didn't fit the bill for the kind of people who would live there, or in Haggard either, for that matter. A certain breed of folk had laid their roots here over the decades. Folks like Cora's blood who had always been here, generations stretching way back before statehood when the Choctaw still owned and ran the show. Them and the witches.

Cora completely believed in all the witch stuff, but for the most part kept it to herself. Polly refused to discuss it, mostly because it got Baba all fired up. Lena, coming from where she did, a place and time far more savage than southeastern Oklahoma, most *definitely* believed in witches. Some of the stories from her homeland she had told Cora, legends concerning fearsome hags, cursed fields, and especially the weavers of wicked *enchantments,* had scared the holy bejeezus out of her. Once Baba got on a tear about the subject she could ramble on for hours, grow progressively more paranoid, believing she saw nefarious activity and evidence of hexing in everything from symbols twisted in the wisps of clouds to necromantic designs in her Spaghetti-Os. At her age, Polly reasoned, it wasn't wise to tax her old, frail heart. Cora had theorized it was really more about Aunt Polly being spooked by the stories then any real concern for Baba's cardiac health.

That night as she readied herself for bed, brushing her hair and listening to *Swap Shop* on the radio, the girl thought about the boy. She thought about him a lot, and she wasn't sure if she cared for it. In spite of the middle school gossips, Cora had zero experience with the male specimens her own age. Never even held a boy's hand, much less let one kiss her or do anything else. This boy, this stranger with the adorable curling mop of rusty gold hair and intense blue eyes, frightened her a little with the frequency of his intrusion into her thoughts. The thoughts were not particularly intense, or even all that interesting. Pretty mundane stuff, really. Cora wondered what his mom was making him for supper. What kind of pajamas he wore to bed. Did he brush his teeth twice a day or just once in the morning? Who was his favorite rock band? Was his mom smart, and if she was what sort of conversations did they have over the dining room table? Matters seemingly so bland any other time which now, with his introduction into her life, had taken on an almost mystical quality.

The girl retired to bed well after midnight, making several journeys from her room to the front porch to gaze out across the pasture separating their properties, hoping for a glimpse of him. Maybe he would be on his porch eating pie or something. Perhaps if he saw her looking he would come over to talk. They could talk about strategies for *Necromania*. Trade notes.

Cora didn't want to wait for that. For him. It wasn't her way.

Before she turned out the lights the girl resolved herself to walk over to the Marley house in the morning, step on onto that ruined old porch, and knock on their door. Maybe his momma would be making breakfast and he would ask her inside, into the kitchen for a seat at the table. Let her share in those deep conversations.

She nodded off while plotting out her invasion of her neighbor's household. For the first time since the Feed Lot hell, she slipped quickly and easily into an accommodating, comfortable slumber. Sleep like when she had been little. Something good for a change.

Cora marched up onto the Hennessey porch just as the front door creaked opened. This deviated from the plan, and she was taken off-guard, something she wasn't good handling. It was almost ten in the morning, a time which she had settled upon when she herself had awoken, like a well-oiled machine, at five on the nose. It had seemed a reasonable time when she had decided upon it. Now, it all felt weird and pushy. Awkward. But there was no turning back now. To flee at this moment would have been disastrous.

Hayder stepped out on the porch, his hair a tangled owls' nest and a light sheen of toothpaste coating his upper lip. He wore a pair of flannel pajama pants that were a little too big for him, a black t-shirt with a peeling iron-on decal of Batman on the front, with bare feet. Cora noticed how large his feet were. Like, Hobbit-level bigness. She tried desperately not to focus on them. In one hand he toted a large white plastic sack of garbage, swollen almost to bursting, his eyes still bleary with drowsiness.

"Cora?" He scrunched up his face. "Ummm…hi?"

"Walk you to the corner?" She smiled, hoping she didn't look too hideous. Nervous sweat had broken out all over her. All of a sudden her light autumn hooded sweatshirt felt like a fifty-pound fur coat. Hayder looked at her questioningly. Not understanding. She jabbed a thumb over her shoulder. "Country trash is picked up at the corner on opposite side of the mailbox. Don't put it where it's supposed to go, and they'll leave it behind."

"Ah yeah. Thanks for telling me. We got a lot more than this in the garage too. I think my mom was going to just haul it off to the dump in the pickup later today." Hayder set the bag down and briskly rubbed his elbows and forearms with his palms. Cora shivered. It felt a lot colder now than from when she'd set out. Now she was regretting the thin black tights and pleated skirt. She was thankful for the thick sweatshirt. Why the skirt anyway? Was she trying to tart herself up? Why? This was just a plain, ordinary boy who had moved into the house next door to her. A regular boy. A human just like her. Nothing special.

She hoped the mascara she had put on earlier hadn't smudged in the nine million times she had touched her face between her house and his.

"Dump's been closed awhile now. At least, the dump close to here," Cora told him. "The next closest one is over in Coffin Mills, which is kind of a drive just to drop off your trash when the Lowry Boys are paid by the county to collect it for us, totally free."

"Hayder? Baby…who is that?" a voice chimed behind him. A light snapped on in the entry way and the pretty redhead emerged to stand by the boy. Unlike her son, the woman was dressed and primped for the day. Jeans that fit her the right way, a red flannel shirt and the kind of boots a fit person went hiking in on her feet. Her thick hair, the deepest shade of red Cora had ever seen on someone not in a cartoon or a science-fiction movie, had been brushed over her shoulders, radiant and full. Cora felt about three shades of troll just looking at her.

"This is the girl I was telling you about." Hayder pointed to Cora. When his mom appeared to not understand he rolled his eyes and turned to address her directly. "For the café. The girl from the arcade across the street."

"Oh, you were telling her about *me*, were you?" Cora cocked an eyebrow, suddenly feeling very forward, and strangely alive with bravado. "Would love to know what was talked about, it being about me and all."

"Ah yes! *That* girl!" Recognition blossomed into the woman's face, her cheeks flushing pink. "Oh yeah. He had a lot to say. Speaks very, *very* highly of you!" She winked at Cora.

Hayder just stood between them, mute and mournful, begging for some sympathetic, unseen entity to put a bullet between his eyes. Nothing permanent, just long enough to forget about this particular moment and its accompanying conversation.

"Maybe we can talk more about that later, then. Wait till he goes to bed and can't interrupt us." Cora giggled, mindful of the gap in her back teeth. She made a fist and hastily covered her mouth.

"Why not now? I can whip you all up something to eat." Mona nudged her son aside and ushered the young girl past him and into the house. "I have to run him into town later to his job. Maybe you can come along. I can show you the café. If it's okay with your parents."

"I don't have parents anymore. So, I can work for you?" Cora asked, trying to hold back her enthusiasm. "For real? Like, work for money and get paid and all of that?"

The woman laughed. "Can you maybe even start today? I'm ready to roll, but could use a fresh set of eyes and perspective. Last minute tweaks and what not. And yes, I am paying money for you to work for me. I can either pay you by the day or the week. Minimum wage and whatever tips you might get." She stuck her hand out. "Sorry, Mona Hennessey."

"Cora Corbucci, ma'am." The child shook the offered hand, noting how smooth and cold the skin felt beneath her own touch. There was something in this chill which sent a coarse ripple through Cora's blood, and a weird feeling to go along with it. Departing almost as soon as it had arrived, but lingering long enough afterward for Cora to recognize the sour taste of bitterness. Yes, that was it. Resentment and lifelessness and even a little drop of something close to fear. The girl pulled her hand back slowly, not trying to alert what she was experiencing internally.

Mona smiled down at her, seemingly unaware of anything extraordinary occurring between them. The feeling was still there but growing noticeably weaker. Pushed down by her mortal rationality.

It was strange.

Cora had felt a lot of things these past few weeks. Things she hadn't felt before the Feed Lot.

Breakfast had been outstanding. Waffles and bacon and even fresh-ground coffee. Cora tried to contain herself but found her sense of restraint and decorum gravely compromised, especially when gazing down at that puffy, butter-drunk square of early morning fried goodness. She'd wolfed down two helpings and close to half a pound of the fried pork ribbons, all washed down with a cup and a half of black coffee. The girl honestly couldn't remember the last time she'd eaten like this. Probably before Baba Lena had begun to have trouble walking and the cooking chores had shifted between herself and Polly. As she ate, she side-eyed the boy she had come to see, not even bothering to hide the said side-eye. He was very quiet, head down and focused upon his meal. But she caught him glancing at her every once in awhile, pretending to look elsewhere upon detection. It was cute. Cute and strange and interesting.

What was he seeing when he was looking at her? A pretty girl? A weirdo? Something gross? A friend?

"So what's your new job?" Cora asked Hayder, swabbing her bacon in a small puddle of maple syrup on her plate. "Why not just work at your momma's?"

Hayder shrugged, cocking his head in his mother's direction. "Dunno. Ask the woman standing over there by the stove. It's her idea I go work at the movie theater. I've even begged her to let me do your job."

"It will be good for you to be out from under my wing, son. Buddy, we've had this discussion twenty dang times." She leaned into Cora, a kettle of hot coffee in her hand. "Top off that coffee for you, kiddo?"

Cora nodded, trying not to indicate what she had smelled when Mona Hennessey had drawn in close to her. There was no mistaking it, as it was an odor she herself was all too familiar with. The reek of booze. Hard, rough, damnable booze. Her eyes found Hayder's and was saddened to see the familiarity reflected back at her from him. He had smelled it too. Mona poured the coffee, smiled, then returned to the kitchen.

"I know. I was yanking your chain, mom." He broke off eye contact with Cora and returned to his waffles, stabbing listlessly at them with his fork.

"The Red Hand?" Cora asked, getting up to take the plate to the sink to rinse it off. After she did she returned to the table and her cup of coffee. "You're going to be working at the Red Hand Theater? For real?"

"Yep. You are looking at the future Master of the Concession Stand. Overlord of the Junk Food." He nodded, still picking around at his mutilated breakfast.

"Sultan of the Snack Bar." Cora snickered, fluttering her long eyelashes. The boy laughed, and she tried not to break her face grinning with delight as she sipped her coffee. "Man, you're a brave person. The Red Hand is spooooooooky! Too spooky for me, and I like scary stuff."

"Haven't been inside it yet. Seen the outside though and it is pretty Hammer horror."

"Oooo...you like Hammer movies?" She paused in mid-sip, very much interested in this detour. "I'm pretty sure I've seen all of them on Creature Feature. I really like *The Mummy*. It's my favorite."

"They're all right, I guess. I like the Universal stuff better, to be honest. They seem more about creating a spooky mood. The Hammer movies are just that. A hammer right on your head with all of the blood and boobies."

Heh heh...he said boobies. Cora giggled on the inside.

"Children, I need to get down to the café and tend to a few things. Cora, you want to go ask your parents if you can go with me? I don't want to just whisk you away without someone at your house being aware." Mona took up Hayder's plate and set into the kitchen sink to soak in hot, sudsy water. She retrieved her purse from the hat rack and slipped its strap over her shoulder. Hayder wandered off to his room to get dressed. With the boy's departure Cora suddenly began to feel very odd. A weird chill settled upon the top of her head and began to ooze a path downward, as if someone had set a plastic bag full of cold Jell-O on her skull and cut a small hole in the side of the bag, allowing for the slimy mess to seep out. This was a deep, strange cold, the kind of cold you felt both inside and outside of your body.

Then, as suddenly as it had manifested, it vanished. The warmth of the dining room returned. Mona Hennessey was staring at her, head cocked in interest. Perhaps even concern.

"Oh! Sorry!" Cora apologized, softly tapping the side of her head. "I space out like that all of the time. My mom and dad are dead. I live with my Baba and aunt. They know I'm with you."

"Baba…what's that?"

"My granny. Baba means that in her language. Granny, I mean."

"That being?"

"Ukrainian."

Hayder's momma seemed to mull that answer over, nodding, then offered a smile. Something in that distortion of her face brought a small twinge of the earlier chill back, then disappeared into obscurity once more. Hayder returned dressed in a pair of red corduroy jeans, a plain black t-shirt, and Converse sneakers the same color as his shirt. He came to stand between his mother and his new friend. Mona ran her hands through his thick shock of hair.

"I like your friend, son. I think she will be a big help to me."

The girl smiled. Why had she been so nervous a few minutes before? It was silly.

Does she drink a lot? She must not. She doesn't act drunk. Not even a little. Heck, everyone could probably use a nip of something now and again. Something to make their problems land softer.

"Still a bit early." The boy tapped his wristwatch. "How about we stop over at The Gates for a couple of games of *Necromania* before she takes me to work?" He looked over at his mother. "That okay with you, momma? Just an hour at the most."

"Of course, sweetie. I can manage on my own for a bit," his mom replied, giving him her patented "hubba-hubba" wink.

Hayder felt like he was going to die today. Death by embarrassment. He was certain of this.

"You better go first, then. My game will last a lot longer than yours will." Cora narrowed her eyes and frogged his arm.

He rolled his eyes and laughed, as did she, and it was not at all awkward.

"Son of a biscuit!" Cora stared at the empty spot in the corner of the arcade where once had stood her revered *Necromania* cabinet. All that was left was a dirty rectangle on the carpet from where the machine had once ruled. Hayder came up beside her, a fresh roll of quarters in his pocket. He walked over to the dirty rectangle, tapping around in it with the toe of his sneaker, as if trying to unearth a clue regarding its unexpected absence.

"Fizzed out last night. Gonna put a pinball machine in there tomorrow."

The unsavory character Hayder had encountered from his previous visit to the arcade was busy polishing bowling balls with one hand and stuffing a cheese coney into his maw with the other. "Wasn't worth keeping around, to tell the truth. Only person I ever saw playing it was you, Corbucci."

"A pinball machine?" Cora practically spat. "Who the heck plays pinball anymore except old geezers?"

"Hey, I like pinball." Hayder shrugged. "But I want *Necromania* back. If anything, so I can show this nimrod here how it's done." He cranked his thumb in Cora's direction. She returned the gesture with an affected, icy glare. Arcade Manager chuckled and returned to his vigorous ball polishing and coney demolishing.

"But I was good at that game. I was good at *something* finally. I had my name on it." Cora sighed, bowing her head, her long black hair curtaining her face. "I guess that's the lesson here. Nothing good lasts."

Hayder found himself unable to speak. His hand itched to reach out and touch her hair. Comfort her and let her know it wasn't that bad. But he just couldn't. It wasn't the right time. However, he did have a possible solution.

"*Dungeon Dwellers* doesn't have anyone playing it for once. We can play that one together. Ya game?" Hayder motioned to the huge double-screened monstrosity with his thumb. Cora lifted her head and peeked over at the game, eyes narrowed, mulling over the proposal. She turned to him and offered a crooked, still somewhat melancholy grin.

"Long as I get to be the Elven Spellweaver, then I'm in." Cora held up her quarter, a pink splash of neon caressing the metallic skin of the coin, then reflecting the shimmering image back into the darkness of her large eyes.

"I like shooting stuff, so I can be the Bloody Minister." Hayder nodded in approval of his choice, then reached up and tapped his coin to hers. "His mace does double damage against the undead."

"Then after you, milord." Cora offered a theatrical curtsey. "Soon the Archfiend of Groth shall know the sting of my elven fire!"

Hayder brought up his hands, fingers interlaced, and cracked his knuckles loud enough to be heard over all of the arcade's countless dings and bleeps.

"A Man of the North be I. The bones of fell creatures shall crumble beneath my blessed steel. Let's rock."

"That was bad to the bone!" Hayder cheered, running his hands through his sweaty hair. "Nobody is going to beat that high score. Nobody!" He walked ahead and opened the door for her.

"You bet your sweet bippy they won't. We have skills, my lad." Cora giggled as she stepped outside, trying to suppress her excitement at having a boy, a real live boy, open a door for her. "We whooped some serious butt!"

It was just a hair past one, and it was as fine an autumn day as Black Knot could offer. Cool enough to be comfortable, a light breeze stirring the clusters of gold and crimson swaying from the boughs and crests of the ancient maples hanging over the arcade like benign sentinels. Hayder could smell good things in the air. Sweet treats baking in family ovens and the clean air of the country. Black Knot felt really good to him right now. He could deal with life here if it was like this all of the time. As he stood beside Cora their elbows touched. The boy was afraid to move. Afraid to speak. Thrilled like he had never been thrilled before.

"I know you've heard things. Things about me." The girl was staring straight ahead now, as if trying to throw up an invisible barrier between them. "I'm crazy. Nutty people in my family. Druggie country people with no class. That I'm not a nice girl."

Hayder nodded. It felt better to tell the truth to her. "That dude at the front desk might have said some stuff to me. But he's kinda weird, I think."

"Well, he would know. He used to sell pot with my Aunt Polly before he got this gig here. He grew up in Haggard, too. And he's a perv."

Hayder remained quiet. He felt like there was more coming.

"If you're gonna be my friend, and I really hope you do want to, you're gonna hear a lot of strange things about me. Some of those strange things might be true." She turned to look at him, her dark eyes gone bible black. "Bail now if you can't handle that. I won't think anything bad about you. Promise."

Hayder found her request absurd. There was only one answer for him, even if all of those horrible things turned out to be fact. He didn't care, and that scared him a little bit. The girl felt both safe and dangerous at the same time, and yet somehow that didn't matter. Maybe a little danger was good. Danger was a dish best served to the young.

The boy tried to come up with something profound to say back. All he could manage was a frail, yet sincere: "We're friends."

Cora looked away, her large eyes shimmering. She removed her glasses and wiped her eyes with the back of her hand.

"You see, Mr. Hennessey, I am a poor person. Poor people have a hard time in Black Knot. I guess poor people have a hard time anywhere they live. There isn't a lot of kindness to spare for folks without money or big friends. People with bad families and bad secrets. When you're poor you don't have the money to just bury your dirty bones whenever you feel like it."

She took his hand over his, her warm skin rippling its heat from her blood into his. A peculiar tremor radiated throughout Hayder's whole body, an exotic strain of joy that he couldn't quite get a handle on. It left him feeling both frightened and euphoric. Hayder wanted to ask her about the Feed Lot, but immediately nuked the idea. At the moment things were feeling good. Like a storm had passed by without thunder.

Hayder interlaced his fingers with hers. It was a bold move, to be sure. But it felt right. The girl held fast to his hand, softly brushing her thumb across his skin. This would come to be a moment to be filed away under the heading of Momentous. A memory to be dredged up in the years to follow whenever he found himself feeling scared or unwanted.

The young boy, not feeling so young at the moment, hoped it would be like this from now on. Black Knot feeling a little more like home with every passing hour.

EIGHT

The Red Hand Theater wasn't just the oldest movie house in Black Knot, but the only one as well. The theater more than lived up to the mental image Hayder had been assembling over the past few weeks. After his mom had dropped him off, promising to return with Cora in a couple of hours to pick him up, Hayder stood on the sidewalk out in front of the Red Hand. Just soaking it all in. The harvest sun, its daily chores settled, had just liquefied into the shadowy ridge of the Kiamichi Mountains, distilled into a cheery mantle of seared orange drifting languidly across the vibrantly colored treetops and gently plunging hillocks.

The theater was the oldest place of its kind Hayder had ever laid eyes upon. It was an odd amalgam of Art Deco flamboyance and gothic Victorian masonry, a lumbering monstrosity of deep gray stone and intricate glasswork completely out of place situated on the main drag of a podunk town. The sprawl of the Red Hand was extraordinary, even a little grotesque. From the outside it appeared to consist of three distinct floors, each demarcated by a trio of large stained-glass windows. The lower floor, obviously, would be the lobby and the main auditorium, the middle story housing the projection booth and the balcony seating. Hayder assumed the uppermost level was storage space. However, a very discernible mote of light flickered behind the motley-colored glass of the top floor's middle window. He wondered about it a bit, but concerned himself no further. Probably just offices for the folks running the place.

Hayder approached the ticket booth and found it empty. He though little of it, as it was still an hour before the first feature. The boy walked over to the entrance and tried the door and found it securely locked. He rattled the door a bit to make some noise.

"Hope you didn't get your days mixed up, mom." He groaned. This wasn't an implausible concern. His mother had been so preoccupied with getting all the kinks ironed out for the opening of the café, he wouldn't have been one bit surprised if she had made a mistake. He gave the door another vigorous shake, following up with an aggressive rap upon the glass. The glass itself was tinted to stave off the glare of both the outside sun and the streetlights. Squinting, he thought he could see a glow, very faint, beckoning from within. He backed away from the door and looked around. Not a soul to be found. The streets of Black Knot's main drag were utterly devoid of anything alive.

Then, an eruption of light! The marquee, normally a dead and dull thing during the daylight hours, suddenly breathed itself to life in an almost vulgar explosion of cinematic phantasmagoria from what appeared to be hundreds of tiny glass bulbs. It was, in a word, magical. As he stood gawking up at the marquee a sudden breeze kicked up, howling down the street and enshrouding him, scattering scraps of garbage and leaves into a dry, rustling wraith encircling his feet. The lurid titles of the double feature loomed before him like a biblical tablet in thick black letters.

Hayder was mesmerized, not hearing the old woman calling to him from the open door. Only when she was standing directly in front of him, snapping her fingers in his face, did his arrested consciousness relent into recognition. The interruption jolted him, eliciting a startled little squawk from the boy.

"Sorry to spook you. Almost forgot to turn on the sign. Always turn on the sign before you open the doors. Rules of the house." The woman, pint-sized and troll-like, apologized. She was one of the oldest people Hayder had ever seen, easily. Stooped and gnarled, how she was not in a nursing home was a mystery. Her head was turnip-shaped and topped by what was obviously an old, very cheap red wig, which hung askew from her skull like a wino's ballcap. There were so many wrinkles furrowing her face Hayder felt like holding a handful of nickels in one hand, over her head, and allowing the coins to roll smoothly through the creases and folds of her cheeks and forehead. However, her eyes, brown as aged hickory, were lively and brimming with ageless pluck. Not a hint of wither or infirmity. She was dressed in mustard yellow slacks, a plain white blouse, and a dark brown vest. A small tag pinned to her vest advertised the name *Vera*.

"That's okay. I was just checking out stuff." Hayder felt very odd. Like how you feel the next morning after being sick with a fever all night. Better, but worn down. It took effort to get the words out of his mouth. Then, before he had a chance to analyze it for very long, the feeling was gone. Had it ever even been there?

"Would I be supposing correctly you're the Hennessey kid?" she asked. He nodded, smiling. His attention kept being drawn to the divine, scintillating magic of the marquee.

"Real beauty, ain't she? That's the original sign, too. We've kept her up pretty dern good, if I do say so. Not even the tornado of '58 could put a dent in this baby." The woman looked up at the sign with him, nodding with unfeigned pride. "I'm Vera Lawson. I tend to this old girl."

"Yup, that's me." Hayder nodded, strangely thankful to have his attention diverted away from the marquee. He held out his hand for her, which she accepted and shook with remarkable vigor. "Name's Hayder."

"Rather just call you be your last name for now, if you don't mind. At least until you've been here long enough for me to know you better. Make sure you are a good fit for the family." She took him by the elbow and began guiding him inside. "You won't be working tonight, of course. Just want to show you around, familiarize you with the old girl. She's an old place, and all old places got habits. You don't tend to those habits, and you find yourself regrettin' it."

Hayder nodded. It sounded a little creepy when she put it like that. Old people could be really dramatic sometimes, so he let it slide. Besides, the marquee was so pretty, so comforting to look at. Its soothing light calmed his apprehensions, like when his mom stroked his hair when he was upset.

Before they entered the theater Hayder noticed something interesting. Something on the front door. Scrawled upon the glass was the likeness of a red hand, a little larger than his own, rendered upon the door in dark red paint. A closer look revealed it to be less of an illustration and more of an impression. As if someone had dipped their own hand in paint and pressed it up against the glass. Smeared, not drawn. He could actually see the swirls and spirals of fingerprints. Or did he? He wasn't sure. Bright lights can sometimes do that. Make shadows gather into funny shapes. Make you think you saw strange sights which would appear totally ordinary in the daylight.

The boy debated asking Vera about it. What it meant. It had to mean something, right? Yet he refrained from doing so.

He hated to admit it to himself, but he was a little afraid of the answer he might get.

Upon entering the lobby of the Red Hand. Hayder was immediately greeted by the welcoming glow of the concession stand, or snack bar as the sign in sparkling purple neon advertised from the wall next to the Slush Kitty machine.

It was a pretty standard setup. A wooden countertop lay across a glass display case, advertising the multitude of nibbles available for purchase. Mostly the predictable brands of candy, with their price tags displayed on a small cardboard label in front of them. Behind the counter there was an enormous popcorn machine, older than the hills judging from the ornate carvings in the tarnished brass skeleton of the apparatus. The contraption was already hard at work roasting kernels of dried corn into salty poofs of joy. The Slush Kitty machine was currently on defrost, and a tidy rack of soda dispensers stood close by awaiting further orders. There was a heated rack for gigantic soft pretzels, a tub of hot melted cheese for nachos, and a conveyor belt rolling and toiling at keeping a handful of hot dogs toasty. On either side of the snack bar was a flight of carpeted steps leading upward, as well as the primary entrances to the auditorium. The carpet was a thin red linoleum. The bathrooms were situated right next to the staircases, men to the left and ladies to the right. To the left of the ladies' bathroom was a Street Hunter pinball machine that appeared to have seen a lot of action. Next to the men's room a flight of steps led down into what Hayder assumed to be the basement.

All in all, it was a painfully ordinary setup.

"I decided last year to relocate the box office to the snack bar. Was a smart move. Food money we been raking in has tripled." Vera ushered him behind the counter and pointed out the various mechanisms of commerce and filled him on the details regarding how to take money, secure that money, then present a paper ticket to the customer in exchange. It all seemed easy enough. Vera then went over the devices responsible for dispensing the edible tidbits. He'd had experience working the concession stand for high school basketball games back home, so this wasn't anything new to him. But he let the old girl run through her entire spiel for the sake of killing time and promoting future goodwill between the two of them.

"Easy enough." Hayder nodded at her. He meant it too.

Yeah…but something's not quite right, is it?

He told that little voice to go away.

Vera Lawson then asked him to follow her into the auditorium. It was here that Hayder began to understand why that little voice had suddenly piped up. It was the same nagging little voice which had cautioned him before opening the door to the basement back home. Told him to stay at the top of the stairs and yell for his mother. Don't you dare go down there by yourself, because you won't like what you find, and you will see something you will not be able to forget about, ever.

Good. You're listening again. Keep your eyes peeled! Be on your guard.

The auditorium was a rambling panorama of folding seats and shadows heavy as cold molasses. Hayder, again, was amazed at the size of the theater. There had to be well over a thousand seats in the chamber, with at least an additional fourth of that tally on the balcony level. He couldn't imagine the place ever being completely full. Not with the sort of bottom of the barrel flicks they seemed to be showing. The screen was probably close to thirty feet tall and double that number in width, enshrouded by a tattered curtain of emerald velvet. It was obvious the auditorium had once been used for more than just showing films, as an ample stage was present beneath the screen, replete with old-fashioned footlights.

"Shoot fire! I gotta go back and lock the lobby door. Don't want folks wandering in before showtime. They'll get into something they shouldn't," Vera told him, her voice echoing through the empty space and returning to them as if she had been casting her words down into the depths of an ancient well. "You just go and have a look-see around and then I'll take you upstairs." She patted his shoulder reassuringly, as if sensing his apprehension, and departed. Hayder didn't particularly want to have a look-see around. The little voice was being noncommittal at the moment, so he reasoned that perhaps a bit of nosing around couldn't really hurt. Taking to the middle aisle the boy began to walk slowly toward the screen, casting a look left to right for any signs of danger.

As he ambled forth Hayder realized the theater was actually rather nice. Pretty, even. At least here in the auditorium. It was clean and cozy, even if the décor was a bit gaudy. The boy began to wonder if the unease he felt had more to do with him than the Red Hand itself. Old buildings had always sort of creeped him out. He was a modern kid and had little appreciation for the history of things. Old stuff made him think of the people who had walked there before him. People who were more than likely long gone from this world now. The notion he might be following in the footsteps of the dead chilled him. His dad had been the same way. Mom, however, had always been a little odd about that sort of thing. Probably because she was an artist. Artsy folks seemed to be extra drawn to peculiar stuff. She had a small library's worth of books on witchy pursuits. Lots of books about herbs and astrology mostly. Mona Hennessey had never been the sort of mom you saw hollering from the stands at ballgames or working PTA potlucks. Hayder couldn't recall her ever hanging out with friends. In fact, he wasn't even sure she really *had* any friends. She'd always been a bit aloof around other adults. Dad had always said it was because she was an only child, and all only children were like that. Withdrawn, shy. A bit moody and guarded, they were perfectly content to be left alone.

Yes, that was his mom to the letter.

Hayder wondered what the screen looked like behind that curtain. He couldn't wait to see a flick here. A good sci-fi movie would look awesome on a beast of screen like this. Or something with a good car chase.

Halfway between the screen and the exit to the lobby was when he heard the first seat fold down. Of course, he didn't identify the noise as such at first. He tried to pass it off as just an ordinary, expected rumbling of the theater's old bones. Another one quickly followed, this time seeming to come from the rear of the auditorium, a nook bathed in a gloom so dense it bordered on unnatural. Afraid to turn around, he just kept walking toward the screen, but the cold sweat had already started to seep out of his skin. Another seat creaked, then another. Then, one more. Once the boy had reached the edge of the stage he had gathered enough courage to spin around and confront whatever trickery was being played upon him. That was what it had to be, right? A prank pulled on the new boy. An initiation. It made sense. Best of all, if it were a joke the punch line would more than likely not be too far off. Better to go ahead and get all of the monkeyshines over with right from the get-go.

"*Ohhhhkayyyy*...I hear you. Good one," Hayder called out, his voice resonating as if he were in a room twice the size of the auditorium. It reminded him of the one time he'd gone to Christmas Eve Mass with his granny in the big cathedral in downtown Dallas years ago. Every little noise bouncing off of every old stone and glass. "Come on out. You got me. Y'all got me real good."

He scanned the rows of empty seats, squinting into the shadows. All of them were in the same compacted position as when Vera had first flung open the doors to the auditorium. A weird, nervous flutter began to rile up in his belly. His eyes gravitated toward the balcony as if someone were whispering in his ear to do it. Drawing his attention to that coal-dark alcove. As his eyes began to adjust to the gloom something began to manifest. Flickers of orange light, winking in and out of visibility. Hayder climbed up on to the stage to get an unobstructed view of the entire balcony, squinting into the disturbing, tar-thick blackness. For what seemed like the longest time in the world the darkness was simply that, but something was off about it all. The shadows wouldn't sit still for long. There was constant movement within the inkiness, a swirling void too deep and vast to be anything close to normal. There were things prowling around within the murk, forms which seemed to shift around, splinter and then re-assemble themselves into what looked like shapes he could almost put a name to.

Was that a tree?

Yes, a tree.

No, a dog.

No.

It was a person.

As if in response the thing detached itself from its shadowy nest, and for a moment Hayder could see it. Although he couldn't discern any distinct facial features he could tell from the build and dimensions it was a child. A girl not far from his age with long ebony hair, snarled and knotted with filth. She was dressed in a grimy scrap of a nightgown, nearly naked, as if she had dressed herself as an afterthought. Her skin radiated a faint bluish cast as if lit from beneath the surface with a slice of cold moonlight. Atop her head, to the boy's horror, a downright mean-looking rack of antlers jutted from the skull, her grubby hair tangled in the terrible prongs. A scream boiled up in his throat, wriggling to make itself heard. Yet he found himself unable to utter a peep, as if a clutch of knobby witch-fingers had curled around his neck and squeezed just hard enough to hold his tongue. She lifted her hand and directed a scrawny finger at him, her slitted eyes glowing jack-o-lantern orange. Hayder could feel in the marrow of his bones she meant him harm, a harm he had no conception of, and the longer he lingered here, in her realm, the worse it would turn out for him.

He closed his eyes and began to pray, something he wasn't particularly good at.

"*Get away get away,*" he murmured. "*Jesus, make it go away. Get away get away!*"

"Who you a-gabbing at, son?"

Hayder opened his eyes and saw Vera standing next to the stage, staring up at him quizzically. To his surprise the balcony was now vacant.

Good God. He was going crazy.

No, you saw that. Quit trying to tell yourself this didn't happen.

"Talking to myself, I guess." He chuckled, leaping from the stage to the floor. "Never mind me."

Vera took a step closer and laid her wizened old hand on his shoulder, her expression grave.

"You just remember what I told you, boyo. It's an old place. All old places got habits."

The boy kept quiet about what he had seen in the balcony. Somehow, he knew Vera would have believed him. This didn't make him feel any better about having seen it, and as he followed Vera up the staircase to the Red Hand's second floor, referred by her as the Administrative Level, he worked very hard at trying to convince himself he had imagined it all. He had seen something, maybe. Certainly not a weird blue girl with deer horns. Talking about it would have only made it more real, and Hayder's mind was still too young and raw to properly manage the experience like a grown-up.

"At the other end of this here hallway are the upstairs bathrooms, which we no longer use for the most part because the floor itself is not open to the public. We only keep them tidy for the VIP movie customers and the projectionist. There's a supply closet up there too. So, if you need extra anything, be it toilet paper or syrup for the Slush Kitty, you come get me and I'll take care of it. But you don't go get it yourself. Remember that." She reached out and rapped her knuckles against the door. "This here is the staircase leading up to the projectionist booth. Old Newt McAlester is the man up there. You don't never, and I mean *never*, go up there, whether he's there or not. He's real touchy about people nosing around in his booth, especially kids. You got no business up there anyway, so this shouldn't be a hard rule for you to stick to."

"Yes ma'am." Hayder nodded.

"I must say, I appreciate your politeness, calling me ma'am and such. Ain't been a ma'am for a very long time." The old woman reached out and slapped his back, smiling with genuine affection. "You seem like a good kid, and I think you'll do well here if you just follow them rules. It's decent moolah for not that much work."

She walked him back downstairs. Outside it had begun to rain a little. Just a mellow autumn shower which made the streets shine like polished glass beneath the amber bask of the marquee. As Hayder watched the rain his mother pulled up in the truck, the headlights cutting through a pale film of fog which had begun to grasp and spiral along the sidewalk. Cora's head was visible in the passenger seat, and the boy fancied he could see the glimmer of her black eyes in the obscurity of the truck cab. He waved at his mom, forgetting the tint on the big lobby window made it too dark for anyone to see inside.

"That would be your ma, I reckon." Vera ambled up beside him and looked out the window. "Oh shoot-fire! I need to go get your uniform. Hang tight." The old woman marched back up the stairs to the balcony level and hung a hard left. More than likely to the off-limits supply closet next to the off-limits restrooms, just a hop skip and a jump from the forbidden balcony and projectionist booth. Hayder stared out the window, seeing his mom lift her hand in salute.

Why did we come here? We shouldn't have come here. I felt it before we even left home, but didn't want to bug you, mom.

Vera returned with a nearly folded pair of black pants and an orange-colored polo shirt, both of which she handed to Hayder. "Needs a good wash. Suds it up really good and dry it with something to make it smell nice. Or dry it outside on a line. Fresh air always gets the stink out of really ripe duds."

As they began walking toward the exit Hayder caught a glimpse of a door in a small alcove next between the Street Hunter machine and the ladies' restroom. He hadn't noticed it coming in, which seemed an intentional design choice. Like it was being purposefully concealed. There was a small brass plaque attached to the door which was too far away for him to read. The door itself was interesting. With its lovingly beveled and sanded corners, the ornate woodwork, it looked more like a door you would find hanging from the entrance to an old church. Perhaps the covering for a trunk where a rich person would store something expensive. Or maybe even the lid of an ancient coffin.

It looks really old. A lot older than the other rooms. Like everything had been built around it.

Vera's hand fell on his shoulder and gave it a reassuring squeeze, although it didn't do much in the way of offering any real comfort for him. Hayder turned to regard the old lady to thank her again when he noticed, for the first time, an odd, shallow scar winding around her throat. More like an old, healed-up and haired-over burn than a scar, really. He caught himself right before that glance evolved into a full-blown gawk. But she'd seen him notice it. He could tell.

Another shoulder squeeze, and a little more forceful than the last one. Vera took one of his hands in her own gnarled clutch of fingers and pressed a couple of green paper stubs into them.

"For tomorrow night's show. My treat. Give these to your friends if you got any," she said, then slipping her hands into the pockets of her old-lady polyester slacks. "See you tomorrow night, Hennessey. You be ready, hear?"

Hayder tried not to look at Cora as he eased into the seat beside her. She was planted by his mom, which he didn't mind one bit. He could feel the girl's dark eyes crawling him as soon as he slammed the truck door, perhaps a little too roughly. Mom asked him something boring and he responded with something equally uninteresting. It must have been the correct response, as Mona didn't ask him anything else. As they backed out and away from the parking lot of the Red Hand, the rain really began to come down, pouring with such force the wipers struggled to slosh the relentless deluge away from the windshield. Mom turned on the radio and began to sing along to some goofy song from when she had been a kid. Most of the songs she had liked as a child were like that. This lightened the mood considerably.

Cora's eyes remained glued to him, but he refused to return the look. He didn't want to talk about it right now.

Her cold little hand slipped into his and squeezed, then slipped away again.

He scooted a little closer to her, their shoulders touching. Something about being close to the girl made him feel safe. Reaching into her lap, he retrieved her hand and wove his fingers into hers. Even in the dark he could see her smile.

She smelled really nice. Like flowers and soap.

Good, normal smells.

NINE

Cora stood beside Hayder at the barbed wire fence separating the Hennessey property from her own. It was almost nine o'clock, the rain had stopped, and it was now full dark with a cloudless heaven. A gentle harvest breeze wafted through the pasture's rippling lake of yellowed grass and the barren thickets of oak and maple trees, filling the air with the scent of wet leaves and decaying hay. They talked easily with one another. The conversation felt a lot more natural than it had the day before, as if they had been pals for years instead of a mere collection of days. He didn't have a lot to say about his evening with Vera Lawson at the Red Hand, which Cora found a bit weird given the colorful reputation of the place. She related how her evening with his mother had gone down, although she too, like her new friend, didn't provide all of the details either. At that moment, when the world felt so fine and right, it didn't seem like a nice idea.

"It went good. Your ma is real nice and cooks a mean chicken-fried steak. You're super-duper lucky." Cora plucked a tall stalk of charnel thistle and popped it into the corner of her mouth, gnawing on it a little. Roseanna Lavera, the town's resident character, had told her the weed possessed mystical properties, most commonly imparting a sense of wellbeing to the chewer. The young girl knew this to be accurate, like most of Roseanna's guidance. As the spicy, slightly sour juices from the stalk flowed into her mouth and down her throat, Cora immediately began to feel soothed. She was used to applying natural concoctions at home for various complaints, and could confirm the reliability of their potency. Cora found it all very romantic. She loved the idea that it was magic, and that magic was real. It helped smooth out the rough edges on everything else.

"Yeah. I suppose I am." Hayder shrugged. "She's been through a lot too. Losing my dad and sister and then having to take care of me by herself. It's not normal for her. She's used to having money and not having to work."

"I think she's doing as good as can be expected. Probably better than you know," Cora commented. She had something else she wanted to say but hesitated. It was a matter perhaps a little too personal for the two of them to discuss right now, but it had been weighing heavily upon her. Deliberating the outcomes of bringing it up versus not, Cora leaned more toward the former. "Look, I don't wanna be butting my nose in your life or anything. I was just curious if…I mean…does your mom…"

"Yes. She does," Hayder interrupted, nodding and looking away from her. The girl immediately regretted saying anything.

"How do you know what I'm talking about?" Cora plucked the thistle from her mouth and tied it in a knot around a rusted fence wire.

"I smelled it on her the other night. Right before bed she was tucking me in, and I could smell it then too. I think it's something called tequila. It's what she used to drink a couple of years ago when she was really bad. I recognized it right off." The boy's voice quivered, and he cleared his throat several times before he continued. "She and my dad were having some problems and it was because of the drinking. She went away to some place where they help people who drink too much, and she got better. Or so I thought."

Cora thought carefully about what she wanted to say next. "I get it. Polly, that's my auntie, she's had problems like that. Still does, really. Not just drinking but drugs too. It seems like something that never goes away. On again and off again. Coffee one morning, then beer the next. I can tell when things are about to get bad with her because she starts acting real sneaky. Like she's hiding something, but it's obvious to me what she's doing. She does the same thing every time. She's gone a lot. Stays out all night, even if she's got to work the next day. Comes home with the same smell, all of the time. I don't know what it is, but I know it's got something to do with bad things. Drinking. Weed. Other stuff I don't know about except that none of it's good. My Baba Lena told me it's the smell of sin coming off of her. Not sure I believe that. Baba can be a little spooky sometimes."

"I keep telling myself maybe it's just a slip. People can do that, right? Everyone slips up. I know just walking away from it all and hearing them say they're done with it forever never really sticks too good. It's something in their blood that makes them want it. With dad and sissy gone I guess I shouldn't be surprised."

Cora knew all about the slip. The slip almost always led to a slide, and at the bottom of that slide very hard days and even worse nights awaited. She playfully frogged his arm.

"I bet that's what it is. Y'all are just going through a rough patch. Once things start to settle down, you get used to living here, maybe she'll stop again. Maybe meet a nice guy to have as her boyfriend." Cora plucked another couple of stalks of thistle and began weaving them into the knot she had tied to the fence. "Sometimes all a sad and hurt person needs is someone to be a little bit nice to them. Let them know there are good things in the world, and they're worth getting to have those things."

Hayder still wouldn't look at her. He stared at the ground and nodded. Cora knew this was the time to end this particular branch of the conversation and move on to something else.

"Say, you want to come over to my house tonight?" she asked suddenly, awkwardly.

Hayder didn't understand. "It's already night. You mean right now?"

"No. Later on. Like, after everyone's gone to sleep." She scooted closer to him until her hip was touching his. Her nearness both terrified and comforted him. "I'll be up for a long time. I don't really sleep all that much anymore."

"Sure. I guess I can sneak out for a bit. Mom sleeps so hard I could bang a drum in front of her bed, and she'd keep right on snoring." He looked at her out of the corner of his eye. "What are we going to do? You have some board games or something?"

Cora giggled. "Nothing that exciting. I know you like *Warriors & Warlocks* and that kind of stuff. I like those things too. You see the mural on the outside of the arcade? The pictures on the window?"

Hayder had noticed. He had assumed the owners of The Gates of Mordor had paid a professional for artwork of that caliber. He turned around to face the girl fully. "You?"

"Yessir!" She beamed proudly. "Paid me seventy-five dollars for it too! I was a high and mighty lady with that kind of money in my pocket, let me tell you!" She didn't tell him where that money had gone. All of it, every single cent, had gone toward paying both the water and the phone bill. Not that it mattered. She had earned the money fairly, and that was that.

"That's really cool! A lot better than I could ever do." Hayder shook his head in sincere admiration. "I guess I can swing by for a little bit. How will I know when it's okay to come over? Won't your grandma and aunt mind? Me being a boy and all."

"*Pffft!* Aunt Polly is working graveyard at the ammo factory, and Baba will be in bed right after *Six-Gun McGee* goes off at twelve-thirty. You got yourself a flashlight?"

He nodded.

"Okie-dokie. Then you get that flashlight of yours and be at your bedroom window around one. I will flash my light at you three times when it's cool to come over. You flash it once if you can't come out, twice if you can. You then hustle your way over here, to that window over there on the back side. The little area beside the well shed." She pointed over to a pitiful, slouched shack listing on the western perimeter of the house. "I'll have the window up, so you won't have to knock or make any noise. We can even play the radio a little if we keep it low. I can show you my drawings and maybe we can work on something together. Something for *Warriors & Warlocks?* Maybe we can start us a game of our own."

All Hayder could do was nod in assent. He didn't want her to know he was aghast at the thought at being in a girl's bedroom after all of the grown-ups had gone to sleep.

"*Kora ... Kora?*" A voice called out feebly into the darkness. Cora could see Baba Lena standing on the porch, lantern in hand. The child sighed and rolled her eyes.

"Ugh! It's my Baba." She told Hayder. Cupping her hands around her mouth she called back to the old woman. "*Bud' tut zhe, baba Lena! Ya v hostyakh u susids'koho khlopchyka.*" The lantern swung back and forth in the darkness. Within its shifting radiance Cora could see Lena waving at her, confirming the message had been received, then ambled back into the desolate house. She turned to Hayder. "I gotta go. The old lady's ready for me to read her *Reader's Digest* to her before the news comes on. Remember, one o'clock. Flash the light twice if you're coming."

The girl reached down and plucked another strand of thistle, this time handing it to the boy. "Try it. Supposed to calm your nerves. A real-life witch told me this, so it ain't just my imagination."

Hayder accepted the offering but kept it in his hand, studying it. The trust between the two of them appeared to have its limits.

"Maybe later." She narrowed her eyes, tilting her head. "Hey, listen."

Hayder cocked his head. He didn't hear anything out of the ordinary.

"Cicadas." She smiled. The boy nodded. Cicadas. Or frogs. But no, it was too late in the season for either one. Yes, cicadas.

"I love the sound of cicadas. Cicadas in October, imagine that." She leaned against a fencepost, closing her eyes as if absorbing the sound. "Remember, one o'clock. Flash the light twice if you can make it."

"I'll be there. I'll bring my game books, and maybe I can show you how to play." He smiled shyly at her. "If you're interested. *Warriors & Warlocks* really just needs at least three people to make a good game. But we can do fine with just the two of us."

Cora nodded and grinned. She liked that idea a lot. She could feel the blood warmly blossoming beneath the white skin of her cheeks.

It was the most romantic thing anyone had ever said to her, and with that she took her leave of him.

The child took her time walking home, sticking to the pasture between their houses rather than the road which ran alongside the front of their properties. She wanted to avoid walking past the Jacobsen farm if she could help it. Although now she had pretty much convinced herself what she had seen over there, the wolf-masked man holding the corpse of her dead friend in one hand and a smoking shotgun in the other, had all been in her head. A nightmare endured while still wide awake. The doctors had told her that her mind might do funny things for a while after the accident. The pills were supposed to help with that. So she took the pills, and as far as she could tell everything felt much better. Yet the fear of that old house across the street held on to her, and she felt it best to just avoid it. No sense in tempting fate, even if it was all just her imagination.

He was so cute, the boy. So nice. She liked his shyness. Hayder was nothing like the other boys at school who were constantly wanting to sneak a feel of her chest or tried lifting her skirt with a stick to see what color of underwear she was wearing. He actually wanted to know her. Include her in the things he liked. Cora was glad she hadn't told him everything about the time she had spent with his mother today. About how Mona Hennessey had been pleasant but noticeably chilly toward her. Nothing like how she had behaved at the house before they had left for town. At the café she had gone over what was to be expected of her new employee, which really wasn't anything Cora hadn't expected. Mostly keep the tables clean, work the register as needed, help a bit in the kitchen if asked. A reek of strong liquor came and went, often obscured by a minty aroma which Cora assumed to be mouthwash or chewing gum. The woman would disappear into the bathroom for several minutes at a stretch, always emerging flustered, scatterbrained and even a little testy. Cora had spent the majority of her time helping take inventory in the stock room, mostly itemizing how much flour and sugar and other supplies were currently available. It wasn't difficult for her. The child was good at that sort of thing, being a very tidy and organized creature by nature.

That was when she had come across the books.

Cora had found them while sifting through some sacks of cornmeal in the rear of the supply closet, packed away in a couple of unremarkable cardboard boxes. The books appeared to be very old, some of them close to crumbling to pieces, each encased in thick leather and bound in some kind of tough twine. Almost like baling wire. When she had reached out her hand to touch one of them, she felt a very real, very present chill exuding from the tome. She opened the cover and looked at the first page, which was fashioned from some kind of heavy paper that took real effort to lift and turn over. The first few pages were passages written in a tongue she didn't recognize, which really wasn't saying much given the only languages Cora had any familiarity with were English, Ukrainian, and a smidgeon of Spanish. Staring at the script for very long made her temples throb and head smart. But she found it difficult to not look at the words, to not want to read them. As if the book *wanted* to be read. Its contents absorbed. She had been so engrossed in her analysis she hadn't heard Mona wander into the storage closet, standing just a few feet behind her.

"You don't need to worry about those."

Cora had shrieked, startled. She began to come up with an excuse but could only stand there, jawing wordlessly, embarrassed at being caught snooping.

Mona had told her the books were for the house and for her to come back up front. They were almost finished. Cora nodded and did as she was told; on pins and needles for the remainder of the time spent in the café. On the way to pick up Hayder from the Red Hand the woman hadn't said one word to her. They rode together in silence for the five-minute drive from the café to the movie theater. But Cora felt like Mona was looking at her somehow. Observing her in a way she couldn't understand. She was grateful for Hayder's company when he finally climbed into the truck to sit beside her.

Yet something wasn't right with the boy. She could sense it immediately. Cora knew he wasn't being entirely forthcoming about his evening spent in the notorious old movie house. That was part of the reason she had asked him to come over later. Maybe she could get him to open up.

However, now that he had agreed to come over, Cora wasn't so certain she wanted to know anything else. She was afraid it would be like if she had continued to read that book, that to know too much would be bad for her. A black Jeep was parked in the front yard, just under the withered cedar tree. Cora had never seen this Jeep before.

Although it wasn't out of the ordinary for visitors at this hour, it was unusual for those said visitors to be complete strangers. Polly's friends, her crowd, were usually the same collection of mugs from her aunt's rogues' gallery of colorful characters. There was Honest Abe, whom Cora knew to be Polly's favorite drinking buddy and one-time flame. Abe was normally accompanied by Bentback Jim, a knobby troll of a man with an affable smile and a fast, dry wit. Sometimes Abe and Jim were accompanied by Lucy Lavera, a tall macaroni noodle on two legs whose constant tangles with the law had all but exiled her from her family, the notorious Lavera clan. The woman had once been the dispatcher for the Black Knot police department when she had been just a teenager. Cora was certain that Lucy was the connection to their shared poisons, for it was country gospel the Lavera dynasty was the wheelhouse for all of the petty drug shenanigans occurring in Black Knot.

These visitors were outsiders, and they felt like it.

At the kitchen table, seated with Aunt Polly, were a trio of strangers. Two men and one woman, each of them dressed in identical, spotless and well-tailored red satin business suits with black silk ties. Individually, none of them looked particularly distinctive, which struck Cora as strange. When she tried to center her attention upon each of them individually, her head began to feel funny. Her focus became clouded and confused. When she would look at one of them, center her attention and try to cling to the memory of what she had just seen, she would immediately forget every single detail, the memory slipping through her brain and into nothingness like melted butter. The three of them smiled at her, and for a palmful of seconds she remembered it, then immediately began to question if it had happened at all. Polly smiled at her too. Much to Cora's relief she was drinking a cup of coffee. Baba Lena was standing by the stove smoking a cigar and chatting amicably with all of them. Baba hadn't smoked since Cora was in the third grade, and the fact the old gal was standing at all, without visible discomfort and actually appearing to be sociable, alarmed her granddaughter. Lena rarely budged from the comfort of her La-Z-Boy unless absolutely necessary, and even then, she never went without a recital of grumbles.

But even that wasn't the freakiest thing. The freakiest thing was she was chatting with her guests in English. Baba Lena, when she spoke at all, *never* conversed in any tongue other than her native Ukrainian. Cora wasn't sure Lena even knew enough of the language to string a single coherent sentence together, much less engage in a spirited conversation like she was right now.

"Hey doll. Where you been?" Polly chimed, smiling between sips of coffee. "Getting kind of late to be wandering around. You ain't running at a hundred percent still neither. Better you take it easy. You'll be all worn out and find yourself in bed again before school starts back up on Monday."

The three strangers nodded as if in agreement, still smiling.

"It is good to see you, kiddo. Yes?" Baba nodded at her, dragging hard on the cigar and pursing her lips to allow a coil of discolored white smoke wiggle out. "Looking strong, you. Like living person again."

"Uh…I went with Hayder and his momma into town. Remember, the boy next door?" Cora was still bewildered by Baba and her apparent newfound eloquence in a language which had been a dead tongue to her up until this moment. "I told you guys about this last night before bed. She's giving me a job at her café across from the arcade. Helping her out with restaurant stuff."

Both Polly and Baba appeared confused, posing no further questions but simply maintaining the unsettling, slightly stilted smile they shared with their mysterious visitors.

"What're *you* doing home, auntie? Thought you were pulling graveyards all month," Cora asked. She ventured a baby step into the kitchen, lingering close to the front door.

"Decided to take the night off. We have guests, you see. Old friends from out of town." Polly tipped her head in the direction of the trio. She rose from her chair and walked over to the stove, pouring herself another cup of coffee. "Stopped by to say hello for a spell. Been waiting on you before they head back out. I've been telling them a lot about you."

The child looked back at the visitors. Each had a cup of coffee on the table before them, their vessels still filled evenly to their brims with dark liquid, untasted. She wanted to ask more about them. Where they had come from, where they were going and what they wanted. It was at that very moment Cora realized she could actually *see* into them. See that these were not people at all but presences, which looked and talked and, for the most part, behaved like real people. Yet it was all a costume. A nifty card trick. Wool over the eyes. Worst of all, Cora felt in her bones that these things knew this. They recognized her power to peer behind their curtain and didn't care. Their purpose for coming to her house at this late hour had simply been to play with her, to spook her, and it was working.

Why can't I run? Why am I just standing here? I need to scream!!!

"We've been wanting to meet you, Cora. See what all the hullaballoo is about." The woman spoke, her voice flat and devoid of any personality, any hint of where she might have come from. She traced a long white finger around the rim of her coffee cup. "One should get to understand things about people who are special. Special people need to get to know other special people. Ya think?"

Cora opened her mouth, unsure whether an answer or a scream was going to emerge, when things began to change in the Corbucci kitchen. For just a crumb of a moment Cora was able to observe the terrifying chain of events transpiring before she had arrived.

The entire kitchen and dining room, the stove, the table and chairs, the countertops and the five people standing and seated before her were completely blanketed in a nasty, glutinous mess very much like a spider's web, but clotted and soggy. Wetter, almost like a meshwork of slime or mucous. The three strangers were no longer sitting, nor did they look like anything even discernibly human. Still garbed in the chic and showy business suits, each of their heads had shifted and morphed into the likeness of an enormous, fiendish bug. Praying mantises with chitinous husks of burnished black and bulbous globes, ignited from within by Stygian lanterns, for eyes. Where their mouths should have been a long beak-like appendage obtruded, translucent and effervescing with a noxious brown solution, terminating in a deadly tip very much like the proboscis of a mosquito. The three strangers were assembled around Polly, who was seated at the table, the same cup of coffee before her, their hands pressed upon her shoulders and beaks stabbed into the base and peak of her skull. The vile ichor collected in their beaks bubbled and sloshed from their maws and into Polly's head. Her aunt's eyes were rolled back to their yellowed whites, fluttering madly in their sockets like trapped moths as the profane three deposited their obscenity into her body. Clearly no longer alive, Baba Lena lay sprawled out upon the floor, a pool of urine spreading from beneath her, her eyes electric with the horror of someone who had finally beheld that one damning sight they had been dreading for all of their lives, a horror suddenly made flesh.

Then, the vision evaporated like condensation on a windshield.

Cora knew right then Baba and Polly were no longer here. Something had come and got them and was now making them walk and smile and drink coffee and smoke cigars. Their skin and bones and all the stuff inside of them was still there, but the powers that made them who they were—their souls, she guessed—had been yanked free and dumped on the side of the road. Dead, but not dead.

Play it cool, girl. They got no power over you right now. They're here to feel you out. Sniff around you like nosy dogs. Sniff out where your weak bits lie.

Why did she think that?

Just tail it on over to your room. Be nice. Smile like you mean it and say your goodnights. Then make your plans to get out of here by morning. Your mind is off-limits to them, and they know it. They want you to crack. They are counting on it.

The best Cora could come up with was a barely convincing, "Real good to meet y'all." She offered a wonky smile and an awkward little wave.

"Y'uns have to excuse her. She's a bit shy with folks she don't know," Polly apologized to them. "Ain't that right, sugar?"

Cora nodded. It wasn't true, of course. There wasn't a bashful bone in her whole skeleton.

"You come sit and have pyrizhky. I bake apple for you special like. Got cheese in fridge to melt on top. So good." Baba Lena patted the seat of an empty chair beside the woman, who then scooted it toward Cora with the toe of her shoe.

"No thanks, Baba. I ate at the café and it's kinda late."

"Oh, come on. It's the shank of the evening and I want to hear everything about this boy next door." The woman grinned wolfishly at her, provoking a small step backward out of the child.

"I seen him getting the mail yesterday. He's a cutie pie." Polly winked at her, the gesture turning Cora's stomach. There was something weird, even illicit, in the way it came across.

Cora didn't know how to respond to that, or if she even should.

The two men accompanying the woman remained silent, their faces grim and stony as they sipped their coffee, seemingly completed uninterested in everything around them. Now that the girl was closer to them, she realized they were twins, completely identical right down to their matching blond flattops and clean-shaven lantern jawlines.

"I'm beat. It was nice to meet y'all. Have a safe drive back to wherever you came from." Cora nodded, offering another half-hearted grin and a limp wave, inching sideways from the kitchen into the living room. Every muscle in her body tensed up, as if anticipating some sort of surprise attack. The five of them said nothing, just smiled back with all of the amiability in the world as Baba began dishing out the pyrizhky for each of them. After she cleared the kitchen, then the living room, and into the archway of her bedroom, she felt like she could breathe easier now. Once in her room she closed the door and locked it.

From the kitchen the sound of laughter resonated throughout the ancient shotgun house. A house built by good people who had somehow lost their way and turned bad. It was not the laughter of sane people.

Five voices in unison screamed out to her. They sounded completely unhinged, perhaps even given to violence. The disordered hilarity of maniacs.

"SLEEP TIGHT! DON'T LET THE BEDBUGS BITE!!"

Cora scurried over to her vanity, retrieved the rickety wooden chair in front of it, and shoved the back of it below the doorknob of her bedroom door. She bunched herself up into a corner of the room, shivering and holding herself.

It looked to be the beginning of a very long night.

As Cora sat huddled in her room, knees drawn up to her chin and eyes narrowed, she had time to think. To burrow deep into herself, her mind and whatever it was which conveyed mobility to her skin and bones. The child finally came to understand, at last, what had *happened* to her. As a result, this newfound clarity allowed her to comprehend the terrifying events transpiring now with a greater degree of clarity.

Something had happened to her that day at the Reverend Billy Tim's Feed Lot. A dark blessing imparted to the rare mortal who sets a toe over that flimsy gray line between being both stone dead and still breathing, ventures a step forward, is labeled a trespasser whose time for eternal sleep has not yet arrived, and is gracefully booted back into the kingdom of the living. However, she had returned with an eerie souvenir. An arcane insight into the way things worked on the other side of the fence. The comings and goings of death itself. Cora could now feel stuff normal people, *living people*, couldn't. She could see the invisible and hear sounds on both sides of the coin. Her eyes were newborn, and they could part the illusions of like creatures and see into their very black centers. That was why she could see the unwelcome visitors in her kitchen for what they were: Monsters, pure and simple.

The little girl began to cry. She knew Baba Lena and Aunt Polly were gone. Not only that, but they were possibly languishing in a very bad place. Such gloomy knowledge would have shattered the mind of a weakened, less hardened child. Cora had been dreading a day like this for a long time. Baba had been in terrible health for many years and Polly had been, with every passing day, one step away from being found dead in a dealer's shack with a needle in her arm. Death had always been close for both of them; it had just come a little earlier than expected.

This was a lot worse than death.

She dried her tears, locked in, and began to formulate a plan.

Cora knew she had to get to Hayder. No way she was going to have him come over here now. God only knew what these freaks might do to him.

Her chest really hurt.

Sometime just after twelve-thirty the kitchen fell quiet. The peeling out of tires soon followed, and Cora heard the creak of Baba Lena's bedroom door closing. The child peered under the gap beneath her bedroom door and found the kitchen draped in darkness. The stovetop light was on, which meant Polly had departed for the evening as well. Cora didn't want to venture a guess where her aunt had strayed away to, but she didn't want to wander out into the kitchen to roll the dice on what she might encounter in the shadows.

Cora slipped her fingers into her bedroom window, carefully prying it clear from the sill, allowing enough space for her to throw a leg over it and roll out of the house. She tumbled to the lawn hard enough to put a smart into her shoulder. It was very cold, and she played with the idea of crawling back into her room to retrieve a hooded sweatshirt, then decided it an unwise decision at that juncture in her jailbreak. Keeping low she crept across the pasture, the high weeds and grass totally obscuring her slight form beneath the moonless night sky, slipping under the barbed wire fence to Hayder's bedroom window. She peered inside and found him sleeping peacefully, uncovered with a flashlight dutifully placed on his nightstand. Cora smiled. At least he had been prepared to rise to the challenge. She rapped her knuckles against the frost-stained glass, praying his mom wouldn't hear. For some reason she didn't want to see the woman again right now.

The boy must not have been out for long, as it only took a couple of knocks to rouse him. He squinted at her, bleary-eyed, and ran a hand through his dense shock of hair. Cora felt a funny little tickle in her belly. He was awfully cute when he woke up. Hayder ambled groggily over to the window and slowly, quietly opened it. Offering a hand, he helped her inside but left the window cracked in case a quick getaway might be required. They sat on the floor beside one another, their hands slipping together easily.

Cora related everything that had happened back at her house, black jeeps, bug-people and all. The girl knew she sounded crazy and had surprised herself by how forthcoming she was about it all. Even more surprising, not only did Hayder listen patiently, never interrupting, but he believed her. He then told her a story. A story detailing the terrifying sights he had encountered at the Red Hand Theater the night before. An event he had not, for even a second, doubted he had experienced. After he was done they linked arms as well as hands. Cora, feeling brave, rested her head on his shoulder. A few seconds later he, somewhat hesitantly, laid his cheek against the top of her head. She closed her eyes and felt calm wash over her. It had been a very long time since she had felt like this.

"I could tell you were holding something back. I could feel it," she murmured to him. "I don't know why. I would have believed you if you told me. That place has a reputation for things like that. A whole lot of awful things have happened there. Polly told me they've been telling spooky stories about it since before she was even born. I've only been there a few times myself. Costs too much."

Hayder squeezed Cora's hand and rubbed his cheek against the top of her head. She breathed a quiet, sweet sigh which rippled through him. The sound touched him with a weird, almost fearful sensation. He opened his mouth as if to say or ask something more, then cut himself off. Still emboldened, the girl reached up and stroked the tips of her fingers across his cheek, then quickly pulled back.

"What is it? You can ask me anything you want to."

Hayder gulped and then did as he had been instructed. He asked her about the Feed Lot, which she was surprised had taken him so long. Cora, in return, told him everything, sparing no detail, no matter how terrible. She included what had happened to her friend Crystal and the man in the gruesome wolf-skin mask, and how she had also seen that same terrifying character standing across the street in the field beside Old Man Jacobsen's abandoned farm just a couple of days ago. She had been trying to pass it off as a hallucination, a figment. After last night, she now knew better.

"Are you better now?" He asked, hesitantly. "I mean, are you still hurt?"

"I'm not at full speed ahead, but tolerable enough, I guess. I get tired pretty fast, and I got a *really* crazy-looking scar." Cora bit her lip, excited, and pulled away from him. "You wanna see it?"

Hayder scrunched up his face. "See…what?"

Eye roll. "My scar, goofball. Pay attention!"

The boy nodded, petrified.

Cora swept her dark hair aside, pulling the neckline of her t-shirt out enough to reveal her bare shoulder, her skin nearly bloodless in pallor, until a thick, almost serpentine pink scar was exposed. Hayder marveled at it. It reminded him of the roots of a plant, crooked and lumpy and invasive. A wound which could never be hidden properly and would always be a source for inquiry. He reached out and traced his finger across the scar. It was both smooth and rough at once, and he wondered how far down it went. The boy then noticed the girl's bra strap for the first time and jerked back his hand as if he'd stuck his finger into an electrical outlet, mortified beyond comprehension. Cora hadn't seemed to notice anything. She'd kept her head turned the whole time.

"What did I tell you? Horrible, ain't it?" She smiled grimly. "But that's not all. I got something else to go with this scar."

Cora related her earlier revelation concerning her recently acquired gifts. How surviving being killed had imparted a specific, peculiar insight into supernatural matters. Hayder listened patiently, his brow furrowed thoughtfully. Of course, he believed her. She hadn't really worried he wouldn't. He wasn't certain why he had done it, but he felt compelled to tell her about Dad and Brandy. What had happened to them and why they had moved here. The girl listened patiently with slowly glistening eyes, her bottom lip trembling. When he was finished Hayder collapsed into her arms, the tears unstoppable and cleansing. The best kind of tears. Cora soothed him, stroking his hair and whispering all of the comforting words she could offer and trying to keep him as quiet as possible. She still felt strange about waking up his mom, and didn't want her anywhere near the two of them. After he was all cried out they clasped hands once more and leaned back against the bedroom wall, together.

Cora looked over at the nightstand. It was nearly three in the morning now.

"I guess I can sleep under the bed," she remarked, only half kidding. "I can't go back home ever again. I do and I won't come back alive."

"Naw. The closet. It's real big, and I can get you some blankets and a pillow. After mom gets up, I want you to slip out the window and then knock on the door. Tell her I told her you to come over early to work on some stuff for *Warriors & Warlocks*. She'll just be so thrilled I have someone to hang out with she won't care how early it is." He turned to look at her, his face almost comically serious. "What are we gonna do, Cora?" he asked her. "We're just a couple of dang kids. We can't fight whatever these...things...are. Heck, my momma doesn't even own a gun."

Cora placed her fingers under the boy's chin and turned him to face her. Something in her eyes charged him with courage. She no longer looked like a child, but something much older. Whatever she was about to tell him, he was ready to believe her and do whatever was asked of him without question.

"I know someone who can help. Hopefully, he's okay. If they got to him, our gooses are cooked," she told him. "He's a cop, but not like a normal cop. It's the sheriff, and he's really nice. He was so sweet to me when I was laid up in the hospital. He grew up with Aunt Polly, so he's been kind of keeping his eye on me for a while now."

"But will he believe us? It's pretty incredible." Hayder looked dubious.

Cora shrugged. "He's lived here a long time. Even before all of this, Black Knot was a weird place. He's probably seen a lot of weird things, I reckon."

"Oh! Almost forgot," Hayder exclaimed, rising to his feet. He opened the nightstand drawer and dug around in it, unearthing a few small stubs of red paper. "Vera gave me tickets for the Halloween movie tonight. A double feature. Freebies."

Cora was confused. "You really wanna go to the movies with all this going on?"

"Might not be a bad idea, really," Hayder reasoned. "I think whatever is going on over at your place is very likely to be mixed up with, in some way or another, the creepy stuff going on at the Red Hand. I mean, how could it not be?"

Cora seemed to mull it over, deciding it was a good idea with an affirmative nod. "So…this is like a date or something?"

The boy collapsed into a rambling, borderline incoherent mess of gibberish. Not really a *date* date because he would be working. He might be able to take a break and watch a little bit of the movie with her, maybe. Cora stood up and laid her fingers across his mouth, silencing the poor fool.

"Shush. I get it." She giggled.

That settled, the two of them stood looking at one another for a long time. At least it felt like a long time. One would smile, then the other, then both would stop, and it would start all over again. It was as if they were trying to make things awkward. To keep from being too comfortable. At last, beaten by fate and instinct, they collapsed together into a sweet and tender embrace. The shared comfort of the kindred.

"I'm not ready for school on Monday," he confided into her ear.

"I'm not ready for school again, ever," she confided back.

INTERLUDE TWO:

Within just a few hours after the appearance of the dual tombstones at the intersection of Belladonna and Lavera, unspeakable things began to happen in Black Knot. Atrocities, some of which would not be discovered until it was all over.

Judith Livesey, music teacher at Mandrake Creek Middle School, had always been something of a prude. At thirty-six she was a steadfast virgin. She'd never even been kissed, much less allowed some grubby man to claw his way between her golden arches. To her the sex act was a clinical, mechanical activity meant only for procreation. In spite of her vocation Judith really despised all children, so the far-reaching benefits of a potential intimate relationship with a man held very little allure for her.

The morning the tombstones had sprouted up from the earth Judith had felt an overpowering itch to get into her car and just start driving, an impulsive decision very much contrary to her predictable nature. The spinster took to Highway 69 and drove until she found herself in the parking lot of the Dew Drop Inn in Rust River some two hours south of Black Knot. Once inside she found a table and ordered an entire pitcher of Hagshead Lager for herself, which earned her the consideration of a few unsavory gentlemen. She promptly ordered another two pitchers for herself and her new admirers, the four of them becoming quite tipsy and amorous.

The revelers lingered at the Dew Drop until closing time, all of them piling into her car for the long jaunt back to her place in the western half of the Knot, a cozy little lake house on banks of the Hootchyfalala. Until dawn's first light the four of them indulged in every act of carnality the men could devise until they were all exhausted, sore and, in her case, bleeding. Another round of drinking followed. Cheap vodka she had kept hidden in the back of the freezer for the days when she was feeling a little wayward. The men, still quite drunk, accepted the libations without question. They had no way of knowing Judith had tapped out an ample measure of horse painkillers into each glass, almost half a bottle's worth left over from when her prized mare, Bella Morte, had gone through knee surgery last year. Each dose, although seemingly modest, was more than enough to send each man hurtling headfirst into his own grave.

It only got more gruesome from there.

Although the teacher had never dressed a deer in her life, she had no problem dragging each man out to the barn behind the house, stringing him up by his ankles to the rafters within, slitting him from crotch to chin with a pair of scissors, and collecting the gore and viscera into whatever was handy. An ice cooler from the attic, a water pail from the garden, a salad bowl from the kitchen, and a big jug used to store oats she'd found in the back of the barn.

Crows and other birds given to feasting upon the meat of the dead circled overhead, screeching and biding their time.

The music teacher dragged the vessels to the front porch and bathed herself from head to toe in their grisly contents, until she was slick with stinking gore. Judith, jubilant, then pleasured herself vigorously, painfully, until she blacked out.

Upon awakening, Judith went back inside her house and cleaned out the contents of the refrigerator, throwing everything into a big pile on her living room floor, even removing the shelves. Not bothering to unplug the appliance, she balled herself up as tight as she could, wedged herself into the now empty container, and closed the door behind her.

The next morning, when she emerged, she would find herself much altered.

The episode with Ms. Livesey with just one story out of several. It would take too long to chronicle everything, and I don't want to frighten you away now. Not after you've already come this far.

Here's one more. Remain calm.

The Black Knot Soccer Club's fall season was set to end the first week in November. Although it was only the final week of October, the weather had turned much colder. Because of this, only a handful of parents had turned out to watch the two teams play. These were the kids in the earlier grades of middle school, mostly sixth graders. Nobody really came to see this group of youngsters play, the larger crowds drawn to the high schoolers. Less than ten grown-ups and as many children, five to each team. Most of the adults chatted while the kids went at it, not really paying attention, only there because they felt they had to be.

If they *had* been paying attention, the adults would have noticed the kiddos were remarkably hostile today. A little too aggressive. When they went after the ball it looked a lot more like a pack of wolves bearing down upon a wounded elk. Some of them even growled, which a few adults took note of, responding only with a perplexed cock of their heads.

"Wow, those kids are really in the zone today," one man remarked. "Go get at 'em, Scotty!" He then went back to reading his home improvement magazine, unconcerned.

When little Bart Gordon, the goalie for Cairn Brothers Salvage, killed Marshall Weatherby, that was when things started to get heated. Bart had tripped the child when he had grown too close to the goal. Then, his eyes blazing and mouth pulled down into a contortion of hatred, Bart had gripped Marshall by his mop of curling blond hair, dragged him over to one of the goal posts and repeatedly bashed his face into the reinforced concrete surface of the pole. Yanking the poor tot's head back and forth, back and forth, until the boy's face had completely collapsed back into his skull, sluggish rivulets of blood and gray mush oozing from his ruined eye and nose sockets. Shocked, taken off guard, a few of the adults started screaming while the rest sat rooted their seats, aghast. Seconds later, every single child on the soccer field dropped to the dead grass, writhing and clawing at their throats and heads, some yanking handfuls of hair from the scalps and gouging their thumbs into their eyes. One woman, coming to her senses, jumped from the bleachers and began running toward her car. Something grabbed her by the ankle and began dragging her back toward the field. She turned to look at it, and what she saw fractured her sanity, degrading her to a slobbering, incontinent simpleton in an instant.

Nobody could move, their screams gagging in their throats, suffocated by horror. The host of children, now unified, turned to regard the assembly with dead, cursed eyes. The mob advanced, arms outstretched, mouths open in yearning hunger, with little Bart leading the way. What followed next, taking only mere minutes, was unbelievable and revolting. When it was over the children, in perfect unison, turned to look toward the east, beyond the swells and slopes of the Kiamichi Mountains, their eyes glassy with fiendish piety.

The corpse of Marshall Weatherby rose from the field and turned to regard the mountains as well. He staggered to front of the flock and raised a pale hand, stretching out his index finger. His eyes, once a beautiful shade of robin's egg blue, had been mashed into useless pulp against his cracked cheekbones. But he saw, nevertheless. Taking his rightful place before the flock of his fellow pilgrims, Marshall began to stagger ahead, heading north with the rest trailing close behind him.

Behind them, a few minutes later, the grown-ups rose up to follow the children. Dead no longer, but not even close to alive. Parents, grandmas, aunts and uncles, they shadowed the children into the woods, up the hills and crags, on their way to the Church to await further guidance.

The day after the emergence of the tombstones, sometime just after three in the morning, an old and expensive car, a long crimson Studebaker, pulled up to the corner of Belladonna and Lavera. The car sat idling for several minutes, a plume of leaden smoke trickling out from behind it like the breath of a slumbering dragon. The rear passenger door creaked open; a long shapely leg sheathed in a black fishnet stocking emerging. The leg belonged to a tall, coldly beautiful young woman with flowing golden hair and eyes black as an empty well. She wore a dark purple cocktail dress and a matching leather jacket, her hands thrust into the pockets to shield them from the chill. Her pretty face, her burnt honey locks, were all an illusion. It was a glamour. A powerful enchantment woven to cloak the true flesh of the person or thing cast upon it. The woman was far older than she looked. Far less human.

The driver opened his door and stepped out, joining the woman at the monuments. He wore checkered slacks, sheepskin coat, a plain white polo shirt, and a ball cap covering his shaggy blond hair. Like the woman, he too employed witchery to conceal his true shape.

"Glad to see she kept her word. We've been waiting a long fucking time for this," the man remarked, tapping one the gravestones with the toe of his boot.

"Our blood is strong," the woman responded, then elbowed her companion. "You curse too much. Stop it. It isn't refined."

The man rolled his eyes but didn't argue.

"So, what comes next? She speaks through you, after all." He shivered, buttoning up his coat and slapping his gloved hands together. "Damned cold out here. Not even November yet."

"We wait for the congregation to be complete. Once we have enough vessels gathered at the church, the wedding party will be ready." She knelt before the tombstones, holding on to the hem of her dress, and laid her hands upon both of them. "Then, the wedding."

"You think she'll be happy with us?" The man also knelt and laid his own hands over the woman's. A pleasurable vibration rippled through both of them.

"Oh yes. It's all going as predicted." She laid her head upon one stone, muttered words, then moved over to the other and repeated the words. "Soon, Seamstress. My Goddess. Your servants have arrived, and the true work has begun. Sleep in peace. The cogs are moving. *Ciao*."

Returning to the car, the witch slipped back into her seat and ordered the man to crank up the heat. The two then drove off and away, into the thick shadows of the Oklahoma autumn morning.

TEN

There were a whole mess of back roads snaking throughout Grinning Goblin Forest, the majority of them being downright treacherous. Matheson was familiar with most of them. He selected a route he was used to exploring from past shenanigans, an approach accessible via the squad car with a little creative maneuvering. He took to the old stagecoach trail between Coffin Mills and Lamplight Falls, just a few miles east of Black Knot. The lawman was confident nobody would be out this way at this time of the night, at least nobody he needed to concern himself over. Townies usually stuck to the main highway leading into and out of the State Park, for it was well known the outlying paths and byways were to be avoided for many legitimate reasons. Mostly because these secret trails were used by folks living outside of the law, away from the bustle of town. People who didn't want to be bothered, and if they were to be bothered it would not go well for the intruder nosing into their affairs. A great deal of Haggard's weed trade was facilitated through these dense thickets of evergreens and cedar. The presence of law enforcement was tolerated for the most part, so long as nobody didn't set their snout to sniffing and digging around too deeply.

Matheson kept the headlights dimmed, drifting along at a relaxed slither, always on the lookout for strange lights gleaming from the woods or a black Jeep coming around the bend ahead of him.

The trip back to the counselor's lodge at Camp Azalea took a lot longer than if he had come in like usual, adding a good fifteen extra minutes of driving to his journey. He didn't mind. It gave him time to think. He kept his .44 revolver on the seat next to him, within close reach, and in the trunk of the car a shiny pump-action Mossberg was wrapped in a leather tarp. In the glovebox he kept his old survival knife, a cherished memento from a not so cherished episode in his life. Matheson treated the blade like a holy relic. It had saved his ass more than once during the war and was never far from his person. In short, he was more than prepared.

The night had suddenly turned very cold, prompting him to switch on the defrost to keep the windshield from glazing over. Matheson was thankful he had remembered to snag his winter coat from the kitchen rack before he had left. It had been a few years since he had been out this way, so he had found himself confused a few times at certain spots on the trail. The way he remembered taking before was so thoroughly overgrown he feared it would be impassible. Gritting his teeth, he soldiered ahead, expecting the car to go plunging down into one of the numerous ravines and gullies. But that didn't happen. He gripped the wheel and tuned out, focused, and soon he found himself where he needed to be. When he arrived, he killed the engine and both the interior and headlights.

This particular spot emptied out on the eastern end of the counselor's lodge, this being the rear of the building instead of the front. The lawman had taken this route with the purpose of setting up his approach upon the property. A better scenario to observe undetected. Matheson urged the car forward, rolling quietly through a lake of yellowed cornstalks, until he could just glimpse the ceramic tiled roof of the building. It was an excellent vantage point; however, due to the thick foliage around him, a fast getaway might prove problematic. He didn't care. The lawman had gone into this adventure knowing full well things might get ugly, and he wasn't leaving until he returned either with answers or in a body bag. Retrieving his revolver and knife, he quietly opened his car door, leaving it ajar, and retrieved the Mossberg from the trunk. He ensured both guns were loaded and pocketed several rounds of shells for both weapons, also collecting a small flashlight from the emergency kit.

Matheson hunkered down, shotgun racked and ready, and began wading through the looming towers of dead corn toward the lodge on the hill.

There had been no tripwires set up, or any booby traps for that matter, for which Juston was both relieved and wary. Moonshiners and crank-cooks commonly set all kinds of nasty snares out around their areas of commerce. This meant who or whatever dwelling in the lodge had a different kind of business going on within, and that scared him.

Tonight, there was someone inside of the lodge. A sickly greenish-yellow light burned from behind the cracked windows, yet there was something off about it. It wasn't the calming glow of a fireplace or a battery-powered lantern. This illumination *radiated*, pulsing in hazy and hypnotic wrinkles of splintered light. Matheson felt himself being dragged, firmly yet gently, toward that light, his fingers slowly uncurling from the stock of the shotgun. Why did he need it, anyway? He really should put it down, shouldn't he? And the knife, the revolver, what use would they be? He didn't need them. He wasn't going to hurt anyone. Nobody was going to harm him, so there was nothing to fear here. Nothing more than a very old building with a faint, welcoming light to usher a cold man to safety.

You should come closer, hoss. Get warm. Take some supper. A nice, cozy bed to rest your weary bones. A strong drink.

WAKE UP!!

Matheson slapped himself. This immediately snapped him out of whatever dark force was trying to slither its way into his head. Now, he felt genuine terror. There was something truly awful out here haunting this cursed place, a place where the soil had borne witness to atrocity and drunk the sweet, untainted blood of children. An honest-to-God boneyard for innocence.

Christ, what is it? the lawman wondered. *Satanists? Some crazy cult of Christians gone off the deep end? Aliens?*

The sheriff of Black Knot slung the shotgun over his shoulder, dropped to his belly, and began to slowly worm his way toward the lodge, grateful for the black sky above and the high witchgrass below. As he crawled he swore he could hear voices, secretive words being passed back and forth through the shadows from hushed mouths to unseen ears. He paused his crawl to listen, to pay attention. Yes, it was voices all right. The high-pitched voices of children, their words indecipherable yet infused with an unmistakable shade of malice. The voices of children who would drown beasts and kill their mothers in their beds.

Matheson thought about the little girls who had died here over a decade past. The three Pixie Scouts. An icy shudder coiled up his spine. He wondered if the vengeful ghouls of those children haunted that defiled patch of woods. Ages nine, nine, and ten, each girl had been raped, choked, then put to the knife. The crime scene had become the stuff of law enforcement legend, the butchery from which had sent even the most seasoned and stonehearted cops into the brush to retch and weep. The killer was never apprehended, and not a lot of effort was put into the case. This was right before Matheson took the reins from his predecessor, G.K. Orr. Orr had been a beloved yet feared figurehead for small-town justice for close to three decades, a lantern-jawed, beer-bellied dickswinger of old who chewed on a toothpick and wasn't above terrorizing a weaker-willed human being into doing what they were told.

The old salt had also been a loyal company man for the OSBI, a torch Juston had a hard time carrying along. He had a rough time with letting a hard truth slide into a cold lie, which hadn't earned him much affection from the fed side of the schoolyard. Orr hadn't cared so long as he was paid. Everyone knew the case would never be solved, so why cry about it? After a few months of media insanity, the matter was quietly broomed, shoveled, then dumped into a very quiet grave. When Matheson had tried to wheedle a secret or two out of the departing constable, he was answered with an uneasy grin, a shake of the head, then a segue into an unrelated conversation.

The day after he had officially pinned on the tin star, Matheson had asked to see the case file for the Pixie Scout Murders of Camp Red Hand. He was informed all of the files resided on the OSBI side, which was more than a little odd. There was not one shred of information in the evidence room pertaining to the case, and repeated calls to OSBI went unanswered. The new sheriff had even reached out to the parents of one of the girls for help, only to hit a dead end. The mother, now a widow, had no interest in stirring old bones and had told him this verbatim. The call had ended with not so much as a goodbye. Just a dead, flat, dial tone.

He soon began to receive phone calls. Always in the small, hazy hours of the morning. On the other end of the receiver a barely audible, frantic whispering of gibberish. Even though Matheson didn't understand what was being said, he sensed the underlying threat of it bubbling in his blood. Somehow he had known these nocturnal calls were related to his continued nosing around on the Pixie case. Being green to the job at the time, Juston was easily cowed into silence. As soon as he stopped asking, the phone also went quiet. He took that as a good sign and dropped the subject altogether. Orr had been right, it didn't matter. Nobody who mattered cared any longer, so why should he?

Except for those three dead little girls. They might care plenty. Especially right now, out in the dark, out in the wild.

The lawman reached the outer edge of the lodge. Here the witchgrass was not so high and he would have to devise a plan to reach the back door of the structure without being spotted. He felt something now, for certain. Something was watching, keeping guard, and he would have to move quickly and decisively. Surveying the layout of the lodge and yard, Matheson spotted a little nook between the side of the building with the chimney and a gardener's shack listing a few feet to his right. There was a narrow corridor of shadow between the two constructs. If he continued to belly-crawl within that patch of cover he might be all right. Any other approach from this side of the house was useless, and he felt a sudden urgency to get the show on the road. As he crawled his elbows sank into the cold mud, soaking through his shirt, making a soft squelching noise that sounded, to him, loud as gunfire as he crept along. It only took him a few minutes to reach the chimney, at which he rose up on his arches and unslung the Mossberg.

He had two options, either the front door or the rear exit. Both might be guarded from within, but for now there appeared to be nobody standing watch outside on either end. The light appeared to be glowing a bit brighter from the rear portion of the lodge, and his gut kept directing his attention in the opposite direction. The lawman opted for the front entrance. It was a risky move, but his gut had never failed him before. Pressing himself close to the outer wall of the building, Matheson unsnapped the button on his holster, freeing the revolver. He drew in a very deep breath, then exhaled slowly.

Then, slowly, as quietly as he could, he racked the shotgun and made tracks toward the forsaken lodge.

The sheriff of Black Knot encountered no opposition as he edged into the common room of the lodge, his shotgun raised and ready. This was the same chamber where he and Raab had found the dead child. The room had much altered since them. It had been cleaned up to the point of being not only livable, but downright cozy were it not for the menacing bite of old evil pervading the air. The slime and sticky alien webs had been pulled down and swept away, and even the walls had appeared to have been wiped down. Not a stick of furniture remained, and along the wooden slats of the floor dozens of muddy footprints had impressed chaotic, confused configurations. Some of the prints appeared to be from a bare-footed traveler, others in shoes and what looked to be boots. There was a definite reek of bleach or some sort of heavy action cleaner present.

The air felt weird. Weak and sickly, as if spread too thin. In the lodge's fireplace a great blaze roared, yet the crackling flames within were unlike anything Matheson had ever seen. The tongues of fire spitting and undulating from within the stone cavity of the hearth had been the source of the eerie greenish-yellow radiance he had witnessed from the field. The conflagration called forth no heat but cast plenty of shadows, hostile dark shapes swarming up the wooden plank walls and rain-rotted ceiling like thirsty leeches in search of an opened vein.

A sunken, crooked archway beckoned from the left of the hearth, the room beyond engulfed in a fearsome gloom. Matheson knew this to be the kitchen area, as all of the counselor lodges bore the same floorplan. The sheriff slung the shotgun over his shoulder and drew the revolver, using his free hand to retrieve the flashlight from his pocket. The man's teeth ground and chattered in his jaw. He was freezing, not from a cold breeze but from the breath of a deep, arcane dread. Struggling to steady his weapon, he switched on the flashlight and crept into the kitchen.

"Not a very smart man, are you?" he murmured. "A smart man would have never come here. But you've never played a very smart game. Not as a kid, not as a cop, not now."

For a moment all he could do was look at it.

It was a door.

A door in the floor.

At least where the floor should have been. Matheson glanced at his feet, his breath snagged in his lungs. It appeared as if he were walking on a pane of clear glass covering up a plummet into a yawning, galactic oblivion.

He tapped the floor with the toe of his boot. It was solid, whatever it was. He considered reaching down to lay his fingers upon it but stopped short of doing so. Best not to mess with it, he reasoned. The door itself was nothing exceptional. A plain old brown wooden thing with a shabby knob meant to look like brass but more than likely being hard plastic. Rather like a door you might find in a single-wide mobile home or a cheap apartment. No ornate markings. Probably not a hundred percent real wood, either. Yet Matheson knew this was no ordinary door. He didn't have to lay flesh upon it to feel the power radiating from it, an almost a palpable crackling of incarcerated energy. He could feel every hair on his arms and head standing at attention.

"What to do here?" He thought out loud. He'd come this far, so why not just go ahead and open the door? Matheson knew this was what needed to be done, but he was afraid of the consequences, and there *would* be consequences. Somehow he understood this was not a regular door, but a portal. A portal not meant for use by everyday folks, human beings like himself, to breach. This was a doorway for passing from one world into another. Or, perhaps, the door was keeping something *in* rather than out. The prospect of this scared the lawman more than any other scenario he could imagine. Without question, though, Matheson understood whatever world lay beyond this door in the floor was meant neither for the living nor the sane. Not that it mattered much right now. He was here, he'd come this far, and he couldn't just walk away. Juston reached out and brushed his fingertips across the knob, settling them across its cheap surface. He curled in his thumb to meet the fingers, and applied the slightest pressure, and began to turn the knob.

At first he had passed off the sound as just the wind. The grieved moan of a breeze whispering through the trees and crags of the forest. He'd encountered the same disturbance often enough camping in these woods over the past three decades, and he knew well how the noise of it could easily unnerve those unfamiliar to its melody. Matheson shrugged it off and returned to the portal, revolving the knob far enough to feel the strike plate begin to relent and the door give a little. Another wail drifted in upon the heels of the first one, louder, closer and more needful than its predecessor. The sheriff's mind was darkened with fleeting visions of ravenous tomb bugs rippling beneath a banquet of putrefying meat, endless prairies of mounded carrion and smoldering pyres of effigy. Great black iron cauldrons bubbling with broth strained from the bones of discarded infants. Entire cities and highways enshrouded in a spider's web. A web spun of a spider hungry enough to swallow up the whole world.

Another howl rippled throughout the shadows of Grinning Goblin Forest. This outburst wormed directly into the workings of his policeman's gut, rattling his entire body with a shriek. A warning. Most definitely not the wind. Matheson whirled around and found he was no longer alone in the lodge. Indeed, he had visitors, and they had come to deliberate upon the awful things which could happen to a trespasser disrupting the sanctity of their profane house of worship.

The living corpse of Scotty Raab shambled into the common room by way of the front archway, staggering upon wrecked ankles and bare feet, his white and wasted arms outstretched in menace. The rot of the grave and the appetite of the forest's wild things had rendered his face nigh unrecognizable, the slack gray flesh beneath his eyes and mouth seeming to drip from his skull like melting clay. His jaw hung open, the jaws unhinged and useless, as his tongue, swollen purple and pocked with peeling ulcers, slavered and licked at the air. The dead man was naked, the flesh around his arms and legs and the rest of his body much like the state of the tissue of his skull. Sloughing slowly away from the muscle and bone, more like a shedding shell than skin. Raab's entrails snaked and curled out from a ragged cavern in his belly like a cluster of tentacles, possessed of their own hellish half-life, behaving as legs would for a living man, dragging him slowly along the floor in the direction of his former superior.

It was the eyes. That was all that remained of the deputy recognizable to Matheson. Although coated with the muck of death, those same brilliant robin's-egg blue eyes. It made him all the more hideous to behold.

Raab-Thing lurched closer, its wilted arm outstretched in want, a gargled, earthen snarl rumbling from deep within its shattered chest. Matheson then realized it wasn't alone. Trailing behind it another horror shuffled along, this creature far more perverse and grotesque than its compatriot. This poor soul, in life, had once been a nurse, judging by the moldering white uniform, peeling gray support hose and sensible shoes now shredded into uselessness. A plastic name plate was pinned to the breast of its worsened blouse, spattered in dried crusts of brown-green gore, rendering the name illegible. The beast's head was swathed in a covering Matheson could only distinguish as some kind of beehive or bug's nest. A flat gray carapace shaped like a walnut, the surface riddled with pulsing crimson furrows and spidery channels, the covering seemed to be possessed of its own life. He could actually feel the vile energy welling from it, reaching out and shoving a hungry hand down his throat to collect his breath one little gasp of air at a time. As it entered the common room a pair of thin, white arms dropped down from between its legs with a sodden squish, lifting up the nurse's skirt, dripping with mucous and clotted matter. The knobby, hideous fingers attached to the arms yearned out to the lawman, craving, hungry for the blood flowing through his skin and bones.

What were they? Demons? Ghosts? Matheson recalled something his Granny Mabel had told him when he had been a small fry. Something about things called haints. Haints were anything which couldn't be defined by a normal person, a passage in the Bible, or a science book. Right now, if ever there were such things as haints, they were here, ready to feast upon his flesh and then drag what remained of him back to whatever hell they had journeyed to this world from.

The lawman holstered his revolver and unslung the Mossberg, racked it hard, and delivered a blast of buckshot smack into the belly of the Raab-Thing. The blast tore a massive chunk of meat away from the monster's ruined abdomen in a deluge of gelatinous sludge, revealing the crooked and deteriorated spine. The creature howled, its oily tentacle guts trembling in time with its outburst. Matheson pumped the shotgun again and aimed for the Nurse-Horror's head, the roar of the gun deafening his ears. The monster staggered back, only a small chip of its carapace chipped away from the assault. Both beasts advanced closer, and Matheson understood immediately this was not a fight he would be able to win today. Not with these measly human toys. He had to get back to town. Back to someone he could talk to about this. Someone who understood the ways of darkness and witchery.

"Sorry this happened to you, old buddy." Matheson nodded at the Raab-Thing and the Nurse-Horror. "And to you as well, ma'am. I'll make them pay, whoever did this. And I *will* find out who did this."

With that the sheriff scrambled back through the lodge. Finding an open window, he hoisted himself over the sill and tumbled out of the window, gun at ready, and into the obscurity of the cold October night.

He lingered in a wary crouch as he beat a path back to the squad car. A sharp crack split the silence, the bullet barely missing him, the hot slug actually singing a hair or two from the top of his head and blasting away an ear of corn from a stalk not a quarter of an inch away from him. Matheson dropped to his belly and quickly rolled to the right, stopping as another shot rang out.

He rested the shotgun out across his arm and listened, knowing the next few moments were critical. Crunch of footsteps coming closer, then another volley of fire. The lawman heard the echo of a spent shell clink against something metallic. Whoever it was, they were armed with some sort of semi-automatic handgun and were standing close to the squad car. He'd heard the casing eject from the weapon and bounce off the body of the vehicle. Another crunch of weeds and leaves beneath a steady, light footfall.

Matheson grinned.

Closer now. Almost right in front of him.

The grin deepened.

I know where you are. Sleep tight, asshole.

Whispering a prayer, Matheson held his breath and squeezed the trigger of the Mossberg, the stock pummeling his shoulder and the blast sounding like a clap of springtime thunder. A howl of agony rippled throughout the cursed corn fields of Camp Red Hand, a succession of pistol blasts shooting into the void, then the telltale sound of a body dropping to the earth. Juston exhaled slowly, afraid to move. He allowed himself a few minutes to gather enough sack to get up and review his handiwork. The man shouldered the shotgun and returned to the comfort of his sidepiece, the revolver speared out in front of him as he drew closer to the thing twitching and moaning on the ground in front of the squad car. The assassin's pistol lay on the ground several feet away from them, easily retrieved by the lawman. He had plugged them square in the chest, a very lucky shot.

What lay sprawled out upon the scarlet-showered grass before him appeared to be human. Either a woman or a very delicately built man garbed in a natty business suit of red satin, the breast of which had been completely shredded by the chew of the buckshot, the flesh beneath reduced to ground-up beef, the tips of a shattered ribcage gleaming through the soggy folds of savaged tissue. The would-be killer's face was covered by a strange mask. Bending closer, Matheson realized it to be the facade of a pig. Not a Halloween mask, but the actual hide of a beast. As if someone had taken a blade to the creature and sliced the visage clean away from the skull. The thing behind the mask coughed, blood gurgling in its throat and spraying from the edges of the jaw of the mask. Its hands clawed feebly up at him, trembled, then drifted slowly down to rest upon its pulverized chest.

Wary, the sheriff knelt beside the thing and poked at the mask with the barrel of his revolver. He slipped the barrel into a snout-hole of the mask and pulled it free from the face, flinging it into the depths of the cornfield. He caught his breath, stood, and took a quick step back. For a moment, all Matheson could do was stare down at it.

It was still a shock to behold, even with all of the other unbelievable sights he had encountered in just the past half an hour. Beneath the mask was nothing more than a small heap of fine white ash and a few lingering wisps of long black hair. A single tooth, a molar. The rest of the thing's clothing then began to collapse, sinking into itself as the body within had been nothing more than a balloon, now slowly deflating. Matheson toed it with his boot, still struggling to believe what he had seen. He knelt again and brushed his hand across the mound of dust. It felt no different than the ash you'd find in any run of the mill hearth in any man's house. He dug around a bit more, studying his kill, his fingers encountering something new. An oddity. Brushing the ashes to one side revealed a trinket. Some sort of amulet carved into a flat oval of rich dark blue wood engraved with a weird symbol. The lawman didn't need to know what the symbol meant to recognize it as the calling card for something unwholesome. He slipped the trinket into his pocket and stood back up, drawing in a deep breath.

"Roseanna's place, as soon as she opens up," he told himself. "If she doesn't have answers nobody will."

From within the house a chorus of moans lamented. Shadows gathering at the window he had crawled out of. More shadows than before. Apparently the party inside had just begun.

"Y'all keep it up. Groan and carry on all you want," he called out to them. "I'll be comin' for you. You can bank on that shit. And when I do, I'm gonna bring some fire back with me. Gonna take that fire and burn this fucker right down to the dirt and rocks like it should have been done years back."

Matheson returned to the squad car, cranked it to life, and hauled himself out of Camp Red Hand like the hounds of the Devil himself were chomping at his ass.

The sheriff had time to clear his head a little while driving away from Grinning Goblin Forest. He decided it best he not return to his trailer in town, but make tracks for his cabin out on the lake instead. Stay as far away from town as possible tonight. There was a lot to do, a lot to plan, and he didn't feel like there was a whole lot of time left.

Maybe check on the Corbucci kid?

He took the old moonshiner's exit off of 75. The road looked as if it hadn't felt a pair of tires in years. Weeds growing thigh-high in some places. No lights. Perfect.

Tomorrow. Do it tomorrow. A little sticky out there for you right now, in case you didn't notice. See if you make it through the night, through the dark, then you can swing by and check on her before you see Roseanna.

Matheson didn't encounter a single headlight as he rumbled along the one-lane road skirting the shores of the Hootchyfalala. He hadn't expected to, but with things being the way they were at the moment he had to be ready for absolutely anything. The lawman hadn't been out to the cabin in almost six months, a choice he was already regretting when he recalled the past problems with the water well. The propane tank probably had at least enough juice to keep him warm tonight. No matter. Only a few people even knew about the existence of his daddy's old hunting bungalow, so it was the safest bet. He could handle living without his creature comforts in exchange for staying alive a little while longer.

About a mile away from the cabin, just as the car began the steep ascent toward Bootlegger's Bluff, the police radio began to chirp. Matheson stared down at the device, his blood curdling, almost veering off of the road. He rarely received calls on the radio unless it was from the station, usually from either Mrs. Priddy or Raab. Of course it wouldn't be Raab, and he was fairly certain old Priddy, by now, had been taken care of in a similarly macabre fashion. He braked to a halt at the crest of the Bluff and waited. Hopefully, it would stop, and he wouldn't have to answer it. But it didn't stop. It kept chirping, blinking, calling, and he realized it would never stop until whatever was on the other end of the line got to speak its piece. He snatched up the mike and pushed the button on the side, working to smooth the tremor out of his voice.

"Matheson here."

"Oh, boss, you just won't let it go, will you?" The voice on the other end was sexless, almost electronic. Flat, each syllable warbling clumsily forth. "I'll give you a gold star for persistence, but come on. It's time to walk away now. This is not your concern, and you have angered those who should not be angered. They only have so much patience. You are fortunate they like you. They admire your bravery. They would rather not see you harmed."

"*Awww*...ain't that sweet." Matheson sneered. "Lucky me, I guess. Just answer me this. Who are you? Who are they?"

"Myself, a mere messenger, constable. Nobody of great concern. They, as you call them, are very much the opposite." The voice was calm. Bored.

"Fill me in. Tell me more," the lawman said. "You're gonna have to do an awful lot of tap dancing to convince me to walk away from my people. My town. I did swear an oath to protect this little burg and the folks that live in it." Suddenly Juston didn't feel quite so shaky. Obviously, he was a more of a threat to them than he realized and had more power to throw around. Otherwise he would have been doornail dead from the beginning.

"This is family business, and that is all you need to know. I don't think I need to tell you what family I am talking about, either. You've seen the graves. You know well the name etched in those stones."

"Sure. The Fulcis. I get it. They're a big noise here, but they ain't the only big noise." Matheson shifted back into drive and continued his ascent up the Bluff. "Tell me what they want. What's coming next. Maybe we can shake a deal out of this mess."

"There will be no bargaining, constable. No deal. Not tonight. Not tomorrow. Not for a thousand lifetimes. The wheels are in motion and the ritual cannot be stopped. It's too late. We've been waiting a long time for this. Nigh two centuries. This time the terrible vows *will* be spoken. The Bride and the Groom *shall* be joined by the blood of a witch. By the spilled blood of a witch the door in the floor shall be flung open, the vessel prepared, and the Seamstress shall return in all of her terrible glory to reap her grim harvest. The faithful, at long last, shall be rewarded for their loyalty." The voice had begun to affect a slightly malevolent quiver. "You will leave Black Knot, Sheriff Matheson. You will leave Black Knot right now. You will turn that car around and drive in any direction you wish. Your reward for compliance shall be your prolonged life. To not be devoured at the marital feast."

"Wait! What witch? What blood?" Matheson bellowed into the mike. The mention of the door in the floor sent him into an unexpected panic. Who…what…were they talking about?

"Oh…no…no. That's quite enough for you, mister man. We think it better for you to let this particular flower blossom it its own good time. You be a good boy and get gone." The voice giggled. A few seconds of static hissed, the broadcast seemingly suspended. Then, faint at first, a crackle of slowly gathering energy, culminating in a horrible bestial howl rumbling forth from the radio speakers. The baying of a mad wolf gripped in the delirium of stirred-up bloodlust. Deafening, as if the beast snarling from the other end of that radio transmission had crawled through the wires and into the car with him. Every inch of the vehicle was alive with the hideous sound, as if the lawman were trapped in a cage with something savage and hungry.

Matheson, barely managing to stifle a scream, snapped off the radio and threw the squad car back into drive, mashing the accelerator with his foot, the harsh scrape of gravel beneath the warm rubber of his tires wailing through the stillness of the night.

It took Juston a little under an hour to board up all of the windows, doors and secret nooks of the cabin. Luckily there had been an abundance of spare wood and nails in the toolshed left over from the last time he'd performed routine repairs on the place. He kept a small fire going in the hearth, a couple of busted chair legs wrapped in old rags close by in the wood bin in case a torch was needed. He kept the Mossberg on the couch, always within reaching distance, his sidepiece holstered at his side, and a hunting rifle retrieved from the back bedroom laid out across the kitchen table. A lot of ammo as well, stuff he had been stockpiling for a few years in case the Russkies attacked.

To his surprise, the phone still worked. He dared not use it. Not right now.

He was so tired. But there would be no rest right now.

He had to plan.

He had to check on the Corbucci kid.

He just had so much to do.

None of this is real. Stop believing, you.

Matheson sprawled out on the couch and closed his eyes. Not to sleep. Just get still and quiet long enough to pull himself together. Even trying to think clearly, let alone form a coherent plan, felt impossible.

Sometime just after sunrise the lawman fell in a very deep sleep. He did not awaken until it was almost full dark.

He was still alive.

That was good. It was a start.

Matheson was appreciative of the siesta. He felt refreshed and a million times more clearheaded. He just wished he hadn't slept so damned long. God only knew what had happened in that precious stretch of hours and going forward there would be no time to waste. He gathered up his gear and made for the front door, quietly unbarring the portal.

Before he left he cut a look over at the telephone. He wanted to make a call.

Probably not a good idea.

She would just laugh at him. Call him crazy and make him think he still cared something for her.

Of course you care about her. There was a time when you would have thrown yourself into the path of an eighteen wheeler to spare her the slightest scratch.

The sheriff picked up the receiver and dialed Becky's number, cussing himself for an idiot with every spin of that rotary dial. The familiar ring drifted through his ears several times. He wasn't even sure what needed to be said. Anything out of his mouth would sound not only unbelievable, but ludicrous. No matter. In all honesty, this was more for him than Becky anyway. He had lost count of how many times he had let the other end ring. After what felt like forever he sighed and went to hang up, only to have the tolling of that tiny unseen jingling cease and the other line come alive. Nobody spoke, but Matheson could discern movement. Shuffling. Breath.

"Beck?" he mumbled into the receiver, the void between the two of them seeming to span all sense of time and place. A familiar gnaw nibbled at him. It was exactly how he had felt back at the lodge. Something was happening. Matheson could feel the unreal assembling of flesh, stealing breath and life and gathering power from a dark fountain. He knew he should hang up the phone, but couldn't bring himself to do it. As if he needed to hear what was to come next.

Giggling, girlish and teasing. The way Becky had laughed when they were dating, and everything had been carefree, fun, and loving. Yet there was a sinister nuance to the mirth which upset him. A sleazy, deranged undertone which served to mock the memories of their intimate moments. Moments he still clung to for comfort now and again. He repeated her name once more, realizing it was too late now. The sons of bitches, whoever they were, had already gotten this close to him, and the knowledge of this filled the lawman with true horror. It made him wonder just how far down they were willing to sink to get their message across.

On the other end of the phone line Matheson heard terrible things. Depravities. Noises no sane man should ever have to hear come from of the mouth of a woman he had once loved. Becky, it was clear, was not alone, and he didn't need to wonder much about who she was with. He heard the laughter of many voices, men and women and the things trapped in between, sick with madness. Interwoven through the repulsive din, the whines of agony and mewls of rapture from the mouth of his former bride, the slapping of diseased flesh and the damp gurgle of aroused juices.

She no longer sounded human.

Matheson slowly laid the receiver of the phone back in its cradle, jerked the line from out of the wall jack, and departed from the cabin without another word.

Town was surprisingly lively for a Sunday evening. Matheson took this as an omen for possible trouble and kept to the side streets where he could see everything he needed to without attracting any unwanted eyes. On the way into town he had stopped at his trailer to swap out the squad car for his old flatbed Ford. Only a few people in town would recognize the truck, but everyone and his dog would know the squad car. True, the truck was older than God and twice as unpredictable, but the cover it provided might prove to be, in a pinch, a tiebreaker between staying alive and dying like a dog.

There was quite a crowd gathered around the tombstones outside of the arcade. Some leaning up against them, the hands and foreheads pressed against the unnatural stone as if engaged in some unholy act of communion. Others were milling about aimlessly, mouths agape, stricken senseless. In the window of Mona Hennessey's café a light burned behind the red curtains, her truck parked in the alley adjacent to the building. Something about the light put a bother into Matheson's gut. It reminded him of the weird radiance he'd seen gleaming earlier from the lodge. He didn't dare venture into town to investigate. Not right now.

The sheriff drove up to the crest of Beltane Hill so he could get a clear view of the police station without being noticed. Even from this distance he could see the black Jeeps, the same ones he'd noticed at the Tarantula Arms crime scene and outside of the hospital. Leaving the truck running, Matheson grabbed the hunting rifle and squat-walked over to the grassy edge of the precipice, using the weapon's high-powered scope to better observe. If there was any funny business going on it was more than likely going on inside, behind closed doors. All of the lights were on, and swarms of shadows could be seen flitting and swishing about behind the drawn shades. He saw Priddy's car parked in back behind the dumpsters. This was not the old woman's usual parking spot, and this filled the lawman with queasy dread. If Priddy were down there she was no longer the same sweet old lady he had known since she'd been his kindergarten Sunday School teacher. Juston swallowed the lump in his throat and angrily mopped his eyes with the sleeve of his flannel shirt.

"How dare they come here. Here. *My* town. How dare they just take people from my town. How dare they just *take* them." Matheson growled under his breath, his fists curled so tightly against the barrel of the rifle the metal bit, unnoticed, into his flesh. He returned to the truck and guided it back onto the road, formulating in his head what was to be done next. The sheriff had to play his cards very wisely going forward, and there was no room for a poorly played hand at this juncture.

Although it was probably not the smartest thing to do, Matheson knew heading down into Haggard to check on the Corbucci kid was going to be his next move. He didn't understand why, but the child was special to him. Keeping her safe, if at all possible, had become of paramount concern for him. If he found any of those goddamn black Jeeps down there he was going to bust into that house and die screaming in a hail of blood and lead if need be. He veered off onto the Mandrake Stream exit, which would take him, briefly, through town. It was the only way to reach Old State Highway 270, itself the only accessible route to Haggard from his current location. No matter. He was confident the truck would provide him sufficient cover for the journey. If not, well, that would be the end of things then and it wouldn't much matter.

Matheson had to struggle to keep his cool when he veered onto Coldcraven Avenue. The sidewalks were absolutely jam packed with people, kids and grown-ups alike, most of them either walking in the direction or loitering outside of the Red Hand Theater. Matheson had forgotten about the Halloween double feature, always a huge draw, going on over the weekend. He rolled up the windows and slumped down in the seat as much as he could and still drive safely. Nobody paid him any mind. Although Halloween was tomorrow, many were dressed in their costumes, a veritable sea of sheet ghouls, red-faced and plastic-horned imps, possessed scarecrows and cloaked bloodsuckers. Candy satchels in hand and flashlights bobbing. Ordinarily the sight would have brought a smile to the lawman's face.

But things were different in Black Knot, and nothing he saw or heard was to be trusted.

As he wormed the truck past the Red Hand a loud bang thundered through the cab of the Ford, startling Matheson enough to where he briefly fumbled with his grip upon the steering wheel, almost veering off onto the sidewalk. The lawman instinctively slammed on the brake, the tires squealing to a complete stop in the middle of the road. Someone had flung something hard, probably a rock, at the truck. He could tell from the sound. Regaining his wits Juston shifted back into first and began to urge the truck back into an easy coast, not wanting to draw any more attention to himself. He had only rolled a few feet forward before his ears caught another sound. Someone calling his name.

Officer Matheson! Officer Matheson! HELP!

The sheriff of Black Knot recognized the voice immediately.

Cora Corbucci.

Matheson glanced at his rear-view mirror and saw the girl running toward the truck. Another kid was running alongside of her, a boy he didn't recognize. The terrified look shared by the both of them was enough to jolt the sheriff into throwing the truck in reverse, hammering the brakes, and flinging open the passenger side door. The kids booked it over to him as if their lives depended upon it. Once they were all seated the two of them began talking all at once, over each other, their voices just a hair below screaming. Matheson made a gesture with his hand for silence and opened his own mouth to demand answers. Behind them another voice hollered. The eyes of the boy Matheson didn't know widened, his face draining ghost pale. Both Cora and the other kid were shivering so badly the leather seats felt as if they were vibrating. The sheriff looked over his shoulder and saw Mona Hennessey running toward them, right down the middle of the street, her eyes wild and hands flailing.

"You get back here with my boy! You get right back here with my son, you bastard!" the woman screamed, tripping over something in the road and rolling off to the side. Within seconds she was back on her feet and running full tilt in their direction. *"Give me that boy or I will see you hanged, you vagabond! Your blood will soak the earth. We will give your flesh to the dogs! We will eat your heart and baptize ourselves in your blood!"*

Matheson looked at the stranger boy, eyes narrowed. "Your momma, son?"

The boy nodded, not meeting his gaze. "Not anymore, I think."

"Can you just drive, and we can talk about this later? Please?" Cora pleaded, shifting the truck back into first for him.

Matheson floored the truck and blazed down the road like a silver bullet sniffing out the heart of a werewolf. The needle of the speedometer never drifted below seventy until they were well beyond the Black Knot City limits, past Coffin Mills, and well on their way to Matheson's cabin in the safety of the Kiamichi Hills. The lawman began to relax and eased down on the accelerator. He felt like he could breathe easy again and he relished the sensation. Very soon, moments like this would be few and far between.

He felt a cold touch on the back of his hand. Cora's eyes were as wide and round as an owl's in the gloom of the truck's cab.

"Something's wrong with his momma. I think something's wrong with everybody," she squeaked. She looked very tiny and frail. Matheson took her hand in his and squeezed it fondly.

"You're right, sweetheart. Something *is* wrong with everybody. Right now, something is wrong with everybody, everything, in this whole goddamned town."

ELEVEN

Hayder's plan had worked perfectly.

Just before seven that same morning he had roused Cora from her bed in his closet, had her roll out of the bedroom window, and sneak up to the front door. As instructed she knocked, his momma answered, and after a brief exchange of pleasantries the girl was admitted into the house. When he came stumbling into the kitchen, pretending to shake off the remnants of slumber, he found the two of them seated at the kitchen table, sipping coffee, eating hot monkey bread, and listening to the radio. He helped himself to a generous portion of the sweet treat and sat with them. The conversation between the three of them was banal, innocent. Mostly about school on Monday and how they felt about that. Mona asked a few questions about Cora's life. Her granny and aunt and what life was like over at her house. Of course the girl lied, saying all of the right things to avoid future discussions. It didn't matter at this point, he figured.

After breakfast, the kids retired to Hayder's room and pretended to be hard at work creating their characters for a *Warriors & Warlocks* campaign which would never happen. Instead, the two discussed what had transpired all over again, as if trying to dissuade themselves from the reality of it all. It didn't work. Around lunchtime Hayder's momma left to pick up some lumber from Coffin Mills, indicating she would be gone for a while, but back before Hayder had to go to work at the Red Hand Theater. Cora whipped up a fast but tasty lunch of bologna sandwiches, potato chips, and sweet tea as they devised a plan to go forward. Food always brought together folks in the middle of a crisis, Cora reasoned. It must have been some sort of country person ritual, the boy reckoned.

"Okay. First thing we need to do is reach Sheriff Matheson," Cora mumbled between bites. "I'll call up to the police department and get him on the horn and ask him to meet us somewhere. Hopefully before you have to go to work. Have him meet us somewhere like Wolfbane Park. Nobody ever goes there and it's just a few blocks away from the Red Hand. I think it's best we try not to draw too much attention to ourselves until we get him on our side."

"What if he doesn't believe us? Or they, or whatever it is, already got to him?" asked Hayder, sipping his tea. "Not farfetched, really."

"Well, if he doesn't believe us, then we go on back home like normal, for tonight at least, and hope we stay alive until tomorrow." Cora turned to regard Hayder. "I'll have to spend another night in your closet, of course. That seemed to work well enough, I think. Then, tomorrow after school, we'll book it over to Roseanna Lavera's shop after school. She will know something, I guarantee it. She's a witch and everybody knows it. And if the sheriff has already become one of them, I guess that will be the end of the whole thing right then and there."

"What...do...you...mean?" Hayder felt a skein of ice travel up his spine. He already knew the answer to that.

"He'll kill us, of course. Duh."

Neither child said anything for a very long time after that.

"Tell me more about this Roseanna person," Hayder said.

Cora finished her sandwich and wiped the crumbs from her fingers on the edge of the table. "It's too long to get into, but Black Knot has two families of witches running the show around these parts. The Fulcis and the Laveras. The Fulcis are mean witches, and the Laveras are still not nice witches, but they aren't as nasty as the Fulci bunch. That's been the noise for as long as I've been alive. Aunt Polly told me it was the same story when she was little, and her mother was little, and all the way back as far as anyone in my family can remember."

"Go on." Hayder was starting to feel worse about the whole enterprise. Witches? What was next, vampires? Werewolves?

Cora's eyes gleamed. This was a topic which appeared to excite her. "The Fulcis got here first, a long time ago, followed by the Laveras. All I know about them is both fams came from somewhere in Italy. The Fulcis own a lot of businesses here and other places. The Laveras not as much, but still enough to have made a name for themselves in the Knot."

"Why did they come *here*? I mean, leave Italy for this, I'm sorry, dump?" Hayder was interested. "And this Roseanna lady is a witch too?"

"Dunno the answer to the first question. About Roseanna, that's what's been said about her. If she is a witch, then she's a nice one. I heard she helped the Tulsa Police find a missing kid's dead body once. It was in the paper here," Cora confirmed.

Hayder didn't want to know any more about that. At this point he felt it best to just accept everything told to him as the truth. He'd seen too much over the past few days to believe just about anything."

After they were both done eating, Cora called the police station to get Sheriff Matheson on the phone. She was going to ask him to meet them someplace safe, out in the open, as soon as possible. Nobody was answering at the station, which rattled alarms all throughout the girl. She could feel something was amiss. Setting down the phone, she waited a couple of minutes and tried to call again. This time the connection failed immediately, a recorded message indicating the number was no longer in service. Cora set the receiver down into the phone cradle, her hands shaking. Her chest ached abominably, her lungs fluttering behind her ribs like a pair of drowning birds.

Don't let Hayder see you like this. It could scare him off, and then you'll have to deal with this all alone. You can't do this on your own. You can't do anything on your own right now. Fib your tail-end off. The truth is bad, bad, bad.

"He's out on patrol, they said. Might be back tonight," Cora lied, trying to look calm. She was good at that.

"So revert to Plan B?" asked Hayder. "The witch lady?"

Cora nodded. As she opened her mouth to speak, the front door opened. Mona Hennessey walked into the room with her arms full of paper sacks stuffed with all sorts of things. The two of them jumped, Cora squeaking out a startled yelp. The woman smiled and came into the dining room, setting down the sacks on the kitchen counter.

"Everyone okay?" Mona asked, eyebrows crinkly with concern.

"Yeah, mom. We just were really in the zone with our game stuff." Hayder answered. They both nodded, Cora struggling to offer a grin.

"You sure?" Mona persisted. She turned to Cora, reaching out a thin pale hand and stroking the child's cheek. "Cora, you like someone just gave you a fright. A very bad, awful fright."

"Nuh...no ma'am. It's like Hayder said. *Warriors & Warlocks*, when you get to playing it, it just sucks you right in," Cora answered, trying not to pull away from the woman's caress.

"Fair enough." Mona scrunched her lip and nodded, seeming to buy it. "We'll have to go back up to the café, I'm afraid. I got so busy at the lumber yard I didn't have time to swing by there and get Hayder's uniform. About an hour, so y'all start wrapping up your little game." With that Mona retrieved her paper sacks and walked through the kitchen and out the back door, heading toward the supply shed where she kept her tools. The duo breathed a collective sigh of relief. Then, they shared a smile.

They had a plan. The best plan they could ever hope for.

For the remainder of their time at Hayder's house the couple sat out on the porch sipping tea and sharing a package of zebra cookies as the sun began to melt into the mountainside. The two of them didn't speak a word. It was a really pretty sunset. Neither of them could ever remember having seen a sunset quite this glorious. It was perfect, and the porch was the best place to watch it from with sweet tea and cookies.

This would be the last time either of them would sit on the porch of this house ever again.

"Well, I would say here's all the proof you'll need to convince your policeman friend," Hayder remarked dryly. He reached out a hesitant hand to touch the stone, then pulled back.

"Yeah…this is definitely a bad sign." Cora stared down at the pair of ornate tombstones jutting up from the shattered asphalt of the street. People walking past them seemed to either not notice or not care about the grave markers. Every so often a person would stop and regard them, maybe even reach out and touch one of them, then go along their merry way. Hayder noticed whenever someone would actually touch one of the monuments it would be in a way that seemed really personal. Like it was the marker for the crypt of a loved one sleeping below the hot tar and concrete.

"Pretty much confirms your suspicion as to who's responsible for all this." The rust-mopped boy rubbed his chin thoughtfully.

Before Cora could answer, Mona Hennessey came out of the café holding Hayder's uniform on a clothes hanger, locking the door behind her and coming over to stand beside her son. She put her arm around his shoulders and hugged him close. Hayder struggled to work his face into a pleasant, convincing grin.

"Wow…ain't that something?" The woman nodded at the monuments. "Streets a wreck. Hope they get that fixed soon. Might keep folks away from the café. Can't have that." Mona walked away from them and back toward the car. The kids looked at one another, looking for an answer. Cora turned to Hayder, locked eyes with him and took his hand in hers.

The boy's eyes were wide with fright. Cora squeezed his hand harder.

"I know." She laid her forehead against his cheek. "I know."

Apparently the Halloween double feature at the Red Hand Theater was something of a big deal. Two movies for the price of one was probably the main allurement, but the evening itself was something of an event to boot. An assembly of colorful tents had been set up outside of the theater, spreading out along the sidewalks and into the street, stretching both ways a good two blocks. The streetlight bulbs had all been replaced in honor of the occasion, the generic warm yellow lamps replaced with moody, pumpkin-spice spheres. A light mist drifted through the air, carried by a gentle, smoky autumn draft. The miniscule droplets of water became a slow cascade of shimmering orange crystals, and through the haze the voices of game barkers and hawkers of cheap wares called out to the foolish. On the afternoon of the hallowed holiday itself a big parade would be held promptly at three-thirty, giving children a chance to get home from school and change into their costumes. Activities would be held throughout the evening until well after midnight. Pie-eating challenges and cake walks, fishing for prizes, bingo, a big and often rowdy street dance, with live bands playing throughout the duration of the revelry.

Under different circumstances, it would have been a lot of fun.

Although Vera had told Hayder this wasn't a normal crowd, it didn't cushion the disheartening realization for him this was going to be a job where he would always be very, very busy. Maybe too busy. The action at the snack bar didn't seem to let up for even a second. The lobby seemed to always be packed to capacity, the occasional drunk fool having to be ushered out the side exit. Vera worked double duty, lending a hand to her young employee while taking money, giving tickets, then taking more and more of each. Hayder had to admire the old girl. She had a system that worked, and she had it down cold. It made his first night a lot easier and helped distract him from all the madness of the past few days.

Not that any of this really mattered all that much now, he told himself. The job, school, everything else. Come tomorrow their world would likely be very different indeed.

Halfway through the first feature Hayder was commanded by Vera to take a break, which he consented to eagerly. A blue raspberry Slush Kitty in hand, he slinked into the theater and quickly located Cora. He found his friend seated in the farthest back row, in the center aisle, in the seats closest to the exit into the auditorium. Cora sipped on a pop, an untouched small tub of popcorn in her lap. When she saw him her eyes lit up and she drew her legs up into her seat, spreading her skirt out over her knees. She patted the seat next to her, into which he slid gratefully.

"Man, it sure feels good to sit down. My dogs are a-barkin'!" Hayder leaned in close and whispered to her. A wild lock of the girl's dark hair brushed against his cheek and sent a furious blush through him.

"Anything happen? Even something that might seem kind of small?" she asked, offering him the tub of popcorn.

"Other than the sheer number of dang people packing into this theater to see a really bad movie? Nope. Nothing." The boy scrunched a handful of slickly buttered popcorn and shoveled it into his mouth. "I ain't never seen this many folks at a movie. Not even when the last Galaxy Champions movie came out last summer. It's crazy!"

Cora shrugged. "Any movie here, even a trashy one, is an event. This isn't Dallas, Mr. Texas." Hayder laughed, nodded, and helped himself to more popcorn. He was ravenous in spite of the squirm horror toying with his guts.

"How's the movie?" Hayder cocked an eye at Cora. "Folks are coming back to the snack bar looking like they might puke."

"I'm not really watching it." She shrugged. "I think things are scary enough for real right now without having to make them worse with pretend scary stuff." The boy nodded and the two of them fell into small talk, as if silence were poisonous. Deadly.

At some point Hayder found himself holding Cora's hand. He really wasn't even sure how it had happened. One minute he wasn't holding her hand, and the next he was. That was what he liked about it, and what alarmed him the most. How easily it just *happened* now. Just a few days ago the thought of holding a pretty girl's hand like this, like a boy and not like a cousin or his mom, would have sent his nerves into a DEFCON-1 state of panic. Now, their hands just found their way back to one another naturally, effortlessly, and merged together into something better than affection. It was understanding. Shelter. Something he would forget in the years to come, as all of those who grow up are inclined to do, and have a hard time remembering its lessons when salvation was needed the most.

Cora was watching him the whole time he was thinking all of this, a faint, anxious smile trembling upon her lips. Hayder met her eyes and really looked at the girl, truly *seeing* her. It was as if it were the first time he were seeing *anybody*. The boy offered his own awkward grin to match. Cora's lips parted and she really smiled for him now. The kind of smile where the joy is reflected in the eyes and soothes the person they're looking at. He noticed the small gap in her back teeth and loved it. The spray of freckles dusting her milky cheeks, he loved them too. That lazy dark eye of hers magnified almost comically behind the lens of those thick glasses was the most beautiful thing he had ever seen in his entire life. Her scent of soap and a faint trace of sweet sweat. Before he knew it he had reached out, slipped his fingers behind her head and gently drew her face to his. Her lips were shy, full and ready to be kissed. Cora laid her hand over his and brushed her thumb across the back of his fingers, their mouths working sweetly with one another. It was a memory Hayder would return to time and time again in his life, particularly in moments of hurt and uncertainty. A moment he knew was big. Bigger than him and everything else around him. A remembrance of perfection most never get to touch, let alone hold flickering in their hands.

Hayder felt a tap on his shoulder. Woozy, he turned to regard Vera smiling benignly down at him. The old lady winked at him and fondly ruffled his mop of crazy hair.

"Time enough for sparking later, tiger. Got a whole 'nuther movie to slog through. Back to work with you now."

Hayder grinned at her sheepishly, then turned to Cora. The girl's cheeks were blushed a visible neon pink in the pooled shadows of the auditorium. She cut him a bashful glance, then stared down at her popcorn, smiling sweetly. The boy stood up, letting her hand slowly slip from his, and followed after his boss.

Right after the credits opened on the next movie, an Italian Western, Cora decided she couldn't hold her pee urge any longer. After hearing Hayder's story about his first visit to the theater, she didn't want to leave the auditorium unless she absolutely had to. The child had always possessed a persnickety bladder, and she had known that large Slush Kitty would return with a bill for services rendered sooner than later. She indulged herself one last slurp of her drink and set off for the ladies' room.

The theater lobby was only half full when she walked out, most of the customers gathered around the snack bar or the arcade area. She tried to catch Hayder's eye with a weak little wave, but he was hard at it trying to construct a flawless pyre of nachos for what appeared to be an especially grouchy and particular old fart. Cora couldn't explain it, but she felt a weird need to look at him whenever she could. Like she was keeping him safe somehow. Without another look she passed beyond the swinging door and into the lavatory.

It was empty, thank goodness. Cora had a history of pee-coyness in public facilities, even with places she had peed at previously. This would cut down on the time she had to spend in the room. She scurried over to the closest stall, entered, locked the door behind her, dropped trou and settled herself into place. When the urine began to flow forth, out it roared like a salvo of river water blasting from the trunk of a boisterous elephant. She didn't even bother to stifle a very contented, very satisfied sigh.

As she sat there taking care of business, Cora thought about the kiss. Actually, that had been all the girl had been thinking of since it had happened. She had been wondering when, or even if, it would happen. She really hadn't counted on it happening when it did, that was for sure. Maybe that was what had made it extra sweet. Unlike everything else happening around them, there had been no urgency in that kiss. Hayder had kissed her like they had all of the time in the world to work at it. Everything else had been forgotten. Now it was all she could think about, and she hoped that wouldn't become a problem. They needed to focus. *She* needed to focus. There was a plan in place and everything, if possible, had to go as designed going forward.

But oh, it had been everything she had imagined her first kiss to be and so much more. She hoped there would be more kisses to come.

The bathroom door creaked open. The sound of shuffling feet. A shadow passed beneath the door of her stall, wandering past her and into the next cubicle, opening and latching the door shut behind them. Cora, now finished, realized, to her horror, there was hardly enough toilet paper clinging to the roll to blow her nose on, much less to wipe with. She wasn't surprised. This sort of predicament seemed to birddog her any time she had been forced to use a bathroom not in her own house. There were now three options available to her; refrain from wiping, which was a last resort tactic she didn't wish to even consider; waddle over to the sink and see if any paper towels were handy, then retreat back to her stall and close up shop; last, ask the hopefully kind-hearted soul in the stall next to her to help her out, providing of course they weren't in the same sad boat. Cora opted for the third approach. She'd been in a similar bind before, and this was usually the swiftest, most efficient tactic in a situation like this.

"Hi…uh…ma'am…er…miss. I know this is kinda awkward, but can you spot me some toilet paper? I just need enough for the basic stuff, not to get too personal." Cora spoke into the stillness. She allowed a couple of minutes to pass before repeating the question. This time her words elicited movement from within the stall, if not a direct response. The girl could see shadows moving beneath the partition of the stall between them. Rambling shadows. She went to repeat her request for a third time, the first sentence failing on her lips. Suddenly, Cora was afraid to move at all. Slowly, the child rose from the seat, trying to not to breathe too loudly. The air in the room had changed. It was humid, heavy, making it hard to catch a breath. The clotted, oppressive air of a secluded bog where the bones of the criminal dead had been laid to rest beneath rancid green waters. Her head began to swim, her vision blur.

She needed to get out. Now.

Cora reached out to unlock the door to the stall. As her fingers brushed across the surface of the cold metal knob she became aware of a funny noise. Muffled…indistinct. Like it might have been coming from some abandoned upstairs room. She focused upon the noise and ascertained it sounded like someone crying. Maybe either a lady or a kid. The kind of soft, exhausted weeping of someone whose grief had worn them down straight to their marrow. It was the lamentation of the weary, the mortally exhausted. As she considered the sound, Cora became increasingly aware of its mounting volume, its spreading intensity. Before long, the child realized the crying wasn't coming from any upstairs room but from the stall right next to her. Moreover, there was a familiarity to the lamentation she couldn't quite put a finger on. A unique quiver in the moan, a hoarse catch in a particularly long, drawn-out sob. Cora had heard it before, she was certain of this, she just couldn't connect the dots all of the way and name who, or what, it belonged to.

"Hey…you okay in there?" Cora knew this was a peculiar question to hit a stranger in the toilet, upset or not, but she didn't really know how to approach the situation any other way. "Are you hurt? Do I need to go get the manager?"

A low, glugging moan responded. Cora froze, realizing now she should have never left her seat to come in here. Should never have come to the Red Hand Theater for the Halloween Double Feature. Neither she nor Hayder should have come; they had been tricked, and now it might be too late to do anything about it. Whatever suffered at the other end of that gargle was most definitely *not* okay, and it didn't want her to be okay either. As in response another moan rumbled throughout the cramped narrows of the bathroom, solemn and dense as if encased in thickening blood, trailing off into whimper, dissolving at last into a shrill, high-pitched sigh, only to blossom once again into a perverse chuckle, flowing at last into a fully molded cackle. Wicked, girlish laughter. Here is where it all finally clicked with Cora Corbucci, recognition, and her mind came very near to shattering at that precise moment.

The severed head of Crystal Compton, once her best friend since church preschool and now quite dead, rolled under the gap in the partition, coming to rest against the toe of Cora's sneaker, face up and eyes staring. The spoils of the grave had already gnawed deeply into the meat of the murdered child's face, the gummy flesh blushing pale green and wilted away from the chin and cheeks, revealing the denuded bone glistening beneath. What little hair remained clung in several matted dirty blonde strips clinging to the cap of her skull, Crystal's signature silver butterfly hairclips still securely held in place. Her withered earlobes seemed to drip from the side of her sunken face, and to Cora's horror she saw the little pink diamond studs gleaming from the ashen earlobes. Cora had helped her pick out those earrings just a month before the Feed Lot horror. They had been a birthday present from Crystal's mom and dad, something she had been practically begging for since she had been ten. Cora wanted to run, knew that she had to run, but her legs had grown too heavy to even twitch a toe, as if her muscles had been injected with freshly mixed cement.

Crystal's lifeless eyes froze Cora her right where she stood, shivering. The ruined mouth opened, a nauseating belch of rank graveyard breath fanning up and sending Cora into a retching convulsion. The dead lips curled into a hideous, malevolent grin, the teeth grinding and chattering against one another like knucklebones rattling within a wooden mug, its tumor-pocked tongue lolling and lapping obscenely at her. A thud slammed against the bathroom stall separating them, the somnolent and demanding fist of a forgotten thing newly awoken from a long hibernation, ravenous and irritable. Another thud followed, this one powerful enough to violently tremble both stalls, then another. Cora saw a clutch of bony fingers, the flesh upon them shriveled gray and leathery, curl around the top of the partition separating their stalls, another pair joining them. The fingers themselves might have been decayed and thin, but the nails upon them were wicked sharp and mean-looking as any beast roaming the wilds. The talons of a carrion bird slathered in purple glitter nail polish. A silver ring with a red birthstone encircling a wasted, whittled thumb.

Cora glanced down at Crystal's head. As if delighted at being noticed, its eyes rolled back into the skull to reveal flat yellow orbs shot through with a spider work of black veins, rivulets of creamy brownish pus oozing from their corners. The living dead thing grinded its charred teeth at her, hissing, as the entire stall began to shake again, the mushy splat of dead bare feet against the side of the wall as if the thing on the other side meant to scale the wall. To join their friend in her cubicle to discuss matters only known to those who have died and did not care to stay dead.

Now her legs found their fuel! Cora dropped to the dirty floor with a panicked yelp, rolling out to the left, under the stall and back into the sink area, just a few feet from the door. A hateful, cheated snarl echoed back and forth against the four narrow walls, so loud it momentarily threw Cora off balance. The girl quickly regained her wits and flung the bathroom door open, not immediately realizing the portal didn't empty into the lobby of the Red Hand at all, but instead funneled her into a tapered, seemingly never-ending corridor of smoldering red carpet, the floor illuminated by a procession of floating electric candelabras. The child immediately understood what she was seeing wasn't real, but couldn't quite get her brain to convince the rest of her body of the illusion. All she could think to do was run for her life, flee like the dogs of the Devil himself were snapping after her, and the breathing dead thing dressed in her best friend's purloined shell swiftly joined her in the nightmare.

Cora dared a brief glance behind her, immediately regretting she had done so. She knew she would never be able to rid herself of the sight of that dreadful ghoul loping after her, garbed in Crystal's ragged pink burial dress, now putrefied to flimsy rags barely clinging to its soggy green flesh, the chattering head held out before it, crowing forth the vilest of profanities.

This all you got, kid? You gonna let this here sliver of a dead goddess' dream shovel the dirt on your grave? You got more salt than that. You didn't survive a buckshot kiss to the tits and gut to let it all just END here. Did you?

Whose voice was that?

Don't you worry about me, little gal. Do what I say. Disbelieve it. That's all you gotta do.

But that was impossible. Cora's legs were so very tired, too. It was only a matter of time before her knees finally buckled, the ankles failed, and she went toppling headfirst and vulnerable onto that nasty carpet. Cornered prey.

Listen here, you, again. It. Isn't. Real. But you keep feeding it with your fear and craziness and it will be more real than you know. After that I got no more skin in this game.

Cora hadn't realized she had skidded to a dead stop on the carpet, contemplating the voice. The fetid devil slammed into her, hard, knocking all of the wind from her lungs and sending a horrific stitch of agony through her chest. If it wasn't real, it made a pretty good argument otherwise. The girl could feel its awful weight crushing her, pinning her to the floor, those terrifying clacking teeth growing closer, its breath of mildewing crypts flowing into her nostrils, into her skull, making her head swim with amnesia and a petrifying cold flooding through her body.

OUTSIDE OUTSIDE OUTSIDE! GET YOU GONE, GONE, GONE!

Cora didn't recognize her own voice at first, but when she did it was like hearing the first cardinals of spring chirping at the end of a long and dreary winter. Somewhere a church bell tolled, and the high, shrill laughter of a woman rang out. Jubilant, coarse laughter. The corridor dissolved around her, banishing the hungry ghost with it as if both had been nothing more than wisps of cigarette smoke. She found herself standing outside of the ladies' room door, in the lobby of the Red Hand.

Then, finally, Cora Corbucci screamed. Screamed loud enough to wake the dead.

Once Hayder got Cora outside, in his arms and calmed, she told him everything. Of course he believed her. He knew. As she sobbed and chattered, he kept a watchful eye around them, looking for any sign of trouble. Aside from the two of them the sidewalk outside the Red Hand Theater was empty and quiet.

"Guess I got me a big dose of believer medicine tonight. Like I needed anything to make this stuff more real." Cora wheezed. Her entire chest felt like a cage full of writhing, hungry rats were trying to gnaw their way to freedom through the skin.

"You okay?" Hayder soothed, stroking her hair. "You act like you're hurting."

"Yeah. That spot where I got shot is going to be hateful till the day I croak, I think." The girl nodded. "I'll make it."

"What's the plan, chief? We try to get the sheriff again?" Hayder asked. "I don't think we counted on things turning bad this fast."

"No! Not there. Not now that it's dark." Cora wasn't sure why she said that. Especially the part about the dark. Based upon her earlier attempt to call the police station, a place that always answered their phone, she had a sinister twinge in her gut about it. "I know you're not gonna like it, Hayder, but I say we hightail it to Roseanna's shop first. Hope to Jesus she's not gone bad and get her on board."

Hayder shrugged and then nodded. "I trust you."

The girl suddenly tensed up in his arms, gently pushing him away. Her eyes were wide as a pair of softballs. The boy turned his head to see what she was looking at, his own eyes following her lead.

There it was, the familiar old flatbed truck parked at the end of the block, illuminated by one of the sidewalk gas lamps, smoke puffing from the muffler, the headlights darkened. There was a fuzzy shape behind the wheel. He knew it was his mother, and the thought of this didn't quite instill the feeling of comfort like it should have when a boy sees his momma. But something made him want to go to her. To talk to her and tell her everything. Get into the passenger seat and let her take care of everything. And she would take care of everything, for she was the woman who had brought him into this world and would never let harm come to her little boy. Hayder began walking in the direction of the truck. Cora quickly snaked him by the elbow and pulled him back.

"Hayder, no!" The tone in her voice immediately brought him to attention. Her eyes were filled with a genuine panic. "Listen, I don't know how to put this and make it sound nice, but I think something is wrong with your mother. Something bad. I think she might be part of all of this somehow."

"What do you mean?" He cocked his head, eyes widening. "Did something…happen?"

Cora then told him, quickly, about the weird books she had found stashed in the café. How they had made her feel when she had touched their ancient covers and how strangely Mona had acted when she had caught her nosing around. The general feeling of unease she experienced when she and his mother had been alone together. The boy didn't want to admit it, but his mother had been behaving…differently…since they'd arrived in Black Knot. Every smile seemed fake. Forced laughter. Up until now he had been attributing it all to her just being sad, but now he could see things a bit more clearly in light of recent horrors. It felt more like she had been wearing her mask of sadness to distract his attention away from something else. Something wrong that had nothing to do with melancholy. It was a bitter pill to choke down, and when the tears came it was damn near a flood. Cora took him in her arms and laid his head against her shoulder. She would comfort him now. The two stood there together, the girl letting her friend have his cry. Cora was loath to stop him, but she could feel eyes upon them. Eyes with wicked designs bubbling within their deathless hollows.

They had to move.

"This way." She grabbed Hayder by the hand and led him down the street toward the Hemlock Lane Farmer's Market. There was a drainage canal behind the livestock area which provided a shortcut to Northtown, where Roseanna's shop was located. They walked fast, reluctant to run and draw attention to themselves. When they reached the corner they heard someone yelling, almost screaming. The three of them turned to see a shape forming from the shadows, too far away to make out but there, nevertheless. The shape screamed louder, and Hayder immediately recognized the voice of his mother. Her voice was shrill, angry, her footsteps growing more rapid, the heels of her boots clicking rapidly against the concrete like a metronome in a madhouse. She was cussing, something his momma never did.

"Haul butt! Now!" Cora shrieked, releasing his hand in preparation of bolting away into a full-blown sprint. As she turned a pair of headlights flashed against the rain-slicked street, blinding her. Headlights belonging to a truck only she could have recognized. She'd only seen it a handful of times, but it was his. It belonged to *him*. She felt like dropping to the ground and weeping with joy. The truck was moving fast, and it had the windows rolled up. He wouldn't be able to hear her yell! She *needed* him to hear her yell!

The girl reached down and grabbed the biggest rock she could throw, which she did. The missile sailed through the air like a silver bullet and banged hard against the top of the cab. The truck slammed on its brakes with a squeal of worn-out rubber. The driver's side window rolled down slowly, and a familiar, blessed face appeared. Cora could tell immediately the man looking back at her was scared too. He looked like he had aged a hundred years, and that gave her hope everything would be all right.

"Officer Matheson!" Cora Corbucci yelled, almost laughing with a maniacal joy. "Officer Matheson! HELP!"

Matheson's tale was, perhaps, even more horrifying than theirs, and when he finished telling it the three of them grew very quiet, soaking in the unbelievable. He too had been headed to see Roseanna. As they drove along, Cora then related their story, all the way from the beginning. Matheson listened thoughtfully, his knuckles gripping the steering wheel so tightly Cora feared the bones might break. When she was done, the three of them stayed quiet for a good piece.

"How do you think your momma is involved in this, Hayder? She was making an awful racket back there." Matheson broke the silence. Hayder turned to Cora, who proceeded to tell the lawman about the strange books and the odd behavior of Mona Hennessey. Hayder filled in a few blanks here and there. The sheriff reached across the three of them and opened the glovebox, retrieved his pack of smokes, shook one out and lit it. He opened his mouth as if to speak but stopped short. He drew on the cigarette and chuckled, shaking his head.

"What's so funny?" asked Cora.

"This town, is all," Matheson said. "It's never been right, and I know it. Sad thing is, I've always known it. I just never wanted to really see it. Really deal with it. Maybe that was part of it all. Some kind of witchcraft. Those tombstones sprouting out of the damn ground kinda sealed the deal for me."

"Well, we have to deal with it now. There ain't another option," Cora insisted. "There ain't no getting away from it! This stuff, it's not from our world. Not *of* our world! We don't end it now the things to come will look like nothing."

"You're right." Hayder nodded, his face solemn. He suddenly seemed much older-looking to Cora, unnerving her a little. "If we don't stop it now it's just gonna grow and grow and grow. Like a weed left alone in a garden to kill the rest of the flowers. It won't just quit at Black Knot. It knows we know about it. It will come looking for us, and it won't stop until we are not around to talk about it anymore."

"Agree with you there, kiddos. This is evil has come a-knockin' from another world, as silly as that sounds for a grown man to say out loud. An evil a human being can't ever hope to understand. Whatever it is, I got a gut feeling we can't just kill it. We got to find a way to get rid of it. Send it back to whatever dark hole it came slithering out of." The truck rattled over the worn-out railroad tracks that divided southern Black Knot from Northtown. "Hayder, I also agree with Cora. Something isn't right with your momma. It pains me to say it. I paid her a visit back before she first opened up. You know, just to introduce myself. I could *feel* it, whatever it was. It was more than just the bashfulness of a lady meeting a strange man for the first time. There was a feeling of…hostility…coming off of her. Like not only was she wanting me out of there, but she might actually hurt me to get me gone."

Hayder didn't respond, just nodded and looked at the truck window. Cora slipped her hand in his and laid her head on his shoulder. That was enough for now.

The truck rattled over the old railroad tracks separating new Black Knot from the old. In that old part of town there lived a witch. Matheson prayed that witch did, in fact, turn out to be a real live witch. A witch who, if she wasn't already a part of all of this, would know what to do and would help them.

Roseanna's Swap Shop could be found at the western edge of Northtown, right across the road from Twisted Oak Cemetery in a strip of derelict structures where it was the sole surviving business. With its wrought iron second-floor balconies, burnished brown brick façade, and floor to ceiling windows, it more closely resembled a swanky New Orleans residence rather than a flea market. It was one of the oldest buildings in Black Knot, having once been a saloon back in the days before statehood when Confederate soldiers seeking refuge from Yankee bounty hunters had erected a small settlement there. It would have flourished too, were it not for the Laveras. Once those damn witches had arrived everything changed. They quickly expelled the Reb squatters and reshaped the land into what they wanted. To this day it was common knowledge that every inch of

Northtown belonged to the Lavera family. Even the Fulcis steered clear of the territories north of the railroad tracks, relegating their nefarious dealings to the southern and eastern slabs of the county. The Swap Shop had been many things over the decades. An Italian restaurant and grocer, still remembered fondly by many of the Knot's older residents; a hardware store which had doubled as a speakeasy; a gentleman's club; and now repository for cast-off odds and ends owned by Roseanna Lavera, the daughter of Augustino Lavera, the one-time mayor of Black Knot and one of the most successful importers of antiques in the entire Southwestern United States. Roseanna herself was something of the black sheep of the clan, having kept her nose relatively clean for most of her life and sticking to a somewhat more low-key existence. She was renowned for her famously friendly and charitable disposition, and if she really were a sorceress, she was most definitely closer to a Glenda than a Wicked Witch of the West.

And, as it turned out, the witch was not home tonight.

Matheson stared at the piece of orange construction paper triple-taped to the front door of the shop. He sighed and ran a hand through his hair.

"Well, shit fire."

"What's the matter?" Cora called from the open truck window. "What's it say?"

"Says she gone. Be back tomorrow on Halloween." The lawman chuckled. "Well, she *is* a witch, after all." He gave the door a soft kick and returned to the truck. The three of them sat together in silence.

Hayder spoke first. "So, what do we do then?"

"Mulling that over, bud." Matheson laid his head against the steering wheel and sighed.

"Better mull quick, boss. I get the feeling we won't be safe out here for much longer. Can't y'all feel it?" Cora shuddered. "We got to get out of town. Once we're out of Black Knot its power, whatever it is, isn't so…powerful."

"How on earth do you know that?" Hayder asked.

She turned to him and kissed his cheek. "Hey kid, I'm the girl who died and came back, remember? I got superpowers now."

"I think she might have something there. We're in witch country right now. Once we get out of witch country their witchiness gets less…witchy. Let's head to my cabin and lay low. It's outside the city limits and nobody knows about it. Raab didn't even know about it. Let's just hope it's far enough. We can try Roseanna again sometime in the afternoon."

Matheson keyed the truck back to life and threw it into reverse, shifted into first and took to the alley behind the shop he knew would lead to a series of back roads. Those back roads would take them into the hills of Grinning Goblin Forest, then eastward toward Coffin Mills, where the cabin lay just over the county line.

Hayder spent most of the journey with the window rolled down, breathing in the autumn night air. It smelled so clean out here. It was so quiet. So unlike Dallas, in the city, where the stink of gasoline never went away, and the meaning of silence was a completely foreign concept. He found himself missing it terribly, for despite all of its cleanliness the air in Black Knot carried with it the bite of winter death. The threat of waiting coffins. The taste of doom.

INTERLUDE THREE

Series of notes found in a family bible written by Barney Driscoll, Black Knot County Coroner from 196- to 198-, provided to author courtesy of Joan Benoit, Registered Nurse at Shadow's Retreat Nursing Home in Coffin Mills, Oklahoma circa 202-.

A heads-up. My prose leans a bit on the purple side. My wife always told me I missed my calling as a writer. Whether or not she was right or wrong about that is up for debate. You be the judge, although if you lean toward the latter keep your damn opinion to yourself.

I'm gonna start off by saying I have seen some strange things in my day. When your line of work involves tending to the dead, that's just kind of a given. The dead have their own strange ways, and dealing with them is, often, a tricky enterprise. Whenever I encounter these strange things, I like to write them down, mostly because I have the attention span of a gnat, and if I don't write them down, I might forget about them. There are some things you don't want to ever forget. I have learned over the years, and I am an old buzzard now, when you forget the past, you can find yourself making big, sometimes tragic mistakes. This is a case of writing down something that happened mostly because it was more than strange. It wandered into the territory of what some people might label as supernatural. Something spooky.

Let me just say that I believe in ghosts. I believe in them completely. I also believe there are things in this world much, much worse than ghosts. I know this, because I have seen these things with my own eyes and heard them with my ears.

I had only been the coroner for a few years when that whole business with Mariana Fulci went down. Her being a Fulci, it was nasty business, of course. I just had no idea how nasty it would turn out to be.

Mariana was a real looker, even by the standards of Fulci women, who are all damn near legendary for their beauty. She was a famously heartless and vain thing, even having let two men shoot each other to death in the parking lot of the Sizzler over a dispute on who would pay her bar tab that night. Wives had a habit of up and vanishing whenever Mariana happened to be buzzing around their husbands, and sometimes even the opposite scenario. The woman seemed to devour humans like cotton candy at a carnival, never satisfied with just one bite, having to eat every wisp down to the bottom of the box.

Back in the early 1970s our little local television station, KBLUD (cute, huh?), got a little extra cashola from the state for something they labeled as "cultural improvement". Whatever that meant. The head brass at the station thought pooling those funds into the development of a late-night horror show was the most culturally significant investment they could come up with, and so it was done. Thus, *Madame Luridia's Plenty Scary Movie* was born. Friday nights at 11:30, it quickly culled a committed audience among college and high-school students high on weed and sozzled on booze you bought by the gallon. It mostly aired bottom of the barrel spooky movie garbage, occasionally throwing in an old Universal classic to maintain respectability. But I think the main draw for a lot of folks, especially the male viewers, was the ample, pale and powdered cleavage of Mariana. Not sure who thought it fit to install her as the host for the program, her being the titular (hehehehe) Madame Luridia, but her being who she was, where she came from, it probably was a choice forced upon whoever at the station was put in charge of making those sorts of decisions. Now, to her credit, she wasn't too bad. She was actually entertaining and quick-witted. Mariana had a charming way about her, like most women who are born peacocks, and seemed to actually know things about the so-called movies presented so they could be mocked properly. Mariana, or Luridia, was a macabre wraith of flowing black hair in her damn near see-through gown of flowing silk crimson, enshrouded in a billow of dry-ice fog as she glided through the flea market set of dime-store tombstones, flim-flam cardboard mausoleums, and twisted trees lifted from high-school drama productions.

The show ran for a few months just shy of three years. When it came to end it had nothing do with bad ratings or a want of crappy movies to gag its loyal subjects with. It ended because of a death. The death of Madame Luridia.

I got the phone call on a Tuesday afternoon, the day before the show was supposed to air. A lot of people don't realize a lot of programs back then were either broadcast live or taped a couple of days in advance. Not that it was a masterwork of technical enterprise, but it was a complicated enough endeavor requiring a few days to fix all of the blubs and missteps before showtime. I remember it well. I was at Tully's BBQ eating a pig sandwich (hotlink, pickles on a bun piled with slaw, onions and a very sweet barbecue sauce, the recipe guarded like a government secret), when Mabel Carmichael, the town bullhorn, came tear-assing into the dining area. She was nearly incoherent, in tears. After getting her calmed down with a coffee cup filled up halfway with bourbon Mabel began to tell us about something she had seen. A terrible thing. After she told us this, I called the police station and got Sheriff Matheson on the horn. This would have been Gerald, the daddy of Juston (a damn good boy). I told him to meet me up at the television station. You see, Mabel's son Gordon (the very definition of a dim bulb) worked up there as one of the guys who worked the microphones used to record their shenanigans for the horror show. When he had arrived for duty, he had found something and had called up his momma. Why neither one of these fools hadn't thought to call the police first eluded me.

Now, Gerald was reluctant at first to check it out. He'd had several run-ins with the Fulcis, none of which had gone well for him. The last tangle with them had almost cost him his badge. But him being the man in charge of law and order, he decided he better do the job he had been elected for and stopped by the hospital to pick me up. Ordinarily I wouldn't have been notified until a body had indeed been found and the deceased state verified. Perhaps he had felt something in his gut and had decided I would be required at the scene. Matheson was like that. He often felt things and they would turn out true. Call it psychic powers or just a really refined intuition, I guess.

Upon our arrival I could tell something was off, as could he. Maybe his mojo had momentarily rubbed off on me. I felt scared, and that is not a word I use casually. For a few minutes we had sat in the squad car, neither of us saying anything. Matheson had brought alone a thermos of coffee and we sat there drinking out of it, passing it back and forth like a pair of teenagers sharing some booze swiped from our parents. Matheson eventually opened his door and I followed suit, my legs all flimsy. We walked up to the station and found the door open, nothing looking out of the ordinary. No signs of someone breaking into the place, which filled me with some relief. If what we were to find in there was what had actually been told to us, there was less of a chance of someone hanging around to hurt us. All the same, Gerald drew his gun and ordered me to stay behind him, close. We entered the station.

I have inhaled the odor of blood enough times to detect it immediately. It didn't even have to be a large amount of the stuff. From the intensity of it I could tell there was a lot of blood, a whole hell of a lot of it. I told this to Matheson, and I could see his face go white even in the shadows of the corridor leading from the lobby and into the control room. Despite its dark reputation, Black Knot was not the sort of place people got killed. Vanish into thin air, sure. But few people turned up dead. At least if they did get killed, rarely were their bodies found. Gerald Matheson was a big old boy, a decorated war veteran, and to see him looked spooked scared the jumping bejeebus out of me. We crept along just a quiet as could be, reaching the control room and finding it empty. I knew before we entered the studio that was where we would find what we had come looking for, and I wasn't wrong.

Mariana Fulci hadn't just slashed her wrists, she had gutted herself, yanked out her innards and had them piled up all nice and neat in her lap. I say she had done it because the blade, a butcher's tool responsible for the carnage, was still in her hand. There was a note nearby, read not long after by yours truly, verifying Mariana had indeed been responsible for this grisly act. The dead woman was wearing her full Luridia costume, even down to the black high-heeled shoes, one of which dangled from the big toe on her stiffened foot, and the plastic fangs which hung perched upon her bottom lip. Her ghoul's makeup had been smeared all over her face as if she had wiped her filthy hands all over her cheeks and chin, bathing herself in her own blood. Most of all I remembered her eyes. Wide open, the lids completely swallowed up by the hollows of her skull, the pupils had already begun to glaze over, signifying she had been dead for a while. To this day I have never seen so much blood spilled from a single body. It was as if she had twice as much blood flowing through her veins than a normal human, pooling out beneath the chair she lay slumped in a good fifteen to twenty feet in every direction.

The suicide note, for that was what it was, was damn near a Russian novel. In spite of its length the message behind it was typical. Love lost. Love regained. Love lost again. The wayward lover had not been named, but word had been going around town for years the paramour in question had been her own twin brother, Mario, himself as much an unrepentant shitbird as his sister. It was common knowledge the Fulcis, while in Italy, had intermarried to the extent some of their offspring had been either stillborn or grotesque. Nobody much cared to bring it up. To even utter the name of a Fulci seemed to invite misfortune.

I called in my team to retrieve the corpse. While we waited Matheson and I stayed outside of the studio, loath to even remain in the building with her, dead or not. The body was collected, sheeted, with Matheson relaying the notification of her death to the head mouthpiece for the Fulcis, Fantasma. We were instructed, quite firmly, to return the corpse to where we had found it, leave immediately, and let the family handle their own dead, their own way. Matheson tried to argue, as delicately as possible for a man of his temperament, this was not only very much against policy but a violation of the law to boot. He was then told where he could stick that law and told something else, which he wouldn't repeat to me. I didn't ask, either. Gerald had a wife and kid he was kind of fond of, after all. Those damned witches had a lot of folks in the palm of their hands, and to dispute their bidding attracted bad luck. I had my guys leave Mariana Fulci right where she died, sitting on her gaudy horror queen throne, cold and drawing flies. Matheson and I drove back to town, called it day, and shared a pitcher of Crow Hollow beer at the Skillet. Neither of us mentioned what had happened on that day ever again.

But that wasn't the end of the story. Other things began to happen.

A couple of weeks after Mariana's death, little Jenny Windham disappeared from her backyard. Her momma, insensible with panic, told Sheriff Matheson the child had been playing by herself in the backyard right as the sun had begun to set, something she had done a thousand times before. Mrs. Windham, a waitress at the Skillet and widowed earlier in the year, had been inside tending to the laundry. She had called out to Jenny to come in for supper and received no answer. Another call brought nothing. Mrs. Windham had gone out into the backyard and found no trace of her daughter. All that indicated Jenny had been there was a single sneaker left behind in her little playhouse not twenty feet from the back porch steps. Upon the toe of the sneaker a single, still fresh drop of blood. The child was never seen again, not even the resources of the OSBI yielding a single clue. Mrs. Windham, five years later, would end up at The Oaks, Black Knot's local booby hatch, where she would remain until she passed a few years after.

Two weeks later someone else got themselves lost. This time it was old Mabel Carmichael. Vanished from the annual Church of the Living Water Fellowship Feast at Lake Hootchyfalala. She'd just finished accepting her thirteenth blue ribbon from the pie contest and had excused herself to visit the ladies' room in a nearby rest stop. Several reliable, sensible folks saw the old girl go into the bathroom, but nobody saw her leave it. There was absolutely no evidence of Mabel ever having been present at the festival, and nobody ever found out what happened to her. Not long after her son got himself married and moved away, to Missouri, I believe. There were others as well, and pretty soon word got around about something unnatural was stalking the streets and country roads of Black Knot after the sun went down. People even claimed to have seen it. Some of these people talked to me about it, but I already knew what it was, and who it had once been. When I showed up in Sheriff Matheson's office one night, hours after everyone else had gone home, he didn't have to be told the reason for my visit. He knew.

The two of us shared a few shots of liquid courage, commonly known as booze, and talked it over. About what was to be done. He gave me gun, a revolver, even though I didn't have much faith in it doing much good. Not just because I had never fired a gun in my life, not even a pellet rifle, but because I feared with what we dealing with was beyond bullets and knives and the pathetic weapons of mortal men. But it was better than nothing, and I hoped perhaps I was wrong. I knew damn well I wasn't, but I was so terrified denial tasted a lot better than the sour pill of truth. We set out for the TV station, listening to an old country music station as we traveled in silence. Matheson offered me a cigarette, also a first for me, and I burned that cancerous stick down to the filter in no time flat, trying to keep my hand from shaking. He was scared too, his knuckles gripping the steering wheel, white as a sun-bleached bone.

When we pulled into the muddy furrow of earth that served as the driveway for KBLUD, I could feel the presence of the unearthly horror sleeping within its darkened rooms, haunting the threadbare sets and props which now served as its tomb. Gerald parked and turned to look at me, and I swear he looked like he'd packed on about twenty extra years on his face in that short drive from town to the station. We sat in the squad car for damn near half an hour, gathering enough sack to open our doors and step out. I realized right then how stupid we had been to come out here at night. Maybe it had been the whiskey, maybe something else. It didn't make a difference now. We were here, and I knew that if we meant to see something, and we did want to see something, it would happen tonight. We got out, our big utility flashlights in hand, and began the climb up the hill toward the building.

The station, had, of course been closed ever since the suicide of the Fulci woman. Mind you, this had been only a couple of months, but the place looked as if it had shuttered against the rest of the world for half a century. The summer grass had grown high enough to brush across our thighs, thick and green, the roof slumping dejectedly at one corner, the outer façade thick with moss and hungry, clutching wisteria. I remember it being a very hot night, even for late July. The heat felt like a huge, gloved hand smothering me with its palm. Matheson, no longer a young man but not yet seasoned enough to be called old, trudged ahead of me like a soldier being sent into the trenches, his breathing labored. I feared for his heart, which he had been having problems with of late. I caught up with him and found him holding a flask, from which he took a pull then handed over to me. Just a sip. Brandy this time, much easier to stomach.

As we drew closer, we encountered an unexpected sight. All of the studio windows had been boarded up with several thick planks of lumber, the front door secured with thick chains and huge, expensive padlocks. Shining our flashlights upon the slats and the steel links revealed an assortment of curious trinkets affixed to them. Tiny brass bells with strange markings carved into the metal. Dried herbs and flowers, the likes of which I had never seen before, bound in twine. Little dolls, crude and unnerving, fashioned from corn husks, scraps of bone and old cloth. Upon the door itself was a strange symbol painted in a substance I knew was not paint. It was blood, although whether it was the blood of a human or a beast I couldn't tell. A quick check of the back door revealed a similar scenario. More herbs, more bells, another doll, another symbol.

Matheson looked at me, and I knew we were not, under any circumstances, going in that station.

"Driscoll, this here shit is witch business. You and I both know it," he said to me, lighting a cigarette. "This is why the Fulcis wanted us to stay out of their affairs, to keep away from their dead. They tend to their dead their own way, just like they said. I say, let them."

The curious part of me wanted to fight about it a little, but I let it go. My attachment to self-preservation got the better of me. I agreed with him. Whatever dwelled within that cursed old television station had been contained. What else could all of that mess mean? The dolls, the flowers, the heavy chains? Even the witches didn't want it let loose upon the world.

As we walked back to the car, I heard a noise behind us. A vigorous, almost panicked scratching, like a possum trapped in an attic, pawing at the trapdoor. Matheson heard it as well, although he pretended not to at first. I grabbed his elbow to stop him, and he turned to regard me angrily. I was afraid, for a moment, he was going to give me five across the eyes. The look softened, then gravitated back to the station. He knew we had to go back there. Just to be sure. Just to know. The scratching gathered in intensity the closer we got to the building. Whatever nasty piece of work confined to that blasphemed collection of dark hallways and musty rooms knew it had gotten our attention. It wanted to be heard. Perhaps more.

We approached cautiously, tracing the disturbance to a series of windows on the western side of the complex. These had been boarded and nailed with an extra level of diligence and garlanded with double the number of talismans as the other doors and windows. Extra effort had been expended here, though for what reason only those responsible would know the answer. When we approached the windows, the scratching abruptly stopped; whatever had been trying to gain our attention now quiet. I got the creepy feeling it was now contemplating us. Trying to figure out why we were there. Maybe, if it scratched long enough, maybe squeaked out a whimper or two, we might find it in our hearts to let it out. Take some air.

I was pretty sure whatever prowled the rooms beyond those timbers and talismans had little need for air anymore. Breath, a beating heart, were now concerns for another time, another life.

Matheson ventured a step toward the window, me close at his heels. Behind the boards something scuttled around, the smacking of wet, bare feet upon concrete. The sheriff pulled his gun from its holster, finger hovering near the trigger. I had left my weapon back in the squad car, in the glovebox. This had probably been for the best, I reckoned. I probably would have only ended up blasting my walnuts off. The closer we got to the window I noticed a tiny sliver of darkness between the boards, just enough to something to peep through, perhaps. And something was peeping. I could feel its eyes crawling over us, and now I did want to run. To get out of here and forget about this night. Maybe even cut out of Black Knot altogether. I had a sister in Little Rock who had been trying to get me to come live with her for years. A much bigger city with lots more opportunity. No goddamn witches. No townsfolk who changed from men into wolves. No corpses who refused to stay still.

Eventually I would join her, but not until many years later, after I had no other choice but to leave or, more precisely, escape. But that's a boy's scout tale for another campfire.

Matheson paused a few feet away from the window, lowering his revolver. "This is Sheriff Gerald Matheson of the Black Knot Police Department. Tell me your name and who did this. Don't be scared. I can get you out if you're hurt. But no sudden moves. If you're armed tell me now. I AM armed, and I've zero reservations about shooting somebody who needs shooting."

I looked at him like he had lost his ever-loving mind. Sensing my discomfort, he turned to me and held up a hand, asking for patience and quiet. He was feeling it out, the thing in the darkness. Not sure why. All I wanted to do was to get out, get away. Whatever it was, I didn't think it would be terribly receptive to good-natured conversation.

There was a weird pause, as if the thing beyond the boards and chains might actually be contemplating Matheson's offer. I could actually feel the hesitation as it were a physical thing, something I could hold cupped in the palm of my hand. Despite my fear I took a step closer, as curious as I was scared. An ungodly stink floated around the window, a sour and sickly smell that made my eyes burn and nostrils pinch-up. I was well acquainted with the stench of all things dead and decaying. Even at that early stage in my career I had dealt with corpses in all states of ruin and decomposition. That this smell bore the odor of death was undeniable, but it was unlike any kind of death smell I had encountered before. It was an old stink, festering. Wounds that had healed, been ripped open, then healed over again and again and again. The faintest whiff of infection and clotted putrefaction, a box of bones and chilly skin covered in earth, buried and meant to be forgotten. The smell went up into my nostrils, straight to the brain, and waited. I reached into the pocket of my jacket and retrieved the bandanna from it, covering my nose. The closer I got to the window, the stronger the smell grew. And I knew then and there the stories were true. Behind those boards and chains something vile, forsaken, awaited.

Then, it made a noise. At first, I wasn't quite sure just what it was. It started very low, muffled, like a nervous chuckling held in check deep within the belly, a hand across the mouth. It started to swell with volume, slowly. Now I wasn't so certain it was laughter, but sobbing. The sobbing soon shifted back into laughter once again, then retreated into sorrow. Then a horrid blending of both, culminating in a sinister, doglike snarl. I hadn't realized, in my reverie, that I had wandered dangerously close to the window, not more than a couple of feet away, until the hand had already grabbed the collar of my shirt and begun dragging me toward its owner. I hadn't even heard the boards snapping, the glass shattering. Behind me

Matheson yelped, and I felt his strong arms encircle my waist, trying to pull me back away from the horror behind the window.

He told me not to look. To keep my eyes closed and dig my heels into the dirt and pull away. But I did look. How could I not have? After all, I had come to see her, and see her I did. To this day I do not regret opening my eyes one bit, even though I still wake up screaming, slicked with sweat, in the earliest hours in the morning, the nightmare of her so fresh in my mind I can still feel the coldness of her skin my cheek, the deadness of her. I have no doubt that one day, it's going to be that same dream that punches the clock on this old ticker of mine. She'll have the last laugh. My last thoughts will be of her. I can only blame myself. Indeed, I had asked for it.

My glimpse into the doorway to hell had been brief. Perhaps that was the Good Lord's way of sparing my poor brain from collapsing into complete insanity. I saw Mariana Fulci, dead as dead could be and yet still living, still moving, still needing. Her face was the shade of freshly dried cement bathed in beams of October moonlight, the eyes wild and staring, smeared with black mascara and splashed of dried blood. The pupils were tiny pinholes of sparkling silver set in puddles of electric green, almost glowing, the orbs of the eyes bulging grotesquely from the sockets of her skull. The luxuriant head of dark hair, once so thick and glossy, now stuck out away from her head in crazy, bestial clumps glued together by pockets of filth and crust. Her mouth a dark and peeling bruise upon the pallor of her face. Then, the awful teeth: yellowed, gleaming and curving over her bottom lip, sharp enough to sink through a man's flesh deep enough to scrape across bone. The fangs of a mountain lion. As she drew me in those eyes locked fast with mine. I could see her neck, white as a swan's, and the sensual swell of her breasts, still beautiful to look at even in her cursed afterlife.

Yes…keep looking at them, gravetender. Keep looking at them. Don't you want to hold them? Kiss them? Suckle them…

And I did. God help me. Although I don't remember it, Matheson would tell me later I had begun to struggle, attempting to free myself from him to go to her. There was a moment of blackness and that horrible, horrible smell, and then a scream. HER scream! I felt her grip upon my shirt loosen, then release entirely. When the fog lifted, I saw the hand of the living dead woman withdrawing between the slats of the window, the gray flesh blistered and oozing red smoke. From one of the occult talismans hanging from the window frame, a cornhusk doll attached to a circlet of tiny silver bells and a spray of charnel thistle bound in baling wire, a scrap of singed corpse flesh clinging to it. Apparently, witch magic doesn't discriminate, even among one's own bloodline.

Now, from within the darkness of the haunted television studio, there were sobs. Crying so pathetic, so lost, I couldn't help but pity the poor beast a little. Imagine the horror of undeath. Nights that never end, alone and hungry and angry. Nothing at all like the seductive, powerful monsters of film. This miserable revenant, their own kinswoman, was proof of the cruelty of the Fulci witches. The extent of that family's sickness, in my eyes, had been doubled. Years later, they would pull another prank out of their Satanic bag of tricks which would make the misfortune of Mariana look like a comedy. Maybe I'll write about that mess the closer I get to cashing in my chips for good. Right now, I choose to enjoy what's left of my waning years in peace.

Somehow Matheson and I found ourselves parked in a stall at the Dairy Duke, each of us holding a drink in a Styrofoam cup, me a cola float and the sheriff a cherry limeade. I didn't remember the drive away from the lonesome ruins of KBLUD, through the wooded arches and roads of Grinning Goblin Forest. I didn't care. I wasn't dead. I was safe right here in the front seat of a cop car holding my float, listening to Carter Melvoin trying to set up a trade between a dude selling a CB radio and a lady offering a sewing machine in return. Matheson slurped his limeade, staring straight ahead at the white picket fence which surrounded the restaurant. We both knew we needed to talk about it. Get it all out there. Neither of us had the energy to start, so we just sat there for a long time, enjoying our drinks and the crisp autumn evening air.

"I reckon we'll find those missing folks in there." Gerald spoke finally. "In the TV studio. I bet that's where she took them after she killed them."

"Unless she ate them." I offered. "There's always that possibility."

Matheson paused, nodded, then returned to his limeade. That was that on the subject.

There would be no more disappearances after that night. At least, not ones we couldn't easily pin down to the creature. Neither the sheriff nor I ever spoke of it again. There was no need to. There was nothing to be done about it, but it did sadden me to allow those innocent deaths to go unresolved. The affair had been officially passed on into the annals of Fulci lore, and there was no record of it ever happening. God help the squeaky wheel who ever attempts to go digging a little too deeply.

Nothing like that ever happened to me again. Not until all of that horrible business with Gerald Matheson's son, Juston, who was the sheriff at that time, happened. The witches, again. It didn't take a whole lot of threatening to convince me it was in my best interest to find another situation. Leave, and be left alone. I did leave, and I don't regret it a bit. I figured I had punched in enough hours on the monster hunter clock, and I was done.

These days, I don't do much except sit around and watch TV. Go on the occasional jaunt to the local coffee shop to shoot the shit with the other codgers. I have a couple of beers in the evening, looking out over a beautiful swell of countryside. My nearest neighbor is five miles away, and my sister passed on three years ago. I don't have much time left, I can feel it. That's all right too.

I cut all ties with Juston Matheson many years ago. I do regret that. He was a good kid, a good lawman. Perhaps a bit too softhearted for his own good. Hopefully he understood my decision, or maybe he just thinks I'm dead and buried in some shallow grave in the hills of Grinning Goblin Forest. No matter to me.

After what happened in Black Knot, that final nasty event, I felt it best to pack up and start fresh somewhere else. Somewhere far away from this town. Far away from monsters, nameless terrors, and most of all, all of them goddamn witches!

TWELVE

Matheson lit the wood-burning stove and put on a pot of coffee, anticipating a long night ahead. There was no food in the cabin pantry other than a big glass jar stuffed with beef jerky, several cans of baked beans, and a couple dozen tins of potted meat. The lawman debated starting the generator, then decided they were too far enough out in the boonies for anyone to hear it and cranked the ancient contraption to life. There was enough gas in it, he reckoned, for a few hours at least. The three of them ate quietly, listlessly. Neither of the kids acted particularly hungry, but Juston had insisted upon them eating a little something. They needed to keep up their strength, he argued, and poor Cora looked like she was on the cusp of fainting if she didn't get something in her belly. After supper Matheson poured everyone a small cup of coffee and they sat together on the dusty wooden floor, their backs to the wall, each thinking their private things.

"What do you think it is?" Hayder spoke up, not addressing anyone in particular.

Matheson blew on his coffee, then ventured a sip. The tiny porcelain cup looked almost comical in his huge, callused hand. "The witches. It has to be. Those tombstones have the Fulci name on em. I can't imagine it's not something to do with them."

"But why now? The Fulcis pretty much own Black Knot." Cora slurped at the cup, her face scrunching up. "Dang, Sheriff, you scrape that coffee of the bottom of a boxcar? Nasty!"

The lawman chuckled. "Man up, kid. It'll put hair on your chest."

Cora set her cup down and ran a pale hand through her hair. "That's what's really scary. If it's the Fulcis then it has to be something big. Something bigger than owning every inch of the earth in the Knot and controlling all the moolah coming in and out of it."

"Hopefully, Roseanna can answer that for us. Or at least give us enough to not feel like we're just stumbling blindly along, waiting for the next horrible thing to happen." Matheson turned to Hayder, leaning in closer to the boy. "I hate to tell you this, buddy, but your momma has something to do with this. Cora feels it. I feel it. I felt something was off right away when I first met her. Before all of the shit hit the fan. I think it's best we stay away from her right now. At least until we have a plan in place."

Hayder choked back tears, firmly setting his jaw. "Me too. She's never been normal since my dad and sister died. I know she's drinking again. She did that a lot before dad died. He fought with mom a lot about it. He told

THE COUNTRY GIRL'S GUIDE TO HEXES AND HAINTS

me she had a strange life before he met her. Didn't tell me what he meant by that, and I never really thought to ask. They acted happy for a while after she stopped drinking. Then Brandy…then…"

"Talk to me about it. My daddy passed on when I was about your age. Never lost a brother or sister, but I know what's it's like for someone of your own blood to be taken away from you too soon."

Hayder asked for another cup of coffee, which Cora fetched for him. He then shared what had happened to his dad and sister. Every little horrible detail. The weird funeral they had had for him, a ceremony attended by a lot of people Hayder had never even heard of, much less met. The cool manner in which his mother had dealt with the fallout afterwards. How she had cut off everyone in dad's family and up and moved them to Black Knot, a town she had lived in for only a brief time as a young girl. Cora laid her head on his shoulder and held his hand as he talked. Matheson said nothing, his face completely neutral. Hayder could almost see the gears and wheels inside the man's skull turning, grinding, trying to make sense of it all.

"Let's get a little shut-eye. I'll stay awake for a couple of hours, then the two of you keep an eye on things while I rest a bit. We got a little less than five hours before daybreak, and I say we be at Roseanna's shop no later than nine. Give her time to get back from wherever freaky places witches are apt to wander off to." The lawman walked across to the cabin to his bedroom, dug around in his closet, and returned with a couple of sleeping bags and an armful of pillows and blankets. "Cora, you take my room. Hayder and I can bunk down in here. Couch has a hide-a-bed in it."

Cora nodded, kissing Hayder's cheek before she headed to Matheson's room. She paused at the door and caught the man's eye. For a second or two he fancied he could hear her voice in his head. Like they were talking without their lips moving. The words collapsed into the void and left behind an aftertaste. The ghostly remnants of a sentiment. She was terrified. Not for herself, but for the boy.

Matheson nodded. He agreed with her.

Mona Hennessey, there would be no denying it, was officially now considered the enemy. From that moment forward, she was one of *them*.

By seven the three of them had breakfasted on bland oatmeal and toast, showered without soap in ice-cold water, and were out the door by eight-thirty. In spite of the grim circumstances it was a remarkably beautiful fall morning. A day where the sun lingers in the sky high enough to keep the heat low but the light plentiful and comforting, the faintest pale gleam of frost glazing over the dead grass and flimsy highway weeds. It was a bit on the blustery side, wraiths of crimson and chocolate leaves swirling playfully across the rugged roads winding through Grinning Goblin Forest, floating gently down from the dying branches of their mother boughs.

It was also Halloween, and to the man and the two children traveling in the old truck, the significance of the day was not lost to them. Now they felt the ancient, primal power of the older than old holiday hanging in the very air like a burial shroud wound about a corpse. Everything felt dangerous. Unsettled. Today, the dead and other things could, and just might, walk.

Matheson took the same back road into Black Knot he had used last night to get out of town. He steered the truck into the lot behind Roseanna's shop, relieved to encounter the Lavera woman's bright pink Volkswagen Beetle in its usual parking spot. He parked next to her and ushered everyone out of the truck, keeping his holster unsnapped and gun within easy reach of his hand, his eyes darting around warily. The sheriff walked up to the back door and knocked, his knuckles sounding alarmingly loud. Receiving no response, he rapped again, receiving the same outcome. He didn't want to admit it in front of the kids, but a cold pit of disquiet had already formed in his gut, and it was a feeling he had come to trust without reservation over the years.

"Guess let's try the front. Didn't want to do that." Matheson sighed, drawing his revolver. He tossed the truck keys to Cora. "Anything happens, you shag ass back to that truck and get out. Go south. Drive and don't stop until you're out of the county limits. Rust River is about an hour away. There's a Holiday Truckstop there right when you pull into town. Can't miss it. You go on inside and ask to speak to Rusty Stevens. He's an old buddy who owes me a favor. Tell him what happened here, but y'all stay away."

"He'll believe us? You sure?" Hayder asked.

Matheson nodded. "Yuh. That old boy has seen some shit in his day. He's a conspiracy buff. Believe me, he'll *want* to believe you. He's a good guy, and he'll know what to do."

The group crept around the side of the building not facing the street, Matheson in the lead. Upon reaching the front door they found it to be locked as well, the same note from the night before taped to the glass. The lawman stared at the note, confused.

"Maybe she forgot to take the sign down," Hayder offered hopefully.

"She'd have the door unlocked. The closed sign turned around. I know this lady. If she's here, she's open for business." Matheson felt his earlier uneasiness return, shivering up his spine like a ripple of frost. He turned to look at Cora, whose face had drained even whiter than normal. Hayder noticed as well.

"Cora?" the boy asked, laying his hand on her shoulder. "Cora, what's the matter?"

The girl shook her head, eyes wide as supper plates. "Something ain't right. A bad thing has happened in there."

"You saying we shouldn't go in?" Matheson asked, scanning for any possible threat.

Cora shook her head again. "No. We HAVE to go in. Just saying something doesn't feel right and we better be ready for it, whatever it is."

Before Matheson could say anything further a sharp, metallic click diverted his attention. The knob of the door turned slightly, just enough to loosen the deadbolt and allow the door to creak open a hair. He turned to look at Cora.

"I told you." She smiled cheerlessly. "Get ready, boss."

The lights didn't work, forcing Matheson to return to the truck to get his service flashlight. Once inside they found the shop deserted. He locked the door behind them, and in single file they crept through the aisles and rounded the corners, looking for the owner of the establishment.

They found Roseanna Lavera in her back office, hanging by her neck from a slender shank of rigging rope, her face having already gone purple and her eyelids, which had thankfully remained closed, blushed black. None of them screamed. Nobody even flinched. It was as if Cora's warning before they entered had prepared them for this. Matheson sank down into a chair, laying his gun in his lap and planting his face between his palms.

"Well, I'd say activate Plan B, but I don't have a Plan B," he chuckled. "Some cop."

Cora laid her hand on his shoulder. "You do now, though. See?"

The lawman uncovered his face and looked up Cora. She was pointing at something in the darkness of the empty store. Something he couldn't see. He stood up, gun in hand, and took a few steps forward. Behind him he heard Hayder gasp. All he could see before him was a thick wall of shadows. There was something funny about those shadows. They were too thick, too much in the world. Like he could grab them in his hand and throw them about his shoulders like a cape. The shadows began to shift, meander about, then bubble and burst. The darkness began to form a shape before him. The outline of a small woman. Although the features were indistinct, Matheson immediately recognized the apparition as being that of Roseanna Lavera. The bold, patrician nose, her signature braid trailing down her back. There was no mistaking it.

Cora stepped forward, imposing herself between the sheriff and the ghost.

"Hey, Rosie. Hate to come a-visiting when you're in such a sad state." The child spoke calmly, casually, as if discussing the weather with a gal pal at the beauty parlor.

The phantom shrugged, throwing up its hands. Matheson noticed the mouth moving, wordlessly. He turned to Cora, who appeared to be listening to something, head nodded in assent, mouth scrunched up thoughtfully.

"Sorry to bug you, but what the hell are you doing?" he asked.

"Shhhh! I'm talking to Rosie." The girl shooed a dismissive hand at him. Cowed, Matheson took a step back and rejoined the boy.

The conversation between the living and the dead went on for several minutes. Cora did most of the listening, responding with one-word answers. The ghost bowed her head and blended back into the shadows. The lights of the shop suddenly snapped on, flooding the room in weak, yellow light. Cora turned to her friends, smiling, her eyes damp.

"Follow me. I know what to do. Rosie is helping us, in her own way."

Cora led them through the labyrinth of junk, curiosities, and petty treasures. The remnants of family secrets, bloodlines, and lost dreams. Radios and board games from every era, taxidermied beasts and bicycles, stringless guitars and dolls with missing limbs. Dresses and hats belonging to women long departed to the grave. Record players missing their needles and CASIO synthesizers with jammed keys. Here and there a genuine treasure. An especially ornate thumb ring, a rare jazz record or a book thought to have been long since forgotten. For several minutes they wandered, Cora pausing to dig around in a specific pile of debris, sighing at coming up empty. They took to the stairs leading up to the loft of shop, where another entire floor of junk awaited for their picking.

At the top of the stairs Cora paused, holding up her hands and closing her eyes. The lawman choked back the urge to talk, stepping back and let her do her thing. The child clapped her hands and giggled, striding across the room to a card table piled chin-high with a heap of ancient audio-visual equipment.

"It's in here." Cora pointed at the table. "Help me, fellas."

Matheson tried not to snap at the little girl. This spooky stuff was starting to overwhelm him. "Help you what?" he said.

"Tell us what it said back there. The ghost," Hayder chimed in. Although he was terrified, the mystery of it all had intrigued him. It felt like an adventure, and it helped ease his concerns for his mother. "What are we looking for?"

Cora slapped her forehead and groaned. "Oh yeah. Y'all couldn't hear what we were talking about. In case you were wondering, the Fulcis did kill her, of course. She says she actually didn't mind. She was eager to leave this world to explore other ones." Cora began pawing through the mountain of old VHS tapes and reel-to reel recorders. "We need to find an old reel of film. It's been buried in this mess of odds and ends for a long time. Years."

"I'll pass on that one. I think I got more than enough movie watchin' done over at the Red Hand, thank you kindly." Hayder shivered at the remembrance.

"No, silly. It's not *that* kind of film. When I was talking to Rosie, it was mostly with my mind, passing pictures back and forth. She showed me an old box marked *Mr. Peters*. Not a cardboard box, but a wooden crate like you'd find behind the grocery store. Like, what they would use to put fruit or juice or something you didn't want to get squished."

"And here it is," Matheson said. He was holding up one end of a dusty leather tarp, a large wooden box with the indicated name stamped with what appeared to have been a stencil with a once-over of black spray paint. Lifting it from its hiding place, surprised by its weight, he carried over to a nearby workbench and set it down. Using his pocketknife he pried the lid off with ease and flung it to the floor. The three of them gathered around the box to inspect its contents.

"So what do we do with this?" Hayder reached into the crate and pulled out a tin cover, presuming to contain a reel of film within. The tin bore a sticker made from yellow painter's tape, peeling at the edges. In black marker the title of the contents had been scrawled in huge, almost child-like box letters.

FROGMAN'S FIELD GUIDE TO THE UNNATURAL PHENOMENA OF LITTLE DIXIE.

Beside the reel was an old battered Big Chief notebook, and beside that a reel-to-reel tape recorder, two circles of tape attached and threaded together to the hubs. Hayder retrieved the notebook from the box and flipped through it. Every single page, front and back, was filled from top to bottom with a surprisingly elegant, almost spidery script. Far too much to read at the moment. He handed it to Matheson, who began to poke around in it. After a few minutes he closed the tablet and grinned.

"I remember this guy. Crazy Morton Peters. He worked at the old TV station out on Sugar Hill. He was what was known as the town character back in the day. Always spouting the most random, ridiculous nonsense." He chuckled. "Although in light of certain events, I'm not too sure how much of it was nonsense now."

"Look!" Hayder exclaimed, pointing.

The specter of Roseanna glided into the room, still clinging to the shadowy corners. She gestured to the box, then lifted a smoky finger to her eyes. Cora approached her, their eyes locking again. Several minutes later the phantom melted back into the shadows, and a feeling pervaded the room indicating the ghost had departed. Upon its departure the shop was suddenly flooded with light; the power returned. Matheson trotted over to the front door and locked it, then returned back to them.

"What was that about?" Hayder asked Cora.

"We have to watch the film, of course."

"That was pretty much a given the second we found this," Matheson said dryly. He looked around the room. "Need a projector, of course. Surely to goodness we can find one that actually works buried in all of this crap."

The three of them set to burrowing through the pile of old phones, stereos and turntables, unearthing two ancient projectors. The first projector came to life when plugged in, but the bulb had burned out. Hayder plugged in the other contraption. At first the projector sputtered, choked on grease and grime, then began to whir steadily, the bulb emitting a soft, yellow glow. Matheson struggled a bit with mounting the reels and threading the tape. He got it working, but feared the machine didn't have a whole lot of time left to it. There was no screen to cast the movie upon, but Cora located an old bedsheet, which was still white and thick enough to serve the purpose.

The children sat cross-legged on the hard floor while the lawman stood, arms across his chest. Nobody wanted to admit they were afraid to watch the film, but they were. Damn near scared out of their skins.

Matheson dimmed the lights, flicked the switch on the projector, and pushed the play button on the tape recorder.

The film lasted just a few minutes shy of half an hour. When it was over, Matheson brought the lights back up and they stood together in silence. They were all thinking the same thing, even though nobody realized it.

"So, where's the rest of it?" Hayder asked. "The film."

"Yuh, clearly there's more." Matheson said.

"Dig around a little bit, maybe?" shrugged Hayder.

"I done looked. That's all the reel-film I could find." Cora groaned. "That was a nice spooky story and all, but not sure what we're supposed to do with it."

"What about that?" Hayder nodded at the tablet in Matheson's hand. The lawman had forgotten he had even been holding it.

"You see how much stuff's in that notebook? Damn near fifty pages, I reckon. A hundred if you consider he wrote on both sides," Matheson commented, holding up the notebook. "Either of you kids read fast?"

Hayder's hand shot up immediately. "I read all three *Master of the Shards* books in a single day. Retained everything. I even won a blue ribbon at the middle-school carnival last year. I read…"

"Congratulations, egghead," the lawman cut him off. He dragged a nearby lawn chair over and pitched the tablet to the boy. "Get to skimming, fast. Find something, anything, that sticks out."

Hayder settled into the chair, opened the tablet, and set his peepers to crawling over the writings. It was slow going. At the beginning there wasn't a lot of cohesion to this Frogman's narrative. Detours left and right and everywhere in between. But over time the journal, for that was what it really was, began to acquire some semblance of structure. Made sense. In fact, it read so smoothly, so professionally, it was difficult to believe its author wasn't someone in the academic field. Thirty minutes went by, then an hour. Matheson was about to take the tablet away when Hayder shrieked happily, jamming his finger hard down upon a page close to the very end.

"What?" Cora said, coming to stand beside him. "I hope that horrible noise that just came out of your mouth means good news."

"Damn right it does, baby." Hayder was clearly very pleased with himself.

"Lay it on us." The lawman slapped the boy's back.

"Right here, Frogman mentions he ran out of film and tape and made another one right after." Hayder pointed at the passage in question.

Matheson groaned, shaking his head. "That's all fine and good, but not a lot of help if we can't find the other reel."

The boy nodded, proudly sticking out his chin. "Guess it's a good thing he says right here where it's at."

"Where? We need to go! Is it far?" Cora squealed.

"The place he worked." Hayder turned to the sheriff. "That TV station you mentioned. It's there."

Matheson scowled. "KBLUD? Hell, that place has been closed up for years. Pretty sure something bad happened there. Something ugly enough to get that place closed down for good. My daddy knew something about it, but I could never get him to talk about it. There were a lot of things that happened when he was in my shoes he didn't like to discuss."

"Now you understand why," Hayder remarked.

After that comment, nobody said anything for a long time.

"I remember watching a neat show that came on really late. Think on a Friday or Saturday. Showed scary movies. Mostly either the old classics or the really crappy ones." Matheson seemed to remember this fondly. After a few seconds, his face went pale.

"What's the matter now?" asked Hayder.

"Maybe it's nothing. I just remember the show had a host. You know one of those hosts who dress up all creepy and make smartass remarks throughout the entire movie." Matheson pulled up his own lawn chair and sank into it. "The host of that show was called Lady Luridia. No…Madame. Madame Luridia."

"Okay? This means what, then?" Cora said.

"Madame Luridia was played by a Fulci lady. Real looker too, like most of the Fulci women." Matheson scratched his chin. "Name of Mary or Louisa or something like that."

"Again, that means what?" Hayder asked.

"It means we need to be careful. Real careful," Cora answered. She nodded at Matheson. "Go on. It say where he stashed the other reel?"

"Yes ma'am. In the control room, under the floor. Says here someone got wise to what he was doing, and he was afraid they would get their hands on it. Stashed it under the station and covered it with some boards he painted to match the rest of the floor."

"Whatever happened to Frogman?" Cora asked the sheriff.

The lawman shrugged. "No idea. One day he was there and the next day he wasn't. You got to understand, Morton Peters wasn't just the town character, but the town lush as well. Those people never stay put for long."

"I think we can all guess what became of him." Hayder shuddered.

"Let's move out, then. Nose around a little more and see if y'all can find some tools. A hatchet or a hammer or, hell, even a knife. Something we can tear that floor up with if there's nothing at the studio." Matheson directed the children, each of them, scattering into different parts of the shop. Matheson turned up a couple of screwdrivers, their heads ground down to flat points. He pocketed them anyway and moved on. Cora found an old hacksaw, rusted into uselessness. Hayder, however, had located an old fireman's axe. The wooden handle on it had been almost chewed to death by termites, and the head of the instrument, although looking plenty sharp, wobbled dangerously. He handed it over to Matheson, who put his hand to his temples as if his brain ached.

"You see, I knew I should have brought the squad car. There was plenty of stuff in the trunk we could have used, and I wouldn't be standing here, looking at this damn near useless piece of crap." Matheson sighed. "Pack up the projector and the recorder thingamajig. We won't be coming back here if we find that other reel. We'll scat back to the cabin."

"I'm with the big guy. I don't think this place will be safe much longer." Cora lifted the recorder while Matheson hefted the projector.

The three of them took the back exit this time, Matheson not bothering to lock the door behind him. What was the point? The owner of the shop wouldn't be returning, ever. Roseanna's Swap Shop was officially closed for business, right then and there, and would remain so until every brick, every beam, crumbled to the earth.

THIRTEEN

Nobody could remember why, or even when, that lonesome swell of earth had been given the name of Sugar Hill.

Truth be told, few rarely gave the matter much thought. Even the oldest living denizen of Black Knot, one Mr. Gunther Giacomo, didn't have any insight into the matter. It had been named such since before his time, and none of the moldy books at the Historical Society bore any mention of it at all. The name certainly did not jive with what you saw. There was nothing particularly sweet about the exhausted collection of mounds and heaps. What few trees bothered to grow there seemed to always be in the throes of some sort of withering affliction, slouched like old men shouldering heavy burdens upon their frail shoulders with shriveled, craven boughs. The leaves upon these trees struggled, year-round, to blossom, eager to shrug, detach, and drift down to be devoured by the dirt when autumn came to call. No men bothered to hunt for game. No church ever held a Sunday school picnic there. Nobody came to enjoy the peace of nature, for there was none to be found. It was a quiet enough place for meditation and reflection, but it was possessed of an eerie, off-putting stillness. A silence which made one feel as if something savage and hungry were keeping an eye on them, breath held, ready to pounce.

It was the perfect place for the old television studio, especially now, in its current derelict splendor.

"Jesus Henry Christ!" Hayder said under his breath, his eyes soaking in the uninviting assemblage of sagging, ramshackle buildings. "I'm not so sure that's gonna be safe to go nosing around in there. Roof's liable to fall right down on us, and I'll bet the floor ain't so hot either."

"I agree. I still can't believe nobody has torn the old girl down, even after all these years." Matheson popped a smoke into the corner of his mouth but didn't light it. "Honestly, it's in pretty decent shape when you consider it's been left alone for over a decade. See those doors and windows? Nailed up tight. Even got chains and whatnot over the boards. Whoever did that wanted to make sure snoopers and hobos couldn't get in."

"Or get out," Cora muttered. Nobody heard her, and she was glad for it. She wasn't certain why she said that, or even thought it. It just popped into her brain, and she didn't care for it one bit.

"Check it out. Some of the boards look newer than the others. See here?" Hayder jogged over to a window and pointed at it. The other two approached to peruse the slats of wood. Indeed, several of the planks appeared to have nailed recently, their color and texture still warm and smooth. The three of them wandered around the perimeter of the studio, finding more boards in a similar state, as well as several new-looking shanks of chain. There were other things too which nobody could explain. Funny little trinkets, mostly corn-dollies and bound clutches of dried herbs and silver charms, had been strung, draped, and nailed to the boards and window frames. Some appeared to be very old, coated with rust and weathered from the elements. However, among the old talismans, here and there, a newer bauble gleamed and beckoned. Obviously, someone was taking some care to restrict the building from trespass. They returned to the front of the structure, perplexed. Although the front doors were light on boards and chains, they were extra thick with the dolls and charms.

Hayder stared one particularly ornate corn dollie, his hand reaching out for it. He couldn't help himself.

"Don't touch that!" Cora stepped forward and, not ungently, slapped his hand away. Hayder looked at her with a mixture of resentment and fright. Cora softened and took his hand in her own, rubbing the back of it tenderly. "Sorry to have done that. But, good grief, can't you boys feel it? I mean *feel* it. Those boards, those weird little poppets and dangly metal things, whoever did all that had a reason to put them there. They weren't just hoping to keep out winos and kids looking for a quiet place to make out. There's more to it than that. A whole lot more, I imagine."

The two males paused, each appearing to withdraw to their individual thoughts. Matheson was the first to nod.

"She's right. This setup here, it's not normal. Something's off. These here trinkets are like locks. Not the metal kind, but locks anyway." He pulled at one of the boards as if to test its sturdiness. "Someone's gone to an awful lot of trouble to make sure nothing goes in or out of this building."

"You think something is in there, then?" Hayder shuddered. His head began to swim with a million images of terrible, arcane terrors.

"Oh yeah. Don't you doubt it for a second, boyo. Not sure what it is, but I got a pretty solid guesstimation of who might have slapped those boards and chains across those windows. I know if I were to take one of those charms, or whatever the hell they are, home, and stick it underneath my pillow tonight, it would give me bad dreams. Maybe make me wreck my truck on the way home. Give me nut cancer in six months."

The two children shared a glance, then looked at the sheriff. Yes, they knew damn well who he was talking about.

Cora stepped forward and laid her hands across one of the boards, giving it a firm yank, then another. Several tugs later the board relented and fell to the grass. Another followed, then another, until all of the slats lay at her feet, splintered and powerless. Taking up one of the wooden slats, the girl used it to swat away the bewitched ornaments dangling from the doorknob. Last of all, the chains, with no boards or witch gizmos left to hold them fast, collapsed to the earth with an ineffectual jangling, the reek of brimstone and roses filling the air. Matheson stepped forward and laid his fingertips upon the door and pushed. The portal, although corroded with dust and disuse, yielded easily to his touch, swinging inward with a shrill, mournful creak.

"Hayder, go get my flashlight from the truck," the sheriff ordered the boy. "Make it fast. I got a feeling we better get in and out of there before the sun goes down." Hayder nodded, trotting down the hill toward the truck. Matheson checked his revolver. Four in the chamber and two in his pocket. Probably not enough, even if whatever awaited them within the ruins of KBLUD could be tamed with hot lead.

"Maybe we should pray," Cora suggested. Matheson looked down at her. He didn't like admitting it to himself, but the kid was looking rough. Worn down. Poor thing should have been at home, still in bed, mending herself. She still wasn't healed up nearly enough to handle regular kid things, much less this horror show.

"How about you pray for me?" Matheson shrugged without a bit of embarrassment. "Myself, I've never believed in that sort of thing."

"Me neither, but I think something is out there right now. Listening. It wants to help us. It talked to me in the Red Hand when that thing that used to be Crystal was a-chasing me." Cora took his hand in hers, and he flinched at the chill of the child's flesh. "Let's just throw out something, anything, and maybe something will hear it."

"It can't hurt, I suppose." The lawman sighed, removing his Stetson.

"What can't hurt?" asked Hayder, the big flashlight held in both hands. He handed it to Matheson, who set it down on the grass.

"Y'all, we're gonna pray. Each of us. Quietly," Cora explained. "I don't have to know who you're asking for favors. But when you do it, say it like you mean it. Like you believe in magic. Like you believe in Good versus Evil and knights in silver armor slaying the evil witch in the woods. Like you can draw power down from the sky, ball up your fist, and hurl a bolt of lightning down upon your enemies. Like the blood of a hundred devils flows through your veins."

The man and the boy stared at the girl. The words coming out of Cora Corbucci's mouth, for just a few seconds, had not been her own. Not at all the voice they were accustomed to, but the voice of someone far older, far wiser, and, most unnerving of all, barely human. Her eyes were rolled back to the whites, glazed over, tears trickling from their corners. A heavy sigh gusted from her mouth, her chest rising then plunging down. The whites rolled back to brown, and she placed her hands upon the side of her head, shaking it as if to shrug off the remnants of a strange dream.

"What?" she asked. They were both gawking at her.

Above them a peal of thunder boomed, rattling the earth beneath them like the footfall from a massive, lumbering beast. A drop of cold wet splattered across the lawman's face. Behind it followed another, then a dozen, then came the downpour. In under a minute each of them was soaked down to their skins.

It didn't matter. They gathered together, huddled in, the rain coming down in massive, blurry sheets, hands joined. Each of them prayed, invoking the power of whatever might be listening.

"You feel that?" Hayder breathed, his voice tinged with disbelief. "Holy moly."

"I did." Matheson squeezed their hands. He suddenly felt like he was ten foot tall and bulletproof. Like he might not even need his gun.

Cora giggled. Hayder thought it was the most beautiful sound he had ever heard.

"Amen," the girl whispered, letting her chin fall upon her chest, then lifting up her head. She looked upon each of her soldiers, favoring them with a benevolent smile. The sorceress to her warriors. Her eyes glimmered in the waning daylight like silver dollars. Each nodded back at her, almost reverently. Yes, they would follow her anywhere.

Their hands still linked, the three passed beyond the threshold of the cursed place, walking headfirst into an unknowable darkness.

Matheson led the way, gun drawn. Following him was Cora, holding the flashlight with one hand curled around the crook of his arm, with Hayder bringing up the rear. What little outside light lingered was beginning to fade very quickly, but was still strong enough to peek in courtesy of a random board, here and there, which had slipped away from the window. Yet even this light was weak, struggling, as if afraid to interfere. It was better than nothing, and they were thankful for it.

The first room they walked into appeared to be some kind of lobby. There were a few prehistoric love seats with their leather cushions shredded by the teeth of rats, the consequences of time and settling dust, and good old-fashioned decay. An end table standing on crooked legs crammed between two of the loveseats, stacked with magazines, some of which bore dates from many years earlier and several web-covered coffee mugs. On one of the tables was an ashtray, probably homemade, shaped like a mermaid, the ashes meant to be tipped into a dip in the ceramic where her belly was, a half-smoked cigarette lodged in one of the grooves dented along the sides. Hayder was surprised at how small the room was, only slighter larger than his own bedroom. Every inch of the room was hooded beneath a quilt of phosphorescent gray dust and draped in a shawl of cobwebs, some of the strands as thick as one of Matheson's wrists. Across the room an archway awaited to their right, leading to a corridor burrowing into a deeper darkness. A darkness they would have to enter.

"I got to come up here with my pa a handful of times when I was a squirt. He was drinking buddies with some of the guys who worked here. It's not a complicated setup." Matheson whispered his words. his voice sounding loud as shattering glass in the quiet shadows. "We take yonder hallway, and it will be just a bit of a walk. We'll soon come to two doors, one at the end of the hallway and another on either the left or right. I can't rightly remember. One at the end empties out into the studio where they did all their filming and whatnot. The other is the control room. The entrance to the basement is in the studio. I got to go down there a few times. It had a darkroom in it. You know, for developing photographs and such."

"What we need is in there," Cora stated matter of fact. She looked up at him, eyebrows raised. "I can tell."

Matheson didn't ask how she knew this. After all, this kid, just a couple of hours earlier, had held a coherent conversation with a dead woman. He thought it prudent to not question a single word from her. "I can't think of any other place they would be keeping what we're looking for. It's dry and cool down there. Away from all the dampness up here, hopefully."

"How do we reach the basement? A lot of basements have an outside way to get in too, you know," Hayder said.

"It's on the other side of the studio in a janitor's closet. It's just a trap door you open up with one of them ladder stairs going down into it," Matheson said. He laid his hand on the boy's shoulder. "Sorry, bud. No such luck. Lot of places like this got so much pricey hardware stacked in their basements, it just doesn't make good business sense to have another way to get in."

"Better put a lid on all this jawing and get to moving. Ain't a lot of light left, and I bet when this place gets dark it's some serious dark. So dark not even a flashlight can cut it," Cora whispered, the unease in her voice palpable.

The group took to the hallway, Matheson having to click on the flashlight to guide the way. Along the walls were hundreds of framed photographs, old postcards, and various souvenirs from hazy seasons of showbiz past. Disc jockeys and cowboys and businessmen and actresses and writers and cameramen, each of them looking like nothing special, like a person everyone in the world has known. The pale and faded faces leered down at them, and in the swirling gloom of the hall appeared to be floating through the shadows like sleepy ghosts. The eyes in those faces seemed to be watching them, observing these gatecrashers, vigilant for any shenanigans. As they walked along, Hayder swore he heard them whispering. He would glance up at one of them, and before his very eyes the expression on a single photograph would change ever so slightly. A dour frown would shift into a crooked, lecherous grin matched with a flirty wink. The boy would close his eyes and shake his head, open his eyes again and the picture would have reverted back to its original state. Just like a trick painting you would find hanging in the chintzy spook house of a traveling carnival.

"I see it too, Hayder," Matheson said. "We're being watched, I think."

"Of course we are," Cora commented flatly. "This is magic going on right here. Real magic can do all kinds of bad stuff to your brain. Turn it to mush. Make you see and hear things that might not, or might, be there. Hurt somebody and maybe even kill them."

"Whatever it is, it's trying to keep us away. Scare us off." Hayder shivered.

Cora turned to the boy, a curious expression in her eyes. "No, whatever lives here *wants* us here. It wants us here *a lot*. It's drawing us in. I don't think it has anything to do with what we came here for. It has another reason."

"Either way, I don't think this is good news." Hayder shivered. The corridor had taken on a sudden chill, like they'd just strolled into the walk-in freezer of a butcher's shop.

As they continued down the hallway Hayder began humming to himself as a distraction, and Matheson found the weight of their stare so unnerving he stumbled over his own feet more than once. Cora had now moved to the front of the group, her eyes frozen into a determined, almost obsessed stare. She snatched the flashlight away from the sheriff and held it brandished out before her like a holy effigy. An aura of power, of strange majesty, radiated out from the child. Unconsciously, the other two slowed their steps, giving her room. The sense that something big was about to happen filled their legs with cold concrete and hastened their pulses.

The hallway seemed to go on without end. One foot stretched out to fifty. A minute turned into half an hour. The walls would close in, widen, and then retract again, like the throat of an enormous snake swallowing a rat. When they reached the end of the corridor it was a sudden, startling termination. As if the room simply materialized from the musty ether. The three were now standing in the entryway of the KBLUD studio.

The chamber was bewilderingly generous in size for a television station in a pissant town like Black Knot. The room was dressed in scenery indicating it had served as the setting for a horror broadcast. The floor was coated in a flimsy spool of green carpet, a heavy shell of dust all but smothering out the color, making it look more like sand than grass. Several gnarled trees, clearly cobbled together from baling wire, balsa wood, and papier-mâché, loomed menacingly over a small graveyard of Styrofoam tombstones and particle board mausoleums and crypts. Everything had been spray-painted a flat gray to mimic a façade of weathered stone, but the artist responsible had made a slapdash job of it. Several gaps had been overlooked, a peek of bare wood here, an exposed chunk of Styrofoam there. Somehow, this shabby presentation served to instill a deeper sense of unease in them. There was something macabre in the shadow cast of the phony grave markers and bargain-basement crypts upon the sprawl of pale dust. It felt more real than any genuine cemetery could have. More conducive to the needs of the unhappy dead. A room where things might just die and not stay that way for long. A few old cameras remained, still attached to their tripods with long tendrils of grimy cobweb and scraps of fuzz flowing to the floor like the hair of a shriveled crone. Upon the back wall a large casket had been propped up. At least, this was what it appeared to be. This too had been patched together from the spare parts of various unwanted things: one side a sheet of corroded tin swiped from a shed, the other side wood from an ancient barn, perhaps. The lid was the corroded door of an old refrigerator. Overall, it looked like a sarcophagus for a scrapyard mummy lifted from a frame in a grade-Z terror flick.

"Lordy, I remember what this used to be. This whole setup," Matheson marveled quietly. "I used to watch this show when I was a boy. My mom, man, she hated the hell out of it."

"What was it?" asked Hayder. "Why did she hate it?"

"*Madame Luridia's Plenty Scary Movie*." The lawman grinned, seeming to recall the memory with a great deal of affection. "To tell you the truth, it wasn't really all that scary. Corny more than anything else. Mostly old movies from the 30s and 40s. Stuff that wouldn't raise a single hair on the back of y'uns' arms. But back then, before all these movies come along with all their blood and guts and zombies and tits, it could put a good spook in a kid with a wild imagination. As to why my momma hated it. She…"

"She didn't like that show because it scared him too much," Cora interrupted. "He would stay up all night, and when he finally did fall asleep, he would have dreams so awful they would make him pee his bed. Soak it clean down to the mattress. He'd get a whuppin' too. It was the only time his momma would whup him, and she HATED whuppin' him."

Hayder looked at her incredulously, then turned to Matheson. The sheriff chuckled and shook his head. "She's right. I won't ask how she knows it, and I don't much care to know. Let's just hope that perception, or whatever it is, comes into play should our luck go south in here."

Cora suddenly shrieked, deftly leaping backward to rejoin the group. She gestured toward something revealed in the wide beam of her flashlight. The three of them followed her trembling finger, saw what she was pointing at, and breathed out a collective gasp.

"Well…goddamn." Matheson scowled.

The heap of bones was easy to miss if you didn't have a good source of light, and even then, one could have simply mistaken the macabre pile as theatrical props. But these bones, even to an untrained eye, were clearly not theatrical knick-knacks or abandoned decorations from a Halloween party concluded decades earlier. The grime adhering to the bumpy surfaces of the yellowed bones, the tufts of hair clinging to the skulls, the unpolished flatness of their color. The lawman had seen enough dead things in his day to confirm the remains were a mixture of human and animal, with far more of the former than the latter.

"I count at least eight people skulls." Hayder's voice quivered. He glanced up at the sheriff. "Those smaller ones…those…those are kid ones?"

Matheson nodded, unspeaking.

Hayder whimpered, his breath looping in and out of his nose and mouth rapidly. He began to step backward, shaking his head. Sensing his fear about to overflow into outright panic, Cora dashed over to him and threw her arms around his neck, whispering words of comfort in his ear. After a few minutes, the boy appeared to settle down, his brows relaxed and breathing normal again. He even chuckled and playfully frogged her arm.

"Sorry, guys."

"Don't be sorry. I'm scared shitless. I won't lie about that," Matheson said. "I just hope whatever did this is gone from this world now. Maybe it ate enough, got full, and moved on to sweeter hunting ground. If it were still here, I think it would have made an appearance by now. Our bones would already be piled on top of those bones." The lawman tried to say this with as much confidence as he could muster, and it seemed to mollify the kids a bit. In private, he didn't believe this. Not at all. But there was no sense in getting the youngsters stirred up. A pair of frightened, skittish children was the last thing he needed to deal with.

"I think I see where we need to be. At least, that's what I'm guessing." Hayder took the flashlight from Cora and shined it on a small alcove off to the right of the coffin. He trained the light on a spot upon the floor. A large trapdoor set into the floor was revealed, a coil of sturdy chains mounded on top of it. He looked up at Matheson.

"I think you're right," the lawman said. "Let's get down there, find what we came for and get the hell out of Dodge before any desperados show up. Everyone behind me, single file. Just like when we were coming in."

Walking across the studio floor over to the trapdoor was a nerve-wracking affair. Hayder kept waiting for a clawed hand, covered in thick black fur, to burst from the fake burial ground and curl its craving fingers around his ankle, Cora kept thinking she saw the shadows huddled in the darker corners of the room moving, an odd odor drifting about the room. She stopped in her tracks and tilted her head up and back, inhaling. Matheson cut a look back at her and nodded.

"Yeah. I smell it too."

"What? Everything in here just smells like rat shit and old things to me." Hayder inhaled deeply, considered the smell in his mouth, then shook his head again. "Yah…nothing."

"I can't describe it. It just smells…different. Like something I've smelled before and somehow not." Matheson shrugged.

"It doesn't really stink, but it's not something I'd like to sit around and breathe in and out all day long either. It just smells…off." Cora pondered. "It smells like…some kind of medicine. Or cleaner. Something you would use to keep food from going bad that didn't work all the way. A covering-up smell."

"Now that you mention it, it kind of reminds of the way the root cellar at my house smelled when I was a boy. Damp, kinda sour," Matheson said. "I remember one time a bunch of the pickles my mom had canned had spoiled because the lids on the jars hadn't been screwed on tight enough. The whole cellar had smelled like vinegar and garlic and moldy cucumbers for weeks. Not really a stink, just real pungent. A smell you can't just wash off with soap and water."

Nobody had anything else to offer, and for a few minutes the room became very, very quiet. The three of them proceeded toward the trapdoor without further fanfare. The door in the floor was much bigger and the chain barring it thicker and more imposing when looked at closely.

"That's a big shank of chain there," Hayder observed. "Padlock's gonna need a key."

"Probably on a peg over in the control room, I bet," Cora added.

"No time for that. I got a key right here. Y'all get back." Matheson aimed the revolver at the spot in the chain where a link met the padlock and squeezed the trigger. The blast roared like a cannon set off in a walk-in freezer, leaving them all with ringing ears and fuzzy heads. The padlock had been thrown across the room from the impact of the bullet, the chain ruined. Cora winced and grabbed at her ears. But Hayder was looking around the room, eyes stretched wide open and unblinking, like a barn owl detecting the passage of a field mouse in the dry grass below it.

"You guys hear that?" he asked.

Matheson regarded the boy curiously. The kid was dead serious and scared colorless. The sort of scare a sane person rarely stumbled across.

"What did you hear?" asked Cora. She was loath to admit it, but she thought she had heard something as well when the initial roar of the gun had subsided.

Hayder paused, opened his mouth, and then quickly clapped his lips together. "Nah, it was nothing, I think. That bang was so loud, probably just my head playing tricks on my ears."

"It was a laugh, wasn't it?" Cora pressed. "You heard something laughing."

Hayder gasped. "How did you know that?"

"I heard it too." The girl's voice dropped to a low whisper. "It *was* something laughing. A lady, I think. It wasn't real deep sounding like a man, and not little enough to be a kid. It only lasted for a second, but I know I heard it. I *know.*"

Matheson picked up the pile of metal links and tossed them to the side. "Look, I'm not saying you what you two actually heard was what you think it was, but just in case it was, we need to light a fire under this here field trip. If something is in here, watching us, playing with us, we need to get gone before it turns full dark." He grabbed the iron rung on the trap door and tugged. The wooden square refused to budge. The lawman hunkered down, lay both hands upon the rung and heaved with every ounce of muscle he could muster. Now the door shifted ever so slightly in its frame, coming loose with a few extra hard heaves, and lifted away without any further trouble. A cold explosion of stale air gusted forth and sucked all of the breath from the lawman's lungs. The two children instinctively backed away as the man struggled to catch his breath.

"I think that door has been shut for a really, really, really long time," Cora remarked. "Probably for a very good reason."

"You think?" Matheson grimaced, attempting to laugh, but he only came up with a dry hack in his throat. "Hand me that light, would you?" Holding out his hand, Cora dutifully returned the flashlight to him. He shined the light into the hole in the floor, illuminating a metal utility ladder leading down. It wasn't a terribly steep climb, maybe ten feet at the most. Matheson could see the stone floor of the basement. He hoped the basement wasn't anything like Roseanna Lavera's shop, with junk haphazardly stacked, shoved, and buried under more layers of junk. They didn't have the time to rummage around through a ton of useless crap.

The sheriff took to the ladder first, his gun holstered and the flashlight in his free hand. Cora followed, then Hayder. Once on the floor Matheson swung the flashlight left to right, giving the room a cursory once-over. Nothing too horrible other than stacks upon stacks of mostly unusable nothings. Old ledgers in thick metal binders crammed between ancient tape recorders and empty film reels and moth-eaten costumes. There were hundreds of the fake tombstones down here and about a million buckets of long-dried paint, some of it stacked up eye-level with the lawman. Tons of old lamps and rolls of tatty carpet. It made the zigzagging corridors and overburdened crannies of Roseanna's shop look like an illustration of order and efficiency, and it made the sheriff's heart sink down into his stomach.

"Yup, what I thought. A wild goose chase about to commence." Matheson turned to Cora and found she was no longer standing beside him. Hearing footsteps to his right, he shined the beam in that direction and saw Cora ambling down the aisle closest to them, her gait sure and measured, in no hurry whatsoever. The sheriff motioned to Hayder, and they followed after the girl, giving her ample room to let whatever invisible conductor was guiding her do their job. She continued down the aisle, hung a hard right, and then helped herself to another hard right. Matheson looked over his shoulder and tried to ignore the twitch of panic in his gut. The ladder seemed like it was a hundred miles away from them, and there didn't appear to be any other way out of the basement. They got stuck in here, they were done for, pure and simple.

The girl stopped and knelt before an old ping-pong table draped with a thick plastic tarp, set up on a pair of wobbly sawhorses. She lifted the tarp and crawled under the table, only the backs of her sneakers visible. There was a series of clacks and shuffles, a rough spell of coughing, then Cora came crawling backward out of the gap, pulling a large suitcase along with her. The luggage was made of rat-nibbled brown leather and dotted with stickers of peace signs and huge psychedelic flowers. She stood up and struggled to lift the suitcase, barely able to budge it an inch.

"Let me get that," Matheson offered, walking over to her and reaching down to grasp the handle of the case. For a moment, their eyes connected, and, for a split frame of time, the lawman realized he was staring into the eyes of someone else. Cora Corbucci's body was there, but another person had somehow crawled into her flesh, into her blood, and wormed their way up into her head, regarding him with a new set of eyeballs. These eyes regarded him with a mixture of amusement and maybe the tiniest twinge of contempt.

"Who *are* you?" he whispered, stepping back.

Cora's brows furrowed, then smoothed. She was now herself again. Eyes the same chocolate brown as before. No amusement. No contempt. Just a concerned curiosity.

"What's the matter, Sheriff? You look like a rat just crawled across your grave."

The lawman, shrugged. "Nothing. The light down here is so dim I thought I saw something, is all. Let's get."

"You don't have to lie, Juston. I'm not alone in here, and I think we all know that. Something is inside of me." The child reached out and took his hand. "Whatever it is, it's helping us, right? Nothing to be afraid of. It's something that I picked up when I was dead, and when they brought me back I think it decided to hang on awhile."

Matheson simply nodded, not wanting to pursue the conversation. He set the suitcase down on its side, carefully, and opened it. Within was the prize they had come looking for. Here it was. It was real, and it belonged to them now. Another Big Chief tablet, a single reel of film, and an audio spool tied up in a stained handkerchief. But there was something else. An extra treasure. The lawman reached into the container and removed the relic, spreading it out across the length of the suitcase. He poked at it a little, then reached down and unfolded it, holding it up for them all to look at. Delicate black lace and a flowing skirt. It was a dress, a very old one, and looked to have belonged to either a child or a very small grown-up.

"What the hell?" the man muttered. Cora reached over and relieved him of the garment. She held it up across her chest and smoothed it, almost lovingly. The dress was small enough to fit her perfectly. She looked into the sheriff's eyes, holding them. There it was again, that look. He hurriedly turned away and resumed his rummaging around into the suitcase.

"We best put this back," Cora said, folding the garment and laying it gingerly into the suitcase.

The sheriff picked up the tablet and opened it, fanning through a few pages. No doubt about it, same handwriting. The words of the Frogman. He flipped another page and found himself sinking back into the story.

"We can read that back at your place. Let's go." Hayder slapped the man's shoulder. The sheriff nodded and replaced the tablet, closing the suitcase and latching it. Once again in single file, the three of them headed toward the basement ladder. The suitcase was amazingly heavy. The lawman wondered if he would be able to lug back up the ladder by himself. Once he started up the ladder, this turned out to not be the case. He simply took his time, one rung at a time, until he reached the opening to the trapdoor.

Matheson poked his head through the opening and looked around. Or tried to, anyway. The studio was consumed by full darkness now, the only illumination being the tiniest slivers of orange harvest moonlight filtering through the gaps in the boards. In spite of their best efforts they had ended spending too much time underground, and now the darkness felt much fiercer and foreboding. Like the thickened shadows had transformed into something flesh and bone that could reach out and touch them. Maybe more.

"We gotta move, guys. Now," Matheson ordered.

"What's wrong?" asked Hayder.

"It's dark as heck now, that's what," Cora snapped. "Move your butts!"

The three quickly scrambled up the ladder, Matheson emerging first with revolver in one hand and the suitcase in the other. Cora came next and offered him the flashlight, which he gently pushed back to her.

"You hold on to it. I need to keep this gun ready. Let's take it slow. It ain't that far back to the truck, but we need to not trip over something and break our necks."

Arms linked, the trio took a collective step forward, the floor creaking beneath their tread like a snap of spring thunder. Matheson suddenly stopped cold, causing everyone behind him to trip upon the heels of the person in front of them. The hollow clicking of the revolver's hammer being drawn back disturbed the quiet of the dark room. All of them then heard what had made the sheriff of Black Knot hold up and ready his weapon. The creaking of metal hinges, their screws rusted and wanting, then a door slowly grinding open. They knew exactly where the sound was coming from. It was obvious, and none of them tried to convince themselves they hadn't heard it because it happened again, then again. A series of metallic groans and squeaks culminating in a flat, jarring thud. Then, the dank squelching of what could only have been the tramping of bare feet upon the smooth, dusty stone floor. Labored, clumsy, as if the legs attached to those feet were struggling to walk, learning to move themselves again after a long and crippling slumber. It was impossible to tell where they were at any given moment. For a second they seemed to be drawing closer, then were heard tiptoeing around on one side of the room, then skittering over to the other side in less than the time it took for them to draw a breath.

"Cora, you shine that light of yours just a little bit to the right now. Take your time. Go easy," Matheson said.

"Y—you mean on that c-coffin?" the girl quivered.

"Please don't call it that," Hayder whined. "It's just a nasty old icebox someone made up to look like that for a movie or something. Probably nothing in it but a moldy sammich and some gross veggies."

"No matter what it is, I want that light on it. You kids stick real close together now, and keep those hands linked up tight. Don't let go for nothing if you can help it. Cora, you get ahold of my belt there and hang on tight." The lawman slowly eased his gun over in the direction of the coffin-thing, waiting for Cora's light to guide his aim. The flashlight's yellow beam swerved and stopped upon the improvised crypt. The door had been flung wide open, barely hanging upon a ruined hinge. Much to their surprise the sarcophagus, for the most part, was empty. Its smooth plastic walls were tarnished from what had more than likely once been eggshell white to a bruised brownish yellow. Collected at the base of the compartment were scraps of shredded cloth, bundled-up branches and run-of-the mill filth commonly found in an abandoned building. It looked no more menacing than an old refrigerator tossed away to rot in the town dump. This certainly didn't look like a box meant for the sheltering of dead things.

"That was closed up before. I know it. I saw it," Hayder whispered.

"I heard it open. All of us did, even if we don't want to admit it," Cora said. "Something opened it and got out. I heard it walking. Didn't you all hear that too?"

Matheson didn't say anything. It was true, the door *had* been closed and he *had* heard it swing open. He knew that with one hundred percent certainty. And those sounds, he had not imagined them. Footsteps for sure, and not an animal either, but something closer to a person. Behind him he felt Cora's fingers slip under his belt and squeeze tightly around the leather strap. The lawman took a hesitant step forward, keeping his eye on the beam from the flashlight, then ventured a second step. The children followed suit, each of them matching him step for step as if they were practicing some sort of weird, shuffling dance routine. Eventually they reached the center of the room, a bone-gnawing cold enveloping them as well as the sour, medicinal stink from when they had first entered the studio, now much stronger than before. Matheson turned to say something but stopped short before he could get a word out.

There was someone else in the room with them now. He could feel it.

Then, he heard it.

It was a woman, or a girl. He wasn't sure which. The voice was small, delicate, and pretty as crystal wind chimes stirred by a soothing summer draft. It seemed to be coming from everywhere, and Matheson couldn't make out any distinct words. Just rambling. Mumbling. He set the suitcase on the floor and put his hand out behind him to put the brakes on the train.

"What is that? Is that...someone talking?" Cora laid her head on the man's back, her voice quivering. "Oh God, it is. It is. I can hear it."

"Good, you hear it too." Matheson wasn't sure if he was relieved by this revelation.

"So do I," added Hayder. "It's a lady. I'm sure of it."

"Well, this at least proves we all can't be crazy at the same time," Matheson said, picking up the suitcase. "Just keep at it. Slow, now. Heel-toe it. The way out is just up ahead."

As if in response the muttering gained in clarity. The voice grew stronger, louder, closer. They could make out individual words now, one at a time, until those words began to form, congeal, and fuse together into coherent sentences. Indeed, it was a woman. She seemed to be having a very heated conversation with herself, and something about the way she was speaking, what she was saying, indicated to them this woman was truly, deeply insane.

"*The fake blood, it always bugged me so. The taste was revolting. Like cough medicine.*" The tone, the inflection of the words sounded peculiar. The woman was speaking as if English were not her native tongue, boasting a thick, syrupy accent. "*I told you, Jerry, all I need is a decent script. The right script.*

Something I can sink my teeth into. I could be as big as Bette Davis! Why can't you see it? Why don't you DO SOMETHING?"

Matheson felt a wave of terror surge through him. He understood and accepted, without question, that they were listening to the former occupant of the box, now set free. Whatever it was, it was going to go from confused to unpleasant very quickly if they didn't get out now.

"Haul ass, kiddos. Move!" he hissed. "Hang on tight and run! Run!"

There was a whoosh of icy air, that insidious dank stench hammering them like a brick wall. A lonesome wailing sliced the darkness, the terrifying screech of something in the throes of unimaginable anguish, compelled by devils of wrath. A lost soul diverted from the doors of salvation into its own personal pocket of damnation. Beneath all of these layers of monstrosity slithered a pervasive aura of sadness. A lamentation of needs and dreams never to be tended to again, buried in the madness of sorcery gone wrong. Matheson, for the first time in his life, felt the cold teeth of true horror bite deeply into the very marrow of his psyche. For a moment he totally forgot where he was, who he was, and what he was doing. By the time he had recovered it was already upon them, eyes blazing crimson against green flesh and lupine teeth bared, confessing to an unholy hunger.

Not only was this woman insane, but she was also very, very dead.

Before the lawman could react, a white hand flashed, a swift blur against the watery beam of Cora's flashlight, the nails upon each finger slashing the tender flesh of his cheek like a handful of straight razors. Matheson felt his feet leave the floor, his body lifted and flipped ass over head until he thudded flat on his back like a gunny sack full of flour, the breath kicked out of his lungs. Cora shrieked at the walking spook show stepping into the light, leaping backward to collide with Hayder.

It was obvious the woman, if that were what you could call it, had once been beautiful. If one looked closely, they could see it still, buried deeply within the blasphemed, infernal husk. Dark hair tumbled from a high widow's peak down across shoulders the color of spoiled milk in snarled, viscid thickets. You could tell her skin, now darkened to a corroded green, had once been as smooth as warm summer butter and her lips plump like ripened blackberries. Now the lips were bleached the hue of a weathered tombstone, the bones like cut glass behind the emaciated membrane stretched across the cheeks. The eyes burned with the ferocity of a blood-maddened animal, and what little remained of its clothing, some kind of evening gown, hung shredded and stained from thin, birdlike arms. It grinned wickedly and lapped a long black tongue across each finger, considering the flavor of the lawman's blood with a thoughtful expression.

"*Ummmm…*" it croaked. "*Deliziosaaaaaaahhhhh…*"

Matheson's eyes widened beneath the dripping veil of blood running into his eyes. He recognized *it*. He remembered late Friday nights staying up with his dad, a Tupperware bowl piled high with popcorn and a big glass of orange pop to share, to watch this beautiful woman play at being dead, who had indeed once been beautiful. It was the one night of the week when he had been allowed to stay up past ten o'clock.

Madame Luridia's Plenty Scary Movie.

He recalled one night, when the show was scheduled to come on, his dad hadn't come for him. He lay awake in his bed for over an hour, waiting. When he slipped out from under his covers to investigate, he found his dad in the living room, nodding off in his Lay-Z-Boy, a beer in his hand and an episode of *Space Voyagers* muted on the television. Gerald Matheson had jerked awake, sloshing his beer onto his lap. At first Juston had thought the old man was going to yell at him, and for a moment there was a look in his eyes like he was ready to light up his son's ass with the palm of his hand. But then his eyes, always set hard, softened. Juston wanted to ask why they weren't watching the show. *Their* show. Yet there was something about the way his father looked at him that scared him quiet.

"Get on to bed, son," his father told him, offering a forced smile. "It's late."

The two of them would never watch the show, nor would anyone else, ever again. It soon vanished into the ether of forgotten leisure. He and his dad settled comfortably into another show to watch, a western called *The Man from Hangman's Gulch.*

It was Madame Luridia. However, she was much altered now. She was no longer among the living. No longer human.

"The juices of a man. It has been so long for me." It purred. *"Tell me, my dear, does your flesh taste as sweet as your blood?"*

"Come and get it, lady, or whatever you are. You come on down here and watch me kick your dead ass through that goddamn window," the lawman gasped, aiming his revolver at the dreadful life-aborted thing and pumping the trigger. The shots rolled through the blackness like captured claps of thunder, the room lighting up with every muzzle flash. The beast roared as the slugs tore into its mottled skin, staggering it back with every leaded thud into its body. Matheson, with dismay, saw the holes where the bullets had burrowed into the malodorous flesh, drawing not a single drop of blood. Luridia stared down at him, its eyes smoldering with an enraged fairy light, nostrils flaring and lips curling into the cruelest of smiles.

"Why is camera two not on me? That shows my best side." It leaned in closer, fangs dripping with saliva. *"Do you have my fan mail? So much mail to tend to. I get hundreds of letters every week. Sacks of it. Sometimes men ask me to marry them. Sometimes women ask for strange things too. People want me to send them locks of my hair. Can you believe that?"*

It leaned back and cackled, an unnerving and chilling sound, then it vaulted toward Matheson fast as a jungle cat, grabbing him by the collar and lifting him off of the floor to meet it at eye level. It giggled and opened its mouth, the jaw unhinging and pulling downward, the dead skin stretching with a dusty mausoleum door scrape, and the horrible, sharp teeth seeming to protrude further from the gums, eager to savage the throat of this interloper. A moist, slimy sound intruded upon the darkness, and from the creature's open jaws a long, oily tentacle slithered out. At the end of the terrible appendage snapped and buzzed a protrusion which reminded the lawman of one of those plants that gobbled up flies. A Venus Flytrap. Yes, that's what it looked like. The tiny mouth at the end of the slippery vine of flesh hissed and nipped, growing closer and closer as the undead beast drew the human morsel toward it.

As he stared into Luridia's hell-touched eyes, Matheson felt his own eyes begin to slowly roll back, the gun slipping from his hand to rattle uselessly to the ground. Upon the side of his throat, he felt the cold scratch of teeth, the veins enticed to the surface of the skin beneath the ghastly seduction of her corpse breath in his nostrils.

"Hey, you get your grody dead person mitts off him!" Cora yelled, dropping the flashlight. She grabbed a microphone stand and made a beeline for the walking dead woman. Smelling the irresistible nectar of child blood, Luridia hurled Matheson across the room like an unwanted doll, sending him crashing headfirst into an old camera, one big enough to conk his head against and render him unconscious. The vampire swatted the stand away from Cora and snatched her up by her long hair, exposing the girl's smooth, white throat. Hayder, a righteous fury erupting within him, took up the microphone stand, now bent into the shape of an L, and charged the damned thing, swinging the stand at it with every drop of strength he could collect from his small body. The attack proved to be in vain. Every dull smack of the metal against the devil's skin only seemed to rile it rather than inflict any real harm. Beaten, Hayder lobbed the stand at the unholy beast, missing her by a mile, then jumping back and away from it, his eyes scanning the darkness for something, anything, he could use as a weapon. Luridia strode toward the boy at an alarming pace, too fast to see until it was already upon him, its breath upon his face the reek of bones rotting in a hot, swampy grave. Hayder felt his sneakers detach from the earth, his body lifted as if he weighed less than a feather. Their eyes met, the living and the dead regarding one another. Luridia giggled again, the tentacle slowly retracting back into her mouth.

"*She shall be my meat! You shall be my cake!*" It swabbed a hungry tongue across its vile, dripping fangs. "*This shall be my grandest performance yet!*"

"I don't think so, death breath!"

Luridia whirled around to see Cora charging at her, a large Styrofoam cross held out before like a cavalier's lance. Styrofoam over a frame of metal. One of the graveyard props unearthed from beneath the Astroturf during the scuffle with Matheson. The monster's eyes widened, a distressed moan rumbling in its chest.

"*You get that away from me, monello.*" It hissed, a silvery string of thick drool seeping from the corners of its mouth. "*Take it away, and I promise to make your death much easier to bear.*"

"You don't like this, huh? Hmmm. Too bad!" Cora ventured a step closer, emboldened. "This here is gonna send you right back down to the Devil where you belong!"

"*What do you know of hell, little girl? Of devils? Of hurt?*" Luridia snarled, dropping Hayder to the floor, its arms stretched out to Cora, almost in a gesture of supplication. "*There is no leaving this place, my honeylamb. This is a house stuck between two worlds where the living are not meant to linger. Come with me. I will give you a kiss. Let me hold you…*"

Cora shoved the cross at the fiend, feeling the righteous power surge through the decayed Styrofoam and rusty metal. The girl had never believed much in God, nor had she really not believed, either. Truth was, she had really never cared one way or another. The girl wasn't sure if it really was the power of a deity working through her right now, but whatever it was, she *believed* in it. She believed the grungy B-movie relic could do damn near anything. Slay dragons, charm beasts, and maybe even call the dead back to life. She held it in both hands, swinging it back and forth like a sanctified broadsword. The creature hissed hatefully and took a step back, holding up its dead hands before its hideous face.

"You get back in that bone box of yours. Hear me, sister? Get out of here before I really let you have it."

"*Now look what you've done, little fool! I am running late for my broadcast. My fans are waiting!*" Luridia mumbled, averting its gaze. "*Camera two…camera two…I am ready for my close-up. Roll the camera. I am ready, Charlie. Ready for my closeuuuuuuup!*"

"Here's your close-up, you dead bitch! Now!" Hayder roared, his voice booming through the darkness. The boy rushed the living dead woman from behind, shoving it with all of his might. Cora sensed his plan and charged forward with a gleeful, barbaric shout, the cross lowered before her. Luridia lurched forward and had no time to even think, no chance to recapture its bearings, until the metal tip of the shabby cross speared it through the dead center of its chest, the Styrofoam shredding away from it as the metal ripped through layers of corpse skin and meat, shattering the ribs and piercing the silent heart behind them. Luridia bellowed in agony, swinging an arm and sending both Cora and Hayder sprawling back into the darkness. The fiend pawed and tore at the cross embedded in its breast, the sacred energy from it spewing arcs of blue electricity into its hands and eyes, filling its open, wailing mouth with a deadly, elfish fire. An odd sound blended into the vampire's awful wailing, seamlessly stitching them together. A noise which reminded Hayder of a teakettle whistling on a hot stove burner. Hissing, swelling, growing louder and sharper by the second. The two of them barely had time to drop to the ground and cover their heads before the whistling reached a fever pitch and the undead horror ruptured into a thousand chunks of bone, innards and shredded hide, a deluge of cold gore soaking them both through their clothes right down to their skin. Blood and limbs and viscera splattered across the studio, painting the festering walls in black ooze, the force knocking over the fake mausoleums and standing cameras and whatever else had the misfortune of being in the passage of the eruption.

The howl of the beast began to slowly trail away, as if the abomination were being sucked up and into an unseen vacuum. Trailing, diminishing, until it faded out completely leaving a blessed silence behind it.

Hayder lifted his head, seeing the flashlight close by and snatching it up. He scanned the room. Matheson was still in the same spot, unmoving. He feared the man was dead until he caught a glimpse of his chest rising and falling. Cora lay close by, groaning and holding her head before she too collapsed and lay quiet and unconscious.

"Gotta get us out of here. What if she comes back? What if she ain't dead all the way?" Hayder stood up, wobbling. The flashlight flickered, burned extraordinarily bright, then sputtered out. The child's heart leapt up into his throat. None of it mattered. He was too tired to do anything about whatever might be coming next.

"God, Big Guy Up There, whatever, please let her be dead. Finally dead," Hayder prayed as his brain began to disconnect. "Please don't let us die. I got too much stuff to do."

Within seconds, the boy collapsed to the floor unconscious, and for the first time in over a decade the halls and chambers of KBLUD felt something close to ordinary again. Now it was just a normal place. An assemblage of boring walls and corridors and nooks housing the remnants of common, everyday junk. A place meant for the living, where the damned had no place any longer.

Cleansed.

Hayder had recovered and taken a step forward toward Cora when he felt a sharp sting in the side of his neck. Before he could cry out a flood of warm, sweet numbness flowed through his veins, mushrooming through his bones and swaddling his brain in quiet. His arms flopped at his sides, struggling to lift themselves. What arms? They had vanished with the sweetness flowing through his body. What body? It was no longer here, just like him. All of it, everything, was gone. He collapsed to the floor in a boneless heap of useless.

The boy felt his head being turned. Warm fingers lifted his chin. He opened his eyes, closed them, then opened them again. He could manage that, at least.

Mona Hennessey smiled down at him. It *was* her, wasn't it? Something had changed. Gone wrong. His mother's smile wasn't the smile he was used to. It had become something unsettling to look at. There was an uncharacteristic remoteness to it. A surgical chill. The eye of a hunter about to put the carcass of her kill to the edge of a blade.

"Hey kiddo. You just catch a few winks, whydontcha?" his mother whispered to him. There was no gentleness to her words, just a statement of facts. "We're going on a little drive. Got some family for you to meet. Folks that have been away for a long, long time."

Hayder tried to smile, and perhaps he did. He then drifted easily into the deepest sleep he had ever known. The kind of slumber so deep, so consuming, a boy might do well to never wake up from it.

Matheson was the first to come to. Awakening to total darkness panicked him, jolting him completely alert. He collected himself and willed his brain to calm down, to work with his breathing on getting that terror pushed off someplace else. He heard someone coughing nearby him. Then a groan from what felt like the other side of the room.

Breathe, he told himself. *Keep breathing until you feel sane again.*

"Who's that?" he called out, fearing, for a moment, what would answer back.

"Me." Cora squawked weakly. She sounded very close to him. "Feel like I've been drug behind a trash truck for a week, but I'm still here."

"What happened? I just remember that woman and then the lights went out," Matheson said. "Hayder, you all right, buddy?"

"It wasn't a woman. It was something that used to be a person. Whatever it was, it's dog crap on the bottom of a shoe now. Hayder and I killed it, I think." Cora wheezed. "Hayder, say something so we can know where you are!"

"So much for being the big brave grown-up standing watch over the kids. Damn if you brats ain't got nuts the size of Texas." Matheson chuckled, his ears still ringing and a sizable goose egg swelling up on the top of his skull. "We need some light in here. Maybe Hayder's out cold and can't answer us."

The sheriff belly-crawled across the floor until he reached a wall, feeling up and along the surface to locate the bottom of a window frame, then moving further up to confirm the glass. Rising to his feet, he set his elbow against the window, reared back, and drove it hard against the glass. The window shuddered, buckled, then the glass gave way, revealing the nailed boards outside. Matheson used the flat of his hand to bust the boards outward, the corn dolls and their tinkling talismans dropping uselessly to the ground. Their enchantments, meant to restrain the unhappy dead housed within, were no longer needed. Outside the rain had finally passed, the clouds thinned out to reveal a whopper of a harvest moon, its scarlet-tinged radiance flooding the studio. Matheson grunted appreciatively and turned to inspect his kids.

Cora…check.

Hayder, however, was not here.

"Where is he?" Cora demanded, rising unsteadily to her feet. She wobbled over to the lawman and grabbed him by collar of his shirt, her eyes glistening with tears. "He was here a minute ago. We pushed that monster into that cross together. I know this. I *know!*"

"Maybe he was hurt and found his way outside," Matheson suggested, wincing as he ran his fingers across his wounded face.

"No. *No!* He wouldn't just leave us in here." Cora shook her head. "He wouldn't leave us here. He wouldn't leave *me*. That's not the way he is!"

"Maybe he was hurt and was confused. Dazed. He might have wandered out," Matheson stammered, trying to come up with something comforting to say. In the pit of his gut, he felt that something was wrong. The worst kind of wrong, which bordered on the outer rims of despair.

"Doubt that. It was dark as heck until you busted them boards away." Cora sniffled, hugging herself. "Maybe he's still in here, then. He might have crawled over where that basement is and fell down the hole. It was so dark. So…so dark."

Matheson laid his hands on her shoulders, giving her a gentle shake. "Let's check everything out here first, then. You go up front, then outside and look around. I'll hit the basement and the closets." The girl nodded and did as she was told. The lawman already knew she wouldn't find anything. Nor would he. The boy was gone. Something awful had come into this equally awful place and spirited Hayder Hennessey away. He had a pretty solid idea of who was responsible, too. In spite of this, Juston collected his revolver from the floor and made for the basement, checking every nook and corner of the studio as he went.

As expected, the basement was empty of all life. No boy. No anything. Just dust and the piled trash of decades. Not even the squeak of a mouse or scuttle of a roach.

Matheson took his time walking back. Before he exited the studio, he became aware of an odd noise, so faint he had almost mistaken it for the rustling of autumn leaves carried by a wild October draft. This was not the passage of dead leaves across the windows and roof, but something more substantial. Something with a distinct heaviness. His attention was drawn to a patch of ruined wall on the other side of the room. He squinted his eyes and moved closer. Something dark, a shape, a blob of something seemed to be traveling up the wall, slowly. Sluglike. The lawman reloaded his gun with the meager ammunition from his pocket and walked toward it. He had never seen anything like it. Nothing living, anyway. Whatever this was, it was alive in that it could move on its own, sluggishly dragging itself up the sheetrock, trailing a greasy brown slick behind it. It brought to mind the dead child from the campground, a crawling pile of raw meat, trembling protrusions, and spoiled excretions. All of it swaddled in the same oozing shawl of loathsome, otherworldly cobwebs.

All of that seemed as if it had happened many years ago. Happened to someone else.

"Gonna have to light up this son of a bitch. Just to be sure."

With that the lawman departed from the ruins of KBLUD, its final broadcast having gone down as its most memorable. One for the ages. A fitting send-off for the leading lady of *Madame Luridia's Plenty Scary Movie*.

Cora was crying. Hayder was not outside, as Matheson had predicted. The man comforted her, something he was not used to doing with a child. He assured her they would find the boy. In his heart he felt he wasn't lying to her. Somehow, he knew Hayder was out there, alive, for the time being. But time was not on their side. Time was now the enemy.

Now only an army of two, they made plans to take the film and its tapes with them someplace safe. Somewhere they could review them without fear. The lawman had decided returning to his cabin might not be the wisest decision. God only knew what evil had transpired in Black Knot since they'd left. If the cabin was even still there. Coffin Mills was still a little too close for his liking, so Matheson decided upon Rust River, a middling-sized town in north Texas just a few miles over the Oklahoma state line. He recalled a decent trucker haunt he had spent a couple of nights in years ago called the La Grange Motor Inn. It would be far enough. Or at least he hoped so.

But first, a little housecleaning was in order.

In the bed of the pickup were several empty mason jars and pop bottles in a wooden crate. These had been intended to be taken to the dump, dropped off, and then forgotten about. Now they would serve a greater purpose. Matheson stripped off his flannel shirt and shredded it into thin ribbons of fabric. The man always carried a spare gas can in the back of the truck in case of emergencies. It had just enough juice in it to fill up two bottles and one mason jar. More than enough to get the barbecue started.

Cora wanted to throw the first one. She insisted upon it. Matheson agreed with her. Indeed, she should be the one to throw the first cocktail, aiming for the outer wall of the studio. After her the lawman lobbed his own projectile through the same window he had broken from inside the studio. Despite the recent rain on the roof, one side of the exterior went up like the Fourth of July. From within they heard the satisfying report of glass shattering from the intensity of the heat, crackling wood, a burnt amber glow welling from deep inside like a railroad signalman's lantern.

Matheson laid his hand upon Cora's shoulder, giving it a reassuring squeeze. She turned to him, and he started at the fire reflected in her dark eyes. The little girl smiled, and again the sheriff of Black Knot saw someone else looking back at him. A stranger. Someone he wasn't entirely sure he liked all that much, or wanted to meet in the flesh, ever.

FOURTEEN

As a little girl, she had heard the name of Bava more than once. This was a very long time ago, you see. Years before she'd even bled, slowly on her way to becoming a woman, her hair still in braids and her thoughts not yet completely consumed by arcane predilections. Most of the children in the Fulci family were like this until they were old enough to be legitimately identified as men and women, be this age nine or sixteen. Until that happened, most of the Fulci youngsters led somewhat normal lives. The elders of the clan thought it best to keep their younger members better in tune with the rest of the world. It made it easier to hide in plain sight, slithering into the mortal world like a copperhead nesting beneath a hen house. Back then, the name meant nothing to her. Just an overheard muttering from time to time. It wasn't until she was well into her teens before that name became tied to an actual person, a myth which would eventually turn out to be very real, very frightening indeed.

On the morning of her fourteenth birthday, not more than a week after her first lunar blood had come and gone, her granny had gifted her with a book. The girl knew what the book was, and what it meant for her. Only select members of the family were presented with the honor of serving as steward for the *Adulphina Libro Sequuntur Somnia et in Sartrix*, a combination of grimoire and genealogical chronicle of the Fulci dynasty. Receiving this tome was a great honor, and twice as prestigious for one as young as she. Under most circumstances, the responsibility of becoming the guardian of this manuscript would have gone to the eldest child of the household, particularly if that child had displayed a specific talent in the deeper eldritch energies of their witchery. She had been awarded the book partly because her brother, technically the next in line to own it, had been born a simpleton, barely able to wipe his nose or feed himself with a spoon, let alone fathom the cryptic knowledge inscribed within its yellowed vellum sheets, and partly because his baby sister had been gifted with exceptional abilities, particularly in the discipline of divination.

Encrypted between its covers, rumored to have been bound in the tanned flesh of some unknown beast long lost to antiquity, the entire saga of the Fulci bloodline had been diligently detailed and chronicled. Warts and all. The book made many things clear about where she, where they, had come from, and the purpose for the presence of an ancient lineage of sorcerers having settled in, of all places, southeastern Oklahoma. It told of a black monolith obscured in a treacherous lap of land between Black Knot and Coffin Mills, and how the monument had called out to Fantasma Fulci all the way across the ocean in the vineyards of southern Italy, upon the eve of her seventeenth birthday. According to the family lore, the monolith had spoken to Fantasma in a dream, claiming to be the tomb housing the spiritual essence of Adulphina, a goddess dwelling within the Deepest Dark, the plane of demonic energy from which the Fulcis drew their power. Adulphina, commonly referred to as the Seamstress of Nightmares, had been thought long since departed from this dimension.

Along with her brother Infestato and several younger members of the family, Fantasma had crossed the sea, braving plague and starvation and storm. They docked their schooner somewhere near the coast of Florida, then took to carriage across a savage land to arrive in an untamed frontier governed by savages who lived off of the bounty of the wilderness, clinging to alien traditions and bloodthirsty rituals. In short, not so far removed from the European interlopers as one might think.

The hallowed monolith lay deep within the campground of the Shogomagra, an offshoot of the Choctaw tribe long forgotten by civilized men and almost never spoken of even by their former Indian brethren. There was a good reason for the latter. According to Fulci lore, the Choctaw maiden who had discovered the monolith had made the mistake of laying her hand upon the rock, not knowing it would flower a dire transformation not only in her flesh, but within her very soul as well. Whatever resided within that smooth slab of polished rock, be it a goddess thought long dead or the very Devil himself, it assumed complete control over the maiden. The entity haunting the monolith had used the girl to step halfway into this world, and in exchange for this taste of liberty imparted marvelous blessings upon the young woman, spitting forth a sorceress of formidable potency upon the earth. The monolith as her mouthpiece, the maiden called out for others to join her in the forest. Many did follow, and those that did not knew it was in their best interest to at least not meddle. At one time there were rumored to have been close to a hundred members of the tribe, newly christened as Shogomagra, which, when interpreted into the white man's tongue from their own means "Those Who Drink Darkness." As it would turn out, the name would prove itself to be fiendishly appropriate.

Years after their untimely extermination, many bizarre legends circulated regarding the Shogomagra, a great many of them being quite unsavory to civilized ears. Their tribal hoodoo, which they referred to as *mojaga*, dipped deeply into the loathsome realm of necromancy, and many survivors of their notoriously brutal raids all provided eerily similar stories about things seen whilst among them. Gruesome things. It was told that not only did these savages consume the flesh of the dead of both friend and foe alike, but also entertained a carnal predilection for the embrace of the dearly departed as well. Because of this, the Shogomagra were so intensely feared by other tribes, especially the Choctaw, they never had to worry about having war waged against them or their horses stolen.

Eventually, the pale interlopers from across the sea would take care of that.

It should come as no surprise the hex upon the Shogomagra lands was the direct result of the antagonism of the Fulci witches. Even the black magic of the Indian reprobates was no match for the gunpowder and even darker witchcraft of these white-faced monsters. Within a mere month of their intrusion into Indian Territory, Fantasma and her entourage had all but annihilated the Shogomagra, with only a few bands left alive to fight another day. Yet this was only the beginning of the grim fairy tale, for as she lay dying the priestess of the brutes made a promise, a grim vow delivered in a spray of blood from her mouth upon the dainty boots of Fantasma herself.

One day, you whiteskin whore, someone will come. A mighty witch. A witch of fearsome power, and this witch will lay down a horrible curse upon these lands you have consecrated in our blood, and this curse will not be dispelled until the last drop of this witch's bloodline has been drained dry.

Fantasma had mocked the woman, cackling like a lunatic as she drove the heel of her boot into the face of the priestess and stomping until there was nothing discernibly human left to look at. The witch put on a brave face for Infestato and the others, but the words of the dying priestess had struck a nerve. She was loath to confess it, even to herself in the privacy of shadows, but Fantasma knew that, in time, this curse would come to pass. She could feel the weight of its truth, the purest of hatred infusing it as if it were a noose hanging from a tree limb before her. Maybe it would come a year from then, maybe fifty. But it *would* happen, and when it did, the family had to be ready.

This prophecy would not be fulfilled until almost another century had passed. By this time, the Fulci heathens and their diabolical sacraments had become deeply embedded within what would one day be southeastern Oklahoma. The end of the War Between the States, with its deluge of shell-shocked and broken Confederate soldiers pouring into the region, provided the perfect cover for the supernatural shenanigans of the Italian occultists. The family welcomed them with open arms and devious sorcery, and upon the backs of these men the town of Black Knot rose from the earth like the hand of a worm-nibbled corpse. The monolith in the forest, now fully attuned to Fantasma, had granted both her and her kinfolk long lifespans, a decade passing before their eyes like a month to a mortal man or woman. This relic significantly amplified Fantasma's thaumaturgical gifts to almost the level of a demigod. There was nothing the witch was not aware of and nothing, absolutely nothing, the woman held in fear. It was she who had named the town Black Knot, not the Choctaw as legend had purported.

The name had been put into her head by the voice dwelling within the monolith, and even she did not comprehend its significance. The stone spoke, she listened, and she obeyed. The name of Fulci was the law, the way, the last word on everything.

The monolith stood watch over them, guiding them, jutting up from the stagnant waters of the black pond where it had stood for a thousand years like a gloved fist striking back at Heaven.

Until the day Sugar Bava drowned herself in the black pond.

Then the monolith stopped talking so much to Fantasma. Its mighty roar had diminished to a whisper, and along with that whisper a gradual, maddening waning of the Fulcis' supernatural dominion over the land. The passage of their stolen years slowly returned to leave its corrupting mark upon their flesh, the brittle infirmities of age eating into their unnatural bones. Their magic, although potent still, was beginning to die. *They* were beginning to die. Now no one, not even the mighty Fantasma herself, could even approach the monolith without fear of bodily harm, as if the stone itself had been attuned to something else and turned against them.

Something like a witch, perhaps. A mighty witch. A witch of fearsome power.

Fantasma had been dreading this day, even though she had foreseen its arrival over a hundred years before. The prophecy of the Shogomagra medicine woman had finally come to collect its bill for services rendered. The voice of The Seamstress had been reduced to a fragile murmur, and so it would be in Black Knot for decades to follow.

Enter one Mona Fulci into the story.

As a little girl, Mona had been brought up on the exploits and escapades of Fantasma Fulci. Belonging to a branch of the family dynasty having fled to Canada around the expiration of the 19th century, Mona, much like Fantasma, had been gifted with an exceptional talent for clairvoyance. Much of this, like most of the true history of the family, was kept very much on the down low. It was now a very different time, and such things were not spoken of casually. She had become the lucky recipient of the *Adulphina Libro Sequuntur Somnia et in Sartrix* by way of her Granny Estrella, who had become her guardian following the death of both her mother and father in a car accident three years earlier.

After she had assumed ownership of the tome, Mona had stayed up all night absorbing every word, every recipe, and every account. However, when she reached the mention of Sugar Bava in the narrative, something within her had perked up. A match struck against stone in a dark room. She realized, at that very moment, why the book had been passed down to her. It had been no accident. The book not only served as chronicle of her family's history, but it had also instilled an immediate sense of purpose to the child. Direction. Whoever this Sugar Bava was—Mona assumed it to be a woman—she was responsible for the decay of the Fulci bloodline's authority in Black Knot. The child was certain if she could unearth the truth about Bava, her meaning in the arc of the tale, the family could be restored to their earlier prominence. This would quickly become her obsession. Her reason to be.

The first entry regarding Sugar Bava had been chronicled in a bundle of yellowing papers, stapled together and sealed in a plastic bag and tucked into the middle of the memoir like a bookmark. Most of the accounts seemed to be tied to a family of bounty killers called The Haints, of which Sugar Bava lorded over as undisputed leader along with her two brothers, no small feat for a woman in that era, particularly one scarcely older than a girl. Snippets from Fantasma's diary, now committed to blurry photocopies, were filled with the clippings of old frontier newspapers and conversations culled from the personal journals of others. Although their time upon the earth had been brief, Sugar and her Haints had accrued an admirable record of cruelty and a downright sadistic affection for violence to boast of. They were bounty killers, true, but their preferred quarry was of a more exotic sort. The Haints only hunted the unnatural things which haunted the world. The strange gathering of shadows in the corner of the parlor. The scratch of craving claws upon a frost-scorched bedroom window. Men long dead crawling from tombs better left forgotten, thirsting for the blood of the living.

Monsters, if you will.

Always a band of three, with no use for outsiders, the Haints perpetrated almost as much evil as they administered deliverance from. Sugar Bava herself was rumored to have been an especially nasty character. By all accounts she was a witch of dreadful talent, supposedly able to summon the phantoms of the damned to fight for her, hold conversations with the bones of the ancient dead, and transform herself into all sorts of unearthly perversions. It was rumored Sugar's mother, herself a formidable enchantress hailing from the hills of Ireland, had actually been the one responsible for the expulsion of the Seamstress from the monolith, or at least setting the wheels of banishment in motion by carrying her own gods with her from across the sea, consecrating the mystical stone to her own dark lord.

However, it was the death of Sugar Bava which sealed the deal with whatever repugnant entity had come to stake its claim upon that deep, cold crater of scummy black water, commonly referred to by the locals from both Black Knot and Coffin Mills as Fulci Holler. Legend had it the gunslinger witch had taken two slugs of pure silver to the heart and had been dumped in the Holler by a rival outlaw with a bone to pick, while others told a tale of her walking into the water willingly, fatally distraught over the disappearance of her beloved brothers. One thing was for certain: after Sugar Bava walked down into that black pool, seemingly never to emerge again, is when communication between the Fulci witches and the monolith fell silent. None of them, not even the almighty Fantasma, could even so much as approach the stone, let alone draw energy from it. It was as if it had been barred by an unseen barrier even the most sincere and impassioned invocations to the Seamstress could not breach. The authority of the Fulci sorcerers, although still formidable, immediately began a slow decline, and the family found themselves having to continuously struggle, year after year, to maintain their hold upon the region.

Fantasma, however, knew damn well the cause of this irksome disruption. The hex of the Shogomagra shamaness had come full circle, at last, and there was precious little the Fulci matriarch could do about it except research and scheme over how to go about un-hexing it. For almost fifty years the Fulci witch used every resource available to crack the secret of the savage juju, the passage of time, no longer suspended by the magic of the Seamstress, taking its toll upon her flesh and bones. When the answer came, it was so simple it was almost galling.

The answer, the key to eradicating the magic of the Shogomagra savage from the stone, was in the curse itself. In retrospect it had been so simple, so obvious, Fantasma had difficulty forgiving herself.

One day, you whiteskin whore, someone will come. A mighty witch. A witch of fearsome power, and this witch will lay down a horrible curse upon these lands you have consecrated in our blood, and this curse will not be dispelled until the last drop of this witch's bloodline has been drained dry.

Will not be dispelled.

The last drop…drained dry.

As long as a single person with a drop of Bava blood in their body walked the earth, the curse would endure. Remove that final drop, the curse would crumble apart.

Emboldened, Fantasma left her brother Infestato in charge of family matters while she scoured the earth for any and all vestiges of the bloodline. It was a daunting task, as it had been almost unanimously agreed upon by all of her available resources Sugar Bava had never married, nor borne any progeny. The Bava brothers were alleged to have died in some adventure gone awry, an event which had led up to Sugar's own disappearance. Yet the curse endured, convincing Fantasma the blood of Bava still flowed in someone's veins, somewhere. She could feel it in her bones, in her skin, and this obsession drove the witch even deeper into madness, her body absorbing the harsh toll inflicted upon it as a result. Her health failing her, the Fulci sorceress returned home with her tail tucked between her legs. Barely conscious upon her arrival, she took fast to her bed and called to her family, the vulture of Death himself perched upon her shoulder. Fantasma provided them direction as to what was to be done after she passed on. No longer were they to focus upon the exploration of forgotten magic to lift the spell from the stone, but actually follow the directions provided in the verbal composition of the curse itself. The hunt for Bava would not end, *could* not end.

With that, the mightiest witch of the Fulci dynasty passed into the hereafter with her brother Infestato following her less than a week later, succumbing to a strange wasting sickness. It seemed one could not exist without the other. The thousands of notes and journals Fantasma had gathered throughout her travels were collected into a rambling monstrosity of a book and passed along from one family member to another. Years went by, summers shifting into autumns, young faces withering away to leathery furrows of flesh, collapsing finally to dust. Another century would pass, every year the power of the remaining Fulci kinfolk growing just a little bit fainter, their hold upon southeastern Oklahoma slackening. For them, the future was now a thing to be feared. Time had become the enemy.

Then came Mona. Once Mona got her hands on the book, everything changed.

Mona spent countless hours obsessing over the contents of the book. It didn't take long for her to pinpoint the flaw in Fantasma's research of the interloping witch. Too much focus had been squandered upon the exploits of Sugar Bava and not nearly enough on her kinsmen, her brothers Micah and Cutter. Delving into the past of Cutter Bava yielded nothing useful. Digging into the comings and goings of the eldest brother Micah, however, was where she struck outlaw gold. One rambling and all too brief entry in the book mentioned, in passing, a woman by the name of Juniper Morgan, who, with a bit of legwork and several sessions of dangerous augury, revealed herself to be what was known as, back in those days, a *sportin' woman.* Juniper worked as a madam for a saloon in a small town not far from where the Bava cottage was rumored to have been located. The Haints were known to have spent a great deal of time in this frontier watering hole. Something about this little nugget plucked a chord inside of Mona. It was a crucial clue, she could feel it, and it was a clue which would eventually prove itself to be the key to a box of wonders.

Pursuing this lead called for a road trip from Canada down to the original Fulci stronghold in Black Knot. By now Mona had changed from a girl to a woman and was more than capable of traveling by herself. Scouring the records and papers housed within both the Black Knot Public Library and Historical Society resulted in a very fast, hard dead end. However, a visit to nearby Coffin Mills, once the hometown for the Haints, proved itself fruitful to the point of predestination. Damn near everyone had a story to tell about the Bava clan, most of them tales of terror better suited for a midnight campfire than genealogical inquiries. At first it had been a series of frustrating dead ends and disproved rumors, deliriums, forcing her to resort to knocking on doors and asking old men in coffees shop and restaurants for any little nugget of lore to spare. This approach proved itself to be wildly lucrative. Weaving together the ramblings and mutterings from several of the old codgers into a single cohesive thread, Mona was led to the basement of a derelict old Baptist church on the north side of town, wherein a treasure trove of information regarding Juniper Morgan was unearthed. All of the birth and death records for the prostitutes of the saloon had been moved here decades earlier from the Coffin Mills courthouse following a terrible fire, stashed there to be forgotten about. Although scorched and fragile, the papers were still quite legible.

The jewel in the crown of this discovery, however, turned out to be a slim little leather volume with the initials J.H. inscribed upon the cover.

Mona knew before she even turned a single page this book was the diary of Juniper Morgan. Only now the whore's last name had become Hennessey. Everything Mona wanted to know was right there. Clear as crystal. It was an amazing stroke of good fortune for the Fulci witch.

Juniper, her narrative surprisingly refined for a woman of her vocation, told the story of a man she had once loved. A strange and dangerous man. A gunslinger by the name of Micah Bava, with sad eyes and a quick draw like a fork of lightning. For many years he had been one of her regulars, an "upstairs gentlemen," as the more prosperous patrons of the saloon were referred to. But it was obvious to Mona, after reading a few choice passages, this Micah was more than just a run-of-the-mill cowboy splurging a day's wages for a bit of female companionship. Juniper had fallen deeply in love with this man, and he with her. Before long there was ever only one customer scrawled down in the pages of her appointment book, and there had been serious talk of their running away together once they had saved enough money to do it properly. Escaping their lives of sin and blood and settling down somewhere out west. Perhaps California. Building a little general store or perhaps starting up a farm with a few head of cattle and horse. A simple life. A *good* life. A life away from his wicked little sister, whom Juniper had become thoroughly convinced was in league with the Devil.

Mona couldn't help but smile at that particular passage. In league with the Devil, indeed.

Then one day, Micah just up and disappeared. In fact, the entire Bava clan had, almost overnight, vanished without fanfare, without leaving behind a single remnant of their existence, as if they had never walked the earth at all. Not long after his departure, a disconsolate Juniper found herself with child, of whom there could only be one man for the father.

Fearing Micah for dead, in desperation, Juniper began to woo a Mister Anson Hennessey, a prominent Coffin Mills businessman who had prospered in the commerce of dried goods and lumber. A kindly and generous older gentleman, he was flattered when propositioned by the young woman, and when her belly began to swell and harden he had no reason to believe the life flowering within her womb wasn't his. After the birth of their child, a boy, Anson took both mother and babe deep into Mexico, setting up shop in a town called El Escorpion, where he amassed a king's ransom providing lumber for the construction of government outposts and other similar enterprises. Juniper's chronicle ended here, but it was more than enough to provide constructive guidance to Mona. She stashed the book in a hastily packed bag, bought a bus ticket to Coahuila, and from there hitched rides with farmers and ranchers traveling the dusty roads until she reached the village of El Escorpion, a spot so insignificant nobody had bothered to pin it to a map or write it down for others to help find it.

At first the trip appeared to have been nothing more than yet another dead end. There were only a handful of people in El Escorpion who called it home, and if it hadn't been for the blind priest, less a man of faith than a fixture at the town cantina, the journey would have ended right then and there. Once the old man's tongue had been loosened by tequila and a few dollars in his pocket, he led the girl back to the chapel to peruse what passed for the town archives. It took some time, diligence, and a lot of rummaging around in filthy, spider-infested crates and boxes, but Mona was rewarded with an armful of registers detailing all of the marriages, deaths, and most important, the births which had occurred in El Escorpion over the past two centuries. It proved to be more than just a mother lode of information; it was the needle in the damned haystack. As it turned out, Juniper Hennessey went on to have had two more children with Anson during their Mexican residency, only to lose both of them to consumption over the course of the next five years.

However, the child of Micah Bava, a son named Steven, survived and eventually migrated to Texas with his mother after the passing of Anson a mere seven years after their arrival in Mexico. The two settled in the town of Eagle Pass, where Juniper carried on Anson's lumber business, a venture at which she proved to be even more successful than her late husband. She would never marry again, mostly because she didn't need to. Besides, her heart had long since retreated to the grave with the memory of her sad-eyed bounty killer. From there it was smooth sailing for Mona. Just a matter of connecting the rest of the dots. Steven grew up and would go on to have children of his own, all of whom had, miraculously, remained in Texas up until that day. After all of the paperwork had been rifled through, the ledgers checked and double checked, there were only two people with the

Bava blood flowing through their veins who were currently alive. A man in Dallas by the name of Richard Hennessey, with a wife named Sabrina, and their son Jackson. As luck had it, Jackson was just a couple of years older than Mona, well into his first semester at Southern Methodist University. Seeing him as her way in, Mona surveyed him from a comfortable distance, moving into an apartment close to the campus and posing as a fellow student, monitoring his comings and goings and habits. Jackson was a very outgoing, popular young man. He was always out and about. Keeping him under her witch's thumb was no trouble whatsoever.

Mona made a plan for her and Jackson to "meet" at a Halloween party being held in the student union. She had learned through observation he tended to gravitate toward girls a little on the rowdy side, which, being who she was, was easy enough for her to pull off. One shared glass of rum-spiked Kool-Aid was all it took for her to coax him away from the party and back to her place. The witch had planned to dispose of him right there and then. Had it all planned out down to the most minute detail, and it would have gone off without a hitch if that pesky gremlin known by some fools as true love hadn't entered the picture.

He had kissed her. That had been what had saved him right then, and after that kiss Mona had to think about a lot of things. She had never met someone so right. So *made* for her.

Mona didn't kill Jackson that night. Or the next night. Or the one after that. Two years later the axe still hadn't fallen, and on one breezy and perfect Halloween afternoon, one year to the day they had met, the two of them stood together in a gorgeous crystal church in downtown Dallas exchanging vows of everlasting devotion. A little over a year later a little red-headed munchkin they would name Hayder was brought screaming and kicking into the world, and a few years later another blessed sprout joined the family, baby girl Brandy. It was a very ordinary time for Mona. A *good* time. She was surprised to find she no longer cared about things like curses and bloodlines and talking stones in the forest. She thrived upon the love of her husband and little ones. The family mission had not only been sidelined, but it had also been ignored, stifled and buried.

Everything remained quiet until Hayder's eleventh birthday. That was when the dream came, a bad dream which put Mona Fulci, now Mona Hennessey, back on track with her macabre fate.

In this dream, which had felt more like a ghostly visitation than some sleepy figment, Fantasma Fulci had paid a visit to Mona, all full of spit and wrath at having the family plans, so many decades in the making, disrupted by something as pathetic and immaterial as love. A battle of wills raged within the young woman's bedroom that night as Jackson slept soundly beside the girl he had pledged to love until death, completely unaware his fate and the fates of both his son and daughter hung in balance. In the end, the blood of the witch within Mona proved too powerful to resist. Reluctantly, she consented to return to her duty. However, a seed had been planted. A seed which, when it was all over, would lead to her own undoing.

Alcohol had become essential to Mona's survival in the weeks leading up to the murders of her husband and daughter. Booze silenced all of the voices in her brain telling her to get it over with. Be done. There had been several half-starts. Close calls with disaster which had nothing to do with fate. Mona would bring them as close to the edge of calamity as she dared, then would pull back at the last minute, agonized. Brandy would say something sweet. Jackson would come home from work with fresh flowers for the dining room. Things that made it very hard for her to destroy them. Hayder, all the while, had been left out of this deadly song and dance. Mona wasn't certain why she had set him apart from the other two. Saving him, in a way. Maybe because he was her firstborn. Maybe because she had, although she would have never owned up to it, loved him best out of the three of them. The two had always been so much more than mother and son. Their bond had been a rare and lovely thing. Something which had gone beyond blood, running very deep.

That fateful August morning, the day she decided it was time to finally fulfill her destiny, Mona had got herself good and crocked. Bourbon, she had found, seemed to be the most effective elixir for numbing her inhibition. While Jackson had been at work and Hayder away at a friend's house for the weekend, she had lured Brandy outside for a dip in the pool. The two of them had splashed and played and laughed, and the more they splashed and played and laughed, the more difficult it had been for Mona to do what was necessary. A few more drinks followed. More splashing, more playing, more laughing. Mother then took her baby girl in her arms, held her close, pressed a tender, drunken kiss upon the satin-smooth cheek, and dunked the child's head beneath the lapping, bleached water. It took less than a minute, and the little girl barely put up a struggle. Perhaps she had thought mommy had been playing a game, realizing until it was too late this had been no game. Maybe she had died before any sense of real terror had set in. Mona had hoped so.

Mona returned to the house and put on a pot of hot water to brew some skullgrass tea. The herb would accelerate the process of purging the effects of the booze from her body, something she needed to get out of the way before she called the police. Mona felt relieved. A monstrous responsibility had been lifted from her shoulders. After that first kill a wall had disintegrated. A wall firmly separating bad from good. The next time she raised her hand in violence, it would not be so hesitant.

Somewhere, a dead witch was smiling.

Mona had waited almost half an hour before calling 911. She had first pulled her dead daughter from her watery grave and made certain the child's life had indeed departed from this world. No pulse, the chest still and the breath stopped like the hands of a clock. Coming up with an excuse for the police hadn't been a problem. Nothing about the scene indicated anything other than a tragic, unforeseeable accident had occurred. She had been inside making lunch for the two of them, leaving her little girl to cool off in the family pool on a hot Texas summer day. Something they had done a hundred times before. Maybe the child had caught a cramp and sunk below the water, taking enough water into her lungs to black out, then drown. By the time the paramedics arrived it was already too late. Brandy had been down for too long, her poor brain deprived of life-sustaining oxygen. But of course, Mona could have told them this.

Instead, she focused upon keeping the tears coming. Offering straggling, messy answers to present and prolong her deception of suffering. She was amazed at how easily the lies popped into her head and rolled out on to her tongue, almost as if someone else had slipped into her skin and was speaking through her mouth. She kept the waterworks flowing, the rambling kicked into overdrive, when she called Jackson at work. At first he hadn't believed her, thinking it all to be a very strange, very morbid joke. But a slight quiver became noticeable in his voice as the conversation continued. Completely out of control, Mona handed the phone over to a police officer so she could lie down. The cop cars parked outside had quickly attracted a steady stream of neighbors into the home, so when Jackson had arrived with Hayder in tow, the house was packed. Jackson's parents arrived soon after. The four of them commiserated as expected, and as they did so the pesky phantom of human remorse began to creep back into Mona's heart. All she could think about was getting everyone out of the house as soon as possible so she could return to her bottle of bourbon. The bourbon made everything be quiet, and when there was quiet there was sanity patiently waiting in the wings.

When they brought Brandy out of the house on a stretcher, her small and sad remains zipped up in a cold black sack, the sorrow and guilt came flooding back, disconnecting her brain and sending her reeling into a darkness she wasn't so certain she would be able to awaken from. But she did awaken, hours later, with her head resting upon the lap of Jackson's mother, who was stroking her hair tenderly and whispering soft nonsense to her. Mona had always liked Jackson's mother. Maybe even loved her a little bit. Killing her was going to be especially tough.

As soon as they left, Mona opened another bottle. Vodka this time. Something to really blast her brains into complete incoherence. Jackson joined her, the first time she had ever seen her husband drink. The witch found she didn't like being drunk with another person. She liked to talk out loud to herself when she was ripped, confess things. It helped clear her head. That night she and Jackson spent wrapped up in one another's arms. Ordinarily this would have made Mona feel safe, comforted. Now, it was just something else in the way. An annoyance like a wasp which had landed upon her kneecap, ready to be flicked away. Through it all, Hayder drifted about in the periphery of reality, ignored, unspeaking, to deal with the trauma alone.

After the funeral Mona and Hayder spent a lot of time together, her pointedly abandoning her heartbroken husband to sort out his own mess alone. Knowing Jackson's day to die was coming up had caused her to completely shut her husband out. The effect this had upon the man was exactly as she had hoped. He became despondent and wretched. So when Mona had led him down into the basement, sinking a syringe full of liquefied hagsbane into the cheek of his left buttock and then persuading him to slip that noose around his neck, it came as no surprise to anyone he had decided to kill himself. This made it much easier for Mona to poison her in-laws' food when she had supper with them a week following Jackson's funeral. Hagsbane again. A little bit of the arcane herb could delude your mind into thinking you had departed this dimension for other, prettier lands. A little bit more would send you straight to Jesus Henry Christ in less than sixty seconds. Unlike Jackson, Mona had left a note behind for them, typewritten and official, looking very much like something Richard Hennessey, Mr. Logical Bank President, would leave behind. The death of their granddaughter and only son within so short a span had been too much to bear. A self-destruction of despondent parents. Nobody even questioned it.

After that, folks started to pay a little extra attention to both her and Hayder, expecting her to perhaps do something drastic. They turned out to be right; Mona Hennessey did do something drastic. She packed them both up and moved away, telling nobody. Not even putting their house up for sale. They just packed their things and moved to a small town in southeastern Oklahoma called Black Knot, a place Mona claimed to have once lived as a young girl. Of course it was a big whopper of a lie, but there was nobody to call her out. In addition, there was an ulterior motive behind the move.

Three weeks before Mona had settled upon her decision to return to the Knot, she and Hayder had been enduring a quiet supper together at the kitchen table. Pizza Barn, their perennial Friday night go-to feast. However, this was no ordinary Friday night. Mona had picked this specific evening to murder her son, although she had no idea how she was going to go about it. There had been nights like this before, each of them ending with her losing her nerve right before she could lay a single finger on the boy's head. She kept putting it off, making every excuse to herself, as if hoping it would all go away if she just shoved it out and away from her head. They munched on their three-cheese New York style pizza, washing it down with orange pop, neither of them speaking. This was good. Talking to her son, engaging him, would only complicate things. When Hayder's eleven o'clock bedtime rolled around she lingered at the dining room table, her orange pop now wired with bourbon, sitting there just pondering the multitude of ways to destroy her son. One hour flowed into another, and when she finally rose to do her duty, she was quite drunk. But she now had a plan. A plan she would have no problem implementing in her current state.

First, a rag of ether over the child's mouth. Soaked through with enough juice to slay the boy painlessly to sleep. So sweet and simple. Humane, even. Mona could hold him close, rocking him and smelling his hair as his heart began to slow, silenced to a murmur, then consigning the boy to whatever hereafter awaited him. Then, a bottle of sleeping pills for her, washed down with a little hair of the dog. Killing herself hadn't been part of the original design, but there was really no further need for her to remain on this planet with the last of the Bava blood flushed away into extinction. Her sole purpose all of these years had been to restore the Fulci name to its former glory, to return the power stolen from them by the Bava witch. But it was more than that. The thought of going through the rest of her life without her family, especially having lived with so much love, so much laughter, the promise of power and eternal life didn't hold much interest for her any longer.

That night, as Hayder slept, Mona prepared everything in the kitchen. She was so ripped she could barely see, doing her best to collect all of her ingredients of murder. Staggering into her son's room, she dropped the rag into the Tupperware bowl filled with ether and stood over him. The boy was so beautiful to look at. Handsome, just like his daddy. Except the eyes. Those he had received from her. The eyes of a witch, with the blood of two of them coursing through his veins. As she regarded her son Mona felt her nerve start to crumble, her resolve diluted. She lifted the rag from the bowl, the stink of the chemical burning her eyes, then dropped it back into the solution.

The Devil can take me, but I won't hurt him. Not my boy. Not ever. Saving him won't bring Jackson and Brandy back to me, I know that. I deserve to pay for what I did to them. This boy, he will live tonight. I owe him that much. I owe his daddy that much.

Mona stroked her son's hair, then leaned down and kissed his forehead. He still smelled like he had when he had been really little. A mixture of playground sweat and something vaguely leathery. Very much a *boy* smell. The witch returned to the kitchen and dumped the ether into the sink, retrieving her pills from the shelf over the stove and snagging a fresh bottle of vodka from the wine rack. Her plans for her son might have changed, but not the plans she had for herself.

He needs a good mother. A real mother who won't have these horrible thoughts. Do such horrible things. A mother who is not a killer. A woman who killed her one true love. Killed her baby girl.

Yes, it would be best for Hayder if she were no longer alive.

Once in her room she scrawled out a hasty note for whoever found her what her intentions for her son were after she had departed from this planet. Full custody was to be awarded to Mrs. Sandra Fugate, Hayder's English teacher and one of her own dear friends. Sandy was single and had no children, but had always wanted them. Mona knew she would be a good momma to her boy. There were no other family members around to lay claim to his guardianship, so the legal hassles would hopefully be minimal.

She hated to think Hayder would more than likely be the one to find her body.

Better him than anyone else, she guessed.

In the palm of her hand, she considered the small pale green ovals.

Ten of them could kill a man. Stir a little booze into the mix and you could put a serious hustle into that sprint toward the underworld.

Yes, twenty should do the trick, and down the hatch went twenty small green ovals, the Angel of Death taking to the wing to give chase.

Mona Fulci was dead in less than thirty minutes.

A voice purred from the shadows of her bedroom. Mona knew it was Fantasma without even opening her eyes to look.

"Welcome back, kinswoman." The dead witch spoke in Italian, her voice gentle, genuine, and sweet. "Now, you should know better than anyone blood trumps death every time. Every. Single. Time."

"So I'm not dead?" Mona was confused. There was no way she could have woken up after swallowing so many of those little pills. She didn't feel all that great, but nowhere close to dead. Just a little groggy and cold. Deeply, incredibly cold. Like she had been submerged in a tub of crushed ice for days Flesh warm, but the bones beneath so very cold. A chill which radiated power.

"Yes, in a manner of speaking. You are talking and can see and hear. You are alive in that way."

Mona lifted her head and opened her eyes. She was surprised to not find the apparition of the regal sorceress standing at her bedside. Just a faint disturbance of bundled shadows in the corner of the room. The entire room had taken on a cloying, claustrophobic air, as if Mona had awoken in a hot mausoleum.

"You brought me back, didn't you?" Mona sat up on the edge of the bed, holding her aching head in her hands. "Just let me die. I don't want to live if I have to kill my son. I don't care about living forever. About power."

Fantasma barked out a mocking laugh. "Well now, isn't that convenient? After killing your husband and daughter, you pause at harming the boy? Where was this love for the other two? Stop giving yourself pious airs about love and family and blood. It's too late for that. You do not have the convenience of delusion now, dearie."

"Maybe I want to salvage some little bit of my soul." Mona rose to her feet, wobbly. She leaned against a bedpost for support.

"Aw, isn't that so very sad? There is no salvation for you. Not for me. Not for any of our bloodline. We exist outside of God, of manmade sacraments of worship and faith. For us, there is only power and pleasure. We are animals of the highest order. We kill, we eat, we rule. That is the duty of evolved creatures. We owe it to these frail mortal things to keep them in line. Thin out the herd when called upon."

"Go to hell. I am not going in there and killing my boy."

"Rest easy for now, my sweet. The child shan't die tonight." The shadows seemed to detach from the corner and draw closer. Mona could feel the chill of the undead intensify the horrible iciness in her bones. "Make no mistake, love: the child of Bava, the last of his namesake, will be offered unto the Seamstress. He is the key to shattering the spell cast upon the stone, and with his spilled blood ours shall be rejuvenated. All you have to do is bring him back home to us. Here, in this land of savages and swine and dust. You won't even have to split a single hair upon his head."

"I can say no." Mona ventured a step closer to the wraith. Her head clear, she felt more emboldened. "You can't hurt that kid without me."

"Oh, that's true enough. That is why you still live. Behold, pet." A swatch of shadow seemed to shift slightly. A phantom limb moving. Mona felt her arm twitch, then jerk, rising up and over her head. The arm lowered, and she felt something slap her hard enough across the cheek to make her ears ring. She closed her eyes and sighed.

"You're inside of me. That's why I'm not dead"

The spirit in the darkness chuckled. There was no reason for anything further to be said. Mona had no other choice but to do as bidden. She plopped back down on to the bed and awaited further guidance, like a good servant of the family.

Fantasma then outlined her plans. The family plans.

Mona was to bring Hayder to Black Knot as soon as possible. Once there, await the proper omens to begin the ritual. Things would begin to happen. Sacrifices made to open up the door between the living flesh and the spirit world, allowing Fantasma and Infestato to return. To officiate the grand ritual to come. It might be three days, maybe three years. But she would recognize the signs upon their manifestation. Her blood would taste the changes in the air. Food would taste sweeter. The caress of a lover's hand more arousing. A door between worlds would be opened, after which the child of Bava would be taken to the Shogomagra monolith and offered to the Seamstress. The ritual would culminate in a matrimonial ceremony between Fantasma and all the other Fulci witches residing in Black Knot. This rite of incestuous wedlock, sealed in the blood of Mona's son, would several all ties of the Bava witch to the stone in the holler. The blackest of wedding nights, a carnal sacrament in which the Seamstress would be reborn through Fantasma's dead womb and poured into an unholy, inhuman vessel. Then, the full and unhindered entrance of their revered Adulphina into the realm of mortals, heralding the beginning of a thousand years of night everlasting. Of darkness given shape and breath and hunger. A shattering of dimensional barriers.

Then, and only then, would Mona be allowed to die. If that was what she desired.

Oh, it was. That would be best. Hopefully, her son would still forgive her on the other side. Perhaps Brandy and Jackson could muster up just the smallest shred of absolution. Maybe it would be okay, once it was all over.

She couldn't help she had been born a Fulci. It wasn't fair.

All Mona could do was nod. Mumble a little and agree. There was really no point in fighting against the blood any longer. The blood of the family would always be there. It would find her no matter where she went, just like it had found and brought her back from the wastelands beyond the veil of the grave. The specter of Fantasma Fulci then departed, leaving Mona alone with her thoughts, of which there were too many to collect into anything coherent.

Mona rose from the bed and walked across the hall to her son's room. Standing beside his bed, she looked down at him. He still slept like an infant. The kind of deep, numbing sleep only very young children are allowed to enjoy. She knelt beside the bed and brushed a stray lock of hair away from his forehead. Hayder scrunched up his face, smacked his lips and rolled over in her direction. He was clutching something against his chest. Mona gently pried his fingers away from the object. It was a framed picture of the four of them together, each of them dressed in some kind of ridiculous Old West get-up. Brandy and herself in frilly hoop-skirted dresses with bared shoulders and huge floppy hats. Jackson and Hayder in matching cowboy duds, right down to leather chaps, deerskin vests and ten-gallon hats. It was a pic from last summer when they had driven down to Arlington to Desperado Gulch for a few days of thrill rides and awesomely unhealthy carnival food. Mona lifted the picture and studied her own face behind the smudged glass. Was this the same person standing here right now? Dead and alive at the same time. Her future out of her hands, destined to kill her baby boy as if he were a sick dog.

No, that wasn't her. Not anymore. She had better get that notion out of her head right now.

Mona sat down on the floor of her son's bedroom, very much the abode of a shy and creative little boy, pressed the picture to her chest and cried quietly to herself until the sun rose, bringing with it a new day. Another day closer to the unthinkable.

FIFTEEN

There were clouds.

No. Not clouds. Fog. Real thick fog. Black fog outlined in neon green.

He was bathing in it. It was all over him like the winding sheet for the forgotten dead. Finding his breath took some time, some focus. His hands reached out and touched the fog, slipping his hands into it and parting it like a set of heavy draperies. An icy gust of air assailed him, bracing and wonderful. The boy could breathe like a normal person again. He started in on his eyes next, willing them to work, to open. This took more effort than regaining his breath. His brain was being stubborn, unwilling to strike up a conversation with the eyelids. After sweet talking it for a bit, his brain began to fall in line, allowing the world around him to creep back in.

A faint glow. The kind of light trapped between day and night. Just enough sun left to make out shapes in the shadows. The more his eyelids parted, allowing the daylight to crawl in, the more his eyes began to burn. Like how a bitter smell can make your eyes burn, water, and sting. The stink of ammonia and decay and smoke. He felt the threat of unconsciousness swirl around in his head. It would have been so easy to fall back into the nothingness. Just let oblivion take the wheel.

"Hey, buddy boy."

It was mom. She slowly emerged from the shadows, smiling. It wasn't the kind of smile that made Hayder feel safe or reassured. There was a rigidity to it. Traces of somberness held in check. He wasn't quite certain it was really her.

"Momma?" he croaked. His throat felt as if it were stuffed with dirt and pebbles. Like he had been catnapping in a shallow grave. He tried to lift his head, failing. It was too much work.

"Shhhh…you just settle down there. I need you to rest." Suddenly mom was holding him, his head settled into the crook of her arm. This made him felt better, though still not quite safe.

Hayder suddenly recalled what had happened. The ghost of Roseanna and the whole scenario with the horror in the television station. He buckled in his mother's arms, squealing with fright. She ran her cold, thin fingers through his sweaty mop of curls. The shivering, the terror, did not go away.

"Mom…mom….I have so much to tell you! I didn't know if I could believe it. Was worried they had gotten to you." He reached up to pat his mother's face, his warm fingertips brushing against her clammy, chilled flesh. The boy drew his hand back as if he had touched something newly slithered from a hole in a tomb. It was mom, all right, but not mom. They *had* gotten to her, but it was deeper, more complex than that.

Mom *was* they.

The sting in his neck. The pitch-black hell of that TV studio and the revenant standing watch over its treasures. Now it was all coming back to him.

There had been that sting and then a really sweet falling apart. Being pulled apart, given to the shadows, then reassembled into where he was now, trapped in his mother's terrible embrace. He swatted weakly at her. No strength. No will to fight back.

"Now, I need you to stay frosty, Hayderbug. No squirming. No tears. Just hold on to me for now and let things happen." He felt her lips upon his forehead. Cold, just like the rest of her. It practically radiated from her. "You are doing something very important. Something needed. You should really be grateful. Not many kids get to play a hand at changing history."

"Where…where's Cora? Mr. Matheson? Red…Rat?" He slurred, a string of drool dripping from the corner of his mouth. It was beginning to dawn on him why he felt so worn out. Someone had made him that way. That pinprick in his neck, now he knew where it had come from. "Did you give me something to make me tired?"

Mom honked his nose playfully. "Sorry, my guy, but yes. I had to. I figured you'd be less afraid this way. I don't want you to be afraid. There's nothing to be scared of. Scout's honor."

Hayder opened his eyes all the way. He looked at his momma for what felt like a very long time. Nothing about her looked weird. Same old momma, still pretty and that familiar, kind of sad half grin. But she felt…different. She didn't feel safe anymore, as a proper mother should. Mona Hennessey was still there, in a way, behind those eyes, but something else was in there too. Hayder decided he didn't want to meet that something else.

"I don't believe you. You aren't my momma." He gathered strength, tried to pull away, only to collapse back into her arms. She sighed and hugged him closer to her.

"The sad thing is, Hayder, I am your momma. And as my son, you will do what your momma tells you to do." Mona was hugging him so tight now it had begun to not feel so good. Like she was trying to smash him into herself. Absorb him. Suddenly, with horror, it dawned on the boy. All of it. Dad and Brandy and now him. Roseanna Lavera. Mom had been responsible for all of it.

"Yeah…I hated to do that. It was really hard. Killing people in the real world isn't as easy as the movies and TV make it look. I couldn't even think about doing that to you. I really didn't want to hurt the Lavera woman either, but I knew she would interfere. She was a super nice lady, so I made sure she went very fast. Her craft wasn't strong enough to resist mine when I made her slip that rope over her head. She felt no pain. Just like daddy.

Just like sissy." Mom smiled grimly down at him, leaning in to plant a peck on the tip of his nose. "Just like you."

Hayder didn't ask her how she had read his thoughts. At this point it really didn't make much difference. Reality had become a very unstable concept over the past few days.

"Why me? You could have just killed me with dad and Brandy."

Mona scrunched up her mouth, as if mulling the question over. "Well, that would have made things a lot easier, I think. That had been the plan. I had come *this* close to doing it before we packed up and moved here. I decided to kill myself instead, only Fantasma stopped me."

"Fantasma?"

"Oh, sorry, bud. Fantasma is the queen of our clan, I guess you would say. The greatest of the Fulci witches." Mona looked away. Her eyes squinted as if pondering some significant mystery. "The stones in town, both her and her brother Infestato, those mark their graves."

"Mom...you're...dead?" Hayder understood now why momma's skin felt so cold, and the realization horrified him.

"Yes, but I live, nonetheless." Momma patted his chest and stroked his cheek with the back of her hand, sending slimy ripples of revulsion through the boy. "Fantasma brought me back so that she would live again."

"So why am I still alive?"

"You have the blood of a witch in you, Hayder. Her name was Bava, a pesky little hillbilly bitch who's caused our family a lot of unnecessary misery for too long. The details really don't matter. It's a long, convoluted tale which I don't have the energy to go over with you."

"Kill me now, then!" Hayder snarled, feeling his gumption starting to come back to him. "I'm as ready as I'll ever be. Just don't you lay a hand on my friends. Don't you dare hurt Cora."

"No can do, pal. They're in too deep, the two of them. Cora, poor thing, will have to be done away with quickly, I'm afraid. You see, she's special. Just like you. Special people like her are the most dangerous to us."

"She's a witch too?" Hayder felt slightly horrorstruck at the notion the strange girl he had grown to care so much for might be a frightful hag of legend in disguise.

"In a manner of speaking. Not a born witch, but more of a made one. She cheated death, you see. Sometimes when people die and then get pulled back into the land of the living, especially kids, they bring stuff back with them from the shadowlands. Souvenirs, kind of. Cora knows things now. She feels things more deeply than a normal person. Now, she has no idea of her potential, and that's a problem."

"So, you're a Fulci?"

"Yup."

Hayder smirked darkly up at her. "You're a Fulci. That means I'm a Fulci too."

"You bet you are. But, you see, you're more than that. You're both family and the enemy, and the enemy blood trumps the blood we share." She lifted his hand to her lips and kissed his fingertips. "Think of it this way. Your blood is like a key. A key that opens a big door. Behind that door is a well filled with a power so amazing, so…overwhelming, you can't even begin to conceive of it."

"Me getting killed is turning the key in that lock." Hayder closed his eyes. Now he was really scared, all of the gumption he had marshaled up draining like dust through a sieve. Mona clucked and ran her fingers through his hair—a gesture which, as a very little child, never failed to soothe him, even now. But this time there was something more to it. A nefarious element that prompted him to struggle. To fight. Mona sighed and wrapped an arm, remarkably strong, around him. Recognizing the bewitchment for what it was, Hayder began to wail and thrash his legs.

"Now, now…you need another shot, I think." His momma rooted around in her purse, struggling to maintain her hold over him, found the needle and sank it deep into his neck. Hayder knew it was useless to resist, but resist he did, cursing, punching, and kicking. He cast his eyes upward to look at his mother, more than likely for the last time, and choked back the tears. Mona's son collected all the spit left in his mouth and hawked it up and onto her face. Unfazed, the woman smiled, even as her son's hateful saliva blinded her eyes. The boy's eyelids drooped, fluttered, cracked open and then slowly drew down once more. This time, they remained closed.

Mona wiped the spit from her face with the tail of her flannel shirt and regarded her son. It was getting harder and harder to remember him. Memories of him were transforming into musings. Daydreams. The fancies of some other weak thing. Not her.

"So glad we spent these last hours together, Hayderbug. I wanted this extra time with you, baby boy. Just us two. Mom and you. Maybe we will see one another in some other place. Some other time. Some other life where there are no Fulcis, no Bavas. No witches. No hurting. Just us. You and me. Mom and you."

SIXTEEN

The two of them reached Rust River sometime around eleven-thirty, dog tired and jittery. By then the town had pretty much closed up shop for the evening. The only places open were a Mexican fast-food dive called Taco Fever, an empty and forlorn Git N' Split, and the La Grange Motor Inn, their home for the rest of the night. The ride to the motel had been, for the most part, unpleasant and tense. Cora was disturbingly quiet, rebuffing all attempts at conversation. She sat slumped in the seat, her pale arms folded across her chest and lips a grim, thin line on her small face. Matheson felt it best to leave her be for now. In truth, the lawman was beyond terrified they wouldn't be able to find Hayder, or that something terrible had happened to him, but he had to be the grown-up right now. Grown-ups weren't always allowed the luxury of panic.

Matheson had checked into the La Grange as Roy D. Mercer with his daughter Melissa. Once they had all of the plunder retrieved from the television studio in the motel room, all set up and ready to go, the sheriff had the child sit on the corner of the bed to talk with him. Matheson knelt beside her, touched her chin and tilted her head up to look at him. Her eyes were glassy and wet, her bottom lip quivering.

"Hey, now. None of that." He grabbed a tissue from a box on the nightstand and dabbed her eyes. "We're gonna get Hayder back. Don't you fret."

"Unless he's dead. He could be dead and that's that and we can't do anything about it."

"I don't think he is, so no more of that talk. Now, I want you to get up, go into the bathroom and wash your face. Get yourself together and have a good cry if you need to. I promise you, Hayder *is* as good as dead if we don't buck up and focus. We got to move." The man took the girl by the elbow and shooed her toward the bathroom, which she then entered and closed the door behind her. He watched after her for a second, slightly ashamed of himself for being so cold. But now was not the time for tears. The lawman did truly believe the boy was still alive, but he also believed the boy wouldn't be alive for much longer.

Matheson double-checked the projector and the tape-playing machine. The film reel was in very bad shape, heavily corroded and brittle, as was the audio tape. He sighed. There was a better than decent chance the film would fall apart as soon as it was threaded into the projector and running. Then what? He tried not to think about it. Thinking too much right now only led to trouble and disappointment. Cora emerged from the bathroom, her eyes red and puffy. She smiled wanly and walked over to him. The two looked at one another, unspeaking.

"I'm sorry, Sheriff Matheson," she said, her voice much stronger. More in charge. "You don't need an out-of-control kid to complicate things. I'm cool now."

Matheson nodded and smiled. No reason to say anything further. The two of them then hunkered beside one another on the bed, using one of the sheets for a screen, dimmed the lights, and flicked the projector to life.

It all went downhill very quickly.

Less than a minute after the lawman had pressed play on the tape machine the audio cut out, the flimsy tape jamming and then spewing away from the reels, ruined. Matheson groaned, his head pounding. Although he had half expected this, he was still pissed. He fiddled with the mess for a few minutes before plucking the shredded remnants from the reels and dropping them to the floor, stomping them with the heel of his boot and cursing under his breath. Cora simply stared, her mouth agape.

"Of course." Cora sighed. "That's about right."

"We'll just have to watch it without sound," the lawman said. "Just pay attention. We got to watch out for clues. Directions. Anything."

The projector, at first, snarled and hissed and popped like it was going to misbehave. The filmstrip seemed to be struggling against the projector. Fighting. Matheson muttered a silent prayer under his breath.

Just come on. Just give us enough. Enough to know where to go. What to do.

The picture splashed across the bedsheet, a grainy and stuttering broadcast of yellowed filmstock. Frogman appeared in frame, haggard and nervous. He was sitting in what looked like a bland, cheap motel room not so different from their own. His eyes drooped, darting left to right. He held something in the palm of his hand, reaching up to his mouth and slapping his hand across it. A glass of water rested on a coffee table, which he retrieved and downed in a one gulp. A pill swallowed, more than likely. Frogman looked as if he hadn't slept for days, unbathed and wild, hands trembling as he ran them through his oily, graying hair. His mouth moved, too slow and clumsy to discern what he was saying. This scene went on for a good ten minutes, the man droning on and on, pausing every so often as if he had heard something, paused to listen, then returned to his silent narrative.

"This ain't going anywhere," Matheson said. "He could be saying anything. Man looks crazy as a dog locked up in a hot shithouse."

"Keep watching! It's not so much what he's saying as where he is," Cora scolded. "Focus on where he is. What he's doing."

As if in response the scene changed from the motel room to outside. The barren trees and dead brown grass hinted at it being sometime in that span of wither between autumn and winter. Frogman, a double-barreled shotgun resting in the crook of his arm, appeared to be standing in some kind of valley or holler. The old man looked exhausted, about to drop, but his eyes had regained some of the pluck and verve from the first film. Determination had returned. Camera in hand, he walked around the perimeter of the indentation until he arrived at a large pool of black water that seemed to go on as far as the eye could see. At this Matheson perked up. Something about the pool and how it related to the earth around it both looked and felt familiar to him. Cora noticed the upturn of his brow and nudged him with her elbow.

"Something's going on with you. You remember something, don't you?"

"Maybe. Gimme time to look at it some more. Let it soak in so I can glue something to it." Matheson reached over to the projector and halted the film. "I think I know this place."

The lawman's eyes crawled over the expanse of the bedsheet, inspecting every inch of fabric. Picking at it for any little crumb. Yes, he had seen this place before, a long time ago when he had been just a boy. That sprawl of black water was unmistakable, and the sloping sides of the holler had a distinctive look to it. Like a gigantic, cupped hand.

Why couldn't he remember it? He wanted to punch a hole in the wall.

Discouraged, Matheson returned to the projector and cranked it back to life. The poor contraption sputtered like an old man choking on a chicken bone, coughing and grinding and struggling. By the time Matheson noticed the reel loosening from the rest of the projector it was already too late. The film unraveled and began twisting and wrapping itself around the supply reel arm, quickly shredding itself into thin, useless strips.

Matheson gasped, yanking the power cord from the outlet to hinder any further ruin. Too late. The film stock, already delicate as a newborn dandelion, practically disintegrated as they stood watching, unable to act. The two of them watched as the treasure they had struggled so hard to recover from that gloomy studio hell, one of them possibly having died in the process, vanished into a mound of shredded celluloid. Trash. Useless, worthless trash.

"Guess that's that then," he said. "We're screwed without that film." He sat down on the edge of the bed and sighed.

"Oh, come on! Let's be honest. It really didn't matter. Without the sound anything useful was pretty thrown out the dang window from the get-go," Cora snapped. The girl plopped her backside on the edge of the bed next to Matheson and sank her face into her hands. She couldn't even cry any more. Didn't want to feel anything. Just crawl into someplace dark and cool and just forget.

"Holy moly!" Matheson suddenly leapt up as if something had nipped him on the ass. He bolted over to the writing desk on the other side of the room. He returned with the Big Chief writing tablet and held it up. "Damn near forgot about this. Don't get all weepy yet. We still have something."

Cora looked up at him, fresh hope putting a shine to her face.

"Best get to reading it then, cowboy. See if you can pick anything out of it that we can use. Any little thing."

Matheson sat down at the desk, opened up the tablet, and began to sift through the mess of notes and scribblings. Luckily, Frogman had never bothered to learn, or had simply never cared about, writing in cursive. His script consisted of fat, almost juvenile block letters strung into simple, easy to follow sentences. Sadly, the old man's inability to focus on one specific topic at a time made a rough go of it. Although the sheriff was not much of a reader, he was an expert skimmer. Reading something and picking out little nuggets of importance came easily for him. He quickly birddogged a passage of interest, hung on to it, and began to read out loud.

"Them Fulci hags had finally met their match. The irony of the situation, them Wop witches getting cockblocked by one of their own, has not been lost upon me. You'd think for all their bippidy boppedy boo-ing and such these Fulci numbskulls could have foreseen the birth of this witch. Could have killed her in the cradle. Done. End of story. I guess the blood of the Bava enchantress, her power, was that strong. It had latched on and begun slowly draining the Fulcis' energy from that goddamned rock before she had even been born." Matheson paused, as if allowing what he had just read to sink in, then continued. "I can't believe they couldn't feel her. A monster like them with that much devil juice flowing through her veins, it's easy for others like them to sniff them out. But somehow Miss Sugar Bava had flown under the radar. To them, she was just another bounty killer. An upstart."

Matheson stopped. Looked down at the tablet. Looked back up. A chord had been struck within him.

"Go on." Cora urged. Impatient.

"Stop a sec. Shhh!" He held out his hands for quiet. "I know that name. Bava. Sugar Bava."

"We don't have time for you to think!"

"Easy there. Gimme a moment here. It's something I remember for sure, just not all of it at once. I'm getting little trickles of remembering every few seconds." Matheson walked up to the wall and laid his head against its smoke-yellowed texture. He closed his eyes and breathed in deeply. He did this for a few minutes, then returned to the center of the room. "My granpappy, my dad's dad, used to tell me stories a lot. Especially scary ones. He was really, *really* good at telling those." The lawman shuddered and chuckled, as that memory had briefly escaped from the past and returned to cause mischief in the present.

"This is important to us why?"

"Sugar Bava and the Haints. Granpappy told me quite a few tall ones about them. Three of them, two brothers and a sister who were bounty hunters. The girl was suspected of being a witch, too, but there were almost no stories about that. Mostly just stories of their exploits. Gory details." The man sank to the corner of the bed. "Again, just ghost stories from an old man. There's no real proof the Haints were even 100% real. It's one of those things where there's just enough truth to the story to make you keep believing, but an extra helping of bullshit to bomb you right back into not believing. I always thought it was a little silly for a cold blooded killer to be named Sugar."

"Her daddy gave her that nickname, if you must know, piglet. And she loved her daddy very much. So be very, very mindful of what you might want to say next."

Matheson turned to regard Cora. Her pale skin had suddenly begun to take on an almost luminescent quality, as if lit from within, a ghost-glow wriggling just beneath the surface of the flesh. The voice which she had used to speak to him sounded like Cora; the resonance was still that of a young girl. The *way* she talked, the manner in which the words emerged from her mouth, were from the throat of another. Something a bit sinister. Feisty. The voice was possessed of a very thick Southern drawl, even more pronounced than Cora's own deeply backwoods twang, thick and languid, almost like a foreign tongue.

"I think we might have a visitor," remarked the lawman. He knelt beside the girl, preparing himself for anything. "I'm not talking to Cora right now, am I?"

"Oh, I'm here. But she's in here too. She's been in here for a long time, come to find out. She's just decided to finally introduce herself to everyone now. Even me." Cora replied. "I don't like her being in here. She's feels kind of mean. It's making me feel sick to my stomach."

"Who am I speaking with, then?" The lawman stood up and moved closer to the window. A strange, upsetting sensation had begun to spread out from Cora. Like some repulsive bug had crawled out of her mouth, scuttled down her chest and leg and then up and on to his lap.

"Aw...I thought you had heard of me, copper. You were just talking about me." Cora smirked up at him, pulling her mouth into an expression of contrived displeasure. Now there was something in the eyes which had altered. An eerie, lunatic gleam. No longer the somber stare of the child called Cora, but something aberrant. Wicked and old and crafty.

"All right then, I'll bite, Miss Bava. If that's who you really are," the lawman said. "You now have the floor. I'll hazard a guess you aren't haunting this here little girl's bones for shits and giggles. What do you want from us? And I'll thank you not to use this child's tongue for talking nasty.

She's a good kid and I won't stand for you dragging her through the gutter."

"*Oooo*...just how I like a man. Cutting right through all the fat down to the meat of the matter." Cora/Sugar cooed. "It's pretty simple to understand, actually. Even for you."

Matheson noticed a bead of sweat form at the girl's widow peak and slowly traveling south, followed by another, then another. Soon the sweat was streaming down in thick rivulets down her forehead. Hey eyes bugged from her skull as if straining to hinder something fighting its way out of her body. Cora's voice then broke through, shoving the dialogue of her uninvited passenger off to the side.

"She's on the up and up, Chief. For the most part."

"For the most part?" Juston cocked a dubious eye. "That doesn't exactly give me the warm fuzzies."

"She wants to help us. That's true. She's deep enough in here for me to feel some of what she's feeling, and she's telling the truth. Or at least she has convinced herself enough of that to fool me."

"That could be. But she's not telling us what she *wants*. That's what I really want to know." Matheson inspected the girl, who at the moment more closely resembled the Cora he knew. It seemed this back and forth between the two spirits housed within the child's body would be going on for time indefinite. "I know you want something you can't get your fingers on. Something you need Cora's body for. A set of living hands to get it for you."

The voice of the dead witch returned. "True enough. These hands can't do much without a little help. Just like you can't see all of the things I can see. Visions and dreams only those who have ripped away the curtain dividing the earth from the Shadowlands can comprehend." She sighed, obviously bored. The girl leaned over and rested her palms in her hands and regarded the lawman thoughtfully. "You feel very interesting to me, Tin Star. It would be quite something to know you in other, more intimate capacities."

"Ah...I see now." Matheson nodded. "And stop doing that. You're in the body of a little girl, for Christ sakes. It just makes you...sick."

"What is it you see, constable? Or what is it you *think* you see? Thrill me with your insight." Cora/Sugar smiled impishly. "My apologies, I reckon. This flesh sack might be young, but I have not been young for a very long time. My manners tend to slip right through the cracks."

"I see that you need us as much as we need you. Don't deny it."

"I won't deny it. There is no benefit to my lying." Cora/Sugar stood up and walked over to the mirror hanging on the wall between the two beds. She stood looking at her reflection for a moment, licking her fingers and straightening her hair up with them. Preening. "Oh Cora dear, you're not a bad looking child. Got to do something about that wandering eye, though. Makes you look like you're simple when you're anything but."

"Enough messing around! We got to get moving! The life of a child depends on it." Matheson yelled.

"Oh much, much more than the life of Hayder Hennessey hangs in balance. More than the fate of Black Knot. This is, for lack of a better way to put it, something damn near biblical. An apocalypse of sorts, if you will." The child reached out and ran her finger down the length of the glass, leaving a trail of smudge behind. "I want to keep what is mine. That is why I choose to help you wretched gut bags. Not a terribly complicated reason, I know, but there you got it."

"What are you talking about? What's yours? The girl?" Matheson stood up and jabbed an angry finger at her. "You think you're gonna be hanging around in that kid's body full-time, you got another thing coming. I will find a way to kick you out of there. An exorcism or something if I have to."

"Oh sweet hell! I am not talking about this broken, cockeyed little fool!" Cora/Sugar groaned, slapping her forehead. "I am talking about the holler! The place the Fulci charlatans have named after themselves."

"There's no such place as Fulci Holler." Matheson shook his head. "I've been hearing that old hunter's tale since I was a sprout. My daddy before me and his daddy before him. Nobody's ever found it, and every single kid in this town has spent at least one summer afternoon trying to find it. Supposed to have buried treasure in it. Under the water. Confederate gold, I hear. All hogwash."

"You say so, love. Guess you're just going to ignore what you watched on that bedsheet just a few minutes ago?" the girl remarked, still messing with her hair. "

"What are you talking about?" Matheson asked, feeling stupid for some inexplicable reason.

"I'm talking about the goddamned film you just watched! The Frog person's home movie. It showed you the holler. Clear as day, right there. It SHOWED you. Ugh!" Cora/Sugar flung herself down on the bed, stretching her arms over her head, yawning. "Little gal, how do you put up with this silly, slow-witted man-child?"

It suddenly dawned on the lawman what the Bava witch was talking about. That black pool briefly glimpsed in the Frogman's film diary.

"I remember! I remember now!" Matheson exclaimed. "Well, kind of. It's not here, though. It's closer to Coffin Mills than the Knot. I remember grandpappy taking me there to squirrel hunt once when I was a kid. I remember us going there and not staying too long. I think he forgot what was out there, then remembered and got us the heck out of there. I can't for the life of me remember exactly where it is."

"A wise decision upon your grandpappy's part." Cora/Sugar commented. "There's nothing to hunt out there any longer. Nothing lives. Nothing grows. It is a domain for the cursed now. My domain. The living have no business being there."

"How long have you been inside of Cora?" Matheson asked.

"A good while now. Ever since this poor thing took that blast of birdshot to the chest. I knew that was the beginning. The men, or whatever they are, that shot her meant to kill her. Her death, along with the folks that died in that place, was the beginning of where we are now. Sacrifices to their goddess. A black candle lit to begin the ritual."

"Why her?" asked Matheson. "Why did you pick her? She's just a regular kid."

"But she's not, you see. Cora is a natural born witch. Just like me. Can't you two feel it? Her brush with dying stirred it up. It *opened* her. It happens like that, sometimes," Cora/Sugar explained. "While she lingered in that between place, I smelled her. I watched her for a spell. I saw my chance and took it. Truth be told y'all, I actually really like her, and I hate, hate, *hate* children."

"Why are you just now piping up?" The lawman was starting to get angry, talking through clenched teeth. "That little boy, Hayder, might very well be dead right now and you could have helped stop it!"

The child-thing shrugged. "I've been enjoying the show. Not a lot to amuse me these days. And no need to worry about the boy. At least for now. He lives still, although I suspect it won't be for very long. His death is the key to the Fulcis getting that stupid rock in my holler to talk to them again."

"What does Hayder have to do with all of this? I need answers! We may not have much time." Matheson had to restrain himself from wanting to strike the child, who with every passing minute had begun to both feel, and look, less like Cora.

"The boy has my blood in his veins. It's a very long story, and if you want, I can tell it to you. The short version, of course."

Matheson, defeated, rolled his eyes and nodded.

Sugar Bava, the dead speaking through the living, began her story. Had they not been directly involved in the same story for the past couple of days, Juston would have never believed it. She told them about her brother, Micah, and the whorehouse he was fond of frequenting. About the slut at the whorehouse he had made with child. A child none of them had ever known until after they had all departed from this world. Hayder's father, although a Hennessey in name, had been a Bava in blood from his connection to that whore. Most shocking of all, it had been Hayder's mother, Mona, who had set this whole dire ritual in motion. Killing Hayder's father, his baby sister, and even his grandparents, framing one as a tragic accident and the others as the suicides of a despondent and heartbroken family.

A lie. All of it. Hayder's mother, a Fulci.

"Jesus, his own mom. I knew something was off about her when I visited her at the café. Of course I had no idea…" Matheson shook his head. "What's so special about the blood? About your blood?"

"Understand this, mortal man. My witchery is far greater, far more consuming, than any Fulci. Any Lavera. Any witch yet born into this realm." The child's voice had taken on a menacing character. The light in the room seemed to change, to shrivel, as if being consumed by the shadows clinging to the walls. "When I departed this planet in that pool of rancid water, before their oh so precious stone, my death energy was so powerful it laid its mark upon it. Upon the stone. Upon the water. Upon the land. A mark which cannot simply be sponged clean. I am a key. My blood, my very lifeforce, is a key. That stone, a doorway. My crossing over into the Shadowlands turned that key in the lock of that door and threw the bolt. Shutting them out. Crippling them."

"But you weren't powerful enough to cheat death," Matheson remarked.

"Oh, but I did. As you can see for yourself, I am still very much in the world." Cora rose and went over to the window, parting the curtains to peer outside. "A lovely evening out. I think I am wanting to take some air."

"So Hayder is the last of your bloodline, then?" Matheson said.

"Indeed. Poor thing."

"The end of your bloodline means the end of your curse upon the holler."

"Naturally."

"The curse gone, the Fulci assholes get their rock, their powers back."

"On the nose, handsome." The girl stared out the motel room window in a daze. "There is currently a ceremony underway. A sacrifice for Halloween, the most sacred of nights to anyone drawing energy from the Shadowlands, as all witches and wizards do."

"Lot of good all this talk is doing. We have no way of finding him. No way of getting to him because we have no idea how to get to this Fulci Holler." Matheson buried his face in his hands. "It's hopeless. We're done."

Cora/Sugar groaned. "Sakes alive! Your head is as thick as your gut, Tin Star. Has it not occurred to you that you don't *need* to watch the film? You have no *need* for the notebook. Your map, your native guide, is standing right in front of you."

"Wait. So the whole trip to the television studio. Dealing with…whatever it was in there. Almost dying. That was all for nothing?" Matheson felt his rage boiling up into his throat. He clenched his fists. "Why didn't you stop us?"

"And miss out on all of that excitement? Please." The girl scoffed and rolled her eyes. She looked away from the window and regarded the lawman imperiously. "Does it really matter now?"

Matheson unclenched his fists, knuckles popping, and sighed. She was right, of course.

"You said you want some air?" he asked.

Cora/Sugar nodded, then returned to gawking out the window. The burnt orange swell of the dawn was simmering on the horizon.

"Then let's saddle up. As of right now, you're the captain of this here ship. You lead the way," Matheson said, starting to gather up their stuff. "We need to find somewhere to dump all of this shit. It's useless now."

"Dump it in the Hootchyfalala," Cora/Sugar advised. "It's used to covering up all sorts of nasty things."

"You would know, right?" Matheson jabbed. The possessed child glanced at him and grinned like a wolf in a calf hutch. His blood froze to a dead halt. "I just want to know something. Why are you doing this?"

The girl raised her eyebrows and cocked her head.

"What are you getting from this? You were a bounty hunter. A killer of men for money. Those kinds of folks don't just do something for nothing. You got a price, and I got a bad feeling when it's all said and done, and if we survive this, I'm gonna get a big old nasty bill sent to me straight from hell."

The child shrugged. "I told you. The Holler. I keep what's mine."

Matheson, for some reason, didn't quite believe that was all there was to it.

SEVENTEEN

Black Knot had never been a good place. Not really.

It had always been much more than just a town. It was like a living thing. A monster. A Venus Flytrap that feasted upon lives and futures rather than insects. Juston Matheson wasn't a terribly trusting man. Life had thrown him enough curveballs to ever just accept that things would go off without a hitch, completely bereft of roadblocks. He had also, over the years, developed an eerily precise horseshit detector. That horseshit detector was squalling like an air raid siren the longer he remained in the company of Sugar Bava, currently squatting uninvited within the body of Cora Corbucci. The witch, although not lying, was most definitely not telling the entire truth. Something, some catch in the deal, was being withheld. Matheson was becoming increasingly concerned what that catch would turn out to be. In short, it was it beginning to feel like a probable out of the frying pan and into another frying pan scenario. A first-rate shit-show.

Rust River's only pawnshop didn't open until nine that morning. Too late for them to wait around for, and there was no way Matheson trusted returning to Black Knot. Especially not with everything going on there and it being Halloween. He suspected all Hell had already broken loose, and better to let the town swallow itself whole than risk their own necks for a handful of bullets. A quick diversion west to the larger town of Cold Nail proved itself to be fruitful. There was an Army surplus store that opened right at six, where Matheson purchased all the ammunition he could without looking too suspicious, and within fifteen minutes they were on the road again, the ghost of a dead witch at the helm.

The drive quickly became more and more unsettling for the lawman. The witch had him driving back north, easing west closer to Coffin Mills. As Sheriff of Black Knot Matheson thought he had driven and memorized every single road, detour, and secret route within a fifty-mile radius in every direction. The road upon which he traveled now, rutted and muddy, was utterly foreign to him, the hills and groves a distorted wonder. He would be powering along, gawking out the window and trying to convince himself he *had* been before. Within seconds something would change to dispel that conviction. A low-hanging bough, a scarecrow listing in a pasture, or a fork in the road. They seemed to climb uphill for hours, the truck almost feeling as if it were airborne, the grind of the tires encountering no resistance as if rolling upon a highway of clouds. Up. Up. Up. Matheson felt his eyelids turn to lead and droop. It all felt like a lovely dream. No witches, no vampires or bug people. He could sleep right now, right here. It was so easy.

"Hey!"

Matheson snapped awake as the truck violently jerked left to right, briefly rolling on just two wheels, righting itself, then slamming down hard upon the road with a jarring jolt. The lawman slammed on the brakes, sending the truck into a skid-spray of back mud and pebbles. He looked over at Cora to make sure she was okay. The child and her ghostly parasite sat quietly, hands folded over lap and legs crossed. Now Matheson's wariness of accepting the guidance of the witch had shifted into overdrive. Something was very wrong with Cora right now, and it was only going to get worse. When addressed directly the child had begun to respond less and less as herself and more as her phantom passenger. Her eyes would dart fearfully around, every laugh a nervous titter. Unhinged giggling. The lawman shifted into park and turned to address the witch.

"Okay, Bava lady, you going to tell me where this is gonna wind up at? Where are we actually *going*?"

Cora turned to him, glassy-eyed, smile a cold thin line. "To the holler, of course. To save the boy. We should really hurry and sit around gabbing about it. Time is of the essence, as you well know."

"Enough *enough* of this! I need to know what you are getting us into here! Stop all this witchy shit and head games and tell me what is going on!"

"But we're so close now, Juston. So close!" Cora reached out and seized his wrist, the chill from her touch biting right down to the bone. Within the space of just a few heartbeats her face had changed dramatically. Her skin had grown even paler than before, white as new chalk, and her eyes somehow larger and slightly slanted upward at the corners. More than anything, the change was in the way the girl carried herself. How she *looked* at him. There was a ghastly maturity in her facial movements, an upsetting brazenness in the way she held up her head, chin lifted, her eyes coring him to his very center. Alarmed, the lawman shut his eyes up tight and shook his head as if to clear the vision from his brain. Upon opening them he found Cora's face had returned to normal, for the most part. The girl looked gaunt and drained. Barely there. Her inner tug of war with the witch's wraith was working its toll upon her. Matheson wondered how long they had before Cora's will finally crumbled. What would happen then? What would he do about it? *Could* he do anything about it?

"I want to see Cora. I want to see her right now," Matheson growled. "You better give that kid some room to breathe in there. Ghost or witch or whatever. Make no bones about it, I'll make you hurt if she's harmed by you barging into her body."

The girl's eyes gleamed, her smile widening into a ghastly rictus. "Ah, you're making me all tingly, constable. I don't doubt you'll do your level best to remain true to that threat." She leaned back against the truck door, a thoughtful expression on her face. "Fret not. Once I am free from this flesh and the Fulci upstarts have been dealt with, I shall return her to you good as new. Better, even."

Matheson narrowed his eyes. He didn't like the sound of that. "What do you mean, free from this flesh?"

The girl dismissed him with a flutter of fingers. "Don't you worry about that. Little Cora is safe. We sit right at the edge of the corridor. The portal between worlds waits to be opened. That should be your only concern."

"Where?" Matheson asked, rolling down the truck window and sticking his head out. Nothing around him, other than being unfamiliar, seemed any different than any other patch of forest or countryside around the Knot. Pastures, overgrown brush and coarse country roads. What was he supposed to see? A portal leading into another world should look…fantastic? A supernatural wonder?

"Right there." The girl trained a long bloodless finger at a vast thicket of pine and cedar a hundred yards or so up the road. Or what remained of the road. The dirt road ended at the imposing barrier of forest.

"Looks like a dead end to me. Sure you're right about that?" The lawman looked at the girl.

"I know my business, man. Do not question the things I know, or how I know them." Cora/Sugar replied flatly. "I must open the door now."

"A door to where? What door? Tell me!" Matheson demanded. Cora groaned, her eyes rolling back to the whites. She slumped back against the seat, unconscious. After a few seconds, the girl opened her eyes and regarded him drowsily. Now she looked herself again. Like Cora and only Cora. The lawman wondered if he had imagined everything earlier.

"She's kind of gone, I think. Not, like, totally got out of me, but she's not in control right now," Cora wheezed. "She has to be out of my body a little to open the door. But she needs my…I don't know…my energy or something to give her a little extra *oomph*."

"Jesus Christ *what door?*" Matheson roared.

Cora nodded at the barricade of forest towering before them. "I only get a few glimpses into her noodle, and when I do it takes a lot of trying to hold on to them. That's why I'm so worn out. As far as I can tell, up yonder where that road ends and the trees begin, there's something like a door. A door leading to something she calls a between place. Could I have some water, please?" Matheson fumbled the canteen from his pack and passed it to her. She unscrewed the cap, tilted the canteen back and gulped sloppily. "A between place is like, I don't know, a pocket of something, some place where what's real and what's a dream get kind of mixed together."

Matheson mulled that over, struggling to grasp the concept. Not being a terribly imaginative man, it was taking some work.

"Let me explain a little, as best I can," Cora offered, sensing his perplexity. "A between place has a door, a way in. But this way in can't be just opened or unlocked with a normal key. You can't *see* the lock, or the key. It takes magic stuff to open it. We can't even see it, but it's there!" Cora sat up, wincing and favoring her side. "Man alive, this old stitch in my side is starting to turn into something really annoying. This running around has got it all fired up."

Matheson took her hand. "You gonna make it, kiddo? Can you soldier through?"

"Don't have much say in that, do I?" she laughed bitterly. "What other choice is there? We have to save my boy. And Black Knot."

"Heck with Black Knot. Black Knot is part of the problem," spat Matheson. "It can go to right to hell." He rubbed his temples. A doozy of a headache was beginning to boil up in his skull. "I think the witch likes *you*, at least."

"Not so sure it's me she likes." Cora leaned back against the makeshift pillow, sighing with relief. "She's too helpful. Too friendly. She's not fooling me, but I suspect she knows that. That's what scares me the most."

"I agree, actually. Just didn't want you to think I was scared about it," Matheson admitted. "She's so confident she's gonna get what she wants, and make no mistake, she wants something, that she isn't really bothering to be too…secretive about it all. She knows we don't trust her, but she also knows we need her. Or at least she's led us to believe that."

Cora shut her eyes and laid her head against the lawman's shoulder. "I just want this to be over. I want to save Hayder and then we can all get away from this bad town and start over. Someplace with nicer weather where we can swim. Swim in the ocean. Like Oregon or some place. But nowhere that gets a lot of snow. Or gets too cold. I can't take being too cold."

"Some place with mountains and woods. I got to have that. Place where I can just drop off the map and not be bothered," the sheriff mused. "Somewhere where the hunting is good and some clean water. Place I can fish and drink beer and get fat as a town dog."

"You're already fast as a town dog, pork rind." Cora giggled.

"Fat and sassy. That's me."

The two of them shared a laugh, then sat good and quiet for a bit. Matheson allowed himself to drop out, if even for a moment. He thought about his dad and wondered how he would have handled this whole mess. Dad wasn't nearly as softhearted as he was, so things would have most definitely taken a different turn under his watch. He had been a company man who rarely rocked the boat. Matheson wasn't so sure the old man hadn't caught on to the Knot's madness, but had instead chosen to do nothing and just let things be. Typical small-town bury your head in the sand until you kick the bucket bullshit. He thought about Becky too. Yes, she had treated him worse than a junkyard dog and screwed that high-school kid and made him look like a complete fool. But she had been his girl at one time. She had been his girl, his best friend, and she had wanted to build a life with him. Something had just gone wrong along the way. Something neither of them understood. The lawman had his theories about it. In spite of his profession, Juston Matheson was a safe man. A safe choice. Coming from the background Becky had grown up in, he figured that had been part of her attraction to him. She had been born a wild girl, and wild girls often grew up to be restless grown-ups. She had needed an anchor, a safe harbor. Yet her innate wildness had been too much to overcome. Juston's nurturing had been like salt sewn into fertile earth. In short, the marriage had been doomed from the beginning.

He thought about the boy. Hayder. Maybe if he could save him he could wash all that mess away. All that failure. Not be so damned useless. He was willing to lay down his life for the kid, which surprised him a little. He barely knew him, and yet he felt as if he had already been a part of his life for a very long time. Both him and Cora.

Matheson didn't realize he had nodded off until he awoke to Cora shaking him, her voice sounding like it were coming from within the depths of a seashell. He lifted his head from the steering wheel, a string of drool trailing from his bottom lip.

"No time for that. Look!" Cora pointed at something beyond the windshield. The lawman could only stare in disbelief. The wall of trees had parted, bent into impossible angles like pipe cleaners or a scene from an old cartoon, revealing a spherical tunnel opening into a frightful darkness beyond. An ominous feeling filled the cab of the truck, the air thick and oppressive. None of them needed to be told the ghost, or whatever it was, of Sugar Bava had returned.

"Miss me, pet?"

"About as much as I miss having crabs," Matheson muttered under his breath.

"You're quite the card, aren't you, Tin Star?" The witch's voice, broadcasting stronger and clearer from Cora's mouth seemed genuinely amused. "That sense of humor will serve you well when things are going south. But the time for such amusements has passed. We must press on. I have opened the door into the world between worlds, and daylight is fading fast."

"We go through that there hole in the woods, then what?" Matheson cranked the pickup to life again. The prehistoric engine emitted a chugging, sickly burp. "Shitfire. I think the old girl is about to punch the last hole in her one-way ticket to the salvage yard."

"Of that, I am uncertain. I know not what terrible enchantments exist within this pocket of unreality. The Fulci dogs, although nowhere near my level of aptitude, are bound to have all sorts of horrors awaiting us. Especially on a night as significant to their survival as this one." Cora/Sugar laid her icy hand upon his shoulder, sending a chill rippling through his blood.

"Look, I know you do not trust me. Very wise of you. But I do swear to you, I will do everything within my power to save your brat. To wipe out these pesky charlatans. When I give my word, it is bond."

Matheson believed her. God help him.

"After that? When we're all done?" He reached over and removed the girl's hand from his shoulder. He didn't want her to touch him in any way.

"Oh love, you really need to learn to live for the moment. You miss out on so many pleasures when you fret so much over the little details." Reaching down, the witch in child's skin shifted the truck into first. "Now, drive."

The road seemed to go on and on, rambling through a mire of gungy black silence. Going deeper, climbing uphill higher and higher, the wheels of the truck lifting up and away from the road and held suspended in mid-air as if being conducted by the cables of a lunatic puppeteer. No sound. Blindness. Deadness. A complete theft of everything that makes a person feel alive. Matheson felt as if he were floating in a pool of utter emptiness, barely a living thing. A corpse worm burrowing through the polluted soil of a graveyard. He felt someone gripping his arm tight, the clutch of a panicked little girl. Matheson lost control of the truck for a moment, shaken up, then realized he had surrendered all control over his fate the second his tires had crossed the threshold of that awful forest, penetrating the arcane membrane protecting the doorway into the between place. He decided it best to just let whatever it was dwelling within this nightmare escort them to their destination. If this was the end of the line, the real end of the line, then so be it.

The lawman suddenly felt his belly drop, then shoot up into his brain, making his head go wobbly. A rush of muggy, mildewed air and the truck slammed down hard, rattling his teeth in his skull, the dry reek of disturbed dust and hay choking him. It took a few minutes for Matheson to catch his bearings. He felt awful, like he had just woken up after sleeping off a long bender. After checking on Cora he opened the truck door and spilled out onto the road, if it could be called that. The road consisted of a crudely delineated pour of gravel spliced between two steeply sloping valleys of lush green grass and closely crowded clusters of ancient trees. It was no longer autumn but summer. Sunlight overhead like a death ray, hot and sticky and suffocating. Weather fashioned for suffering. Yet there was something else. A sense of belonging, of familiarity. Like returning to your childhood home after decades abroad and finding it totally renovated. Little bits of memory here and there. Flashes of yesterday. A corner where a chair used to be where now a potbellied stove simmered. A new back porch instead of the open-ended pasture stretching out as far as you could strain your eyes. Your old bedroom now a chamber for storing useless junk.

A hot breeze slithered through the trees and down through the hills, carrying with it the smell of burning timber and stagnant water.

"This place. This place is familiar." Matheson looked around him, as if capturing every little detail with his eyes might jog his memory. "I think."

"The closer we get to the heart of the between place, where the weavers of this pocket dimension concoct their witcheries, reality as you perceive it will begin to tatter, weaken, then unravel altogether. Memories from the past might return to the now, although you might find the sequence of events, the way you remember those things, much altered," Cora/Sugar said. "Be prepared for sights and sounds and wonders the likes of which mortals have never before witnessed."

Matheson continued to look around, absorbing his surroundings. "I *have* been here. I recognize this road. These hills. But I don't think they're here anymore. At least not like this. Like, they might even be gone completely now."

Cora/Sugar shrugged. "As I said, what has happened before can be called forth from the ethers of the past and repurposed. Such is the influence of a pocket realm. It steals the dreams and memories of others and weaves them out into a new creation."

The sheriff returned to the truck. "Where to, Maleficent?"

The child smiled flatly and pointed at the windshield. "Just drive."

Fighting the urge to groan, Matheson shifted into gear and eased his foot on to the accelerator. Better to take it easy with the truck right now. He reckoned it was going to be a goner before this whole nightmare was finished. They lumbered down the rutted path, the truck banging and clanging like an old junk wagon. If the plan had been for some kind of surprise attack, that ship had already sailed. Sailed, crashed against the rocks, and sunk.

As he drove the nagging sense of familiarity only amplified in power. He could hardly concentrate on the road. He hadn't realized he'd been tugging at the lobe of his ear the whole time. His suddenly ear felt wet, cold, and when he pulled away to regard his hand he could see streaks of blood on his fingertips.

"I warned you about that, didn't I? You're gonna pull that little dude right off one day."

Cora's voice now. Cora and only Cora.

It made him smile.

As they drove along more and more landmarks began to appear. Places Matheson remembered but knew had been gone for a very long time. Up ahead, still a good drive away, he could see the colossal white screen of the old 270 Drive-In. But that was impossible! Hell, that had burned down what, twenty years ago? Man, he had loved that place! He knew a lot of guys who had lost their virginity in the back seats of cars there, himself included. The Old 270 always showed the best scary movies, had the tastiest popcorn, and the juiciest burgers a teenage carnivore could ever ask for.

And there! On the right.

Alfred Bouchard's tree farm! Mom and dad had taken him there every year at Christmas to chop down their very own tree for trimming. Mr. Bouchard's wife made the sweetest ghostberry jam and the best peanut brittle this side of Mars. That farm had been closed since he had been in middle school, razed to the ground and turned into a housing addition. Hereford Lane was what it was called, and there were damn near a hundred ugly as sin tract houses there now. Not a trace of the tree farm at all, and Old Man Bouchard had been dead for damn near a decade now.

When Matheson looked at these wonders it was as if he were not just seeing them with the eyes in his skull, but another set of eyes he didn't know about. Eyes that could see things that couldn't normally be looked at directly. Everything had a fanciful, grainy quality to it, as if he were watching a film about these places rather than actually being present, in the moment, looking right at them. A little past the farm a dilapidated windmill imposed alongside a tall grain elevator, both casting ominous shadows across the road. Matheson recognized this ruin as the R.J. McAlester Grain Mill. The lawman had only ever heard about this place, as it had been shut down sometime in the 50s shortly before he had been born.

"Whatcha thinking about, Sheriff? You look kinda swoony." Cora's huge dark eyes questioned.

"I'm beginning to wonder if we aren't all asleep at the wheel and dreaming right now. All these things around us, the farm over there and the windmill, and if you look up yonder and see that drive-in, they're things from the past, from Black Knot's past, that aren't around anymore." Matheson shook his head in disbelief. "But here they are, all the same."

"I get a feeling time doesn't behave here like it does where we came from. We had better put the lead on it. Hayder may have only minutes to live for all we know." Cora's voice took on an ominous, steely tone. "When

I get my hands on one of them Fulci witches I am going to make 'em hurt bad if they so much as split one hair on his head."

"As you say, little gal. Warp speed ahead!" The lawman gunned the accelerator. The truck griped back with a shriek of metal and clattering steel. Matheson groaned. "Sorry, old girl, but I gotta beg you to go a little faster. Now move, goddammit!"

The ramshackle clunker, as if by sorcery, seemed to be galvanized by his command. The clanking relented, fading out and returning with a mighty, supercharged roar like a truck fresh off of the assembly line. Brave. Mean. Ready to kick shit up. The force of the acceleration threw the two of them back against the seat, the growl of the engine filling up the cab of the Ford like the sigh of a dragon. And it was loud. Loud like a battle cry. Loud like God.

EIGHTEEN

There are times in our lives when we encounter things, happenings, which seem utterly unreal. Completely outside the realm of possibility. Often we pass these experiences off as the remnants of bad dreams. Overactive imaginations. Or, in the worst-case scenario, the first stirrings of a long dormant lunacy. Usually such distressing moments are quickly shaken off like dust from an overcoat kept too long in the closet. There's no meat to them. We can recognize the separation from phantasmagoria and the flesh and relegate the moment to the outer recesses of our minds, where the trivial things haunting us are sent to wither, dry up, and finally crumble to ash.

For Hayder Hennessey, this was not one of those times.

The boy's eyes fluttered, slowly creeping open, struggling to see through lids which felt as if they had been glued shut. His skull felt too full, clogged with clumsy thoughts. He knew he wasn't asleep, but he didn't feel quite awake either. A sliver of amber light crept into his vision, blurred at first, then gradually dissolving away. His eyes were now open. Open all the way. He could truly see, and it didn't take him long at all to realize he was not in a good place. This was so far from good it was inconceivable to fully understand just how bad it was. But he could feel it. Oh, could he ever feel it.

He was in what appeared to be a school gymnasium, long abandoned to neglect and disintegration. The wooden floor had once been a basketball court, scuffed with time and the exodus of decades of vermin across its flaking surface. On either side of him the bleachers had been folded up neatly and sequestered to the sides, out of the way, unneeded. Above, high in the rafters which seemed to reach up longer than architecturally possible, dozens, if not hundreds of iron lanterns hung suspended in the air, bobbing up and down as if conducted upon the wings of a spectral draft, like swarms of lightning bugs entombed in mason jars. On the wall directly in front of him, just a hair above the broken-down backboard and rusted rim of the ancient basketball goal, a tattered purple banner, swathed in cobwebs, stretched across the length of the wall inscribed with the words in a bleached, yellowed script:

GOLGOTHA SPRINGS CLASS OF 1956 SENIOR PROM
A NIGHT TO REMEMBER

All around him were the trappings of a gay celebration gone sour several years buried in the past. Dunes of glitter and papier-mâché lay spread out in shimmering drifts across the floor of the gymnasium, stirred into sporadic dust devils by a stout, musty wind which would howl through the chamber every so often. A table here and there, chairs, overturned. The fragments of a crystal punch bowl and too many shattered glass cups to count. Strips of lacy fabric and hair combs and orphaned shoes. Flat stink of meat left to rot into dried pulp and the penetrating, distinctive odors of melted wax and some sort of spicy incense, all of which blended into a dank, hypnotizing brew which made Hayder's thoughts crumble inside of his skull.

Something on the floor. Brighter than the other debris heaped up around it. Pale. Cold and luminous. Almost glowing. The boy squinted his eyes and craned his neck out as far as he could. He saw it. He looked again to make sure it was what he had thought he had seen.

Yes, it was a skull. A real one. The skull of a person who had once been alive and had met some tragic end down here. Wherever here was.

Of course he hadn't been surprised to see the skull. Not even a little. What was the shock of one little bare bone when stacked up against the walking nightmares he and his friends had encountered over the past few days? It was like a Halloween decoration for the front porch. A dime store gag.

Where *was* he?

Hayder tried to move his arms. Like wet cement. He could almost feel something, then nothing.

Tried again. Nothing.

Wait, a little movement again. Yes? Or had he just imagined it?

He realized, panicked, that he couldn't even *feel* his arms, or his legs. He could tell both of his arms had been pinned behind his back and his knees were bent. The boy focused on moving his legs, and after a few minutes, was able to coax a twitch out of one of his ankles. This seemed to elicit a responsive twitch from a corresponding bound wrist. The boy understood the situation now, his puke gurgling in his throat.

This was something to be very much afraid of.

He had been hogtied, like a goat about to be delivered to the altar for sacrifice, and he was going to die.

"Oh no. Not yet, love."

Hayder strained his neck in the direction of the voice. It was coming from behind him, and the ropes binding his shoulders and armpits prevented him from moving his head more than a half an inch left to right.

"Please do not wiggle so, young man. You might hurt yourself, and we need you in tiptop condition for tonight's service."

It dawned on Hayder the voice speaking to him was not communicating in English. Was it Spanish? The inflection on some of the words that made him think about Spanish-y things. He wasn't sure. Not that it really mattered. Amazingly, the boy had no trouble understanding what was being said to him.

"I shall loosen the knots a bit, yes? You are clearly not going anywhere, I think. However, I do feel the need to warn you in advance that should you decide to run, to escape your destiny, your role as ring-bearer in this magnificent rite of unholy wedlock, things will go quite poorly for you."

Hayder felt the pressure around both his wrists and ankles relent ever so slightly. Blood began to trickle back into his hands and feet, pinprick tingles rippling through his palms and toes. He was able to move his head a little. Just enough to see he was lying on a large silver platter. The kind you would find in some big-city chow house for serving pretentious, overpriced meals to a big gathering of gullible rich folks. The platter had been placed in the dead center of a supper table of colossal dimensions. Stretching a good twenty-five feet from end to end, it was a sprawling monster of polished black wood, nicked with a centuries' worth of knife-play and rowdiness and glossed over with a hardened sheen of God only knew what. Two columns of empty chairs on both sides of the table, Hayder guessed at no less than fifty. It reminded him of the feasting table for a country lord in a sword and sorcery flick. Refined, yet patently barbaric.

He was lying in the middle of the table, trussed-up like a suckling pig to be roasted. The only thing missing was an apple stuffed into his mouth.

He was meant to be eaten alive.

A scream began to gurgle in his throat, only to be silenced by the coarse bellow of rock grating against rock. He turned his head to the right, toward the sound. The floor began to rumble and tremor, large slivers of wood and concrete and dirt spewing up and into the air like a blast of errant steam from an awakened geyser, revealing a wide, seemingly fathomless crater. The crater began to quickly fill with water, dark as a midnight graveyard, and from that pool a gigantic hunk of black stone, as tall as five men teetering upon one another's shoulders, emerged, breaking the surface of the water like the hand of an insane preacher calling down the wrath of a forgotten deity from the sky. The power radiating from the stone was overwhelming. It threatened to steal his breath, siphon the blood from his veins, his very life, from his lungs. Putrefy his bones into globs of cold pudding. Hayder found himself unable to tear his eyes away from the monolith, its obsidian surface so smooth, like silk. Almost like unblemished flesh.

Then, he *saw*. He saw and he understood.

This was it. This stone.

This stone was the reason for all of the nasty things which had been happening to Black Knot. No, that wasn't all the way true. The horrible stuff was already there, but the stone made it even worse. Like a magnifying glass focusing a ray from the sun into a beam of killing heat. Hayder wanted to hurt the stone. Break it into a hundred million pieces. But there was something else to it he didn't quite understand. A weird and unnerving sense of attachment. He wanted to destroy it, yes. But he didn't want anyone else to destroy it or even lay so much as a finger on it. It was *his* stone. It belonged to *him*.

In his head, the delicate, raspy chuckle of a woman. A woman he knew.

No, *she* knew him.

"Mom?"

No…not mom…

The boy didn't have time to mull this over. Within minutes of the stone's emergence from the water further grumbling from the bowels of the earth followed, the entire gymnasium immersed within the confines of a horrific, primordial shudder. From directly behind the monolith, up from the floor, a grand staircase of solid limestone began building itself into existence, demolishing the walls of the gymnasium around it into a ghostly shower of dust and rubble. The ceiling cracked down the middle like a rotten egg, splintering and falling apart in huge chunks of plaster and mildewed insulation, rising up higher and higher until terminating into a portal of swirling crimson and black. As if heralding the portal's emergence, the strains of a peculiar melody began to eddy throughout the room, a sinister mishmash of discordant violins, braying horns and the feral pounding of drums. Out of tune, disorienting, out of sync, yet somehow coherent and provoking. The stone began to emit a low, mesmeric hum. From the heart of the monolith a feeble golden spark began to shimmer, steadily manifesting into a solid pillar of deep blue flame. Pulsing every few seconds, the flame began to throb in time with the drumming. Melding, transforming, into a smooth and hypnotic rhythm.

The stone was singing. Singing a wedding hymn.

The song, the sound, made Hayder feel funny inside. Disturbing images began to swim into his skull to tease at his brain. Moving pictures chronicling repulsive acts he didn't understand but recognized for the perversions they were projecting into him. He shut his eyes and tried to misdirect the attempted confiscation of his reason. He thought about Cora. About Sheriff Matheson and how he hoped he was safe. About Cora some more. The fun times had at The Gates of Mordor and Cora's sweet kiss in the shadowy auditorium of a cursed old movie house.

It was working!

The demented visions began to recede from his memory like a lingering curtain of smoke blown clear from the remnants of a doused funeral pyre, the bones of the dead still smoldering upon the charred and collapsed kindling. His eyes being closed, Hayder didn't see the dreadful portal beginning to open, the glutinous darkness gestating within parting, an organized procession of terrors emerging from whatever nightmare realm lay beyond its alien threshold. The music ended abruptly, a single horn screeching out a chilling wail of welcome for these new arrivals to the feast.

At the scream of the horn the boy's snapped open. He saw them. The witches. They were coming down for supper, and he knew they were hungry for boy flesh.

From a distance they looked like normal enough people. They were marching down the stairs single file, one at a time, each of them carrying a single lit black candle in one hand and some unidentifiable talisman in the other. As they drew closer Hayder noticed they no longer looked so ordinary. Most of them were clothed in the tattered clothing from another era. Multiple eras, in fact. They didn't walk so much as shamble and stagger down the steps, as if they were mere vessels devoid of all autonomy over their limbs, conducted by the invisible cords of a mad puppeteer. This grim parade carried with them a nauseating stench. The odor of treacherous grimoires sealed in jackets of human skin, bound in blood and rot and perverse necromancy. A smell that lingered within his head as well as the hollows of his nose, absorbed into the psyche. Now he could really see them. Every single one of them. Many of them appeared to have been dead for a very long time, several of the wights having mortified into an almost mummified state. Some had withered down to the bare bone, their skeletal visages covered by tattered masks. A shabby orphanage rabbit sporting the fangs of a cottonmouth. A leering harlequin with a flapping, cancerous tongue lolling from the mouth of its mask. An apple-cheeked baby-thing with blood trickling from its eyes. A goggled-eyed fish with a foaming, chittering maw.

One…two…three…twenty. The Fulci family had come home for a long overdue reunion.

Once the procession reached the bottom of the staircase they parted in the middle and split into two groups on either side, unmoving, patiently awaiting guidance. At the top of the stairs a pair of gargantuan louts, each arrayed in leather loincloths with their slavering jaws held in check by tarnished bridles, emerged from the portal bearing a huge sarcophagus of either stone or wood which had endured the world for so long it had become akin to solid rock. Brushing past the revelers, they set the coffin down beside the pool of water, just a few feet away from the monolith, which immediately ceased to sing. Something was about to happen, Hayder felt. This planet was about to be done with him very soon.

"Do I scream?" he pondered glumly. No, that would be a waste of both breath and time. What use was screaming when your death, more than likely to arrive in the next few minutes, was assured?

The boy was a bit dumbfounded he wasn't more…afraid. A glimpse, just a very quick peek, of the horrors moaning and whispering before him would be enough to hammer most people down into a panicked, screaming fit. But he understood the world he was dealing with very well now. The vicious ghosts haunting the nooks and hallways of Red Hand Theater, the horrible living dead thing stalking the shadowy chambers of KBLUD, and now, this. There was really precious little left to stir the cauldron of terror his mind had been dropped into.

He was wrong about that. Very much so.

Another bray from the horn. Louder this time. More insistent.

The grim gathering of ghouls waddled closer to the boy, their intermingled mortuary reek turning his stomach. A crushing mantle of silence drifted across the room. The mob slowly parted to reveal a trio of figures shrouded in shadow at the summit of the staircase, one in the front and two behind them. The one in the front waltzed slowly down the steps, one foot at a time, until it stepped into a patch of stray lantern light. Hayder sucked in his breath, his eyes bugged out of his skull.

It was the Wolf-Man. The vile beast who had blasted a load of lead pellets into Cora's chest, left her for dead, murdered her best friend, and had been haunting her ever since. Here he…it…was, in the flesh.

It was real.

Of course it was. How could it not have been?

It was wearing a suit, impeccably tailored with every available bare spot coated in glittering rhinestones, neatly buttoned and topped off with a perfectly knotted, solid black tie. The beast mask covering its face was something skinned from a nightmare. More of a headdress than a true mask, it did indeed appear to have been cobbled together from the actual head of a large timber wolf. The skull beneath removed, the muscle and fat scraped away and slipped over the face, the smell of hot roadkill and misery radiating from it in a choking, grotesque miasma. Somehow Hayder understood to be grateful for the fact its face was obscured. Behind the disguise, the illusion, he was certain something horrible was being veiled from him. A sight which would have tipped him right over the edge into absolute and irreparable madness.

The creature approached the supper table, paused at the edge and leaned forward. Inspecting him. It cocked its head curiously and inhaled, a soggy and congested wheeze rattling from its chest. Hayder realized with disgust the beast was sniffing him. Imbibing his scent to perhaps appraise a hint of the flavor to come. The stink from the thing was overpowering, the soured contents of his belly lurching up into his throat. From beneath the edges of the mask Hayder saw the scraggly tendrils of a black beard, gnarled with clumps of filth and tied into a series of intricate braids. The drone of buzzing insects accompanied it; however, Hayder didn't spot a single fly or wasp. It reached out a hand encased in black leather and laid the tips of its fingers upon his forehead, smoothing the boy's hair away and out of his eyes. Almost a tender gesture.

"Soon, little brother." It spoke, its voice deep and rich, surprisingly comforting. "Soon you will fill our bellies. You will fill our bellies with your skin and bones and meat, and the door will be flung open. There will be no distinction between the living and the dead. We will take back what rightfully belonged to us before the hayseed witch purloined it." It reached out and gave his nose a playful pinch. "How wonderful for you! To be a part of this momentous occasion. To know that you are the key. You are the key *and* the door. I cry for you. Your jubilation will know no bounds. Your reward is richly deserved."

"You hurt Cora." Hayder spat up at it, eyes alight with fury. "You tried to kill her, but you didn't do it. She showed you and lived and now you're afraid of her, I think. You know something happened to her when she was dead for a little bit. She brought back something with her, something that can hurt you too."

The Wolf-Man folded its arms across its chest and looked down at the boy with a cocked head. Its eyes were a lovely, almost phosphorescent sea green, the pupils tiny pinpricks of silver. "Oh, I won't deny that. Indeed, I am *terrified* of facing that child again. It would have been so much better if she had simply died. Just a minute more of her bleeding on that floor—a minute, mind you—and the Bava witch would not have been able to stow away in her flesh. It would have made things go much more smoothly. The entrance for the Seamstress back into our world without fanfare or melodrama. But now, we must be prepared to deal with the country witch. She must not be allowed to maintain her hold over the stone."

Hayder's brain hurt. He remembered that name. Bava. His mother had mentioned it to him earlier. He had almost forgotten. Here he was now. Hayder Hennessey, once a normal boy from Texas, now a freak with the blood of an evil witch bubbling in his body. An unfortunate peculiarity for which he was about to be slaughtered, chewed up, and swallowed.

The beast chuckled, a dank and raspy sound. It reached down and checked the boy's bindings, tightening them a bit more. "Better these are a bit snugger, my friend. You don't know your own strength, and we can't have you stirring things up right before the ceremony is about to begin. Before you are carved up, sliced to bits, and our cups filled to the brim with your blood."

"My friends might have something to say about that." Hayder struggled against the ropes. He couldn't even twitch a finger now, his skin growing numb once again.

Wolf-Man leaned closer to him, resting its elbows on the supper table. "They'll be dead soon. My word on that one, boy. Although I rather hope the girl makes it. At least long enough for her and me to be reunited. I want to gaze into her lovely dark eyes as I gobble the life from her body. Watch those eyes roll over white from life into death. I have been dreaming of that moment for some time, even as I fear it now. I will make her suffer for denying me the pleasure of her extinction. Her pain will be…glorious."

The pounding of drums suddenly engulfed the gymnasium, loud enough to drown out all other noise. The Wolf-Man's head jerked up, immediately followed by the rest of its body. It clapped its gloved hands together in joy.

"What is that?" Hayder gasped. The boy realized he had to pee badly.

Might as well just piss your pants, buddy. Give these demons something sour to smack their lips on when they eat you.

"Harken, the bride and groom have arrived to exchange their vows," the Wolf-Man rasped, backing away from the table. It gestured in the direction of the stairs. "You are such a fortunate child! How many humans, how many living things, can attest they were instrumental in ushering in the end of all life? The end of the world as they have come to know it. The end *and* the beginning?" The Wolf-Man reared back its head and offered up a somber, ferocious howl, sounding every bit like a savage animal impatient to dig into the carcass of its crippled prey. The Wolf-Man looked back down at Hayder and smoothed the boy's hair back from his sweaty brow. It then turned, walked away from him, and took its place at the bottom of the staircase. The congregated living dead shambled down and took their places at the table, leaving four seats vacant. Hayder was not anxious to see those empty spaces filled. He could feel the eyes of his ghastly supper companions on him, the eerie smacking of their dry, cold, and hungry mouths. He only hoped they at least gave him something before they put him to the knife. Something to help him forget, to not feel it when the dinner bell finally tolled.

"Ordinarily, we are loath to harm a child…unnecessarily," a voice called from the emptiness. Hayder immediately recognized it. It was the voice of the woman, or whatever it was, who had loosened the ropes for him earlier. "I beg your forgiveness, young man. My kinsman. Seeing as the blood of Fulci as well as Bava flows within your veins, the decision to end your life was not made hastily. Please know that as you depart from this world and try not to bear us any ill will."

Hayder's eyes were drawn up the staircase, crawling up each stone step until they settled upon that dreadful ribbon of nothingness. From out of the darkness two figures materialized, stepping out of the void and into this world in a vulgar belch of billowing dark green smoke and charnel reek. The shapes linked hands and began walking down the steps, the pounding of the drums deafening and the mad wailing of the Wolf-Man scrambling the boy's thoughts. The two figures reached the base of the staircase and into the light. Recognition flooded him. He wasn't sure how, but he understood immediately the names inscribed on the twin tombstones bursting through the pavement outside of the arcade belong to them. These two monsters. These witches. The aura of sheer necromantic power rushed over the boy, a cloying and petrifying energy. The drums pounded harder. The horns shrieked as if trying to rouse buried bones from the earth. And the howling…oh…that awful…awful howling!

He knew their names. Blood knew blood, after all.

Fantasma and Infestato. Sister and brother. Bride and groom. The Devoted of the Seamstress.

The witch queen wore a flowing gown of shimmering crimson satin which flowed from her bare white shoulders to the floor like a spill of blood, obscuring her feet entirely. A spiky diadem of some dark metal, a barbed and deadly looking ornament, topped her golden-haired scalp, stray curls twirling around her jaw and the slope of her slender white neck. Beneath the crown a gauzy veil of matching red obscured the witch's face, but Hayder could feel her old, dead eyes glowering down at him. Infestato boasted similar attire, a long gown of sackcloth black with a matching crown and ornate veil of his own. Were it not for the warlock's considerable height and the divergent color of his garb, Hayder would have been hard-pressed to tell the two of them apart. The man took up the hand of his sister and lifted their arms up together in a conjoined gesture of salutation. With their unoccupied hands, both bride and groom began to scrawl arcane symbols in the motionless air before them. This was met by a rowdy chorus of unearthly moans and cackles from the wedding guests below, some rising from their chairs to shake their talismans at the blessed couple or respond by drawing their own invisible commands with their withered fingers. At that specific moment, Hayder could feel the incalculable magnitude of the power contained within the room. The terrible collected energy flowing from these two fiendish messiahs and the tainted, adoring flock groveling at their feet below.

Yet for all of their perceived potency and imposing presentation, something was off. Hayder could feel it. It hung in the air, heavy and desperate. The power of the Fulci witches, already crippled and maimed, was beginning to wane. The unholy atmosphere in the chamber was thinning out, weakening. The witch blood within Hayder could actually sense their infernal enchantments starting to subside. Like the killing waters of a flood receding away from the remnants of its ruin to reveal the surviving life left behind, struggling for air in the layers of mud and debris.

He knew what that meant. This was not good news. It meant his time upon this world would be coming to an end sooner than later.

From the pool of shadows assembled at the bottom of the staircase a silhouette broke loose and began to walk toward him. Hayder squinted, preparing for whatever was to come next. What was it going to be? The edge of a razor cutting into his throat or plunged into his heart? Eaten alive, one tiny morsel of flesh at a time? A ball peen hammer planted firmly between his eyes?

Come on, he whispered to himself. *Come on and just do what you have to do, already.*

It was only his mother. Mona Hennessey. Mona Fulci. Who or whatever she had finally become.

Now the boy *screamed*.

Hayder saw his mother in her true flesh. Her witchskin. The warped and perverse form cursed upon her, upon all the Fulci kinfolk, by their savage deity. And by God he screamed and screamed and screamed some more until he felt his throat was going to bulge out, boil over, and finally burst. The shifting of the shadow play in the room, partly due to the constant hovering and bobbing of the lanterns in the overhead rafters of the gymnasium, had obscured the woman's face upon her initial approach. That didn't matter much to him. Hayder would have known it was his mother even if he hadn't seen her face. That long mane of thick rusty hair, always in that same tightly knotted ponytail strung up high atop her head, was unmistakable. The familiar, easygoing tread of her walk. Heel to toe, never in a hurry, as if time were never a concern. Very much like his own dawdling, laid-back gait. She stepped fully into a rectangle of much brighter, more penetrating radiance, her hands upon the back of a chair, which she then pulled out and settled into, scooting closer to the edge of the supper table. The yellow glow splashed against the virginal white fabric of her simple cloth tunic, and for a few seconds the woman appeared to have been completely engulfed into a deluge of the purest, brightest heavenly light. Hayder squinted into that light, hoping that perhaps things had been wrong. The grim fairy tale his mother had told him earlier about a boy and doorways and witches and blood to be spilled. The light would fade, and his mother would be standing there. Whole again and normal. The woman who had delivered him into the world.

Nothing to fear here, boyo.

Jeepers Creepers…where'd you get those peepers?

He looked up into his mother's eyes.

A horror stared back at him.

What had once been the thin, pale and somberly pretty face of Mona Hennessey had been replaced by the visage of a devil. A pathetic, broken monster eloped from the pages of bedtime story turned to poison, no longer resembling anything remotely human. The flesh of her face had been peeled neatly back and away from the skull, hooked in place by a wicked string of barbs and chains, revealing the gluey roadmap of chalky tendon and livid pink muscle twitching and oozing beneath. Her lidless eyes goggled stupidly, unfocused and swollen, mouth gaping with lips shining like fat graveyard worms. Hundreds of tiny black bugs skittered across the sopping tissue of her cheeks and chin, slipping in and out of the ruined nostrils, some roosted into tiny settlements here and there to nibble and gnaw at the scourged skin. Perhaps concerned over her son's terrified reaction, Mona reached out a quivering, bony hand to him, a low, anxious moan fluttering in her throat.

Strange words began to form in Hayder's mind. Words he understood, but how he came to know them was a mystery. When they hissed from his mouth the effect of them upon the woman who had once been called his mother was to make her recoil, holding up her wasted arms as if to ward off a blow. Rising from her chair, she began backing away from the boy, bowing repeatedly as if projecting sorrow, contrition, until her body was once more enfolded by the shadows, absorbed back into one of the room's many gloomy nooks. Hayder then, for the first time, noticed there were other things slinking around in those shadows. Grumbling, hungry things, impatient to sit down to the wedding feast.

"Ah yes…well done, young man. If ever there were any disinclination on our part to acknowledge your talents, you just put them to rest." Fantasma took up the hand of her brother and the both of them began to descend the staircase together. "Your sacrifice will be remembered by all those of Fulci blood. We will always praise your name and tell our children of your sacrifice."

The infernal groom nodded. "May the Seamstress bless you in your journey into the Shadowlands."

Once the grim pair reached the bottom step, Infestato released his sister's hand, allowing her to come closer to the boy. To be alone with him and have words. Fantasma leaned over Hayder and stroked his damp hair back away from his forehead. Her scent was odd, but not unpleasant. Spicy and slightly musty. It brought to mind head pictures of faraway places and midnight devotionals to thirsty spirits. Behind the living dead witch, lost in the gloom of the gymnasium, a pitiful moan warbled. It was mom. Hayder could tell. For a moment, just a moment, the boy wanted to go to her. Lay his head upon her breast and tell her it was okay. They would be okay, and they could leave this place together and just go someplace else. Start over. They had done it before, right? They could forget all about Dad and Brandy and Sugar Bava and all of the dead folks in between and just do it all over. Maybe even change their names. Dye their hair. Become something in the ballpark of normal.

Except there was no normal now, was there? There would never be a normal again. Not the sort of normal a child would need to grow up as they should.

A sigh from the shadows. It *was* mom. Annoyed, Fantasma turned and hissed at Mona. Hayder could feel the wraith of his mother, cowed, retreat back into the darkness. Hayder knew there would be nothing further from her. This had been the final word. For all intents and purposes, Mona Hennessey had joined the ranks of the faceless dead.

"Oh, never you mind her, *bambolina*. She is just so…what is your word…jealous? A jealous momma is a dangerous thing for a little boy." Fantasma laid her hands upon the child's chest, head cocked, studying him. Hayder was reminded of a praying mantis he had once seen eating a cricket. It had started with the head of the cricket first, gnawing and devouring its way down until there was nothing left. Not even a trace of a feeler or an uneaten scrap of pulp. "Why don't you just think of me as your mother now? When the pain comes, it will make it easier to bear, and I shan't allow you to suffer for long. *Mia promessa*."

Fantasma leaned back, drawing the bridal veil away from her face with a leisurely, almost theatrical flourish. After the gruesome revelation of his mother's witchskin, Hayder was better prepared for the fright he was about to behold. A scream bubbled in his throat, welling up into a choking ball, then unraveling into a strangled gasp. Fantasma Fulci, unlike his mother, appeared completely inhuman. Not a scrap of anything indicating the sorceress had ever been anything remotely of this earth. Her face had been misshapen into the likeness of a deer, sickly, the fur matted and riddled with mange, pocked with clustered covens of bloated gray ticks and scuttling fleas. From the top of her skull a pair of short, wickedly sharp antlers sprouted out, various occult charms and trinkets dangling from the top and rear tines, with strange runes carved into their discolored and grainy surface. The eyes were alight with the fever of derangement, rolling about in their putrefied sockets, unable to focus, and lit from within by a baleful orange glow. Fantasma opened her revolting maw, slimy green filth drooling from the corners and through the slits in her blackened, jagged teeth. Hayder realized, with horror, the witch was smiling at him.

He glanced over at the monolith obscenely jutting up from the pool of water and felt something stir inside of him. A stirring in a place he didn't fully understand. It wasn't something working through his body, although it came across that way at first. After a bit longer, listening and feeling, Hayder understood.

The stone was trying to talk to him. To establish a line of communication. Unite.

I'm listening. He formed the words in his brain and then allowed them to be carried through the stillness, from one world into another. On the other end of the psychic telephone, he heard laughter. The sharp, mocking laughter of a woman. And then, he knew. It was *her*.

His kinswoman. The blood of his blood. The witch known as Sugar Bava.

His fear, his shock, began to subside very quickly.

"Do not be troubled, sweet boy, for I am here now. Here with you." The voice was soft and slightly raspy, with a peculiar inflection balanced somewhere between backwater yokel and European refinement. It was strange, unnervingly soothing, the voice of this long-dead witch. And the power, dear Lord, the power of just her voice filled him with a ridiculous measure of nerve. So much nerve it was almost unnatural, a bit frightening, even.

"I know you," he thought back. He hoped his tormentors couldn't hear the thoughts in his head. If they did, they made no indication of it. *"You're my family."*

"Indeed, lamb. You are the seed of my poor brother, now long lost to me. That makes you like my brother. My little boy. My family," the Bava witch purred into his ear. It was as if she were kneeling at his side, right next to the table. Hayder swore he could feel the coldness of her breath upon his face and neck, stirring his curls. *"I will keep you safe. And never you mind these blundering dullards. The Fulci pretenders cannot penetrate the black ocean of my mind. Just lie still. Do not attempt to struggle or challenge them. Be quiet. Soon the others will come, and I shall manifest fully. I will be as flesh, as the living, and I will grind these carnival hucksters to dust beneath my heel and whet my lips with their ancient blood."*

"Use me!" Hayder implored. *"Work through my body and let's end it all, right here and now!"*

The witch clucked sadly. *"Regretfully, that is not possible. Though of my blood, your energy is not quite…there. Fear not, love. The conduit is soon to arrive. Be warned now. Prepare for a really, really, really bumpy ride ahead."*

The boy's blood went cold.

"The conduit?"

Hayder didn't wait for an answer. He knew who the witch was referring to. The conduit.

It was Cora.

Across the ethers of the cosmos, twirling and dancing within the darkness of death, he could feel Sugar Bava smiling. Laughing.

He felt an icy hand on his chest. The boy opened his eyes to see Fantasma's revolting visage gaping down at him, head cocked, the flies and fleas crawling and buzzing over the decayed and shabby fur of her face.

"Ah, someone else is here, no?" the Fulci witch commented. It wasn't so much a question as an affirmation of knowledge. "That's fine. We're done here."

"What are you going to do to me?" Despite Sugar's warning, the boy struggled against his bonds, gritting his teeth so hard it hurt his jaw.

Fantasma laughed, a weird, almost girlish giggle. "Why, little one, we are going to *eat* you, of course. Isn't it obvious?" She gestured to the old coffin beside the stone. The witch muttered an arcane string of nonsense and draw invisible commands in the air. The lid of the casket unlatched and began to open with an indignant, rusty creak. Fantasma turned back to him and reached down, tenderly cupping his chin. "Behold, mortal, Adulphina! Adulphina, the Seamstress of Nightmares! Through us she will feed and become whole. Your skin and bones will give her the strength to rise from the void and join my brother and me in unholy wedded harmony. I will bear his fruit. *Her* fruit. The Seamstress will then fully enter this puny universe. She will reclaim the stone and be liberated from her cosmic prison. Free…free to rape and plunder the world!"

The witch turned to her brother and snapped her fingers. Infestato nodded beneath the folds of his veil and lifted his arms into the air, his voice loud and strong enough to penetrate and bend the laws of time and space and reality.

"Let the wedding commence!"

A terrifying, glugging cheer rose up from the assembled, hungry flock of ghouls. They banged their cold fists upon the table, impatient for meat. Hayder, slowly losing his grip on his bearings, looked over at the now open coffin, a smoky miasma of mustard-yellow haze hovering above the terrible box. Something inside of it was stirring. Awakening. A faint pounding was coming from within, like a closed fist pounding upon the door of a profaned chapel. The boy turned and watched Fantasma walking away from him and up the staircase toward her brother, her flimsy matrimonial vestments slipping from her shoulders and exposing her nude, ivory flesh. Infestato unbound his garments and cast them aside, leaving only his head covered by the veil, holding out his arms to receive his sister. All at once the seated ghouls rose from their chairs, as if charmed, and began to form a single line at the base of the stairs, patiently waiting their turn for whatever was to come next. Hayder fought to turn away but couldn't. Something unearthly and unforgiving held him in place. He was meant to see this horror unfold. A horror he was instrumental in bringing to life.

"Please, God. Please." The boy whispered a prayer. "If I'm going to die let it be fast. Let it not hurt and let it be real quick and take me up to heaven just as fast as you can. Spare Cora. Spare Sheriff Matheson."

Die? Please, boy. Have some faith. The time draws close. Just a little more. A few moments more and it will all be done.

Her again. He wanted to believe her.

At the peak of the staircase Fantasma and Infestato Fulci embraced, their hands running feverishly over one another's bodies. Insistent, almost frenzied caresses. The warlock kissed a path down his sister's festering body, pausing when eye-level with her sex. The witch reached down and lovingly stroked her brother's cheek with her knuckles, then withdrew and settled her hands between her legs, her bony fingers spreading open the diseased channel of her sex. Hayder gasped as Infestato bowed his head and then inched forward, closer, upward, and nuzzled his head against her opening, the top of his skull melting into that noxious gap in her crotch, as if he were a sewer rat being swallowed by a python. A mushy, slurping sound filled the chamber. The boy watched, sickened, as Infestato's chin vanished, then his entire head into his sister's obliging cavity. By the time Fantasma had devoured her brother up to his shoulders Hayder understood what was happening. It was like witnessing a black widow gobbling her mate alive. Ingesting him. Sapping his strength and power as his flesh was absorbed by his sister, the hellish sacrament meant to appease the craving of the Seamstress. Soon all that remained of Infestato were his feet, then just the toes, then nothing at all. At the base of the staircase the first ghoul began to shamble forth, up the steps, to have their own moment of pleasure, then extinction, with their cherished queen. The wedding was not just a uniting of a brother and his sister, but the consummation for the entire family. A group affair. The ghoul staggered forth, ripping its tattered graveyard cerements off, and repeated the same ritual as its warlock brethren.

Hayder felt movement next to him. In one of the chairs closest to him a shadow blossomed up from the seat, a distinctly human-like silhouette. Another revenant took their turn with the queen witch, and upon its consumption another shadow appeared in another empty chair. The another. Another. The boy was truly frightened now, struggling to compose himself. He knew damn well once the last ghoul was devoured by Fantasma, something horrible was going to happen. This was when the nightmare would truly come to life.

Fantasma moaned and shuddered in satanic ecstasy, swooning and wobbling as if drunk upon the most decadent of wines, her belly purple and swollen to a grotesque, gargantuan proportion. A viscous pink slime dripped from between her thighs and splashed across the tops of her bare feet; a penetrating and bitter stink like dried urine pervaded the room, making it hard to draw breath without choking. Then, the smell of old death, bringing to mind images of settled dust and bones and faded things. A crumbling mansion consumed by time and the wild. Weed-choked cemeteries. Another howl of corrupted ecstasy burst from the mouth of the Fulci sorceress, this time louder than the preceding outbursts. More intense. The witch's belly had swelled to a fantastic, impossible girth, the bottom of it drooping to the floor. Hayder watched the final ghoul, his own mother this time, slide up and into Fantasma's tainted orifice. Across the room, the only remaining vacant chair gained an occupant, a vague sliver of a human-shaped shadow shimmering into existence. A massive spurt of fluids exploded from Fantasma's nether regions, splashing down the steps in a slimy torrent of filth and infestation. And oh, Lord, how it reeked! The spoiled perfume of gangrene and suicide and hymns offered up to monstrous ghosts.

"*Our Lady!*" the seated throng chanted, the gymnasium quaking and rumbling as if some horrible entity were slowly clawing its way up from some abandoned pocket of hell. Fantasma Fulci was completely now unrecognizable as anything which had ever been remotely human. Her skin had been stretched so tightly across the muscle and fat it had split and fallen away from the rest of her like the discarded mortuary sheet for a corpse. Even the bestial head had fractured and sloughed away from the skull, leaving behind a pulsating, faceless blob resembling the hide of a blind, craving insect. The witch's entire body had come to resemble a rot-fattened coffin worm: larval, wriggling, and corpulent from its gruesome repast. Hayder turned from the lewd spectacle, nauseated and frightened. In spite of the Bava witch's assurances, the boy found himself swirling around the drain of hopelessness. Whatever was coming, and there *was* something coming, there would be no way to fight it, much less defeat it. He didn't even feel like praying anymore. God suddenly didn't seem to matter much. This right here was something a lot older than God, a lot meaner, and a whole lot hungrier.

Then the crying started. The inimitable, fragile wail of a newborn child.

The sound was coming from the open coffin.

Hayder turned his attention to the coffin, lonesome and forbidding, his mind struggling to steady itself from toppling headfirst into the deep and dark pool of insanity. From within the coffin came a frenzied rustling. Movement. Whatever abomination resided within the bone box had been stirred, its slumber interrupted.

The crying grew louder, more insistent.

Ravenous.

Ravenous, yes, and impatient.

Hayder watched with horror as a tiny white hand rose from the casket, not quite human yet not totally completely divorced from humanity. The spindly fingers were too long and thin. They reminded the boy of the tentacle of a jellyfish. Flimsy, weak. Almost like the feelers on a curious insect. The fingers stretched out, closed, then stretched out once again, as if the awakening miscreation were testing out the efficacy of a newly sprouted limb. The fingers came to rest upon the side of the sarcophagus, drumming against the ancient wood, the sharp nails tipping the fingers raking obscenely against the side of it.

Hayder felt a shadow fall across the table. The Wolf-Man stood over him. In one gloved hand it clutched a small green vial filled with a small quantity of some milky fluid. The other hand wielded a wicked looking knife. His daddy had owned a knife like that. It was called a deer skinner, and it was used for exactly what its name entailed. The fiend leaned down and nuzzled its peeling snout against the boy's nose, genuinely affectionate. The stench oozing from it was unbearable to breathe in.

"Here, you drink this, little buddy. It will make this"—it brandished the knife at him—"much easier to bear."

Hayder nodded dumbly and opened his mouth to receive the elixir. The Wolf-Man grunted in approval and uncorked the bottle, laying its glass rim against the boy's bottom lip. The boy was actually relieved. All of it, the nightmare of losing his daddy and baby sister, his mother's gruesome transformation into a creature sired from the blackest of magics.

"Know that this is being done from a place of love, young Bava. Young Fulci. Drink."

Hayder opened his mouth to receive the profane sacrament, just as the gymnasium filled with a metallic roar, an earsplitting shatter of glass, and a howl of fury and lamentation from the dreadful thing rising from the coffin.

NINETEEN

The Old Highway 270 Drive-In, in its heyday, had been the place to be if a kid wanted to see a really bad scary movie. The so-bad-it's amazing kind of flick. Mostly grainy black and white B-listers and Technicolor Euro-nightmares. The drive-in season was typically a short one, usually starting in the final weeks of spring and ending just before Thanksgiving unless the weather turned cold faster than expected. Built in the mid-1950s, it had been a favorite among the younger denizens of both Black Knot and Coffin Mills, famous state-wide for its sweet kettle corn and cheeseburgers. The burgers were especially treasured, particularly a culinary monstrosity known as the Gutbuster. This locally-revered repast was a straightforward enough concoction: a homemade bun piled with grilled onions, garden-grown tomatoes, and finely diced hot peppers, with a choice of mustard or ketchup. Two patties were smashed out, a big slice of cheddar cheese inserted between them, then the whole shebang was grilled and sealed together into a mouth-watering pocket of something wonderful. The snack even carried a warning along with it. The potential eater was advised to make a small incision at the edge of the melded patties in order to vent them. Failure to do this often resulted in the Gutbuster actually *exploding*. Enough customers with grease-stained shirts and mild scorching around their mouths and cheeks attested to the combustible nature of the meal. Everyone agreed, however, the pain and mess were more than worth the risk.

The drive-in had been a bit on the scruffy side from the beginning. Speakers for the cars only functioned properly a third of the time. The screen boasted a few noticeable scars which only grew larger and more conspicuous with every fading season. The lavatories were a certifiable fright to be avoided unless the circumstances were truly dire. In the summer, at the hottest summit of its dog days, the gravel parking lot transformed into one huge barbecue grill, the heat rising up and off of the rocks making the cinematic experience so uncomfortable spectators often resorted to abandoning the inside of their vehicles to sit on the hood or in a lawn chair.

The Old 270 had burned down to the dirt less than a decade after it first opened its gates. Nobody ever really figured out what had sparked the blaze. No one looked into it. The fire department had never shown up to douse the flames. Folks rarely talked about it after it was gone. It was almost as if the 270 hadn't even been real, just something imagined, the memory of it cast aside for other empty legend, another meaningless footnote. Oh, there were rumors, of course. Years later, when many of the people alive at the time of the drive-in's heyday had passed on. Most of them very silly. Impossible. Like the trashy plot from one of the thousands of bargain basement cinematic offerings splashed across that fifty-foot-tall mountain of yellowed white wood and steel.

Regardless, it had been discarded by the living. Nobody wanted it. It was done for.

But now the Old Highway 270 Drive-In was open for business once again! Now, in its new forever twilight home, it could show scary movies again, and so it did. *Only* scary movies. Scary movies all of the time, forever and ever, broadcast straight from a nastier place than Hell could ever hope to be.

Juston Matheson remembered the 270 now. Really *remembered* it. Up until that moment, when he finally laid eyes upon it again for the first time since he had grown up, the place had never crossed his mind. Not even once. Yet here it was again, even larger and more magnificent than he remembered. In spite of the urgency of their situation, the lawman found himself slowing the truck down to admire it.

The screen seemed to menace over them like a necromancer's tower, the top of it brushing up against the eternally overcast heavens. No, that wasn't right. It had never been that tall, or that bright. The light from it was bedazzling, rendering whatever revulsion was transpiring on the thick canvas rectangle that much more vivid. The picture on the bill tonight appeared to be a dandy, too. Something with a phantom dragster piloted by a leering revenant in a cruddy dime store rubber mask that looked like a cross between Frankenstein and the Invisible Man. A warty green corpse face swaddled in dirty, gory bandages, one bloodshot eyeball goggling obscenely. Then a scene of a beach party overrun by shambling zombies, each of them looking more like a bunch of folks dressed in raggedy farm clothes with their faces slathered in a cheap gray greasepaint than the actual walking dead. For all its shabbiness there was an unnerving feeling of authenticity to the experience. Matheson felt his nerves tingle as he gaped up at the mammoth screen, watching the second-hand store ghouls stalk a screaming teenaged girl across a ribbon of scarlet-painted sand, overtaking her, tearing her bikini from her nubile body and sinking their rotten teeth and nails into her tender, buttery flesh.

"Holy hell…" the lawman muttered, unbelieving. The Old 270 had never shown a movie like *this* before.

An incredible, oily gout of blood spurted from out of the screen and across the road, spattering across the windshield of the truck with the force of a massive, closed fist. Taken by surprise, Matheson lost control of the wheel, the truck zigzagging crazily along the dirt road, dust billowing up in a blurry brown cloud. Within a few seconds he had command of the wheel again, hitting the wipers to clear the muck away from the glass, succeeding only in smearing the nasty muck further.

"Watch out!" Cora screamed.

Through the blotted glass the lawman just glimpsed the child standing in the middle of the road, missing them by a matter of inches. Matheson hammered his foot on the brake, the tired old truck swerving off of the road and into the weeds. For a moment time seemed to choke upon itself, the Ford rolling down into rut after rut hard enough to rattle their brains and chatter the teeth in their heads. The man quickly regained control of the truck and had them safely back on the road, slamming once more on the brake. He rolled down the window and stuck his head out, looking for the child. Yes, they were still back there, perhaps a hundred feet away, clumsily lurching in their direction. There was a peculiar pacing in their walk. The lumbering tread of a drunkard. Matheson shifted the Ford into reverse and began driving backward in their direction. The closer they got to the child the more Matheson began to feel something was very wrong.

Then he saw it. This was no mere child standing in the middle of the road. The child, or whatever it was, was very much dead, and had been as such for quite a while, if anything in this haunted hollow in reality had ever been truly alive. Its face was scarcely more than a carelessly scoured skull, the flesh withered down to an almost leathery texture, straggling in gluey clumps from the chin and nose cavity. What little hair clinging to its head was knotted with cockleburs and a gummy discharge of flesh moldered to paste, the crookedly set eyes a gooey, fetid mass. The revenant was dressed in the tattered scraps of a fairy costume, a flimsy swath of purple silk trimmed in frayed gold stitching and dulled glitter, stained black with the rancid fluids of death. It croaked out a coarse groan and raised its arms, an orange papier-mâché jack-o-lantern dangling from one withered wrist, and started to trundle toward them.

"Are we...in...Hell?" the lawman muttered, lowering his eyes. "I know I haven't always been the best boy, but..."

"Matheson!" Cora shrieked, gesturing wildly at the windshield. Matheson lifted his head and saw other forms gathering behind the dead fairy princess, a whole lot of them, lurching forward slowly, a chorus of hateful snarls and cheated moans accompanying their passage. An assemblage of no longer living monstrosities was revealed in the eternally autumn gloaming. More dead kids in ragged Halloween costumes, some new and some from a time barely remembered. As they drew closer Matheson was shocked to realize he knew many of them. Kids and folks from town, many of which he had shared supper tables and gossiped over coffee with. Scotty Raab, looking even less human than when the lawman had last encountered him at the Red Hand campground. His former deputy and friend cackled and snarled at them, a large pair of vibrating antennae atop his head writhing and whipping hungrily. And Priddy, dear, sweet old Ms. Priddy. Matheson only recognized her from the dress she, or it, wore. The pink one with the rash of big while polka dots splashed across the skirt. The old girl had worn it every single Friday for as long as he had worked with her. The horror mildewing beneath the fabric no longer resembled that sweet old lady, Sunday school teacher, and crafter of the tastiest cinnamon rolls he had every smacked his lips across. The woman's head was split right down the middle, peeled away from the bone beneath, blossoming out into a mess of slimy tendrils and ruptured, dripping yellow tumors like a blasphemous mushroom, her tightly wound bun of silver hair suspended from a soggy rind of dissected scalp like a mesmerist's pendulum. Her mouth was a tiny, unmoving thing. Like the suckers lining the tentacle of a squid, opening and closing, the purple tongue popping in and out. Licking. Slurping. Needing.

"Good Lord…" The lawman laid his head on the steering wheel. Thought about crying. But he had seen too much, hurt too much, to even care about crying anymore.

Then he saw her. The one person he hoped he would never lay eyes upon ever again. Becky Shoeman, more intimately known to him as Becky Matheson, his first and, more than likely, last love. The lovely, big-haired girl from Missouri he had once made a bride of before the petty struggles of life and reality had torn them apart. Turned them into hateful strangers Recognizing her wasn't difficult. She was nude, her body pale and smooth as frost-glazed marble, and headless. She shuffled toward the truck, her head tucked neatly in the crook of her arm like some manner of ghoulish handbag, the lifeless eyes unblinking. Her mouth moved, a stitched together chatter of nonsense dribbling forth, the words muffled and out of synch with the lips, as if her utterances were being transmitted from a phantom radio broadcast whispering from another, darker country. Juston could only stare. Screaming seemed like an option left behind a long time ago. He understood then, it only for a moment, what it was like to be truly insane. When the mind can no longer discern the true face of suffering and respond accordingly.

He didn't even notice the crowd forming before them, congregating. Preparing for the macabre feast to satisfy the gnawing in their swollen, rotten guts.

Matheson snapped to, his mind sluggish and addled as if awakened from a drugged slumber. Indeed, a veritable mob of the living dead had begun to gather, some of them clawing their way up from the earth, smelling the precious warm life to be lapped up. Matheson shifted the Ford into first. As if in retort, the truck lurched, coughed and then died altogether. The lawman stared down at the steering wheel, unable to speak. He cranked the key in the ignition and floored the accelerator. The engine complained groggily, rattled, then returned to idleness. The flock of ghouls cackled in unison, sensing the opportunity. Soon, there would be blood and meat for everyone. For all of them.

Just like one of those goddamned scary movies. The same ones he'd watched on that monster of a screen at the Old 270. Now, he was a part of one.

"Hellfire and damnation! Let me deal with this. As usual, it takes a woman to save a man's fucking bacon."

Matheson looked over at Cora. She returned the stare, her dark eyes cold. The lawman knew Cora, for the time being, was gone again and the Bava witch had returned. The child's face split into a chilling smile, winked at him, then was crawling out the passenger side door before he could stop her.

"No. You just stay put. Let me do my thing." The witch spoke into his head. "That's why she's here."

Matheson had a very bad feeling about what was to come. If they made it through this, what further terrible things awaited?

She's getting deeper into Cora. I'm afraid. Once the frying pan is removed from the fire it's still hot enough to burn. Just as dangerous.

Cora/Sugar skipped merrily to the front of the truck, standing defiantly before the growing horde of the undead, her hands on her hips. The flock was less than fifty feet away from them, give or take a foot. The witch in the child's body lifted her hands into the air, her fingers fanned out as if waiting for something to fall from the sky and into them. The hungry creatures stopped in their tread, their hunger abated at the arrival of something unholier than themselves. The girl threw back her head and began to sing, a sweet and lilting melody which stirred something strange within Matheson. Something delving deep into his cells, his blood. Vicious and primeval. The ghouls began to wail in unison, a pitiful, mournful noise, and began to slowly back away, some of them scrabbling at the dirt they had just crawled out from. Retreating.

"Oh no, my pretty dead things. You don't get to go back to bed. You've upset me, and now y'all have to pay." The witch-child chuckled, lowering her right arm while leaving the left one aloft. She looked back at Matheson, locked eyes with him, and snapped her fingers. The sound split the air like the crack of a hunting rifle, causing the lawman to flinch. A new sound began to grow, seemingly called forth from the air. The earth beneath the truck began to tremble, just a hesitant little shiver at first, then quickly resolving into a steady rolling grumble. All around another, stranger commotion entered into the nightmare. The snapping and popping of branches, wood twisting and tangling and snarling. Groaning like a choir of wayward spirits desperate for the tongue of a spiritualist to gossip with the living. Matheson snagged his shotgun from the rack behind the seat and shoved the truck door open, rolling himself out. Once his feet hit the ground another tremble rumbled beneath him, and he had to grab hold of the door to keep from falling. Overhead a gathered membrane of shadows thrashed and writhed, as if the sky had been transformed into a squirming crypt of worms. Matheson looked up. He saw and he gasped, his heart pounding against his ribcage like a trapped sparrow.

It was the trees. The trees had come to life. The witch had willed them into servitude with a single dark breath.

These trees were old. Born before Jesus and all of the men who had written about Him in their holy books and hymnals. A heathen grove looming a hundred feet high or more, molded into a druidic steeple, swaying and crooking with a weird, possessed cadence. Cracking and splitting and then reforming themselves. Limbs transforming into the warped shapes of arms and hands and fingers. All the while the witch chanted them into servitude, a frantic and deep whispering of forsaken arcana. Matheson could only gawk as the boughs and branches broke free from one another and became like a hundred angry fists ready to draw blood and fracture bones at the behest of their dreadful mistress.

The girl glanced over her shoulder at him. The eyes looking back at Matheson no longer resembled the sweet, placid brown spheres residing within the skull of Cora Corbucci. These were the eyes of Sugar Bava now, the fabled witch of Fulci Holler, and to stare too long into them was to court bad luck, to invite insanity. He turned away, icy sweat having broken out all over his body from head to toe. A flash of a thought passed from her into him.

Observe, puny man of this world. Behold the power of a true sorceress. A power not even death could chain, and no grave can hold. Observe, and understand!

At that moment the thick arms and misshapen hands of the forest came pounding down upon the swarm of the living dead. Many of the poor wretches wailed and lifted their hands up to shield themselves—a useless endeavor as the oaken fists came battering down upon them like a god-hammer, crushing many into fetid mounds of grisly pulp. Branches became like scythes for reaping grain, swishing back and forth, shredding decaying flesh and lopping heads from hunched and disfigured shoulders. Grinding rotten bones into a reeking mash of convulsing, gasping innards. What few managed to slink away were quickly apprehended by roots as sharp and deadly as barbed wire, erupting up from the earth and coiling themselves around their unnatural prey and constricting them as a serpent would torment a rodent, their unsavory bodies bloating, throbbing, then bursting into a gruesome shower of corpse filth and satanic fluids. Dust billowed up from the road, obscuring much of the carnage from the delicate eyes of the living forced to observe. Then, as suddenly as they had arrived, the trees relented. The wooden claws, dripping with filth, withdrew through the miasma of disturbed dirt and rock and climbed back up toward the sky, reforming the pagan arch. When the dust settled a macabre sea of butchery lay smashed and spread out before the two of them. Unrecognizable remnants of lives enslaved to an uncaring, cosmic madness, unworthy of either burial or commemoration. Nothing recognizable. Nothing to remember them by.

All of these good folks. All of them, just gone.

Matheson racked the shotgun, his face a stone tablet with a sworn oath of vengeance etched upon its impassive surface. He couldn't recall any time in his three-plus decades of existence when he had felt so enraged, so thirsty for vengeance. So angry he no longer cared what happened to him.

"Kiddo?" he called out, taking a few hesitant steps closer to the child. "Cora, baby. You okay up there?"

The girl looked at the lawman over her shoulder. For a hair of a second Matheson saw the feisty spirit of the dead witch burning in her eyes flicker, then return to the familiar mellow coolness of Cora Corbucci.

"I'm so scared, old man." Her bottom lip quivered. Juston could see the sheen of tears shimmering from her eyes from where he was standing. "She's in here, and I ain't sure she's ever gonna leave." The child's eyes rolled back to their whites, and she sank to her knees, swayed back and forth for a couple of seconds, then collapsed into a defeated heap upon the ground. Matheson rushed over to her, slinging the shotgun over his shoulder. He collected the girl, gathering her into his arms carefully, as if she were made from bone china. The sheriff hustled back to the truck, leaning inside and depositing Cora in the seat. The girl was unresponsive, her skin ashen.

"Oh God, is she dead?"

Cora opened her eyes, gulping up air with a series of ragged gasps. She glanced around, drowsy, a little addled. Matheson exhaled with relief. He slid back into the driver's seat. Once inside he smiled and ruffled her hair.

"Sakes alive. You can't keep doing this to me, girl. I got an iffy ticker as it is." He turned the key in the ignition. The first couple of attempts were met with a grinding of metal, sputtering out with a sickly cough and stink of exhaust. The third time did the trick, the old bag of nuts and bolts roaring back to life. Matheson knew it wouldn't last; he just hoped it lasted long enough. He turned to smile at the girl.

"Right up ahead." Cora pointed out the windshield, the witch's syrupy cadence trickling back into her voice. It's almost over. *Allllll...over."*

The doors of Golgotha Springs High School had only been open since the autumn of 1956 before that damn tremor closed them for good.

It had been a fine-looking school, especially for a town of barely more than two thousand people. The Springs, as it had been called, was a city populated primarily by out of towners. People with pockets full of endless cash to build giant, elegant houses with rambling lawns and teams of workers hired to care for both. The downtown area was small but charming. Lots of retired folks running antique and curio shops, quaint cafés boasting blackberry cobbler and chicken-fried steak and great coffee. Golgotha Springs had been a new town. Its citizens had been the first to live there. For all they knew, its memories began, and would end, with them. Few knew the history of the land upon which those houses and shops had been built. Had they known, a single brick would never have been laid.

Few knew the earth where the town resided had once belonged to the Shogomagra, an Indian tribe whose history had long since been surrendered to ethers of antiquity, relegated to the category of knowledge best left buried, ugly bones never to be stirred. The Shogomagra had been an offshoot of the Choctaw, banished from the tribe for swearing a blood allegiance to some secret, malevolent being. What few written accounts existed chronicling their exploits revealed them to be an exceptionally nasty, brutish lot. Tales of diabolical rituals, perverse debauches, cannibalism, and even worse things. It was said the dark spirit they venerated had granted their medicine men special influence over matters of the grave. Rumors of dead things that wouldn't lie down. When their alleged extermination at the hands of government-sanctioned Indian killers and unscrupulous armed forces had been complete, few of those involved in the slaughter would talk about the Shogomagra, and ever fewer wrote about them. It was as if they had been completely shut out of history, which was not a bad thing. The land where they had settled, even after their extinction, was avoided by everyone with half a lick of sense in their noggins.

Nobody would ever know the man who had founded the Springs had been *called* there. How he had conjured forth a dark spirit in the basement of his house who had entered his body, guiding his hand to write down the original location of the Shogomagra camp in a book bound in the flesh of demons who had died by swallowing their own tongues, and under whose guidance had led him to where he was to open a door to allow them entrance into the realm of men. This man then allied himself with other likeminded men and women to pool resources. By 1945, just a few months after the end of World War II, Golgotha Springs had become a reality. It *existed.* For the most part, its denizens were completely unaware, or at least unconscious of, the atrocities of the past soaked into the soil beneath their grand, towering mansions and perfectly manicured lawns. But it was there, nevertheless. Chewing tiny little holes in their minds, one little nibble at a time.

Nobody would ever refer to it as an earthquake, as such a potentially cataclysmic event rarely happened in Oklahoma and had never occurred before at all in the southeastern cranny of the state. Whatever it was, it was big and mean enough to open up a rift right through the dead center of town, sending the churches and stores and the homes of these well-heeled and unsuspecting fools straight down into a flaming, earthen hell. It had happened at the tail end of May, a week after school had let out and on the evening of the senior prom. An evening of enchantment warped into a night of destruction. Just over a hundred people perished in that gymnasium, their lives claimed by crumbling rock and twisted steel. Many drowned. Some were fried alive in their own skins from downed electrical cables. The entire town had been consumed, swallowed up by the earth and entombed in the muddy waters of the Hootchyfalala.

The National Guard had been called in for what was referred to as a "recovery" operation. Some of the lost would be lost forever, and the few survivors of the tragedy quickly moved on, never to speak of the disaster again. Now, only the foolhardy or just plain stupid ventured into the remnants and rubble of Golgotha Springs. Mostly junk-rats splashing around the banks of the lake, scrounging for the trinkets of the dead. Sometimes they would find something of worth. Sometimes people would venture down there and never be heard from again.

What had happened? The fury of an angry God? The Devil? Just plain, good old-fashioned bad luck?

It didn't much matter, for Golgotha Springs High School had returned, existing in a pocket of eternal twilight to pay homage to the gods of death.

"I know this place."

Matheson slowed the truck down, unwilling to stop completely. He didn't trust the shuddering heap of scrap anymore. Before them stood what had once been a grand, ornate structure. Too formal to be someone's residence. It looked like some kind of office building. Perhaps a government facility from long ago, or a museum. It was a full three stories tall, five porch to roof columns standing watch, the white paint discolored to an ugly bruised gray. All of the windows except for a huge one in the dead center of the second floor had been boarded up and chained. A large dome declined sadly in the middle of the roof, its shingles rattling in the poisoned breeze, shuttered from the outside world. As they drew closer Matheson saw the huge brass plaque bolted above the entrance, tarnished with moss and mold. Now he did stop, but left the engine idling. It grumbled like a sickly, wheezing hog. He was right. He did know this place.

"Golgotha Springs High School?" Cora squinted out the windshield, then turned to the lawman. "That sounds familiar. Was that a real place?"

"*Was* would be the right way to describe it. You might have heard folks talk about it." Matheson nodded grimly. "Big old earthquake swallowed that building up, the whole damned town up, a long time ago." He looked at the girl and shrugged. "I would say this is impossible, only that impossible doesn't mean diddly-squat anymore."

"It's not a school now. The witch says it's a church. A church for the Fulcis to do their bad things." Cora replied in her own voice. "Hayder is in there. I can feel it. *She* can feel it too."

"No time to waste, then. Let's roll." Matheson shifted back into first and began to ease the Ford ahead. A second later he slammed on the brakes. He'd been so busy deliberating over the marvel of the school he hadn't noticed the wide, coiling stream of sackcloth dark water dividing their side of the world from the forsaken building. The stream was littered with hundreds of floating coffins and dangerous scraps of junk. Every so often a spout of black water would spurt up, following by the brief sheen of slick, reptilian hide. It reminded Matheson of a moat guarding an old castle, one plagued by a litany of terrible memories.

"Dammit! No way we are getting this old heap across that mess. Sorry, old girl." Juston patted the dashboard fondly. "No wading across it either. There's things swimming in there, and I don't think they'll just step aside and let us just go skipping-to-my-lou in." He laid his head down against the steering wheel, relishing its cool surface. A warm hand laid itself across his. He turned his head to find Cora looking at him.

"There's a way. You just got to let someone else take the wheel for a bit," the little girl said, squeezing her thumb into his palm. "The witch can get us in there. You just have to let her. Trust her and let her."

Matheson chuckled sarcastically. "No thanks. I'd rather trust Satan himself to take the wheel."

"Trust me, handsome. You will need my witchery to transport you across the dark water. I will serve as the ferryman across the rivers of Hell and Death." Sugar Bava was in command of Cora once again. She stroked his cheek with the back of her hand. "You really have no choice, do you? Go on. Take your chances with the water. Stand tall upon the boxes of the dead and hope that terrible thing sloshing around in the muck won't rise up and gobble you whole. Go on."

The lawman jerked away from her hand and sighed dejectedly. Of course she was right. He was afraid she was going to be right about a lot of things.

"Tell me what you want me to do," he growled.

"Up yonder, off the road and up the hill a bit, there is an overhang. It's close enough to that big window…"

Matheson interrupted her. He understood where this was going. "Are you crazy? You want me to drive this prehistoric truck off of this cliff and through that there window?"

"It's an overhang," corrected the witch.

"Overhang, cliff, what the hell ever! If we're lucky we'll crash and be dead in seconds. That is, if the glass from that goddamned window doesn't shred us to pieces."

The witch ignored him. "You just get this rattling pile of metal up there. Back it up as far as you can and get it really cooking. Push it as hard as it will let you. Then start driving ahead and as fast as you can. I will give you wings and cover us in a new skin. Not a scratch will be laid upon that adorable head of yours. Of any of ours."

"I don't believe you," Matheson said through clenched teeth.

"Then we shall all just wait here to die then." Cora/Sugar shrugged indifferently. She turned away and began to whistle a strange, unnerving tune. The sheriff sighed and leaned back in his seat. He had to think for a minute.

Remember where you are. This isn't the real world. Who knows what we can do here, in this place? You're running out of time and options. Do you want to be stuck here, in this place? You've come this far. Finish what you started, you son of a bitch.

Cursing under his breath, Juston steered the truck off of the road and up the swell of the hill as directed. At the crest of the hill was the aforementioned overhang. The leap from the edge of the precipice to the window was a good hundred feet. An impossible gap, even for a leap of faith.

Of course, they did have a witch on board.

The gloom of the approaching night was growing thicker. Once it was full dark, it would all be over for everyone.

He shifted into reverse and began backing the truck up, swerving to avoid the occasional stray rock or tree.

It was do or die.

Matheson threw the truck into first and sank the accelerator all the way to the floor of the pickup. The truck lurched forward at an incredible speed, the earth beneath the spinning wheels crumbling away. Then they were flying. *Actually flying.* There was no more distinction between earth and heaven. Just the emptiness of space and time and the unknown. It was…exhilarating.

Then they hit the glass, and everything dissolved immediately into utter blackness.

TWENTY

Cora Corbucci stood across from the witch Sugar Bava, a name only spoken out loud by old men in cautious whispers, their craggy faces illuminated by the glow of a low-burning autumn campfire. A ghost story come to life, rising from a tomb of dusty, moldering books. Surrounding them was a meadow of rolling, glossy darkness, like a sheet of black plastic laid across a cold and stiffening corpse. No sound. No smells. Just them and the awful, awful darkness.

The girl could feel the power radiating from the evil thing. Even trapped behind the curtain of the Afterlife, so very powerful.

Cora was surprised at how small, how beautiful the sorceress was, at least to look at. She was roughly the same height as Cora, perhaps taller by just a skim off of a hair. Her thick hair fell around her shoulders in unruly, curling waves of scorched honey, framing a delicate heart-shaped face pale as winter's breath. Her lips were full and ripe, her dark eyes too large for her face and set slightly apart, lending a weird and slightly uncanny look to her. She wore a long flowing gown of deep crimson, almost black in the hooded illumination of the netherworld, her white shoulders and tiny feet bare. She was smiling at Cora, a shallow and grim distortion of the face. It was not the smile of someone offering comfort. It was the ruthless grin of a predator creeping up behind a crippled animal, fangs bared and pupils dilating with kill lust.

The child wondered where the name Sugar came from. There was nothing sweet whatsoever burning within those eyes.

"You're lookin' a bit raggedy there, sister," the witch commented, her voice slivered with a stinging mockery of concern. "I think a nap is just the thing. A beauty needs her beauty sleep, after all."

"You think you're gonna swallow me up until there isn't any more of me left. But you're wrong about that. I got my own witchcraft. I can keep you off me," Cora shot back. They were circling one another like a pair of gunslingers now, eyes locked, assessing the other for weakness, a slip-up.

"Oh yes you do, sweetness. I can taste it. You're *delicious*." Bava smacked her lips obscenely. "When the Wolf blasted you, he never counted on you actually living. You tricked that dirty old fucker quite thoroughly. But the witchcraft inside of you has always been there. A planted seed. You had to be touched by death to make that seed go to flower. A flower nurtured with blood."

"You want Hayder. He's the reason for you being inside of me." Cora felt her will slipping. Wavering. The witch was trying to poke a hole in her defenses.

"*Pffft!*" Sugar spat. "That brat will soon wear out his usefulness to me. The witchblood bubbling through his veins means nothing to him. He doesn't understand the power. Doesn't *want* to understand it. The older he gets without using his talents, without testing himself, the more those talents will die a little bit with every passing night."

"You need my boy more than you think. He dies and your hold over that stupid rock will be gone. You'll finally become the mean old ghost you really are."

"Oh, such a brave thing! You are everything I had hoped you would be, and so much more," Bava cackled. She held out a thin white hand to Cora. "I have been watching you for a while now. Since you were very little. I hoped to meet you someday. Lucky me...that someday has come sooner than later."

"Don't get too used to it, lady," Cora sneered. "We're about to tie up loose ends, and when we do you'll be gone. By God, I'll make sure of that."

Bava stopped abruptly, hand still outstretched. The smile on her face had shifted into complete coldness, a surgical expression without a crumb of humanity.

"You keep telling yourself that, little bird. Whatever lies you can tell yourself to make it hurt less. By the time my work is done, when Hayder has served my purpose, it really won't matter any longer. I will live in *you*, and *you* will know the true power of *your* witchery. I will be as your mother, your teacher, your very life. You will beg me to stay. You will pine to feel me burning within you."

Cora began to feel woozy. Like the time at Bible Camp a few years ago when one of the other girls had slipped a splash of booze into her orange pop. It began as a slow, warm balm melting down inside of her, spreading throughout her limbs like sweet concrete. Everything became hazy. Like a dream. Her eyes closed. She just couldn't keep them open any longer.

Such a soft voice. Like slow, warmed molasses trickling into her ears and varnishing her brain.

"Yes, pet. Just a few winks to keep the wheels turning. Sleep for me. Ease yourself. Such incredible, dreadful visions and pleasures await you. Await us."

TWENTY-ONE

The ecstasy was even greater, more overwhelming, than she could have ever dreamed, even in her filthiest, most depraved fantasies. Fantasma felt the penetration of the Seamstress throbbing within every loathsome orifice of her blighted flesh. The glory, the horror, was beautifully inconceivable. As the Fulci children crawled up into the bloated hulk of her body, slowly becoming one with her, she could actually *taste* her power growing. Flowing. Within her purple and distended belly the witch could feel them rummaging around, devouring her, moaning, the husks of their living dead carcasses swelling like seedlings about to blossom into flowers of sickness. Their blood, their reeking meat, merging with her own.

It was her reward for service. For her devotion. Orgasm after savage orgasm rippled throughout every repugnant inch of her corpulence. In the coffin at the bottom of the staircase, the Seamstress had already begun to inhabit the vessel. The tiny pink arms of the miscreation within the box flailed about dumbly, grasping at air. Looking for anything. Indulging in this new breath of existence. Beside the sarcophagus the Wolf stood over the Bava child, the sacrificial family blade held aloft, poised to plunge down into the little boy's baby flesh in search of his beating heart. Once the blood of life ceased to surge through the chambers of the organ, the child's death confirmed, the grisly supper would finally commence. The sacred bell would ring out and both of them, the Seamstress and her faithful servant, would sit at that table and dine together, as foretold. Then the greatest of all witches would offer herself to receive the blessing of the Lady. She would be embraced and consumed, a special blessing reserved only for the most loyal and cunning of witches. So long in the making. So long in its realization.

The stone would be theirs at last. Truly *belong* to them. The Bava whore would fade from the ether like smoke clinging to the timbers of a snuffed death pyre. The Fulci name would be eternal, and the entire world would fall to its bended knee before it.

The blade rose and harvested a gleam of faded twilight sun. The Wolf spoke the words. It was going to work! She could feel the love of the goddess enfolding her. Rebuilding her, one cell at a time.

Fantasma's rapture, her dark delusions, were split asunder with a thunder of breaking glass and wood and a metallic roar.

She knew immediately what it was, what was happening, and then the sweet, contemptuous laughter she had heard far too many times in her dreams.

The cackle of Sugar Bava, the dreadful Witch of Fulci Holler.

Matheson's truck missed both Hayder and the Wolf-Man by just a few feet, slamming down solidly enough to bounce the small boy from off of the table and send him hurling him to the floor. The Wolf-Man was not so fortunate. A shrieking shower of ground-up stained-glass, countless tiny pinprick daggers raining down upon him and shredding through the flimsy fabric of his gaudy leisure suit, calling forth fresh blood from thousands of tiny fissures, ripped into his flesh. He howled in agony, writhing upon the hard floor and clawing frantically at his mask. Behind them Fantasma belched forth a nasty, choking scream as the shriveled abomination nesting within the coffin mewled and gurgled. The old pickup had ended its days tear-assing down the back roads of and country lanes of Black Knot by landing upon the ancient casket, pulverizing its revolting resident into a cold smear of slimy filth. A tiny white arm thrashed beneath the weight of the rear driver-side tire, the spindly fingers grasping feebly at the air, opening and closing, dancing, shuddering, then slowly dropping down to lie still.

Hayder lay stunned upon the floor, his ears ringing. He was covered in dust and powdery fragments of glass, the overpowering tang of blood in his mouth. Through the haze and chaos he heard the rusty creak of the truck door swinging open. Matheson was yelling for him and Cora. He tried to call out to them, to let them know where he was, when his arms were jerked back, pain slivering up through his shoulders. Suddenly his hands were free. Aching, bloodied, but free. The boy rose to his feet and looked around, his eyes drawn to a shadow corner of the room. For an instant—just a blink of an eye, mind you—he saw his mother. Mona Hennessey, the way she had looked when she had been his momma. Beautiful and funny and full of love and strangeness. The woman who had taught him how to ride a bike, who made the tastiest mac and cheese ever, and told the best ghost stories over a low burning campfire.

Now, she was barely here. A watery, fading thing lost forever. The ghost rose a hand up in greeting, nodded its head, then dissolved back into the gloom.

"I love you, momma. Be well," the boy whispered, then smiled.

Matheson called out to them through miasma of smoke and gas fumes, a voice filled with fear and hurt.

Their smiles faded very quickly indeed.

The lawman knew he was badly hurt. He could feel at least one rib poking against the aching flesh of his right side. Not something that was going to kill him right away, but the longer he let it get away from him, or if he got jostled a little too roughly, he was going to go down. He was going to go down hard.

He hollered out to Cora, doubling over in pain for his trouble. He had just glimpsed her crawling out of the truck through the passenger side window, scurrying off into the fray to only God knew where. He yelled for Hayder. All he could hear was the awful, cheated weeping of the misshapen repugnance on the staircase, its plump and ulcerated hands slicing at the air with razor-tipped fingers. He wasn't sure how he knew it, but it was the Fulci witch-queen he was looking at. The one whose name had been chiseled upon one of the cursed tombstones which had split apart Main Street back home. It was badly hurt. Hurt and very, very angry. He waddled over to the truck to retrieve the shotgun from the gun rack and found it missing. Frantic, he searched behind the seats and in the floorboard, even in the ruined area around where the vehicle had crashed. Nothing.

Now he felt true terror, but only for a moment. He fumbled around through the debris and found a splintered chair leg, thick oak almost sharpened down to a spear, and started toward the witch-thing. He cut eyes to the monolith imposing from the pool of greasy water. That was the key to it, to sending these Fulci hellspawn back down to the Devil where they belonged. Fantasma had spotted him now, her goggly frog-like eyes focused, and she began to totter slowly down the steps toward him, leaving a bubbling trail of yellow-green sludge in her wake. The lawman looked down at the chair leg in his hand, then to the stone, then back to the lumbering monster coming to devour him. Matheson's heart sank, the terror seeping into his bones. It was hopeless. He had no idea how to fight the beast, to destroy the rock, to save these kids. To save Black Knot.

Drop your stick, little man. Drop the stick and turn away from the stone. Come and know me better. Join with me. Come inside of me and taste pleasures unimaginable.

Yes, it sounded good. Just follow that voice, understand the words and be done with all of this. Did he really ever think this would work? A man and two children could defeat something half-god...with what? A gun? A scrap of splintered wood? The table leg fell from his hands, and he began to walk toward the witch-beast, his eyes shining with tears.

Yes, come to me. Come to me and I will make it all better. You will be able to close your eyes and forget. Forever. There will be peace at last. Peace...at...last.

It was Becky's voice. No, his mother. His daddy. Raab. His own.

A thundering crack slashed through the pandemonium, Matheson recognized it immediately. It was the shotgun. His shotgun. Another blast, followed by a peal of high, sweet laughter. The laughter of a child who had lost their mind. Sanity collapsed into derangement.

The howling of a wolf.

Cora.

Cora/Sugar approached the Wolf-Man through the curtain of smoke, racking the shotgun. He struggled up from the floor, wobbling unsteadily. His suit was dyed with blood deepened to black, covered from head to toe in a shimmering coat of broken glass. Cora felt the Bava witch withdraw, relinquishing control to her host. It was her time now. A moment long overdue. This monster was going to pay for breaking her body, for killing her best friend and robbing the only family she had ever known from her.

Enjoy, little sweet. This is for you.

The Wolf-Man heard the crunch of glass beneath the soles of her sneakers and whipped around. A low growl rumbled in his throat. The beast dared a step closer, hesitated, and cocked his head. He began to heel-toe backward, his gloved hands held out as if to ward her off, or perhaps beg pardon. Resting the shotgun in the crook of her arm, Cora offered her hand, fanned out her fingers and curled them, wiggling each digit in a gesture of invitation.

"Come to me, little doggie. Come to me and take your lumps like a man."

Unable to control himself, the Wolf-Man found himself lifted from off of the floor and dragged across the room. Toward the little girl he had meant to kill but couldn't. Toward the little girl he had meant to drive insane but couldn't. He found himself staring down the barrel of the shotgun, the black sphere of the muzzle a rip in time and space and unknown galaxies. An abyss to which he would be banished and tormented for the remainder of his unnatural days.

Cora lowered the weapon, placed the barrel against his chest, and squeezed the trigger. The boom echoed through the chamber like the knuckles of an angry god banging upon the door of Hades, the world transforming into a wasteland of sulfur-stink and gnashing teeth. The Wolf-Man went flying back, head over tail, in a rupture of sticky gore and shredded cloth, a desolate yowl trailing behind him. He came to land on his back, hard enough for Cora to hear the bones in his spine splinter and break like winter twigs. The girl beamed with satisfaction and ambled toward him, stopping to stand over him. She reached down and ripped the mask from his face. Cora stared dead into the face of an extraterrestrial atrocity which would have, under normal circumstances, driven her immediately into absolute, incomprehensible lunacy. But Cora was no longer normal, nor would she ever be normal again. That train had pulled out of the station.

The child held up the mask, slick and dripping in her hand. Regarded it. Studied it. Indeed, the flayed hide of a beast. A Halloween mask turned ugly. Cora slipped it over her head, her skin embraced by heat and wetness and filth. The stench within the mask was the ghost of savagery come to life. Of unrepentant bloodlust and the thrill of cruelty. She glowered down at the pitiful creature at her feet, its trembling hands held up and entreating mercy. The child chuckled and lowered the shotgun directly into the gaping void of its unmentionable face. The scrape of the weapon's forestock was the peal of a funeral bell. The little girl laughed. What a joke. Such a puny, insignificant thing to have caused her so much misfortune.

"You're done giving me bad dreams."

Cora pulled the trigger. The blast was the final page of a terrible book being turned and shelved forever. The last shovelful of dirt upon the lid of a coffin. The wolf's arms remained up, reaching for her, shuddered once more, then sank down to rest upon his chest. The girl stared down at the mess of what had been her greatest nightmare. Nothing to fear any more. Pathetic. Now just little more than a bag of skin and worms.

Cora Corbucci flung the gun away and raised her hands into the air, to the burning sky, drunk upon the heady nectar of vengeance, and howled. Howled and howled until her throat was raw, aching, about to burst. Alive at last.

Hayder shuffled toward Matheson, his legs like Jello. He was fairly certain something somewhere in his body was broken. The report of a gun bellowed through the length of the gymnasium of the dead school, followed by lunatic laughter, then the unnerving baying of a wild thing. Matheson came lurching at him through the smoke, his face ashen and weary. The boy staggered over to him and the two wrapped their arms around one another, fiercely embracing.

"That noise…" Hayder started, wheezing.

The lawman nodded. "It's Cora. We gotta find her."

"No need. I am here."

The three of them turned and saw Cora emerge from the smoke, a fright in the wolf skin mask, her arms slick with blood. She gripped the mask and pulled it off, casting it to the side. Her face affected a queer amalgamation of pain and serenity. Matheson smiled sadly at her.

"You take care of things, kiddo?"

Cora nodded, but when she spoke it was the witch addressing them.

"One down, one to go." The child turned and pointed at the stone. "Come, kinsman. Join me at the stone." She held out her hand to Hayder, palm open.

Hayder found himself unable to resist. Disengaging himself from Matheson, he walked over to her and accepted her hand. A shock jolted through his arm and into his brain. He knew what to do, what they had to do. Together, and only together, witch to witch, could they destroy the stone. That goddamned stone, the true source of all of their misery. All of their loss. Just a mere rock. Cora began to lead Hayder away from the others toward the pool. The boy could feel their united energies welling, growing, become more real.

"What are you doing?" Matheson yelled at them, trying to walk over to them and sinking down to one knee, holding his side. He was beginning to think his injury was a lot worse than he had earlier imagined. Breathing was beginning to be a chore, even painful. A punctured lung, no doubt.

"Calm down, Tin Star. Only the three of us can split the stone asunder." Cora/Sugar was half-dragging Hayder along. The boy was beginning to feel an odd disquiet grow within him, something which tasted a lot like distrust going down.

"Wait a minute. We destroy that rock, then that'll keep you from being tied to it. You won't have to haunt it anymore." He ground his heel in the floor and stopped them both cold, jerking his hand free. "What happens then? We'll be setting you free, but I get the feeling there's something else to all that. I can tell."

"Of course there is something more to it, you silly goose. Did you not think there would be a cost for my aid? Payment to the piper?" Cora/Sugar smiled sweetly. "You're right. I shall be free. Free to roam the earth without the shackles of death to hold me. Without bars to box me in."

Hayder looked down, thinking. He didn't like what she was saying. He discerned the smell of something rotten. The girl reached out and took his hand in her own again, lifting up both of their arms together.

"Come. We will only have this chance. This moment. Observe."

Hayder looked up to see the stone looming over him like a forgotten divinity roused from hibernation by words of magic. The awesome majesty of the stone held him mesmerized him, sliding its malevolent tendrils into his brain. Burrowing into his heart, seeking what it wanted and taking it. He turned and saw Cora looking at him, and for a second it was her. His girl. Eyes tender and full of fright. Something in them, almost pleading. His girl knew a lot but couldn't tell him. The witch had too firm a grip on her tongue.

The two turned to confront the stone. Cora closed her eyes and began to sing. The words were in a language alien to him, possessed of a modulation like a kind of eerie poetry, but the melody struck a familiar note. The boy couldn't explain it, but he had heard it before, but not with his own ears. He opened his mouth and began to sing too. The same tune, the same rhythm, the same incomprehensible verses. Immediately the world around them began to melt away like a film of thin ice upon the windshield of a warm car. Phantasmal faces appeared before his eyes, pale and leering, cadaverous. Cora's grip on his hand tightened. She threw her head back and began to scream, transforming the song into a macabre invocation, her voice cleaving through the centuries, pulling power from the tombs of the damned. Hayder felt the spell worm its way into his own head, and soon he was screaming along with her. Together the two of them, holding hands and screaming.

The stone began to tremble. The mighty stone, responsible for so much misery and destruction, was afraid. Afraid of the song and what it meant. Afraid of what was to come next.

Someplace else, in a realm unknown to men of this world, something began to listen.

Fantasma Fulci collapsed upon the scuffed wooden floor, her corpulence pooling out grotesquely beneath her in an indecent sprawl. The floor was cool and comforting beneath the cratered flesh of her flabby jowls. Her leprous black tongue lapped weakly at the floor, seeking substance to provide her strength. The power to punish these upstarts. She cried out to the Seamstress for succor. Just a kiss upon the crown of her head to fill her with enough vigor to rise up and blast these interlopers into oblivion. The witch-queen prayed. Prayed for her dread mistress to enfold and cradle her. To make things right again.

A monumental crack split the air, louder than a hundred angelic trumpets sounded before a doomsday charge. A roar of rushing water and churning, agitated air. She lifted her weary head and saw the Bava child and the little girl, the host for that bothersome country witch, standing before the blessed rock, holding hands and singing. The crack had come from the stone. It was splitting down the middle, and the louder, the higher the two children sang, the deeper the crack spread downward. The pool of black water was a swirling maelstrom, shaking the stone like a viper clasped in the hand of a beguiled preacher.

Fantasma felt the floor beneath her belly begin to rumble, divide, and start to crumble apart.

All she could do was lay her head back down and weep. Weep and wait for it.

Somewhere, Death was laughing. It had been waiting for this precious moment for a very long time.

Matheson watched the scene with fascinated horror. The enchanted stone was visibly vibrating, tremoring with such ferocity it appeared blurry to his eyes. The resonance of unnatural thunder filled his ears, rendering him wobbly and disoriented. He had no way of comprehending the gravity, the magnitude, of the bedlam unfolding before him. How close they had come to witnessing the end of all things, the extinguishing of everything. The lawman watched Cora and Hayder, linked together by the blood sorcery of a long-dead witch, call down the fury of a sleeping god, now wide awake and cantankerous, upon the monolith. The sealing of a door which should have remained forgotten, unrecorded.

"My god comes! The Quiet Lord! Master of Opened Veins! Emperor of the Phantom Nations!" Sugar Bava bellowed triumphantly from the mouth of Cora Corbucci, Hayder dutifully repeating every word after her. Above the stone a hazy gray form began to assemble. At first a mere wisp of errant smoke seeping from the pipe of an old man upon his bed of dying, coalescing and dividing, then adhering at last into the distinctive shape of a tall, slender man with a pair of great shadowy wings like those of a monstrous bat. Its face creased by a sinister smirk, the wraith lifted a spectral arm and hammered a gigantic gray fist down upon the peak of the blasphemed rock, deepening the awakened split in its roughhewn surface. A clap of thunder tolled, loud enough to knock the legs out from under both Hayder and Cora and send Matheson somersaulting backward and across the floor of the gymnasium. There was a dazzling flash of crimson light and an icy gust of arcane wind. The breath of plague pyres and murder. The stone split asunder and began to levitate up and out of the dark water, disintegrating one fragment at a time, each shard transforming into dust as they descended toward the pool.

Flattened and convulsing beneath Matheson's truck, the rotten horror in the coffin began to whimper.

With a final blinding flare of light the stone shattered, becoming a perfect pillar of ash hovering in mid-air, bobbing like a fishing lure on the surface of a lake, then cascading down into the pool to be consumed by the tainted water which had once served as its home, its altar.

The light slowly diminished, blindness now giving way to clarity. In the murky water the ashes of the stone churned and eddied, slowly forgetting its molecular composition. Soon there was nothing but the putrid water, a hazy recollection of the light, and the whimpering thing lying in the coffin. A warm balm of serenity drifted down upon each of them.

Behind them a horrible, pained scream burrowed into their ears. The floor began to quake again, and the balm of serenity receded.

It wasn't over after all. Something was coming. It was knocking on the door of this world right now.

Fantasma had been wounded beyond all hope of mending. When the stone shattered she could hardly raise her misshapen head, a weak croak of protest gargling in the diseased fissure of her throat. She had resigned herself to defeat and had made peace with it, for the most part. The Seamstress could take her now, body and spirit. The Fulci hag would fade into the cosmos, devoured by the ethers of time to wait for another chance. An opportunity for revenge. For a witch, death was never really the end.

When they perished, for lack of a better term, they simply went elsewhere for a while, seeking other realms and other adventures. Biding their time until they found their way back to the world of mortals. Back to recoup the debt of their demise with an icy dose of retribution. Fantasma found comfort in the belief that she would deal with the Bava family once more. Perhaps ten years from now. Perhaps two centuries. A millennium. She could wait. The living dead were a very patient lot.

Then, the floor of the gymnasium rumbled faintly. Had she imagined it?

A second rumble, more insistent than the previous one. Something in the tremor tickled a nerve. The entire chamber began to rock violently, like a rowboat coasting too far out into a discontented sea. Fantasma's dreams of revenge and other worlds began to unravel. She could feel it in the air, feel it all around her. The Seamstress was displeased. Not over the destruction of the stone, but at the failure of her most trusted, most resourceful servant, to protect the stone. Her failure to open the door. And now that servant was going to suffer for her weakness.

The varnished wooden floor beneath the coffin degenerated and caved in, swallowing both the coffin and its occupant, now flattened into a pathetic mass of warbling pulp. From the bowels of the earth a gargantuan glowing blue hand surged forth, sending a hail-bomb of rubble and spoiled earth spewing out in its wake. The malformed appendage, the size of a school bus, lashed out and snatched up Fantasma as easy as plucking a wasp from the shoulder of a terrified child, lifting her up and into the air. The giant fingers curled themselves around her revolting form, and with a single, effortless twitch, crushed the sorceress in a gout of bloody mulch and shredded bone. The sorceress managed a feeble squawk before she was completely enclosed in the spectral fist. Its job done, punishment doled out, the hand of the Seamstress, dripping with slime and congealed globs of fat, slowly retreated back down into the crater in the floor, like a cobra retreating from the snarl of a mongoose.

A cold wind gusted through the gymnasium, no longer a sanctuary for the damned. Everything was quiet and clean. They could breathe now.

It was done.

TWENTY-TWO

The three of them stood gathered around the hole in the floor where the giant hand had hauled Fantasma Fulci down to whatever hell awaited her, staring down into its seemingly impossibly deep gloom. Hayder picked up a small chunk of broken granite and tossed it into the hole. Seconds passed. Then a minute. Nothing. If there was a bottom to the crater, it was too deep to hear the rock hit the bottom, and maybe that was a good thing. Through the shattered window the corn-yellow radiance of a harvest moon shined down upon the ruined gymnasium, now no longer a temple for ungodly devotions. A chilly breeze wafted through the chamber, imparting a comforting tremble to each of them. Nothing nefarious to it at all. Just a common, run of the mill autumn shiver. Everything was silent and solemn, even an attempt at the slightest whisper feeling sacrilegious.

"Thank God for the moon. It would be bad dark in here," Hayder commented. The boy spoke in the drowsy undertones of one so dog tired they were lingering in a state mere minutes from a total breakdown into incoherence.

"Got a camping lantern in the truck toolbox if we need it." Matheson glanced at the ruin of his trusty old claptrap, now officially retired from all future road trips. He sighed sadly. "At least I did."

Everyone remained silent. Matheson looked at Cora for signs of anything. The child was staring at the crater, head cocked, a strange smile scrawled on her face. That smile bothered him.

"So, how do we get out of here?" asked Hayder. "I thought maybe when that witch cashed in her ticket something cool would happen. A portal or something would open up. Like when you defeat the Lich King in *Necromania*."

"This is not a game, piglet." Cora turned away from the depression in the floor and regarded the boy with amusement. "Well, it was. Not the sort of game you are referring to. But a game, nevertheless."

"You're still here?" asked Matheson. He hadn't needed to. The presence of the Bava witch radiated out from Cora in an unsettling, draining aura.

Cora/Sugar skipped her eyes over from the boy to the lawman. "Why…I never went away."

"She's not going to go away, either," Hayder commented flatly. He walked over to Cora and locked eyes with her. "Don't y'all get it? Why she helped us in the first place?"

Realization dawned upon Matheson. "You mean to stay in her body, don't you? You're going to squat in this child's body and do all of your dark magic with it. Through it."

"That's right. I saw it while Cora and I were fighting with the stone. I could read Cora's thoughts, and *hers*." Hayder nodded, his face grim. "She did it so she could have a way to kick a hole in this world and return to life. Kind of."

"Do remember, I had a hand in that fight!" Cora/Sugar sniped playfully. Not really angry. "Were it not for me the lot of you would be dissolving into little piles of shit in the belly of that Fulci cunt. Your wretched little Black Knot would be a ghost town. A bit of gratitude is in order, I think."

"So, it's over?" Hayder wheezed.

"Oh yes, it's as over as over gets." The witch in the child's skin nodded, returning her eyes to the crater. "The Fulci bloodline is as good as dead. A few stragglers will endure here and there. Not enough to pose any threat to us. The Lavera dogs will assume control of things for a brief spell, but we'll deal with them soon enough."

At that moment Matheson understood everything, a comprehension reflected back at him from Hayder's eyes. He considered tackling Cora. Maybe Hayder had enough juice left in him to fight the witch, Bava to Bava. Somehow drive her out of the little girl. He just had to find his chance. Wait for the window.

Cora/Sugar leapt back and away, snatched up a shard of glass and held it to her throat. "Don't be a fool, Tin Star. I know what you're going to do before the thought even tingles the wrinkles in that tiny brain of yours. Twitch a finger and this child will die choking on her own blood."

"Then you'll have no way to do anything. You'll go back to being a sad old ghost like before," Hayder growled, hands curled up into fists at his side.

Sugar chuckled. "Would you like to test that theory, piglet?" As if to drive home her threat she slid the glass across the white plane of Cora's throat, drawing a single crimson bead. "No. You won't do that. None of you will. I will wear down this child until I am in complete control. I have plans not only for Black Knot but Coffin Mills as well. The Mills was my unhappy home a very long time ago. I have unfinished business there. Grave business."

"Cora…she'll be…gone?" Hayder gulped, his eyes welling up with tears. "You're going to kill her?" The last utterance came out as a snarl. The anger in his voice was palpable.

"If need be. But I don't want to. You'll find I can be reasonable. Her power will flow better into me if I keep her breathing and the heart within her beating." The witch cocked the little girl's head, batted her eyes and clucked in mock sorrow. "Oh, peanut, don't worry so. I reckon I can permit your puppy love to endure. Granted, it might feel a tad…awkward. Just pretend it's her eyes when you're looking into mine."

Hayder vaulted himself at Cora/Sugar, taking everyone off guard, including the witch herself. He rammed headfirst into the girl's belly with a roar worthy of a Viking pummeling a hated adversary. A startled burst of air whooshed from her mouth, the shard of glass flying from her hand to shatter uselessly on the floor. The momentum of Hayder's assault carried them both across the floor and into the pool of water where the stone had once stood in government, both of them vanishing into its dark depths. Matheson quickly followed, pausing at the edge of the water, looking for signs from them. A splash or a bubble. The lawman took a deep breath and readied himself to dive in after the two when they broke the surface of the water, Sugar's throat gripped in Hayder's hands, her eyes rolling back in her head, gagging.

"You damn thing! You *damn* thing! You get out of her!" He brought her face up close to his own, screaming, unreasonable. Matheson could feel the eldritch energy radiating from Hayder's body in thick, heady waves, and backed away from the water. The lawman knew he could do nothing more here. This was a battle to be fought between unnatural things.

Hayder dunked Sugar back under the water and held her down, his eyes bulging with rage and hurt. Her face was a faint, pale flicker in the black pool below. "Get out of her! You get out of her! You can't have her. I love her and you can't have her because I love her and she's my girl!"

Sugar got a hand free and slapped the boy across the face, connecting solidly enough to make his ears ring and head spin. Hayder shrugged it off and grabbed her hand and linked his fingers with hers, restraining her. He held her down with one hand and focused every good feeling for his girl he had inside of him into the other hand. All of his love, his friendship, and his faith from within himself coursing up through his arm and into his palm, transfusing it into her. The little white hand gripped in his began to struggle less, easing beneath his touch. The chill of the water began to subside, a definite warmth flowing into the pool. Hayder brought her back to the surface, still gripping her hand with the other curled around her slender neck. Her eyes were swollen with exhaustion, teeth gritted, and mouth drawn down in a grimace of slowly expiring rage.

"Know this, boy," the witch spat up at him. "Know that part of me will live within your precious little doll. A part of me will live forever in *you*. You are a Bava, and there is no escape from that. There will be no escape from *me*!"

Hayder nodded, his wet hair blinding his vision. "Maybe. But for now you'll just be a footnote in the big book. The big picture. Just a spooky story told to scare little kids. A bad dream. I'll make sure of that." He shoved her head back beneath the water and held it firm, every muscle in his body working at keeping her submerged within that watery tomb. The other hand remained clasped with hers. He could feel Cora clinging to life in that hand, fighting her way free from her psychic prison.

"You gotta get out of there. You gotta get out of there, Cora. If I have to kill your body to keep your soul safe then I'll do it. I'll do it, because I love you so much. You're my girl and you're my best friend and I love you so much I will kill you to save you!"

The body thrashing beneath him suddenly stilled. Her hand slid limply from his own in a boneless descent back into the water, floating weightlessly like the shed skin of a jellyfish. Cora's eyes grew fixed, gazing sightlessly up at him from the depths of the dark water like a rejected mannequin. A handful of tiny bubbles drooled from her nose and traveled upward and ascended to the surface, popping upon arrival. Hayder stared down at her, studying her. Remembering. He slipped his arms under her and lifted her body gently up to him, gathering her close, cradled her head in the crook of his arm. Behind him, Matheson was crying.

However, Hayder didn't weep. Not a single tear. He knew there was nothing to cry about.

The boy tilted the girl's head back and pressed his lips to hers. A delicate, faithful embrace. A sliver of electricity hummed through his mouth. He felt Cora smile against his own smile. Her eyes opened, the long black lashes dripping. Their smiles grew wider and returned to one another to share a sweet kiss.

Childhood was over.

Cora broke the kiss. He laid his forehead against hers.

"Not b-b-bad, Hennessey. Not bad at a-all." She turned away and buried a cough in his shoulder. She was shivering all over. "You did all right, b-boyfriend."

"Did I, girlfriend?" he asked. Now he was crying. It was the right time.

"Yup. You beat the Lich King. H-high-score for life, m-m-mister."

Hayder held Cora close and rocked back and forth. Then Matheson's big, burly bear-arms enfolded both of them. They lingered like this for a duration unknown, uncared for. They had earned this moment of peace. It had been hard fought for.

Cora was the first to lift her head. Her eyes widened. Matheson glanced at her, turning his own head to see what the fuss was about.

"Y'all...look!" He released them and stood up.

"Everything's changed." Hayder gasped. "What the heck..."

Matheson helped Hayder and Cora to their feet. The boy was correct. Everything *had* changed.

The four of them were still standing in the gymnasium of Golgotha Springs High School, the room covered in decorations for the Senior Prom for the Class of 1956. Yet there was no hole in the floor. No shattered glass or staircase. No wrecked truck. Just an empty, forgotten orphan of a building surrendered to the ages. It looked a lot less lively now in the present, or wherever they were. The walls were slicked green with oily mold and the standing water sloshed around their ankles. Windows sunk into the sills had become like wet cardboard, sagging and desolate. A yawning hole in the wall closest to the locker rooms led outside into whatever lay beyond, apparently the only way out. Even their clothes were dry now.

"Where the hell's my truck?" Matheson murmured, looking around.

"Where we left it," Cora chimed.

"Where is that?"

"Where we came from. Remember what the witch said. We were in a place like a pocket in your jeans. 'Cept this pocket was in the real world. Someplace set aside for witches and nightmares," the girl explained. "Now that we've come back home to the now, assuming that's where we are, whatever we left behind in that pocket ain't coming back with us."

Matheson shook his head. "Truck was a pile of scrap anyway. Spares me the trouble of having it lugged off to the salvage yard. He looked down at Cora. "You okay, lil gal? You soaked up some hard lumps in there." The child shrugged indifferently.

"I feel all right, I guess." She reached out and touched his shirt where a splotch of red was slowly getting larger, spreading out. "More worried for you, big guy."

Matheson winced and favored his side. "Yeah, pretty sure stuff in there got moved around that needed to stay put. Probably need to get that mended sooner than later."

"You're bad off. We should get moving." Hayder slipped his free arm around the lawman's waist, while Cora attended to the other side.

"Guess that's the only way out of here," Matheson commented, nodding at the hole in the wall. "We're close to the river. Recognize that nasty smell anywhere."

"We're home, just not in a part of home we know about. I can tell," Cora said, pulling away from Hayder and ambling toward the way out. "Traveling old school, gents. Hopefully the old man here can stand the walk."

"I'll manage, but not for too long." Matheson coughed. "We take too long, feel free to just toe me into a hole in the ground. No hard feelings. Promise."

Led by Cora, the three of them passed through the hole in the wall. Transitioning completely, at last, from the land of the dead back into the world of the living.

"I know this place. Kind of?" Matheson looked around, appraising their surroundings. "Those cliffs over there, that's Juniper Point. No mistaking it. I've never been on this side of it before."

"You're right. Wonder why it looks weird from here? Nobody I know has ever talked about this old school over yonder," Cora commented. "Kids knew about that old place, they'd be all over it. Getting into trouble."

"Dunno. This side of the lake has always been underwater. I used to think the place where The Springs took a nose-dive into the lake was further back." Matheson pondered. "Lake's water level's been damned low lately. Kinda pulled back the curtains on the past, I guess."

"Rain's been light. Probably why," Hayder said.

For even a few seconds, it had felt good to talk about something normal. Boring stuff.

"Don't matter. It's here now, and I don't care if I ever see it again."

They began to walk. Hayder turned to look over his shoulder, his pace slowing, then pausing. Barely perceptible, a white form, possibly the dimensions of a small female, hovered in the window. The boy could feel the rage of that wraith, the melancholy and hopelessness, from where he had stopped.

We will meet again, little boy. Soon...soon...

Hayder nodded, unsmiling and silent, then turned back to rejoin his friends, leaving the ghost to suffer in its own isolated abyss.

They had been fortunate; the three only had to limp along a little more than a mile before they were rescued. A young Amish couple had happened upon them on the way home from church. Treated them a buggy ride into town, right up to the emergency entrance of the Morgana Fulci Memorial Hospital. It had almost been too late for Matheson, and he was confident he wouldn't have survived if they had walked just a mile or two longer. One punctured lung and four cracked ribs later, the lawman, after a lengthy wait, was laid up comfortably in his own private room in the hospital with a smorgasbord of little blue pills to take the edge off.

When they had arrived, Black Knot had devolved into a state just a hair's shadow of complete chaos. The streets were strewn with debris and the remains of banged-up cars and glass, fire hydrants upturned and erupting. Folks walking around, some in their pajamas, some gussied up for the office, others buck naked. All of them wandering around dazed, like they had awoken from some fantastic, vibrant and horrible terror of the night. Hung-over from a legendary bender they would never remember. Nobody would ever ask what had happened or even talk about it, not even in the privacy of the own homes, enraptured in their most intimate moments. The influence of the Fulci witches, although currently reduced to the point of complete impotence, would still linger in the town of Black Knot a long time to come. Perhaps even forever. And that was just fine with the dwellers of the Knot. Denial had been the best friend to the town from the time the first brick had been laid upon that once-sacred soil.

Matheson had to admit he was glad for this denial, although it pained him to remember Raab and Mrs. Priddy, the latter of which had gone missing and would, like Scotty Raab, never be found again. A lot of people would be reported missing over the next month. Some of them would eventually be found, having awoken in barns, in dumpsters, in the woods, feeling groggy and confused. Some of them could only recall flashes of things. Fragments of bad dreams. A few returned impaired. Unable to speak or hear. Missing limbs or insensible to the point of having to be sent over to The Oaks, where they would more than likely remain in custody for the remainder of their living days. Both the hospital and police station remained empty. The police station had sustained significant damage. A fire, it looked like. Nothing which couldn't be explained away. Nobody could remember what had happened. They simply accepted it, like everything else.

The lawman, soon to be a private citizen, kept a low profile. He surrendered his badge and gun to OSBI without fanfare. They were in charge now, and none of this was his concern any longer. He had never felt better, more like a complete person, than he had at that moment. Afterwards, he lit a cigarette and stared up at the sky. The clouds were very thick. Crowded together. The way they looked before they began to shed snow.

As predicted by the Bava witch, the Lavera family quickly assumed control over the governmental concerns of the town. The transition of authority had appeared seamless to everyone, as if the Fulci monsters had never existed. Matheson found them friendly enough, much easier to deal with than their predecessors. The primary figurehead of the family, Gable Lavera, had even taken Juston out for bowling and beers. He was about the most un-witchy looking witch you could ever imagine with his trucker cap, oil-stained coveralls and granddaddy-like approachability. He had seemed a decent enough guy, but Matheson knew better than to fully trust him. The Laveras were, for the most part, an introverted and unobtrusive lot. Just do what they asked when asked, keep quiet when told to do so, don't piss them off, and you'd be right as rain. They poured money into rebuilding whatever couldn't be salvaged, getting people back to work and being productive. In other words, flip the world back up on its proper side and pull up your bootstraps. With denial on your side the capricious process of healing was accelerated tenfold.

Of course the Feds had eventually stepped up to stick their nasty little fingers in the pie. Too many big-mouths and gossip-whores running their jaws to outsiders to keep things totally quiet from the external, unknown powers that be. A lengthy but truthfully half-hearted investigation had been conducted and concluded in less than a month. Lots of rumors, most of them not nearly as ridiculous as the truth of the matter, which would never be available for public consumption. Eventually a carefully fabricated line of horseshit had been concocted to appease the thirst for ugliness from the rest of the world. It had been a leak of an experimental medical gas from the tanks at the nearby Army Ammunition Depot. Something to do with mass sedation for the purpose of what would eventually be come to known as post-traumatic stress disorder years down the line. There were lawsuits, of course. There was the settling of those lawsuits. Money passed from hand to hand. Money could be an effective negotiator in matters where a man was asked to shut his trap and turn his head.

The Lavera witches seem to have every bit as much clout as the Fulcis, and their money meant a little more than everyone else's.

Of course Matheson and company knew better. Of course they did. They kept quiet, never to mention it again unless they had seen or heard something not normal. Suspicious things most folks wouldn't give a spare thought for.

Just in case they had to do something else.

In the middle of the town square proper, outside the Gates of Mordor Arcade—which in five years would close and become a record store, then yet another café, a non-denominational house of worship, then finally a pile of brick and busted cement—the strange tombstones weathered and crumbled into nothing. The pale dust collected, stirred, then scattered to the four savage winds.

THE END OF THE STORY

After he had taken a couple of weeks off to recuperate, the first thing Matheson did was ask a Choctaw medicine man to bless the tainted earth of Camp Red Hand.

It had taken a great deal of convincing, him having to resort to sweetening the deal with a crisp twenty-dollar bill. The lawman didn't blame the shaman one bit for his reluctance. It was asking a lot. As it turned out the blessing had perhaps been unnecessary. The medicine man, after walking the length and breadth of the grounds, had seemed satisfied whatever restless horror had been haunting the spot was now gone. Only the hazy aftertaste of a bad memory remained behind. But the shaman blessed it anyway. He'd been paid to do so. After the old man left Matheson lingered behind for a couple of hours, strolling through the woods and listening to the crows. The nip of winter had been very strong that day, the fragile blush of autumn already draining away from bursts of crimson, gold, and purple to a singular dull, solemn brown. He liked that. Matheson loved the cold. He loved winter.

Perhaps they would have a decent snow this year. In all his years living in Black Knot he could only remember one good snowfall. Usually it just stayed cold and dry. Boring. As if winter had couldn't be bothered to visit.

He had forgotten his jacket back at the cabin. He shivered as he walked, but it was a good kind of shivering. A shivering of the flesh, and that was all.

It was fine with him. He loved the cold. He loved winter.

When he finally felt up to going out and about, Matheson drove over to Becky's house. He'd bought a decent used car from a guy in Lamplight Falls he had gone to school with. A little Volkswagen which took a lot of getting used to. He was barely able to squeeze his bulky frame into the driver's seat, but he liked the way the little German rocket booked it down the road. The comforting smell of gasoline and the insectoid growl of the motor. Those foreign cars lived longer than some people. It had been a good deal.

He would never drive a truck again.

Juston knew nobody would be home. It was okay. He had to go. He felt he owed Becky that much.

The front door had been unlocked and opened a crack. He hadn't brought a gun. It hadn't even occurred to him. The inside of the mobile home looked as if a tiny twister had come swirling and smashing through it. Furniture overturned, lamps smashed, and the carpet ripped up. Dark stains smeared across the walls. Matheson didn't look at those for very long. He knew what it was. He ambled into the bedroom. Much to his surprise the room was undisturbed. Tidy, even. On the bed a huge pile of photo albums had been spread out. Their wedding album lay open, as if someone, maybe her, had been looking at them before the bad things had taken over. Had she been thinking of him, maybe missing him, missing them, before the unspeakable had consumed her? He liked to think so. The former lawman stood in the room for a long time, flipping through the book. He paused at a particular photograph, lingered for a moment, then removed it from its plastic sheath and slipped it into his shirt pocket. That photo had always been his favorite. Them on their honeymoon in California, standing on a cliff overlooking the ocean, toasting the camera with cans of beer. Man, they looked so young. So alive with everything to look forward to.

Why did this happen to me? To all of us?

Juston sat in his car for a long time and cried. Sobbing so hard he lost control of his breath, repeatedly punching his fist into the dashboard until he split the skin of his knuckles.

Before he went home he stopped at Roseanna's shop. He found both the front and back doors locked up solid. He peered through a side window and found the inside of the shop empty. Not a scrap of junk. No shelves. Even the floor appeared to have been swept and mopped. He wasn't terribly surprised. The Laveras, like the Fulcis, took very good care of their own.

Let them. The cleaning up of messes in Black Knot was no longer his problem.

Thanksgiving arrived. For the first time in his thirty-four years, Juston Matheson understood what it was to be truly thankful, and it felt like a baptism. He was purged.

By the first week of December, he had a job at a plant nursery in Coffin Mills. Simple labor, mostly. Unpacking bags of seed, sod, and flowers. Maybe a little landscaping on the weekends. Money was decent enough, and the old couple who ran the place were very good to him. It was the best job he had ever had. In time the police station was rebuilt, and a new Tin Star placed in charge.

Matheson was glad for it. The maintaining of law and order, the cleaning up of messes, in Black Knot was no longer his problem.

Somewhere along the way he gained a son, and, briefly, a daughter.

These were the days when adoption was a relatively easy process. You found a kid without parents, told someone about it, and a search would go out for any living relatives. Matheson had a feeling nobody on their end really checked all that hard, which was fine by him. He already knew there would be no other kin to come calling for Hayder in the future, but he had to go through the motions of checking. His being a cop had helped speed things along, as well as keep certain information close to the vest. Hayder had simply reported his mother as having gone missing on Halloween, which wasn't a lie, and indicated wanting to live with Sheriff Matheson. Matheson hadn't even mentioned the possibility of assuming the role of guardian for the boy, but he didn't dispute it. Of course, he was going to take care of him. Of course he would.

They never heard another word about Mona Fulci. Mona Hennessey. Whoever she had been. Hayder never spoke of her, and shut down all attempts by Matheson to engage in the subject. After a while Juston gave him his space and let him be. The boy was a lot like him, he came to find. Still waters that ran deep.

Cora's situation was a little trickier. The tragedy at the Feed Lot had transformed her into something of a celebrity, and everybody in Black Knot knew her granny and aunt. They were the sort of people folks in a small town would have referred to as characters. Again, Matheson's law enforcement connections pulled them through it. It was well known Polly Corbucci had a whole lot of people, mostly thugs in the crank trade, chomping at the bit to help her pull off a vanishing act. For them to just go away was not exactly unexpected, which was the story fed to the public to digest. Cora, however, was fairly certain there weren't a lot of Corbuccis out there in the world at large, and as for her Baba Lena, Lord only knew whether or not there were any kinfolk remaining in the Ukraine. Matheson immediately wrote off that branch of the family. Nobody was going to want to go through the hassle of a very expensive wild goose chase across another continent looking for one little girl's roots, and a little cracker girl at that. Juston put feelers out just the same.

The three of them lived quietly in Matheson's little cabin, Cora taking his bed and he and Hayder crashing in the living room.

For her part, Cora was fine with all of it. Borderline indifferent. This troubled Matheson. True, the girl was a mellow, relaxed kid for the most part. Now, at times, she seemed to be a little too 'go with the flow.' Yes to everything. No arguing whatsoever. Perpetually scatterbrained and drowsy, almost as if she had been both awake and asleep at the same time. It was understandable, he supposed, after what they had been through, for both kids to have issues to work out. Some things they might not ever recover from all the way. Same for him. He thought about getting all of them set up with someone to talk to. A professional person, maybe a doctor, who knew how to deal with things like this. But that was part of the problem, wasn't it? The chance of finding someone who had dealt with things like this would be impossible outside of a looney bin. No, they had to dig their own way out of this hole, even if they had to climb up and out of it one centimeter at a time.

Yet Cora seemed to be buried in a deeper, blacker hole than either of the other two. He kept a close eye on her.

Both Cora and Hayder hated school. If they both had still been somewhat normal children, everything would have been peachy for the most part. But they weren't normal children, not even normal human beings, anymore. By Christmas Cora had been getting into fights regularly at lunch over the littlest, seemingly trite things. Hayder would then get into trouble getting into fights over Cora's fights. It became a vicious cycle, which was only remedied by having Matheson pull them both out of school. He didn't really worry about their education. They were both bright kids and, as it turned out, more than disciplined enough to learn from home. From the cabin. Their secret hideout.

Maybe they needed to do something. Matheson though about that a lot. Maybe they needed to do something like pack up their lives, one box at a time, and get the hell out of Dodge.

Spring arrived in Black Knot, bringing with it dramatic changes for their cobbled together family. Child Services had contacted Matheson on a Saturday morning just before he was about to take Cora and Hayder fishing. They had found someone. A distant cousin from New Mexico named Marjorie. After getting the okay from Juston, Marjorie flew both herself and her husband Jake to Tulsa, then drove an hour and a half south to Black Knot just to meet Cora. They were a good-looking pair, barely in their thirties, clean cut, attentive and childless. The couple owned a very successful renovation business back in Los Alamos, and as soon as Marjorie set eyes on Cora's dilapidated shotgun house, she fell in love both with it and the little girl, immediately Cora was wary at first, but warmed to them both quickly, which kind of wounded Matheson a little. He had been a bit disheartened to find them a very nice, very normal couple. Part of him had hoped they would be losers, unsuitable. Ultimately he was glad someone was taking an interest in her. Giving her the things she needed to feel like a regular kid, something she'd never had with Baba and Polly. Marjorie drove her down to Dallas for shopping and "girl time". Jake doted on her as well, helping her with her innate artistic talents and encouraging her to improve herself with books and trips to the museums in Oklahoma City. They hugged her a lot and said nice things.

He didn't want to lose the kid. Maybe he even loved her. No, not maybe.

Damn, why did they have to be so nice?

Yet there was still something off with Cora. A gloominess. Her new guardians had offered to pay for therapy, which she repeatedly refused. Matheson knew why. It was the same reason he had never followed through with his own attempts at rehabilitation. They could never tell a soul about what had happened. The last thing Cora needed was institutionalization.

The three of them still spent a lot of time together, hanging out at Matheson's cabin for barbecue and badminton. Hiking trips in Grinning Goblin. Sometimes the cousins went with them. They didn't obstruct Juston and Hayder's interactions with the girl, and for that he was glad. They weren't going anywhere anytime soon, and Matheson was glad they were sticking around. He could still keep an eye on the girl that way.

Hayder had taken Cora's leaving Matheson's cabin really hard, even though he still got to see the girl pretty much whenever he felt like it. Juston knew a lot of it was in the boy's head. Having gone through so much with Cora had bonded him to her, and she with him. Not having her around, in the cabin where he could see her all of the time, made him nervous. Emotional. It had been a rough few weeks after the girl moved out. A lot of tears and tantrums over the littlest things.

Matheson missed seeing them together. What they had was something truly special. Something very right. It warmed his heart. It was something a lot of people pine for. Something you only read about. Perhaps he even envied them, just a little bit.

Summer arrived. A sweltering season. Too hot to keep the windows closed. A lot of people left theirs open, hoping to catch a stray, relieving breeze or two.

Some people kept their windows shut all of the time. Almost like they were afraid something might try to climb over the sill of that same window, into their house, to get them.

Cora and Hayder stood beside the fence separating his house from hers. This time they lingered on her side of the barrier, ignoring the rambling two-story ruin of his former life across from them as they talked. Inside of her house the sound of sawing and hammering poured from the open windows, which seemed to go on all day, relenting only when dusk began to fall. They both laughed at the insane amount of effort Marjorie and Jake were putting into cleaning up what Matheson had nicknamed "The Ol' Shithole". Whatever. If Marjorie wanted to dump her money and time into restoring the "rustic savageness" of the sprawling old barn, it was her business. Just let her. She was a nice lady, and one should always let a nice lady have her way so she would keep on being nice.

Cora gnawed on a shoot of witchgrass as they chatted. Hayder was reminded of another moment, not that long ago, when she had been in this exact same pose. He had found her so beautiful then, and even more so now as he stood beside her, trying not to stare. The girl's face had changed a little in that brief span of time. Perhaps a bit more fullness to her cheekbones and mouth. Her long black hair seemed thicker, more lustrous, with a slight hint of waviness which hadn't been there before. She was still a tiny, willowy thing. Probably wouldn't get much taller, if at all. There had been some talk of Marjorie taking her to a specialist in Tulsa to have her trick eye fixed. Hayder hoped not. He loved that strange, oddball sphere rolling around in her skull. It was part of her personality. The stuff that made her Cora.

He had changed as well. In just a few months he'd grown two full inches and put on at least ten pounds of muscle, thanks to Matheson working him like a dog. He'd also grown in other ways he preferred to keep to himself. He blushed thinking about it.

"*Dang, we're growing up,*" he thought. "*I don't think I like that.*"

"I want to be little forever. I want the both of us to be little forever."

He looked at her, astounded. She glanced at him out of the corner of her eye and winked.

Don't ask.

But he had to. They could talk about anything, so long as it was asked honestly.

"How are things, Cora?" He hesitated between each word. He had to find the right way to say what he really wanted to. What was it with being around her that made his tongue not want to work?

"Just say what you feel, sweetie. You're not just my boyfriend, you're my bestest friend." She spat out the witchgrass and plucked herself another stalk to mangle. He blushed again. *Boyfriend.*

She shook her head, rolled her eyes, and kissed his cheek.

"I know, I know." He groaned. "I don't really like talking about all of that. It's almost like something that didn't happen, but I know it did. When I go to bring it up I sometimes wonder if I'm really remembering it. Does that make sense?"

Cora smiled sadly. "Maybe I understand that a little too much. We can talk about it."

"She's still in there, isn't she? Sugar Bava." he asked. She moved closer to him and leaned into his arms, laying her head on his shoulder. He settled his cheek upon the top of her head and smelled her hair. Lemon and something earthy.

"Of course she is. Not super-duper strong. Like a flicker on a candle that's about burned down to the bottom." He felt her shiver. "Sometimes I think I see her. At weird places. Not whole glimpses. Flashes of her. Like, I was at Suds Yer Duds doing the laundry last week and I swear to God I thought I saw her standing across the street, outside the donut shop. I blinked and she was gone. But I could still *feel* her."

"She can't hurt you, you know. Don't get too worked up about it." Of course he didn't one hundred percent believe that. Cora didn't either, and he knew this. He just felt he needed to say it.

"It's not so much about hurting so much as she just *won't let go*." Cora kicked a fencepost. "I think I'm safe, for the most part. Maybe her being inside of me, just a little bit, ain't such a horrible thing."

Hayder cocked an eye. "How so?"

"Well, she's probably most of the reason I can hear what you're thinking, lover boy. I can hear what other people are thinking too. I couldn't do that before. After the Feed Lot I could only hear little blurbs. Patches of thoughts. Her being inside of me, I don't know, amplified those things. Or something like that."

The boy shook his head. "That's not necessarily a good thing. I would hate to be able to hear what someone is thinking, especially if it's about me."

"It is what it is. I'm fine. Stop mother-henning me." Cora elbowed him friskily. The two linked hands and stood together, staring up at the setting sun. The sun was slowly thawing into the horizon like molten rock.

"Someone's got a birthday coming up next week. The big one three."

"I know that. That would be me," Cora affirmed, a slightly mocking lilt to her voice.

"Yes, I know, smart aleck." Hayder softly pinched her side, making her squeal. "I don't know what to get you. How about a few hints? Kinda new at this whole boyfriend-girlfriend stuff."

"Right now I wanna go swimming."

"No, I meant for your birthday."

"I told you what I want. I want to go swimming." Cora pulled away and began leading him toward the house. "Manitou Creek will be totally empty right now. Not even the crank cooks know about it. We can have it all to ourselves."

"Um, I don't have my suit," he protested. Something about the way she was talking made him feel nervous. He couldn't discern if it were a good sort of nervous or a bad kind.

"Me neither. Your underwear will do just fine." The girl rolled her eyes. "Jeeze, quit being so uptight, grandpa."

"What are…you…gonna wear?" Hayder felt his face getting hotter and hotter, like it might just melt right off of his skull.

"My word. If your face got any redder Santa Claus could truss you up and use you to guide his sleigh this Christmas." Cora snickered. "I can strip down to my underwear too and throw on one of Jake's big shirts. Would that make you feel better, oh hunk of mine?"

Hayder nodded. His heart felt like a wild, uncaged thing trying to claw its way out of his chest.

Yes, that would work just fine. Yes, that would be okay.

The waters of Manitou Creek were so clear you could see straight down to its very bottom. It wasn't terribly deep, perhaps only six or seven feet at its dead middle. It hovered at the constant comfortable temperature of, if one had to guess, seventy degrees give or take a number, and tasted clean enough to bottle up and drink. Like most everything in Black Knot it had its very own legend, a ghost story no less. It was rumored a Shogomagra maiden had fallen in love with a wounded Confederate soldier who had defected during one of the countless forgotten skirmishes in Indian Territory. The maiden had discovered him lying on the banks of the creek, delusional and nearly dead from a bullet in his shoulder. Knowing her people would have killed and devoured the flesh of the pale interloper, she began to nurse him back to health, in secret. Neither could speak the language of the other, but this didn't stop the flower of romance from blossoming. After the soldier mended they continued to meet, lying together on the muddy banks of the creek, speaking with their eyes and bodies. They knew they wanted to be together. Neither had to say it out loud.

Of course, like in all legends of this kind, the two lovers were discovered by a hunting party of Shogomagra, of whom the maiden's father was chief. Enraged and ashamed, her father killed them both on the spot, while still entwined in one another's arms, their blood mingling and draining into the crystalline waters. It was rumored the dirt residing at the bottom of the creek had gained its crimson hue from the mingled blood of the two ill-fated lovers who had perished on its mossy bank, and to bathe in its waters would bring one good luck in all matters related to love.

Cora told this story to Hayder as they stood on the bank together. It was too dark to verify the color of the creek bed, but he took her word as gospel. Although barefoot, he still wore his Bermuda shorts and t-shirt. He was going to stay dressed as long as possible. Cora wore a huge green University of New Mexico t-shirt which barely covered the bottom of her panties, and the boy had to make a conscious effort to not gawk. He wasn't sure why he bothered. Of course she knew he was looking. She knew everything now.

"Get those off. Quit being silly." The girl snapped her fingers in his face. "Here. Hold up your arms." He did as she commanded, holding up his arms so she could shuck off his shirt. He was embarrassed to find himself trembling. What the heck was wrong with him?

Cora giggled and took his face in her palms. She brought his face up to hers and pressed her lips to his. The trembling began to subside, and he allowed himself to enjoy their kiss, working his mouth softly in perfect unison with hers. The girl, his girl, broke the kiss and looked into his eyes. Her eyes were so deep and dark he felt like diving into them, allow them to swallow him whole. She kissed him again.

"Don't be afraid."

Hayder felt a strange stirring in a place he didn't want to her to know about. *Oh Lord, don't let her see it!*

"I need to get in the water. Now!" he croaked.

The boy waded into the shallow end of the creek and jackknifed himself into the water. The water was lovely, if considerably cooler than he had anticipated, eliciting a startled yelp out of him.

"Holy smokes! Is it cold?" Cora asked. "By the way, love the tighty whities, boyfriend. I kind of figured that's what you had on under there."

"Ha ha. Just get in here and see how cold it is for yourself." Hayder dog-paddled for a bit before swimming closer to the bank. "Beware, I've been known to dunk unsuspecting girls."

"*Hrmph!* We'll see about that," she sneered comically. The girl slowly waded into the water, splashing her legs and allowing her flesh to acclimate to the temperature. Once the water reached her waist she dunked her head beneath the surface, tarrying within the crystalline depths a few seconds before bursting back up with a delighted howl. "Holy crap! That feels amazing!"

Hayder swam up to her and the two stared at one another for what felt like ages. Something in her eyes bothered him. What bugged him the most was he couldn't understand the look. Couldn't pick it apart to study it. It wasn't bad or hateful, nor was it a hundred percent pleasant. Maybe a little melancholy. Some anger mixed in. Then, almost as soon as it had appeared it had departed. Had he even seen it? Now he was looking at Cora. Cora, his best friend and girl.

"You just hang on to me. I'll carry you around." Hayder turned around, offering her his back. She giggled and clambered up onto him, wrapping her arms and legs around him. Cora's sweet scent filled his head, the warmth of her closeness making him dizzy. The boy began to trudge across the outer rim of the creek, keeping to the shallow end.

"Mush, doggie! Mush!" Cora laughed, hugging him tight and propping her chin on the top of his head. "C'mon doggie, get the lead out!"

"Tryin' to. Quit your squiggling. Still haven't got my sea legs yet!" The boy waddled around the perimeter of the creek, the water sloshing up to just a little below his collarbone, struggling to keep them both upright. For a little while everything was absolutely, unequivocally, perfect. Uncorrupted. The stars in heaven were aligned, swollen with overflowing promise. The person he cared for the most on this cold and selfish planet was right here, with him. She was *with* him. Cora latched on to his back, sweetly hugging herself to him, making him feel so very okay with everything. His future, their future, was wide open. Nothing but open lanes on the highway ahead.

Yet something was still off. He could feel it. When Hayder figured out what it was, he didn't want to admit it. Not talk about it. He didn't want to spoil the moment.

It was Cora.

Hayder waded toward the center of the creek, the water creeping up to the bottom of his chin, then stopping where he was. Cora leaned forward and around, peering up at him. He turned to look at her. She knew. Of course she knew.

She knows everything now, remember?

"I'm happy right now. It's not that." She laid her head on his shoulder, her arms hugging him tighter. "Stop worrying so much about every little thing."

"What is it, then?" he asked. "I can tell something's wrong. Not just today. It's felt like this every day since it ended. Is it me?"

Cora groaned. "Ohhhh *jeeeeeze!* Not that, please!" She frogged his shoulder hard, almost slipping from her perch on his back. "You're such a goofus sometimes. Don't you know you're the only thing that works for me? The only thing that's…right? Can't you understand that and just leave it alone?"

"Don't start going around in circles on me. I can feel it. I know you're not happy."

"It's not that at all. I am plenty happy. You're being a little dramatic, boyfriend."

"Stop trying to lead me away from it. What's wrong? If you really care about what I feel you'd tell me."

For a long time Cora stayed quiet. Hayder sighed and closed his eyes. He focused on the honeyed music of the country night. Cicadas sawing out their placid melodies to be carried along by a peaceful summer zephyr meandering through the valley, disordering the solemn stillness of the water.

"Hayder…I." The girl struggled, her tongue clumsy in her mouth. "Hayder, I hurt. I hurt inside. Everything just…hurts. Hurts to be around. Living here, in this place, this town, it's so hard for me."

"What do you mean?" asked the boy, feeling an unwelcome tingle of apprehension ripple through his belly. He wanted to pry the girl off of his back and make her look at him, but he chickened out. It was better if he didn't look at her right now.

"I just hate it here. I hate that I can't forget any of it. The Feed Lot. All of the dead people. I can feel all of that death, taste it like gross food in my mouth. I can still feel that witch banging around inside of me. It's like she ripped a piece of herself off and buried it inside of my body. Like the seed of a poisonous plant. One day that plant might grow something. Something I might not be able to get rid of. That scares me so bad, Hayder. What will happen then?" She laid her head upon the back of his and sighed. "And that house. That house. I hate that damn house most of all."

She had cursed. It was the first time he had ever heard Cora say a legitimate swear word. It unsettled him.

"Yeah, but it's starting to look real nice. Your cousin is doing a rad job. I barely recognize it."

"It's not how it looks, but how it *feels*. Marji can spruce it up all she wants, but it's still a house with a sad heart and bad memories." Her voice quivered. "Baba and Polly, I can still feel them in there. Smell Baba's bath powder and auntie's perfume. It's a haunted house, and the ghosts in there are ghosts I can't see, and that scares me a lot. It's the spot the house, the dirt, it was built upon, I think. It's soaked through with the blood of things that died when they weren't ready to die. Broken hearts and lost minds."

"It's Black Knot," Hayder muttered. He understood her now.

"It is, and I hate it," she mumbled, her warm breath vibrating against the bare skin of his back. "I hate Black Knot. It's…it's wearing me down."

Hayder wasn't sure what to say, but he could feel her turmoil, her despair, and it made his heart ache for her. He just wanted her to be Cora again. The weird girl in the arcade who had kicked his ass at his favorite video game. The girl he had fought monsters with, and had beaten them.

He laid his hand over hers, their fingers interlocked.

"Don't be scared. I got you," he whispered. It was hard to get the words out, as if they carried actual tangible heaviness. "I'll always carry you. Always."

She sniffled. Hayder could tell she was crying. Should he turn around? Should he leave her be? What was the right thing to do? He felt Cora's lips on the back of his head, then the side of his neck. Warm. Loving. Terrifying. She laid her head on his shoulder, a long tendril of her hair clinging to his cheek.

"I hope you're this way forever, boyfriend. Please stay this way. No matter what happens, please stay this way. Stay sweet and funny and make folks smile and laugh like you do. Be you. Always, just be you and stay that way."

Hayder's throat began to swell. He could barely swallow, and his eyes grew hot, itchy. His heart in his chest felt as if it weighed a million pounds.

They meandered around in the creek for little while longer. They then walked out of the water, onto the bank of the creek, then followed the path hewn through the grass leading to the road.

They held hands.

He loved the way his girl smelled. The way she smiled. The way she looked up at the sky and seemed to gaze into forever.

"Jesus, y'all took long enough." Matheson teased, dropping his cigarette to the earth and grinding it out with the heel of his boot. "I know sparking takes time, but Lordy." The former lawman stood at the end of the driveway with Marjorie and Jake. The three wore matching Cheshire Cat grins on their faces. Cora's cousins were sipping from matching bottles of Chinese beer while Juston nursed a cup of coffee. It made Hayder happy to see that. He hadn't seen anything other than a glass of water or coffee touch the man's lips in well over a month.

"I agree with this, gentlemen. Better get that wooing in hand. Might have to take the hose to you two and cool you off," Marjorie joked, nudging her husband. Jake chuckled and sipped his beer, nodding pleasantly at them. He was an affable man, always quick to smile and reluctant to raise his voice.

"Lil gal, you look good. Getting a little meat on them bones." Matheson slurped his coffee, following up with a cocky smile. Cora lurched forward and punched his arm. Rather hard.

"You calling me fat, old man?" She jabbed a finger into the slight swell of his paunch. "You'd know all about that, wouldn't you, butterball?"

"No ma'am. Just healthy. Glad to see these nice folks here are keeping their thumb on you. Making you behave and such. That's not such an easy endeavor."

Hayder looked at Cora, the both of them then locking eyes with Juston. Marjorie and Jake glanced at one another. They could feel something transfer between the other three. Had they missed something important in the exchange?

Marjorie polished off the remainder of her beer and pitched it the trash barrel next to the mailbox. "It was nice to see you again, Juston. We'll leave you guys to say your goodnights and see you soon." The woman ruffled Hayder's hair and took her husband's hand, guiding him back to the house with a stream of chatter trailing behind them. Matheson followed them with his eyes as they departed, an oddly wistful look to him.

"Being married looks nice. I bet it could be real nice with the right person," he murmured, scratching his bearded chin. "Don't think I could do it again. Not after all that."

"Oh, I think you still might make an all right-enough husband. You're not *too* awful to look at it and you smell okay enough. You know how to fix stuff. That mouth of yours might be a problem, though," Cora snarked, slipping her arm around Hayder's slight waist. "So when are y'all heading out? Early, I guess? Early worm gets the fish, or something like that?"

"Not too early. Got three whole weeks of fishing ahead of us with plenty of early mornings to honor. Probably hit the road after breakfast. The drive to Soledad Point is about three hours or so. Got plenty of time." Matheson said. "Sure you don't want to come with? I make some mean pan bread. I might even let you shoot a gun at snakes if you feel so inclined."

The girl puckered her mouth and winced. "Ick. No! I hate touching fish. I hate worms. Put 'em both together and that's a big fat no sirree bob."

Matheson popped a matchstick in the corner of his mouth. He'd been using this tactic as a deterrent to his chain smoking, and so far it had been working well for him. "You sure? You don't have to fish. You can take care of the campground. Tidy up. You know, do your job as a woman as God intended."

"Oh man. Here it comes," Hayder groaned. "Prepare to get lit up, pops. You asked for it."

"That was actually clever, so I'll let that one slide, you old gasbag." Cora nodded approvingly. "I'm technically still a girl, so that's not a worry of mine at the moment."

"You sure? I'd like it a lot if you went with us," Hayder said. The boy knew he sounded needy and desperate, which was exactly how he felt. He didn't want to go that long without seeing her. Being around her.

"Nah. You two men-people need to go do men-people things. Talk about manly stuff. Run around in the woods like animals and grunt. You know, act like men and what not." She rose on her tiptoes and kissed Hayder's cheek. "I need to help Marji and Jake with some stuff. This old barn here seems to have something falling off of it dang near every day, it seems."

Hayder nodded, disappointed.

"You have fun. Now is the time for fun." Cora smiled up at him. She ran her hand through his curling mop of rusty hair and drew his face down to her own. Her mouth tasted like oranges and wood smoke. She kissed his upper lip, drifted to the corners, and then entertained his bottom lip and the edge of his chin, ending upon his forehead. Their arms looped around one another, squeezed, and lingered. Matheson stepped forward and engulfed them both in his bear-like arms, hugging them fiercely. The three of them stood there for a long time, comforting one another. Each of them so brave, so scared, so hurt and healed over, hurt and healed over again.

Cora broke away first, rubbing the flat of her palm across her eyes. "You take good care of this one now, you hear?"

"Oh, he's in good hands, lil gal." Matheson reached out and pinched the girl's nose.

"I meant you, goober," she said to the former lawman, now full-time angler. She turned to Hayder. "You hearing me, boyfriend? This one over here is a crazy mess and needs a minder to keep him from getting into trouble." She looked at Matheson, reached up, and gave his ear a good, hard tug.

"Hey!" he protested feebly.

"That lobe is red as a beet. You've been digging at it again, haven't you? My word." She looked up at the man, face cross and hands set firmly on her slight hips. "Ain't you ever gonna learn your lesson?

"At my age, I suspect not." Matheson leaned forward and kissed Cora's forehead. "You be good now. See you soon."

"A tall order, old man, but I'll do my best."

Matheson smiled at her, seemed about to say something else, then turned and walked back to the car. Cora turned to Hayder and cocked her head, eyes crawling over his face. She did this for a long time. With her pointing finger she traced the outline of his eyes. His mouth. His jaw.

"What're you doing?" He grinned down at her. Something felt strange.

"Can't I look at my boyfriend?" she asked, continuing her explorations. "I like looking at my handsome fella."

"Oh now." He rolled his eyes.

She tiptoed up again and kissed him. A quick, confectionary graze.

"Goodnight, boyfriend."

"Later on, girlfriend."

Cora kissed Hayder's hand, smiled, and let him go.

As Matheson drove away, Hayder glanced up at the rear-view mirror. Cora stood in the middle of the dirt road outside of her house, her hand raised. He wondered how it could be possible to need someone, to want to be close to someone, so much. It made him a little afraid.

He felt Matheson's hand on his shoulder. He turned to look at the man. Yes, he understood.

The car came to a halt by the stop sign at the end of the road. Hayder looked up at the mirror again and saw the road behind them empty. Cora was gone. Only a delicate stir of disturbed dust swirling suspended in the air, thinning a little more and more with time, until it had cleared enough to reveal further emptiness. As if the girl had never been there at all.

The trip had been exactly what the two of them had needed. What was it about being out in nature, reliant upon your innate human skills for survival, which made a man feel so renewed? Matheson taught Hayder how to fish properly, both by pole and trotline. How to wrangle a bass without getting his hand cut by their fins, and picking the fragile little bones from their meat while filleting them. The oft-mentioned pan bread made an appearance, and was every bit as tasty and filling as advertised. They even shot a couple of squirrels and whipped up a yummy stew using some chicken stock and taters Matheson had brought from home, just in case. They swam in Borgia Creek every morning, using its clean and cold water for bathing themselves. The sheriff used the opportunity as not only a chance to relax and unwind but to educate as well. He had always dreamed about having a son, or just a kid in general, to show these things to. Most of his fondest memories were of doing these things with his old man, and he had longed to pass these skills on to someone else, who would then pass on these same lessons to another. Maybe their own children. Hayder loved the attention, especially after what had happened to his mother.

His mother?

It was weird. Remembering his mom was difficult. Even something so small as what she had looked like. Mona Hennessey felt like something he had just imagined, or maybe had read about. Same for Brandy and his daddy. All of them had been characters in a sad movie, and maybe it was best that way. If there were a God, maybe he was doing him a little favor. Protecting his mind from completely crumbling away into insanity. Matheson never asked the boy about them, or how he was dealing with the loss. If he had it wouldn't have bothered Hayder a bit. They didn't feel real anymore, so talking about them carried precious little emotional heft. It didn't matter. That life was over. It was gone.

Hayder had also been able to put Cora out of his mind, somewhat, at least until the start of that third and final week. It wasn't a purposeful strategy. He had genuinely been busy. When he returned to the real world, He realized he missed her horribly, fiercely, feeling a trifle guilty for allowing himself to enjoy things without her. He told Matheson this, receiving a consolatory pat on his shoulders. They would be home in just a few days and things would be better. Maybe time away was good sometimes. Hayder wasn't buying that last part, and finding ways to enjoy himself and pass the time became something of a struggle those last couple of days.

On the morning they packed up to go home, Hayder was uncharacteristically sullen. Matheson found himself taken aback by this. The boy had been mooning and shambling around for half the week like a lost puppy yearning for his little girl owner to scratch his chin. He thought about asking Hayder what was wrong, but thought better of it. The kid was becoming a teenager in a little over a month, and the former lawman simply chalked up the crabbiness to surging hormones and the general melancholia of that transitional state from little boy to young man. He'd been there himself before. The best medicine was being left the hell alone.

The car had barely pulled into the drive of the cabin before Hayder had the door open and his feet on the earth, barreling toward the porch and into the house. Matheson unpacked the car without a word. Let the boy do what he needed to do. After a few minutes Hayder returned to the porch holding the receiver of the phone in his hand, staring down at it as if it were something he didn't recognize. Matheson's heart began to thump faster in his chest, his throat dry. He set their backpacks on the grass and walked over to the boy, lifting the receiver from his hand. Hayder's face was washed clean of all color. Pale. Drained.

Matheson raised the receiver to his ear and listened.

The number was out of service, the recorded voice said.

The two of them looked at one another.

The number was out of service, the recorded voice said.

That voice was not known to lie.

They drove out to Haggard immediately, neither of them having much to say. It was a gloomy journey. The clouds were swollen with storm threat, and the air was thick and stifling with the odor of turned, ripe dirt. A good day for a nap, which Matheson planned to treat himself to as soon as he got Hayder settled down. He could feel the child's tension, like a loaded mousetrap. The man wanted to reassure the boy. Maybe they had forgotten to pay the phone bill. But no, that wasn't right. Maybe in the days when Polly had been in charge of the house. The current owners were most definitely the sort of people who shirked on paying their bills. People with money didn't forget things like that.

Matheson didn't say this to Hayder. He didn't say anything at all.

As soon as the FOR SALE sign came into view, Hayder turned away from Matheson. The man knew what was going on, and was certain the boy did too. The second they pulled into the driveway the boy made a strangled, wounded noise in his throat and flung the car door open, bolting toward the house. Juston opened his door and stepped out, taking his time. He sat on the hood of the car and lit a cigarette. All he could think about was how much he could use a beer. Maybe a twelve-pack. No, a whole damned case.

It began to sprinkle. The rain offered no comfort. It was too hot and sticky outside for that.

Hayder dashed back and forth across the porch, now restored and no longer sagging into the earth. He peered into the front windows, running along the sides of the house and looking into those as well. Once he reached the backyard he stayed gone for so long Matheson felt obliged to go looking for him. He found the boy inside, having found an unlocked window to shimmy through. Juston came closer and looked through the window. The room was empty and scrubbed so thoroughly the wood floors gleamed like polished stone. Hayder was sitting on the floor, cross-legged, a battered loose-leaf notebook opened up on his lap.

"Hayder?" Juston said.

"It's my fault." The boy drew in a ragged, trembling breath. "I stopped thinking about her for a minute and now..." He set the notebook down and drew his knees up to his chin, resting his head on them.

"It's not." Matheson opened the window a crack further. Thought about crawling through it to be with the boy but decided against it.

"It's empty," Hayder whimpered. The dead, listless tone in his voice cracked Matheson's heart. It was the way a man who'd finally accepted a death sentence sounded, so far beyond sadness they had passed over into the valley of disoriented. Dazed.

"I know, son. It is." Juston reached through the window and held out his hand to the boy. "Come on. We can talk about this at home, Hayder."

Hayder picked up the notebook and walked over to the window, effortlessly clambering over the sill and out. Wordless. He handed the notebook to the man and walked away. The boy stumbled over to the barbed wire fence separating Cora's house from his own former abode. He scaled a fencepost and dropped down into the pasture, sitting down on the grass, his back to Matheson.

Juston looked down at the notebook and opened it. He felt like an intruder, this bound collection of paper not meant for his eyes. Just the first dozen or so pages had been filled out. Mostly pencil sketches of a knight, broadsword in hand, fending off various horrific beasts. Walking corpses. Elephantine bats and skeletal wizards. Good, no, excellent craft. Matheson had seen this artwork before. He recognized the artist immediately.

On the final page was a note scrawled in a childish, yet decidedly girlish script. Huge, looping letters. Clean and organized. Whoever had written it had taken their time. Juston could feel the sentiment and thoughtfulness exuding from the paper.

Remember to watch those gargoyles. The ones that fly. They can hurt you fast and bad if you don't know how to take them out. Remember what I showed you? You got to roll around them, then try and give them a good whack on their back. That rolling around mess is the only way to take them out. If the zombie wizards are around, get rid of them first. They can raise the monsters you just killed back from the dead. If that happens, you're toast. They will swarm you and kill you and then you got to go all the way back to the start of the level. You'll want to give up a lot. Don't. Keep rolling. Keep swinging.

Remember, you get more points for rolling around and not getting hit. It's an easy way to score points and win you an extra man. You'll need that extra man when you have the big showdown with the lich at the end. He's no pushover.

You'll get really frustrated at first, trying to get this all down. Practice as much as you can.

Hayder, you're my best friend. You're the first person I can say I have ever loved, and that's the truth. Saying goodbye to your face would have killed me, and right now I feel like I am half dead already. I told you this place is killing me. Not just this house. This town. This life. Every day I feel every bad thing that has happened here. I feel it every day. I feel it all day long.

You were the only thing that made things good for me. But I know if I stayed I would just bring all that sadness with me. As long as I stay here it won't go away. It will spread to me and into you like a sickness. I can't bear to think of hurting you like that, and it WOULD hurt you. It will spoil all of the things about you that make you so sweet. So amazing. I leave you because I love those things about you and I want to keep them, those memories, with me always.

Please don't hate me, boyfriend. You don't have to forgive me. Just don't hate me.

Just remember me. Even a little.

Your girlfriend loves you, but she has to go.

Matheson closed the notebook and glanced over at the boy.

Hayder was staring up at the gray clouds hanging overhead. A funeral shroud in heaven.

This time, it was the man who turned away from the child. He began to weep softly as to not disturb the boy.

The man cried for Hayder, for Cora, for Becky, and for Black Knot.

Juston dried his eyes on the sleeve of his shirt and looked back at the boy.

Yes, it was time.

When they got back to the cabin Matheson offered to phone the number listed on the FOR SALE sign in the yard. Maybe find out something. Hayder shook his head no and retreated to his room, the notebook under his arm, shutting the door behind him. Juston left him alone and called the realtor anyway. According to them, the old Corbucci place had been posted for sale for over a month, the sign only having gone up officially just a day shy of a week ago. The sellers had provided no indication where they were going, and they hadn't asked. It wasn't their business. The realtor confessed they were not terribly optimistic about getting the property sold. Haggard was not exactly a desirable place to live, no matter how beautifully the home had been restored. Matheson agreed. Haggard was, and would more than likely remain, a shithole until God himself decided to wipe everything from the face of the earth. He had thanked the person on the other end of the phone for their time and hung up.

He went to the stove and began whipping up some lunch. Pork chops and green beans. He cooked the beans with a generous dollop of bacon fat, just like his momma had for him. If you didn't simmer those green beans in the bacon fat it just didn't come out right. They added some body, some bite, to the blandness of the beans. Mostly he liked it because it made him think about good things. Being a boy himself and how it felt to have someone take care of you.

Around ten that evening Hayder finally emerged from his room, the notebook in his hands and his eyes swollen to slits. He sat down to supper, picked at it for a few minutes, then decided it was actually delicious and wolfed down three helpings of green beans and two whole chops. Matheson felt a little better. A boy eating was a boy wanting to get better. Yet he didn't say a word while he chowed. Juston kept quiet. It was the right thing to do.

When they finished they sat together at the kitchen table, only the stovetop light on, Matheson smoking and Hayder working on a jigsaw puzzle. Something they had both done a million times before.

Hayder wanted to start a bonfire outside so he could burn the notebook. When he told Matheson this he said it between clenched teeth. The man told him, firmly yet gently, no. He would keep the notebook for him, but he refused to destroy it. He knew the boy would regret it. It was anger talking, and you never make decisions like this when you were mad. The child handed the notebook to the man and walked outside. Matheson left him alone for a spell while he finished his coffee. He smoked another cigarette. So much for quitting.

Juston found the boy standing on the porch, staring up at the sky. The clouds had departed, taking their storms with them. There was a coolness to the air that purged the filth from the lungs. A whisper of autumn kindness.

Matheson walked over to Hayder and put his arm around him. He drew him close. The boy stiffened, then loosened, finally relenting. He leaned his head against the big man's side.

They stood like that, comforting one another, until the darkness grew too deep. The night too long. They then returned to the cabin, their home, and drew down the curtain upon a very long, very trying, day.

EPILOGUE

A year later Juston Matheson and his son Hayder moved to Lenzi Bay, Oregon. It was a long ways away from Black Knot, which was the idea.

Both of them came to love the climate of the Pacific Northwest, and Matheson found great pleasure working as a foreman for a lumber company out of Portland. It was simple work, which was what the man had been looking for. He knew what was expected of him, and he needed that. No drama. No vile things to hide from. No guns. Blessed, sweet banality. Hayder, of his own volition, returned to brick-and-mortar school, where he did quite well. He found a group of good kids, mostly nerds like himself, who remained friends with him well past graduation. They both thrived, and their former lives in southeastern Oklahoma seemed like something that had happened to someone else. Other people.

Upon graduation Hayder declined Matheson's offer to send him to college and went to work instead for a construction company. He liked doing things with his hands, and that's what he wanted to do. Matheson tried, quite unsuccessfully, to hide his pride in this decision. Unless you wanted to be a doctor or a biologist, the former lawman regarded college to be a monumental waste of time, not to mention money. But if the boy had wanted to go, the man would have sent him without question. He would have done anything within his means to make the kid even the least bit happy.

Somewhere along the way, Hayder met a girl. They dated for five years, and Juston liked her very much. She was going to school to learn criminal forensics, something the man happened to have some familiarity with, and the two of them got along very well. The man was relieved when Hayder had first met the young lady that she looked nothing like someone else. He never mentioned this to Hayder. They never spoke of those days, even though those days were often very much on their mind. Hayder would eventually quit the construction company and open a bistro in their little town, much like his own mother had done a long time ago. Matheson wondered if the boy saw the connection. Maybe he did. Maybe not. The café was a great success, and Matheson was glad to see the boy grow into a man with a purpose, with a dream. Not many who had gone through the things he had could put those broken pieces back together again into something that worked right.

A week shy of Hayder's twenty-fifth birthday his father, Juston Matheson, former sheriff of Black Knot, passed away in his sleep.

It had been a peaceful departure, which Hayder had been thankful for. Probably his heart, the doctor had said. It wasn't too much of a surprise.

The old man ate bacon three times a day and drank enough coffee to peel the chrome off of a trailer hitch. He had died happy, Hayder told himself, and it was probably true. The last decade of Matheson's life had been a fine one. He had no complaints. How many of us can attest to that?

Two years after Matheson's death, Hayder and his new bride, Jenna, welcomed a little girl into the world. Her name was Melissa, named after Jenna's granny. Something about the child's birth stirred something within the young man. A longing to tie up loose ends.

Impulsively, he booked a plane to Dallas and paid a visit to the graves of his father, or the man who created him, and his baby sister. It had been the first time he'd laid eyes on the graves since he was eleven years old. It was an odd experience, one that would never be repeated again. It was a strangely unemotional reunion. Like laying flowers across the tomb of a stranger, the dead nameless and unknown beneath the stone.

That wasn't really why he had gone. He had known damn well from the beginning it had been a cover. Dallas, after all, wasn't that far from someplace else.

A three-hour drive northeast. A mere jaunt.

On the drive back to the airport he thought about hooking a right on Old Highway 69, northbound.

Come on, it's just up the road a piece.

He cranked the radio up and drowned out that little voice in his brain. Mercifully, it worked.

Leave those things be. If Matheson had been here, sitting next to him, he would have told him the same thing.

Ghosts needed someone to haunt them. Better to let them sleep in their tombs where they belonged.

Halloween arrived.

Autumn in Lenzi Bay was achingly beautiful. Hayder had never seen such vibrant, scintillating colors in either Texas or Oklahoma. There, autumn seemed to just be passing through. Here, it came to life. It dug in and stayed. He liked that. It anchored him.

The boy, now a man, stood on the back deck of his house sipping Old Raven from an icy tumbler. The bourbon had been Matheson's favorite until he had given up drinking altogether. Finding a store this far out west that sold it had been a lost cause. Hayder had a case of it shipped in from Oklahoma City, only breaking out a bottle when he felt particularly sentimental.

Like tonight.

Hayder lifted his glass to the cold harvest moon and toasted the memory of his father, a damn good man. He toasted the memory of the boy he had once been.

He drank to a girl he had once loved and killed monsters with. He wondered where she was and what had become of her every single day. Sometimes thinking about it made him hurt.

It was a good night. Maybe, after everyone had gone to bed, he would take the notebook out of the old footlocker he kept in the attic. Maybe it was time.

Jenna called to him from the kitchen window. Supper was ready. Beans and cornbread with sweet tea. He loved the sound of his wife's voice.

The wind suddenly died down as if drawing in its breath. The trees no longer rustled, which allowed him to hear something.

A marvel.

Cicadas.

Cicadas *in October*.

Imagine that.

ACKNOWLEDGMENTS

Thanks and love to Annie and the boys, to whom this book is dedicated. Special nods to my wonderful editor Scarlett R. Algee and everyone at JournalStone, and my beta reader Rachel Dawn Drenning. Special fist bumps and big thank yous for Matthew M. Bartlett, Jonathan Raab, Jared Collins and Alan Sessler.

ABOUT THE AUTHOR

Mer Whinery is a storyteller of the rural macabre from Southeastern Oklahoma. He loves the smells of burning leaves and something sweet baking in the oven, sunny autumn afternoons and shabby carnival spook houses. He currently lives outside Tulsa with his wife Annie, his two sons Kameron and Harper, and a mob of unruly critters.

He is the author of the short fiction collections *The Little Dixie Horror Show* and *Phantasmagoria Blues*, and the very, very weird western *Trade Yer Coffin for a Gun*.

He can be found on:
Facebook: https://www.facebook.com/merwhinery
Twitter: https://twitter.com/MerWhinery
Instagram: https://www.instagram.com/merwhinerythewriter